THE PSYCHOPATH CLUB

The Psychopath Club
SANDRA BOND

THE CANAL PRESS

THE PSYCHOPATH CLUB
Sandra Bond

Copyright © 2021 Sandra Bond. All Rights Reserved.
Published by The Canal Press, Bethesda, Maryland (*www.thecanalpress.com*).
For information, email *editor@timespinnerpress.com*.
Author's website: *www.sandra-bond.com*.

BOOK DESIGN | John D. Berry
COVER DESIGN | Sandra Bond & John D. Berry
AUTHOR PHOTO | Oliver Facey

For Henry and Jo Hamilton, sine qua non

1

Darroll Martock's sixteenth birthday fell on the eleventh day of June, 2003, which was why he was going to kill somebody on the tenth of June.

He had been planning the deed for plenty of time, of course. Even before his fifteenth birthday the idea had been in his head, bouncing around like a pinball ricocheting between bumpers. All Darroll had to do was to hit the flipper button just right, to send the ball shooting up the pinball table into the target, and kapow! JACKPOT, the machine would blare, and everything around him would explode into flashing lights and a cacophony of sound.

But Darroll wanted the flashing lights and the noise to remain safely in his head, not to take on reality. Police sirens and strobes did not figure in his plan. Well, they did, of course; but it was vital for him to be well out of the way before they came on the scene. Darroll didn't want his ass hauled off to jail before his victim's blood had even had the chance to congeal.

Because Darroll didn't intend to stop at one victim. Darroll wanted his trail of death to be more than one corpse long.

And if he was to achieve that goal, Darroll had to make sure he got away with his killings, every single one of them, for as long as he could. He wanted his game of murder-pinball to clock up plenty of extra balls and replays. Darroll, in other words, had to be smart; smarter than the average psychopath.

His plan had been growing inside him pretty much since his parents had separated. Before even waiting for the divorce, they had moved almost as far apart as they could without crossing an international border. His father had gone south to Georgia, while his mother had gone north, with a reluctant Darroll in tow, and fetched up here. Here in Muldoon.

Darroll hadn't lived a week in Muldoon before he realised that he despised the pissant little town from the bottom of his heart.

And with a heart as black and villainous as Darroll knew his own was, there was room for a lot of hate in it.

The discovery hit him as he woke up one morning with cold feet. He curled them back under his bedclothes in an attempt to find some warmth for his toes, and as he did so, he realised that he had done the same damn thing every morning he had woken up in Muldoon. It didn't help that he was five feet eleven inches tall and his comforter was only five feet six long, because his mother hadn't quite yet realised that her son was a young man in all but name, rather than just a kid.

But the main reason was geography. Muldoon was a stupid little town in a stupid little state, where it snowed every time you farted, and froze solid for six months of every year; so no matter what he put on his feet, or how many layers of it, his feet were always cold. Always. His feet were never not cold.

Once he'd taken note of this, every day began the same hateful way. Darroll would awaken to the ache of cold feet, each toe a tiny, misshapen ice cube. As the days passed, the state of his feet began to turn into an obsession. Even wearing socks to bed didn't solve Darroll's problem; the feeling of them, confining and awkward, on his feet before he went to sleep annoyed him, and he always ended up kicking the socks off in his sleep. And in the morning, that meant cold toes for Darroll Martock again. Ten cold toes.

Why ten?

He didn't know the answer. Ten was an arbitrary number and that was how many toes you had. And fingers, of course. Except for Rodney Liebscher's big brother, who managed to cut one off while he was chopping logs for the furnace. See, that was the kind of state he had to live in. A state where you had to keep furnaces going all the year round, burning up wood and oil and gasoline, and causing pollution and deforestation, and you needed to cut your fingers off into the bargain to make their fires keep burning.

Or you could freeze to death, as the other alternative. Your toes going colder and colder and colder and colder, until you couldn't feel them any more, and then they became gangrenous. Dead, in other words. They'd turn black, like the polar expeditionaries of a hundred years ago. Darroll had read a book about some of them. They froze all their toes off trying to get to the south pole, and some other guy reached it ahead of them, so being British these guys just said "Pip pip" to each other, and smacked each other on the shoulder heartily, and trudged off into the snow with their toes turning black until they couldn't walk any more, and then they died. With their ridiculous moustaches turning white from the snow, and their feet black as hell, from the ankles right down to the end of their toenails. Darroll always pictured it as a greeny black, with a bit of blood here and there, only not very much blood, on account of how their feet were so frozen that the blood could scarcely get into them any more.

Of course, they could have been Americans. Now Americans wouldn't have just shrugged and let the ice grow on their moustaches. No, they'd have looked meaningfully at each other and gritted their jaws. Perhaps one of them would have rolled his chewin' tobacco from one cheek to the other and spat on the ground, just to show where the South Pole was. And then they'd have gone after that varmint Amundsen and his Scandinavian creeps and shot the bastards full of hot lead. Yeah.

And then they'd have died from the ice, with black feet. But in a manly, frontiersman, all-American way. No crawling into a tent saying "pip pip" or "Tell the people back home we did it for the Queen". They'd crawl on till they couldn't crawl any more, and then die with their bodies pointing back towards America and civilisation.

Civilisation. Hah. If this was civilisation, why were his feet cold?

Why did he have to have feet, anyway? Why couldn't he have wheels? Or hooves? Feet just looked stupid, like deformed hands.

So Darroll was glad to welcome his murder fantasy into his mind, simply as a means of distracting him from his cold feet in the morning. He had daydreamed of killing his enemies for quite some time; but now he was forced to live in Muldoon, and wake up with cold feet every day, he found the fantasy changing from a vague, occasional reverie into a regular daily event.

Soon it began to develop further, to mutate into a swampy

morass below the surface of his mind, always there, always at the edge of his consciousness, ready for him to slide into whenever he was bored, or some jerk at school annoyed him. There were a lot of jerks at Darroll's school, and a lot of boredom in his life, because Muldoon had so little to occupy an active mind.

And upon his fifteenth birthday, when he hadn't bothered to hold any kind of celebration, because he didn't see any point in marking the fact that he'd kept on breathing for another twelve months, he had spent half the day fantasising about blood and mayhem. Finally he had confronted himself, somewhere within the grim passageways of his own mind, the narrow corridors whose walls seeped sweat and greenish bile, and struck a deal with himself.

By the time he was sixteen, Darroll Martock would either be out of Muldoon, or he would kill someone.

And now Darroll was fifteen years, three hundred and sixty-four days old, and he was still in Muldoon. So that was that. No point in running away; where would he go? To his father in the south? Not a chance.

He had been planning his murder for weeks, honing and refining the scheme. The choice of victim was a tough one. There were so many people in his life whom he despised.

His parents were both prime candidates, but after a while he rejected them both. His father was in Georgia, well beyond Darroll's reach, and had made it plain that visiting his son and his ex-wife in Muldoon was not high on his list of priorities; not on it at all, in fact. This suited Darroll fine in one way, because he hated his father, but at the same time Darroll resented his father's abandonment of him. It wasn't logical, and he knew it wasn't logical, but since when did logic interfere with emotion?

His mother, now... He despised his mother, too. He despised her for marrying his father, and for having given birth to him, and for giving him a candy ass name and then spelling it an unusual way, so that every time he had to give his name, he was forced to spell it out, D-A-R-R-O-L-L. It was the O that threw people. They would look up at him in confusion, their mouth ironically in the shape of an O itself, and he'd have to repeat himself, every damn time.

He despised her for not being good enough in bed to keep his father around, and for being weak enough to let his dad mess around with other women, and then leave her for one of them. And he despised her for bringing him to Muldoon most of all.

Yes, his mother was the obvious target, living in the same house and seeing him every day. But that was the problem, he realised. If his mom turned up murdered, who the hell else would the cops look for when it came to obvious suspects? His mother hadn't formed any new relationships since his father had quit the marriage; she didn't go out to work, or leave the house at all most of the time. She spent most of the day in the easy chair in front of the television, drinking coffee in the mornings and switching to alcohol at some point after lunch.

It wasn't much of a life. Darroll had more than half convinced himself that it would be no less than humane to put an end to her routine. But how he could he do so without going straight into the frame for the crime?

Reluctantly, Darroll had started to consider a wider range of potential victims.

There were plenty of pretexts for one person to off another. Racial hatred was a biggie, but Darroll didn't know any people who weren't white in Muldoon. That was the sort of town Muldoon was; white as the snow that blanketed it from fall to spring.

Likewise, gang violence was always listed as one of the biggest causes for the deaths of guys aged under twenty-five, but Muldoon didn't have any gangs. Unless you counted some of the cliques at school...

School.

There was no shortage of people he despised at Isidor Straus High. There was hardly a member of staff in the whole place, from Principal Tidmarsh downward, that he wouldn't have loved to shove a gun into the mouth of and pull the trigger. Spatter their worthless academic brains all over the nearest wall. But Darroll Martock did not possess a gun, or the means of acquiring one, and he somehow couldn't see himself overpowering a grown adult male with his lanky, unmuscular frame. There was Mrs Patterson, who was in her fifties, but she was made of rawhide and concrete blocks and Darroll suspected that if he swung a punch at her, all he would get was sore knuckles. No, not Mrs Patterson. Nor Ms Krukowski, who was younger and less of a dried-up old harridan than Mrs Patterson. Darroll knew that Ms Krukowski attended judo classes, and it would be not only disastrous but embarrassing if he went for her with a knife or something, only for her to pick him up and dump him on his ass.

By this process of elimination, Darroll had narrowed his field of potential victims down to one group; the idiots from Muldoon and other nearby towns with whom he had to share classes at Straus High. And from that field he had come down to one. Ed Crowe.

Tomorrow, Darroll Martock would be sixteen years old; and so, today, Ed Crowe was going to die.

2

It took Darroll Martock nine minutes to walk from his home into the town of Muldoon. He turned left at Fifth and Main and headed down to Third, where Muldoon's only public parking lot hid behind the wall with the civic mural painted upon it, and then turned again for half a block to reach Celebration Burger. Celebration Burger was about the only place left in Muldoon where you could buy some food, sit down, and eat while you watched the world go by outside the window.

Not that there was a lot of world in Muldoon to go by; that was the whole problem with Muldoon, of course.

After he had decided on Ed Crowe as his first victim, Darroll had spent a whole month or more planning how to off the guy. Ed was bigger than Darroll, and stronger. He was easily the biggest guy in their grade, and Darroll supposed it was inevitable that Ed should have fallen into the role of bully. He fitted it the way a hand fitted into a baseball mitt. There was hardly a kid in school whose life Ed had not pushed his unwelcome way into at some point and made into a misery; hardly a kid who hadn't been beaten up or pushed around, or had Ed shove his dirty jockstrap into their face, making them choke on his stink while Ed and his sycophants snorted with laughter.

If Ed Crowe were to turn up as a corpse, who would the police suspect first out of the dozens of students turning cartwheels of joy in Straus High?

Darroll still had the problem of choosing a murder method. Physical violence was out, of course. Ed could break him in half with one hand. The only possible way he could take Ed Crowe down was by stealth, and to get him on his own wouldn't be easy; he always seemed to have his girlfriend Patsy Young around him, and generally some of his male hangers-on too.

That put paid to stabbing, strangling, and similar methods involving manual force.

He had already discounted the use of a firearm as impractical, and he couldn't think of an easy way to poison Ed, either.

Darroll sat in Celebration Burger as May turned into June and the end of the school year loomed up, pondering his options. Local farmers would pull into the little parking lot behind the store and come inside to eat, or to grab a bag of hamburgers to go for their family out on the farm. Straus High kids would hang around the place, joking and pushing each other around, or throwing French fries at each other from table to table. Ed Crowe himself was a regular customer. Darroll wished he knew how Crowe could stow away so many hamburgers without any of his goddamn muscle turning to fat. How the hell was he going to put Ed Crowe six feet under, without the risk of either failing to kill the jerk outright, or being picked up for the crime afterward?

When the answer came, it almost made Darroll laugh out loud at the irony of it.

He had been sitting toying with a milkshake in Celebration Burger when Ed Crowe had come inside from the side door, the one that led to the parking lot. Ed was already sixteen and, of course, had a truck to drive where Darroll was still reliant upon his own feet to get him about town.

Darroll watched Ed swagger up to the counter and order, then turn around and survey the room like he owned it. Ed's eyes met Darroll's for a moment, and there was contempt in them. Darroll looked away, but not quickly enough.

Ed pushed himself away from the counter, ready to come over and crush Darroll into atoms. Darroll didn't hang around for Ed. He grabbed his milkshake and scooted out of the main door, not quite at a run. A glance behind him showed that Ed Crowe had returned to the counter, rather than pursuing him. Exhaling in relief, Darroll swung round the corner of the restaurant building and found himself in its parking lot. He quickly walked past the side entrance, through whose glass he could see Ed Crowe still leaning on the counter like a hoodlum, and paused to take stock among the parked vehicles.

That was when he noticed that the car he was standing next to wasn't locked.

Of course it wasn't locked. This was Muldoon.

In Muldoon, you could leave anything unlocked. Forget murder; there was no crime in Muldoon at all to speak of. No robbery, burglary, rape, sodomy or arson. Darroll had even heard Mike Barker, whose daughter Darroll shared classes with, boast that he'd lost his latchkey three years ago and never had to worry about it. "I never lock my front door anyways," he'd said. "I mean who the hell is gonna come inside and steal my television, this is Muldoon, right?"

The plot began to coalesce in Darroll's mind. He stood there, his milkshake forgotten in his hand, thinking, for several minutes. Only when the side door to Celebration opened and Ed Crowe came out with a big brown bag of burgers in his arm did Darroll quickly vamoose out of sight. Ed crossed the lot to his truck, threw the burgers in through the passenger window, and climbed into the driver's seat. Not only had he, too, left his vehicle unlocked, but the windows had been down all the time.

This town, thought Darroll. This goddamn fucking town.

He remembered the milkshake he had been clutching for fifteen minutes. His warm hand had been around it and he expected it to have separated into an unpalatable mess, but before he threw it into the nearest trash can, he gave a tentative suck at the straw. The shake was still good, still tasty.

Of course it was. This was Muldoon. If a thing was cold in Muldoon, then it damned well stayed cold.

Darroll leaned on the back wall of Celebration Burger and finished his milkshake, thinking of how Ed Crowe was soon going to be cold.

And staying cold.

3

The plan was quite simple, but that was good, Darroll reasoned. The simpler the plan, the harder it was for something to go wrong.

Over the next week, he haunted Celebration Burger, both the building and the parking lot behind. He sat in the window eating, pretending to look at the mural on the other side of the street. What he was actually doing was scoping out the clientele and getting to know the people who habitually left their cars unlocked and stealable, keys sitting temptingly in the ignition, because who the hell would steal a car in Muldoon?

The plan was clear in his head. He needed to hover around the restaurant, waiting for Crowe to come in. Then Darroll would scurry round to the parking lot, steal one of the unlocked cars, and when Crowe emerged, drive a nice big chunk of Detroit iron straight into his body. Send him flying. Maybe reverse over him a few times. Make the big, burly Crowe so flat and skinny that even Darroll's lean body had more breadth to it.

Then he'd race out of town, find somewhere unobserved, and use the gas can he had purchased and filled in readiness. Torch the murder weapon till it was no more than a mass of twisted metal. Scorch every fingerprint, every trace of himself, completely off the thing.

And then, all he had to do was walk back home, wearing an innocent expression, and act surprised at the news that Ed Crowe had shoved his last jockstrap into someone's face.

Okay, they might ask if he'd been around at the time of the accident (surely they'd think it was an accident; whoever heard of murder being committed in Muldoon?) But that was the other reason he'd been hanging out in Celebration Burger so much; if he was in there every day, it made it harder for the staff and the regulars to recall what time he arrived and departed. What's that, officer? Darroll Martock? Well, there was one day he left around the same time as Ed Crowe, but was that today or yesterday or a week last Thursday?

And so, on that cold June day, Darroll Martock, one day shy of sixteen, was sitting near the front door of Celebration Burger, nursing the end of a portion of fries. His heart thump-thumped against his ribs and his kidneys pumped adrenalin into his bloodstream, his whole body acting in unison to back up his brain, ready to commit his first murder.

All he needed was for Ed Crowe to show up.

And finally he did. Darroll pushed his fries away, and walked out of the door and into the parking lot. Old Petersen was eating inside, still, plenty of food remaining on his tray, while his Mercury sedan sat unattended in the lot.

He strode round the side of the building and over to the Mercury. He held his breath as he approached it. What if Petersen had actually locked it this once?

He hadn't. The driver's door was open, and the keys sat in the ignition.

Darroll threw himself into the driver's seat, closed the door, and turned the key. The engine sprang to life immediately.

There were seconds to go, just seconds. His hand was ready on the transmission, his foot on the gas.

Ed Crowe appeared round the side of the building, brown burger bag in hand. It couldn't be easier. He even had to cross in front of the Mercury. Darroll ducked his head slightly, lest Ed see him there, in someone else's car.

Three seconds, two.

Crowe stepped into open space, twenty feet from the Mercury and directly ahead of it.

All Darroll had to do was shift into gear, gun the gas, and Ed Crowe would go flying, arms and legs breaking from the impact, first with the Mercury, then with the hardtop of the parking lot. The bag of hamburgers Crowe was carrying would scatter to the four winds. Within ten seconds Darroll would be out onto the street. Within twenty, he'd be out of sight, and within a minute, he'd be out of town, scattering to the four winds himself.

For one second, then another, Darroll sat with Ed Crowe in his sights. Come on, come on, his mind screamed. Everything is perfect. You can do this. You are a psychopath. You were born to kill, to murder, to destroy –

His hand and his foot remained exactly where they were.

Crowe was past the Mercury in three seconds, and in a couple more, he had reached his own truck. He tossed the bag of hamburgers in through the open window, opened the door, and joined them inside.

Darroll sat in the Mercury for perhaps two minutes after Ed had driven away. It was only the thought of what would happen if Petersen came out of the restaurant and saw him sitting there that made him kill the Mercury's engine and make an exit.

He walked for half a block, then broke into a run, fists clenching as he cursed himself for a coward. Then he caught sight of his reflection in the wing mirror of a parked car. He flinched away from his own face, revolted, and came to an abrupt stop, gasping for breath. Then he reached out to grab the mirror, and gave it a savage wrench. For a second it resisted, before force prevailed, and the mirror snapped clean off in his hand.

He hurled it into the doorway of a boarded-up shop, and began running again.

Once home, he threw himself onto his bed and stared at the ceiling.

What the hell kind of psychopath was he? What the hell kind of psychopath chickened out of their first murder?

He broke into tears, suddenly and unexpectedly, muffling his sobs with his pillow. He'd failed. He had shown up chicken when the chips were down. He wept bitterly for ten minutes, crying for himself, crying for all the corpses he'd hoped to line up against his name and would never create, all the murders he'd planned so lovingly and was never going to commit.

Next day, Ed Crowe's birthday present to Darroll was to shove him down the steps outside the library, and damn near break his leg.

4

When Darroll arrived home on the afternoon of his sixteenth birthday, limping thanks to Ed Crowe, his mother was in the kitchen drinking coffee. She drank only coffee and alcohol, and normally by this time, she would have moved on to alcohol.

Darroll hated her on coffee because she was bright and positive and optimistic, and he hated her on alcohol because she was morose and sat staring at the television night after night after night. He'd hate her on water too, but she never drank that, as far as he could tell.

"Happy birthday, sweet pea," she said, as he poured himself a glass of milk.

He hated being called sweet pea, too. Hated her, he corrected himself. The hatred wasn't just random. She made him hate her, when she called him sweet pea. Or cherub.

"Thanks, Mom," he said into his glass of milk.

She looked at the milk, and he looked at her. He knew what she was going to say. She was going to grumble at him for drinking milk in the afternoon. Point out that he'd had milk on his cereal that morning. As though there were a milk shortage, like in Africa. Maybe she thought they were living in a desert. Muldoon was surrounded by farms, cows dotted all over them, mooing and eating grass and depositing huge cowpats everywhere, cows that were all full of milk the way his mother was full of shit. There was no way this fucking state was ever going to have a milk shortage.

But she didn't say it.

"Got you a present," she said instead, awkwardly.

He nearly choked on his last mouthful of milk.

"It's round behind the house," she said.

He pushed his glass away, so hard that it practically fell off the edge of the table.

"Come on," she said, with one of the little smiles he hated, because he knew she thought they were something special that they had between them. When all the time he knew that there was nothing between them. Nothing at all.

They climbed the stairs to the rear door. Darroll looked at the back of his mother's legs. They had veins in them. Ugly veins. And ugly feet at the bottom. Feet still looked stupid to him. These days, feet always looked crazy and wrong.

Mom reached into the pocket of her apron and held out a key to him. "Happy birthday, Darroll," she said.

Darroll stared at the big black car that was sitting in the lot. The big old black car.

"It's yours," she said, still holding the key out to him.

He took the key without a word and walked up to the automobile, hesitating slightly before he took the last step, as though he was afraid it was suddenly going to jump on him and squash him. Then he circled around it.

He already knew what he'd see on the back, but he looked at it anyway. OLDSMOBILE.

His mother had bought him a fucking Oldsmobile for his sixteenth birthday. A brand so ancient, it wasn't even being made any more.

As he walked around the car he composed his features into the kind of expression she'd be expecting. Surprised and pleased and a bit shy. "Awww. Mom," he'd say to her.

He turned away from the car, gave her the expression. "Awww. Mom."

"Is it okay then?"

She knew nothing about cars. Jesus. When he turned up with this at Straus High, he was going to die. If not from having his face beaten in for having such a lame-ass car, then from sheer embarrassment at having to go around town in this ancient heap of wreckage. It wasn't vintage, it wasn't retro, it wasn't cool. It looked like it had taken a wrong turn on its way to the scrapyard to turn itself in, and somehow wound up outside the Martock house.

"It's great, Mom," he said, and came close to her so she could peck him on the cheek. He shuddered inwardly every time she did that.

"I wish it could have been newer," she said. So do I, he thought.

"Well, hey," he said, retreating before she could give him another kiss. "It's... cool. It's better than anything Dad got me, anyway," he added, giving her a grin, trying to lighten the situation.

Instead she wouldn't meet his eyes for a moment.

He swallowed hard. Of course, she had bought it with his father's money. For a moment he'd been surprised enough to let himself forget, but his mother's money came from his father. All of it. The money that bought his car, the money that bought his milk, the money that put a roof over their heads; it all came from his father. His mother hated his father so much that she'd brought him halfway across the country, to this fucking lump-of-ice state, to get away from him. But she didn't hate him enough to refuse his money.

She looked back at him, and he didn't look away in time. Not only did he know, but she knew he knew.

Her cheeks grew a little pink. "Well, you could say that," she said, in a voice so artificial it should have been made from 1950s plastic. That cheap crummy sort. Like the instrument panel on the car was probably made of.

He wanted to slap her. She was always saying things like that. Things with no meaning, things that she only said to give her mouth something to say. She didn't understand that Darroll liked silence when there was nothing to say. Which around here, was most of the time.

"You going to go for a ride?" she said. "There's insurance, and plates, and everything. I sorted it."

Well, of course she had. She wasn't going to spend five dollars and sixteen cents, or however much she'd laid down for this rust-pile, without him being able to drive it. He was going to have to go out in this thing, and be looked at.

"Sure," he said. He clicked open the door (he was amazed that something as old as Noah's Ark actually had central locking) and sat behind the wheel. He realised he was holding the keys so tightly that the dealer's nametag on the keyring was pressing sharp metal into his palm, so he got rid of them by pushing them into the ignition. He looked at the controls. Windshield washers, lights, turn signals. Horn. Air conditioning, which was set to top heat, of course, in this goddamn iceberg state. No button, more was the pity, to turn on the laser beam and annihilate other road users, or indeed to blast his mom into atoms.

Darroll had already gotten his first licence, six months ago. That was one of the few good things about this state; they had enlightened ideas about how old you had to be to drive. Of course, this was only making a virtue out of necessity. Around Muldoon, there were plenty of kids Darroll knew who had been driving since they were about twelve. Not just cars, either; tractors and farm machines. Darroll allowed himself a brief fantasy of running down Ed Crowe with a baler, and depositing his mangled body out of the back of the device, neatly trussed.

Then he realised his mother was looking expectantly at him.

Time to face the music, time to test out his birthday present.

He left her standing, looking worried, as he guided the big Oldsmobile away from the house and onto the county highway. The transmission was soggy, like the dregs of milk in his glass, and the engine grumbled whenever he put his foot down. Laser beam? This thing couldn't power a flashlight beam.

The highway entered Muldoon on Fifth Street. He didn't meet another car all the way in. He turned right on Washington, right again on Fourth, right again on Parsons, and back to Fifth. Then he tried a left turn, back onto Washington and up to the traffic lights, one of only a couple of sets in town, on Seventh. Which were red. He stopped, even though there was no other traffic about. Even psychopaths have to stop at red lights, he told himself –

"Hey!" Someone knocked on his window.

He wound it down, and ducked his head to look through and see what jerk was knocking on his window like they owned his car, the car he'd only been given ten minutes ago.

"When'd you get a car?" asked the window-rapper. It was Chuck Milne.

Darroll relaxed. Chuck was an asshole, like everyone he knew; but he was a dork asshole, rather than a jock asshole like Ed Crowe, or a psychotic asshole like Darroll himself. Chuck wasn't going to hassle him over his wheels.

"Today," Darroll said, nonchalantly.

"Wicked," Chuck said. Chuck was the sort of guy who thought you could say "Wicked" and not make yourself sound like some asshole who was five years behind on how people actually talked. He was also the sort of guy who thought anything which had a wheel at each corner and moved under its own power was 'wicked', including a black Oldsmobile 88 that had been made when Darroll was still learning how to get to grips with solid food. Or maybe it was older. Maybe it had been made when those gallant British explorers were all dying with their moustaches full of ice and their feet turning the same shade of black as the paint on the car. A solid matt black, with paler bits and scrapes here and there. And some rusty spots, where the paint had fallen off totally. Rust coming through from under, like blood coming out of a polar explorer's gangrenous foot.

"It's okay," Darroll muttered, trying to sound as though it was nothing much to him whether he had a car or not, and whether Chuck Milne liked it or not.

"Can I..."

Chuck didn't finish the sentence. He didn't even raise his voice to suggest that it was a question, or rather, a request. He just seemed to materialise in the passenger seat, with his fat ass taking up the whole damn thing, and his grey eyes giving the interior the once-over from under the greasy beanie hat he always wore.

The lights had turned to green, but there was still no other traffic, so Darroll was in no hurry to move on. He considered ordering Chuck to get the fuck out, but it was something to have a guy who looked up to him for having a car. Even if it was only Chuck Milne, and even if the car was only an Oldsmobile 88.

Chuck peered at the instrument panel. "So how fast you been?"

"I told you, I only got it today," Darroll already wanted to slap Chuck's fat face, for being so fucking annoying.

"What, you haven't taken her out and opened her up?"

The image made Darroll wince. This car was not female. And especially not an opened up female.

"No. I on-ly got it to-day." Darroll said it for the third time, slowly, and emphasising the neutral pronoun this time.

"Well, you gotta try!"

"Why?"

"Because it's what you do when you get a car for the first time!"

"Must have missed the period they taught us that in driver's ed," Darroll said to Chuck, with a minor sneer, small enough that Chuck wouldn't spot it and realise Darroll was mocking him. Which he was. And which Chuck did indeed fail to observe.

"Aw, man!" protested Chuck. "You have to! You gotta take her out of town! Go down to the interstate!"

"The interstate?"

Darroll hadn't thought of that. The interstate was three miles out of town. You could drive onto the Interstate and go anywhere. You could go to Chicago. Or New York. Or you could drive all the way to Georgia, to his father's house, and punch him smack in his left eye. Punch him for bringing Darroll into existence sixteen years and half an hour ago, and punch him again for the way he sent his mother checks every month, like she was some kind of employee on a payroll.

"The interstate," Chuck repeated.

"What the hell," Darroll said. "Let's do it."

"Whoo!" yelled Chuck as they finally rolled past the lights. There were still no other vehicles in sight, which was Muldoon all over. Jesus, it was a wonder Darroll's father's checks ever arrived. It was a wonder the postal service knew the damn town was here at all.

They drove south, out of town, and buildings soon gave way to pasture. And cows. Cows to the left of them, chewing grass and standing there like idiots, as brainless as the farmers who bred them, and milked them, and would sell them to be killed for pet food as soon as they stopped giving enough milk. Cows to the right of them, turning grass into milk and cow shit. You could smell the cows. Everywhere in this state you could smell the cows.

A mile south of town there was the railroad crossing, over tracks that were orange with rust and hadn't seen a train since before the Oldsmobile had rolled off the production line. Then there was a bar. Then a gas station, and then the interstate.

"Which way you going?" Chuck asked, sounding wildly excited. Maybe he'd never been on an Interstate before, the fucking hick. Darroll answered with a shrug.

"Whichever way the wheels go," he said, and turned up the first on-ramp. Which was westbound.

"Go west, young man!" yodelled Chuck. Darroll again suppressed an urge to smack him in the face.

The interstate was as empty as Muldoon had been. Darroll looked at the speedometer. The numbers went all the way up, past the speed limit, into three digits, up, up and away to 180.

"Well," Darroll said. "You wanted to see how fast this thing'll go." He pushed his foot down.

The big old engine lumbered into life and the speedometer started to climb. "Oh yeah!" Chuck exclaimed as the movement pushed him back in his seat, making his fat cheeks wobble.

Fifty. Fifty-five. Sixty.

"And she breaks the limit!" Chuck gasped, like he thought he was commentating on the Indy 500. "Darroll, dude, you are now a criminal."

"Big fucking deal," Darroll muttered, and pushed his foot further down. Sixty-five. Seventy.

"Wow," breathed Chuck. "This old babe's got a motor in her all right…"

"She's not a babe," Darroll said. Cold anger gripped him, and he imagined for a second tweaking the wheel and smacking the rusty heap of shit into the next bridge support, delivering a concrete pillar into Chuck's face at seventy-five miles an hour. The thought made his heart pound.

His foot stayed down. Eighty. Eighty-five.

"Jeez, Martock, take it easy. There are cops along here sometimes…"

Ninety.

"Martock!"

Ninety-five. The engine was growling like a tiger in a zoo, a tiger having stones thrown at it by jeering teenagers. A tiger waiting to spring free from its cage and devour everything it saw.

"Darroll... shit, you're gonna do the century?" Chuck's eyes were bulging, as round as empty cartridge cases. And as devoid of any charge.

Darroll's foot stayed down. Ninety-eight, ninety-nine –

"DARROLL!"

– one hundred.

An overbridge flashed past them and was left behind. They bore down on a suburban Honda in the other lane, were beyond it in a trice, its driver's face a pink blur as Darroll left it in their dust.

"Shit, Martock!" Chuck howled in fear and glee. "You're crazy! You're mad!"

And Darroll grinned wildly all of a sudden, because for once in his stupid life, Chuck Milne was right. He was mad. And he didn't care a damn.

5

Darroll woke early next morning, but he didn't get out of bed; he lay there, thinking, as the crack of light that edged between his curtains grew brighter. Now and again he looked at his feet, musing once more on how wrong feet looked. He'd read about how some guys had a foot fetish, how they could only get a boner if they were looking at a woman's foot. Or sometimes, even, just a woman's shoe. Darroll couldn't understand that at all. He found normal sex hard enough to comprehend. Sometimes he wondered what it would be like to actually be that close to a girl, body against body, skin against skin. The thought aroused him, but at the same time, it horrified him. Getting that close to another human being? Him?

When his alarm rang, he switched it off and kept lying there, until his mother had to come and order him out of bed. He threw some clothes on, grabbed a bowl of cereal and poured milk on it, then took a glass and filled that with milk too. His mother gave him a look, and he looked back at her defiantly, daring her to make an issue of his milk consumption. As he ate breakfast, he pondered making milk his trade mark. Leave a milk bottle next to every corpse he created. The Milk Bottle Murderer.

Except he wasn't going to be creating any corpses, was he? He'd allowed Ed Crowe to keep on living.

He arrived at school in the Oldsmobile and hid it in a remote corner of the parking lot. The parking zone at Straus High was enormous. Muldoon wasn't big enough to justify having a high school, really, but the same thing went for all the other dumb little hick towns in this part of the state. Years ago, the education board had closed down the other surrounding schools, and amalgamated them all into Muldoon, buying up a bunch of ground at the edge of town and building a new campus there, big enough to accommodate all the previous little schools' pupils. More than enough, in fact, which was why the parking lot was never full. Probably half of the local high schoolers came in by bus, a whole network of big lumbering yellow things grinding their way between little towns and outlying farms, trudging their way along the roads, tired but uncomplaining, like the cows on the farms where the buses picked up their passengers.

He was glad to slide out of the Oldsmobile and head into school without anyone coming to examine the automobile; he'd wondered whether Chuck Milne might have told people. Of course, Chuck Milne wasn't the kind of guy people were interested in hearing gossip from.

Darroll had a study period before lunch. He headed to the library, and found Chuck already sitting there on one of the computers. Chuck waved at him and pointed at an empty seat next to him. Not knowing quite why, Darroll sat down, trying not to look at Chuck's pants. They were always one size too tight, his stomach bulging over his belt line at the front, and his ass crack showing whenever he leaned forward, giving you a good look at a forest of sweaty little black hairs.

Darroll spent five minutes trying to get the computer to deliver him pornography, and failing. Last year, some kid in a high school in the next county had managed to access, print, and distribute to most of his class several ultra-high-quality photographs of a woman engaged in an act of intimacy with a Clydesdale stallion. Word had leaked out and lawyers had become involved; the lawsuit was still live. As a result, the computers at Isidor Straus had been fitted with a security program so fierce, with its settings turned up so high, that if you so much as tried to download a page that contained the word 'abreast', the nuclear attack warning siren would sound. Then the entire Library and Information Technology staff would descend on you, wearing contamination suits, and drag you away to Mr Tidmarsh's office on the end of a great big hook.

He was about to abandon his quest and click over to a television review page, when Chuck nudged him to draw his attention.

"Shit," Chuck said. "This guy killed so many women he said he couldn't even remember how many. They think forty-six at least."

"What?" Darroll looked over from his own screen to Chuck's.

Chuck pointed a fat finger at his monitor, where a picture of an undistinguished, scrawny man with a straggly mustache stared gloomily out of the screen.

"He's serving eighteen life sentences," Chuck said in a low, awed voice. "But they aren't gonna kill him, cos in his state, they got no death penalty."

Darroll stared at the murderer. He'd read about this guy before, but he was surprised to find Chuck trespassing on his own sacred turf of killers and killing. He needed to make time to figure out how to respond. "Creepy eyes," he said.

Chuck leaned in closer to his screen. "Nah. Photos always look like that when you know someone's put away three dozen prostitutes. You know they're a freak, so you imagine they look like a freak. If someone took a photo of me right now," he went on, "and put it on a website saying I killed eighteen women and chopped them up and made a stir fry out of them, then people'd say I look like a freak."

"You do look like a freak."

Chuck punched Darroll on the arm, not hard enough to hurt, but hard enough to warn him against further wisecracks.

"So," said Darroll, leaning over further to look at the text Chuck was reading, "is this guy like in the record books for killing all those women?" He knew the answer; he just wanted to know how well Chuck knew the topic.

"No way," Chuck replied. "There was this dude in England, a doctor. He killed hundreds and hundreds of his patients and nobody ever figured it out for the longest time. Because he mostly killed little old ladies, see? Who nobody was going to miss, and were going to die soon anyway. So by the time they finally figured him out, he was nearly at five hundred."

"What about 9-11?" Darroll objected. "There were three thousand people killed in that." Darroll always remembered the death toll. He'd thrown a spitball at Martha Kloofman during the two minutes' silence on the first anniversary of the Twin Towers, and Mrs Patterson had erupted in the biggest fury anyone could remember. He was dishonoring the memory of three thousand people, she yelled, and ought to be ashamed of himself. Darroll had pretended to be, though he wasn't; it was simpler to look shamefaced and say sorry, and let it blow over.

"9-11 doesn't count." Chuck shook his head firmly. "That was all in one go. Those guys in the planes didn't know how many people they were gonna get, it was all a big guess. Hell, I heard that that Bin Laden dude said he hadn't expected to kill anything like as many as that, he hadn't thought the towers would actually come down. No, these guys, the truck driver and the doctor, they chose to kill each and every one of their victims, separately and individually. Every goddamn time they thought to themselves 'I'm gonna kill someone today', and they went out and did it, and came back home, and a week later they did it again. That's way more twisted than killing thousands of people in one go with an airplane or a bomb."

"You know a hell of a lot about this weird shit," Darroll said, leaning back in his chair, and wondering whether he had misjudged Chuck Milne.

"Everyone needs to have a hobby," shrugged Chuck.

"You're sick."

"Says the guy who killed his pet cat," Chuck pointed out. "Dude, mistreating animals when you're a kid is an absolutely classic sign of a serial killer."

Darroll's heart gave a sudden thump.

"My cat was about a million years old and senile. She pissed all over my comic book collection," he said. "It was a mercy killing."

"That's what that English doctor probably said."

"Fuck you."

The irony was, Darroll hadn't killed his cat at all. She had taken the final trip to the veterinary surgery with kidney failure. Darroll had claimed afterwards that he'd killed her, just because he knew killing or torturing pets was the sign of a psychopath. Nobody had commented at the time. To find that Chuck had not only swallowed his lie, but drawn the conclusion from it that he wanted people to draw... Darroll felt very pleased with himself, all of a sudden.

Chuck was clicking his mouse, looking up one serial killer after another. Darroll knew most of them already. He let himself drift off into a fantasy where Chuck Milne was giving an interview to the television about how Darroll should have been caught before he killed all those people, how the warning signs had all been there but nobody had taken any notice. Except for Chuck, of course.

For once, Darroll was disappointed when the bell rang.

6

That afternoon in class, Ann Barker passed Darroll a note.

People were always passing notes in class, and Mrs Patterson never noticed, being kind of old and short sighted. But Darroll never wrote any, and very seldom received one.

COME SEE ME IN RECESS. COOL STUFF TO DO, it read. The writing was Chuck Milne's.

Darroll glanced along the row of desks at Chuck. Chuck had chosen to sit next to Vanessa Murchison instead of him, so Darroll had figured Chuck was pissed at him because of their exchange of insults in the library that morning. But Chuck gave him a sly grin.

Vanessa Murchison looked back at Darroll too. Vanessa was about the only other kid in the class who had as few friends as Darroll. She was a fat Goth and painted her fingernails black. Darroll's mother made tsk-ing noises when she first saw Vanessa, and said it made her look like she'd hit her own fingers with a hammer. This had sent Darroll into a pleasant five-minute reverie in which he kidnapped Ed Crowe, tied him up, and slowly broke every one of his fingers with a hammer till he screamed for mercy and pissed his pants from the pain.

Darroll somehow doubted that Chuck had any 'cool stuff' for him, but before he could decide whether to seek Chuck out at recess, Chuck came looking for him, practically as soon as he exited the classroom. Fat Vanessa was there too, her breasts wobbling like a sad old cow's udders as she walked along. She had a sketchbook under her arm. Vanessa was always drawing; weird, surreal cartoons and twisted landscapes that made Ms Pulleyn, the art teacher, make little cooing noises of appreciation. Darroll never got the time of day from Ms Pulleyn, because he couldn't draw worth shit.

Vanessa was always yammering on about how she was going to go to art camp next year. Darroll despised camps of all descriptions. Camp was just a way for his father to pay off yet more of his guilt debt with money, while forcing Darroll to hang out with a different set of jerks and losers who were as bad as the usual set. He had only ever made one friend at camp, a guy from Nebraska with terrible acne, called Milton. For a week they'd hung out, eaten at the same table, shared their entire repertoire of bad jokes (and Milton had a pretty impressive repertoire), been basically inseparable. At the end of camp, they'd pinky-sworn a vow to stay in touch; Milton had even hinted that Darroll might come visit him some day, warning him that Omaha was terrible. Darroll had assured him it couldn't be as bad as Muldoon.

Darroll had written Milton an eight-page letter and mailed it excitedly, and then he waited and waited, until it became clear that he was never going to hear from Milton again.

"What's this shit all about?" Darroll asked Chuck, ignoring Vanessa.

Chuck wouldn't talk until he dragged Darroll and Vanessa away from everyone else, into the little space opposite the school janitor's office that smelt of disinfectant and mashed potato.

"I want to form a club," he finally said.

"Who'd join a club with you?" asked Vanessa, pushing a piece of chewing gum into her fat mouth.

"You two, to begin with," said Chuck. "You're both pretty goddamn miserable at this school, aren't you?"

Darroll nodded, and Vanessa grunted an assent.

"You both get left out of the cool things that everyone else does because of their stupid little cliquey games?"

Again, Darroll and Vanessa agreed that it was so.

"Yeah. Me too. I'm starting a club for everyone who's not part of a clique."

Darroll was about to point out to Chuck that to do so would only be forming one more clique, and actually perpetuating the whole clique system; but he kept his mouth shut. Something about Chuck's air was getting him interested, despite himself.

"The reason we're not in a clique," Vanessa said, slightly indistinctly through her gum, "is that we're outsiders. We aren't social animals like the jocks and muscle guys, or even the chess club. We enjoy our own company because we see through the falsity of traditional social structures. We know nobody outside us can come close to matching the fascination and complexity of our inner monologues."

Darroll didn't know how he managed to keep himself from laughing aloud, or how Vanessa managed to even say that with a straight face.

Chuck, however, nodded at Vanessa as if she'd come up with some pearl of utter wisdom. "See, that's why you're perfect for the club. You're special."

Vanessa gave him a sharp look, and Chuck shook his head. "Not like that, special. Unique. You don't conform."

"Wouldn't if I could, couldn't if I would," Vanessa said smugly, and bit down on her gum.

"You're the same, Darroll," Chuck said to him. "You can't or won't fit in and people don't like that."

"Fine," Darroll said, speaking at last. "I don't like people." And that includes you two assholes, he added silently to himself.

"So. There's a couple more people I want to ask. Can you guys meet at five o'clock tonight in Celebration Burger?"

Darroll's instinctive response was to tell Chuck to shove his celebration burger up his fat ass, but he squashed it. Curiosity was rising in his mind. He shrugged. "Sure."

"Celebration Burger is evil," Vanessa protested. "All fast food just rots. It's a symbol of how the western world's values are becoming sicker and more homogenized."

Chuck rolled his eyes. "Fine, fine. If we want to meet someplace different the second meeting, we can. This is just an obvious place, that everyone knows, for us to meet up and talk. You don't have to eat a rotburger if you don't want to."

Vanessa pulled a face that was plainly meant to indicate that she was giving the question serious thought, as though it were an issue of life and death, or survival of the human race. Finally she said "Oh, what the hell. We're all going to die horrible deaths anyway, soon enough."

I could arrange that, thought Darroll.

7

Celebration Burger was owned by an old couple. They had resisted all the burger chains' blandishments over the years, and kept it resolutely independent, a mom and pop show. When one or both of them died, the chains would swoop in and make Celebration Burger their own. The old laminated yellow paper menus and superannuated milk shake machines would be swept away, replaced by the best and newest and blandest upgrades that money could buy.

But for now, Celebration endured. It sat on the corner of Third and Main where Third ended, opposite the long brick wall covered in a big civic mural, of which Muldoon was disproportionately proud. You got a good view of the mural from the windows of the restaurant. It featured a big railroad train, some American Indians in unrealistic buckskin clothing, some World War II GIs, and a clump of smiling kids who apparently represented The Future. You didn't get many smiling kids in Muldoon these days. For that matter, there were no GIs or warpainted braves about, either. And the rail line through Muldoon had been abandoned years ago.

There were five people waiting when Darroll arrived at Celebration Burger, ten minutes late. None of them were smiling.

They were in a corner booth. Vanessa Murchison was squashed into it, her fat belly squeezed by the table edge, like dough being divided by a cookie cutter. She had a burger in front of her, despite her protestations earlier.

Next to her was Chuck, and next to him was Joe Boardman. Boardman was a year younger than Chuck and Darroll, and although he was on the football team, he was nailed into a box labelled 'pariah' because he had red hair, and because he was gay.

Alongside Boardman was another girl, a skinny little thing with big round glasses and no tits. Darroll didn't know her, didn't even know what grade she was in, though if she was next to Boardman, he guessed she might be the same age as him.

Lastly, there was Rowdy Serxner. Darroll wasn't surprised to see him; he knew Rowdy hung out with Chuck sometimes, playing Dungeons and Dragons and stupid lameass escapist stuff like that. Rowdy always had dirt under his fingernails and smelt like cow shit, because his folks were farmers and made Rowdy help on the farm after school. So Rowdy would pretend to be a hobbit in the middle ages, or something crazy like that. Rowdy was too dumb to realise that in the real middle ages, everyone had to help look after cows and get cow shit under their fingernails.

Darroll squeezed into the booth next to Vanessa, making six around the corner table. It was a round table, being in the window bay, and Darroll had a sudden crazy thought that Chuck had brought them here to declare them all Knights of the Round Table and say that they had to go around robbing the rich to give to the poor. If he did, Darroll was going to take his burger and walk out.

"Well, hey, guys," said Chuck, sounding nervous. It was probably the first time he'd ever tried to address as many as five other people at once. Certainly the only time he'd done so, Darroll figured, without someone smacking him round the head or throwing things at him to shut him up.

"Hey hey," said Rowdy. Darroll grunted. Nobody else said anything.

"Firstly," Chuck said, "I'm going to ask you all to swear yourselves to secrecy."

Boardman gave Chuck a look. So did the girl next to Boardman.

"Y'see," Chuck went on, "the thing is, if this club takes off like I'm hoping it will, we aren't going to want people to know about it."

"Why?" asked Rowdy. "Is it gonna be popular?"

"Hell, no." Chuck picked up a long French fry from his tray, and waved it at Rowdy to emphasise his point. "It's going to be way, way unpopular."

"So instead of us being asocial loners who live inside our own heads all the time," Vanessa said, "we're going to be asocial loners who live inside each other's heads? Pardon me, but it hardly sounds an improvement."

"That's not the reason I want you to swear," Chuck said, starting to sound irate. "It's because... well, you guys remember Columbine?"

There was a general hubbub round the table. Vanessa started to shove at Darroll, trying to get out, but she was wedged too tightly to use much force. "No way," Rowdy said, with a horrified air, and Boardman gave Chuck another of those looks.

"Shut up, and take a chill pill!" Chuck slapped the table, and the sound of it shocked the little group into silence.

Chuck went on, speaking very quietly, and glancing around as though he feared eavesdroppers. "We are not going to shoot up Isidor Straus High, much though it may deserve it. We're not going to assassinate Mr Tidmarsh or Mrs Patterson, much though they may both deserve that. But if people hear broken-telephone gossip about us, they... might get the wrong idea and think we are. So we all keep quiet as the grave about it, okay?"

"I don't get it," said Rowdy, and the girl between Rowdy and Boardman spoke for the first time. "I don't either," she said in a little voice.

"So come on," Chuck said. "Even if some of you don't want to join the club, you still have to swear you'll never tell. Really swear. Swear, like, on the Bible."

"I'm not swearing on the Bible," Vanessa said. She'd stopped trying to push Darroll onto the floor and escape from the booth, and was picking the gherkin slices out of her burger. "The Bible is a tome of hypocrisy and lies, that distorts any truth it once held by reflecting it through a mirror of hatred, held up by the middle classes and middle Americans."

"Are you a Satanist?" asked Darroll.

"I fucking am not. All religions are the crutch of the weak and ignorant," began Vanessa.

Chuck slapped the table again. "Hey! I don't care if you actually swear on the Bible or not, long as you swear by something you hold dear, something that means as much to you as anything else you can think of."

"Hey, Vanessa can swear on that hamburger, then," said Rowdy, and snorted with laughter. Vanessa picked up the discarded pickle slice and threw it at him.

"Guys!" pleaded Chuck. "I just want you to swear."

Boardman was the first one to shrug and assent. "What the hell, it doesn't hurt me. Who'm I gonna tell anyway? I swear – what do I swear, Milne?"

"Swear never to discuss the club's existence or doings with anyone outside the club. Or where you can be overheard by those not in the club."

"Fine. I swear that." Boardman put his hand to his chest and thumped it gently, over his heart.

"What about you, Beth?" Chuck asked the quiet girl.

"I swear by almighty God," said the girl, as though she was about to give evidence in a court case.

Rowdy looked at Darroll and Vanessa. Darroll looked back, staring him in the eye, and Rowdy looked away.

"Oh, what the fuck," Darroll said. "Like Boardman says, it doesn't do any harm. I swear on my life I'll keep the secret."

"Yeah, okay," Rowdy muttered. "I swear by the Lord Jesus and the Bible, I won't speak about this stupid bullshit to anybody."

Chuck looked about to fire a verbal rejoinder at Rowdy for the 'stupid bullshit' remark, but Vanessa got in first. "And I vow by every fibre of my mortal being that if I break the oath of silence, may I be ripped apart and subjected to the most extreme anguish and agony ever known to man or woman," she said, closing her eyes and holding not one but both hands to her chest. Her wrists crossed between her boobs, her arms emulating a support bra.

"And I too vow by all I hold dear to me to keep forever secret the existence of the Psychopath Club," said Chuck. From the way he said it, it was clear that he hadn't waited till last by accident; it had been part of his plan to reveal the clique's name as the closing words of the oath, for dramatic effect.

Darroll suppressed an urge to reach out his leg under the table and kick him.

Five pairs of eyes fixed themselves on Chuck, who grinned back at them. For once he was the focus of attention, and he obviously relished it.

"I hear you ask, what is the Psychopath Club?" Chuck went on, even though nobody had asked him any such thing.

"What is the Psychopath Club?" asked Boardman, in a stupid nasal voice that was an obvious attempt to emulate Chuck's.

"The Psychopath Club," Chuck said, speaking more softly still and taking another wary glance around, "is a celebration of everything that is dark, antisocial, and morally repugnant in the so-called human race."

Vanessa visibly perked up and started paying closer attention. Darroll could see her mentally filing away some of Chuck's turns of phrase for recycling.

"I think it's fair to say that we have all known what it is to be an outcast from our peers." Chuck looked around the other five. "Some of us have tried to overcome it. Some of us have revelled in our status as loners. Some have possibly pretended it isn't going on. But it is. Let's face it," he said, dropping out of his pompous mode and back to informality, "we are all having a fucking rotten time at Straus High. Right? It's people who get treated like this, people who get shoved around and bullied and our clothes ripped and bottles of soda poured into our book bags, that go on to do… well… pretty terrible things. Some of them shoot up their schools and kill people for revenge. Some of them make it out of school but then go around killing people afterwards."

"Now I'm not saying," Chuck hurriedly went on, waving a finger at Rowdy, whose mouth was already open to protest, "that any of us would be at risk of turning into the Unabomber or Ted Bundy or anything like that. But those jerks who make our life hell, our families who don't care or understand, our teachers who turn a blind eye? They don't know that. For all they care, we could be half a dozen mass murderers in training, sitting right here in Celebration Burger chowing on hamburgers like normal people. It would almost serve them right if we were."

Darroll listened in silence. Chuck's words rang in his brain like a fire alarm; an unwelcome sound, a sound to scare the hearer, but a sound that wouldn't go away and couldn't be ignored.

"You all know I enjoy reading up on psychos," Chuck said. "The study of abnormal psychology is fascinating in its own right. Look how many damn books people still read about Jack the Ripper. Look how many books Ann Rule sells."

"Ann who?" asked Vanessa.

"She writes true crime books," Chuck explained. "About Ted Bundy, and the I-5 murders, and cases like that. Go into a bookstore, you'll see shelves of her writing."

A silent, thoughtful nod from Vanessa. Chuck spoke again. "You can't tell me that everyone who reads Ann Rule, or watches that movie about Columbine, is sick in the head."

"Can so too," interjected Vanessa. "Western society is sick in the head, every last member."

"Fine," sighed Chuck. "You know what I mean. I mean, it's normal people who do that. People who work nine to five and come home to their wives and kids. Not just misfits. But... I don't want to have to explain that to old Tidmarsh. Or to the cops. The Psychopath Club stays secret because... well, you know teachers. They always pick on the outsiders. They'd be bound to whip up some conspiracy theory, say we were going to blow up Straus High or shoot the Mayor or some bullshit. No, we're strictly a study and social group. Every meeting we have, we talk about sociopaths we've been reading up on... how they got that way, how they expressed themselves, what they did that gave them away to the law... that kind of thing. We are gonna study those people because they're fascinating, and to learn how we can prevent ourselves being like them, yeah?"

An obvious sneer formed on Joe Boardman's face. "This sounds like anti-queer camp to me," he growled, and Darroll snorted at the mention of camp.

"Nuh uh. We are not judging anyone, or setting ourselves up to say who or what is right or wrong. We are neutral. Our aim is knowledge. Shit, Joe, I wouldn't try to talk you out of being... like you are. Apart from anything else you'd kick my ass for trying," said Chuck.

Boardman nodded. "Damn right I would."

The table fell silent. Rowdy picked up his burger and looked at it, as though hoping it might give him inspiration. It was the skinny girl, Beth, who spoke.

"Well, I'm in," she said. "I love reading about things like that. I know it's sort of icky but it's amazing to find out other people are into it too. I didn't think anyone else in school was till I found you, Chuck."

Rowdy was obviously happier to follow someone else's lead than to go out on a limb himself. "Sure, why not," he said. "I totally know who Jack the Ripper really was. He was the Queen of England's doctor and they hushed it up, like they hush up flying saucers and pyramids."

"Meh, I'm in," Boardman said without further elaboration.

"This could be the start of something never before seen in the annals of history," Vanessa began. Chuck rolled his eyes, and Vanessa pouted. "Well, it could! We're going to be delving into the depths of the psyche and questing through the furthest levels of the id. Who knows what we're going to find?"

"Gonna find that your ideas about psychology are decades out of date," yawned Boardman, and Vanessa pouted again.

"Well, Darroll?" asked Chuck. "Gonna make it six?"

Darroll's heart was still thumping, as though he'd run all the way to the burger joint. He wasn't at all certain that he liked the idea of a group whose avowed purpose was to talk people out of being a psychopath, rather than the reverse.

On the other hand, he had never been part of a clique; certainly not one with a vow of secrecy and a hidden agenda. And after all, why did he need to worry? How could they talk him out of being what came naturally to him?

"Sure," he said. He was astonished at how nonchalant his voice sounded, how completely calm, as though he were responding to a waitress asking if he wanted regular or curly fries.

Chuck seemed delighted at the hundred per cent sign-up, as though he hadn't expected it. Quite likely, he hadn't even expected anyone to turn up at the meeting at all.

"Then, ladies and gentlemen... the Psychopath Club is hereby formed."

He lifted his glass of soda in front of him, then put it back down again when nobody showed any sign of joining in the toast.

8

The second meeting of the Psychopath Club took place that Saturday.

They had agreed to hold it at Boardman's place. Chuck and Rowdy both lived out of town, inconveniently difficult to reach. Darroll nixed any suggestion of holding it at his house; he couldn't stand the thought of them meeting his mother, though of course he didn't say that. Vanessa also vetoed holding it at her place, with no explanation, and Boardman had finally offered his house.

Darroll couldn't be bothered to drive to Boardman's; he could walk it in five minutes. It took him more time than that to get there, though, because for reasons he couldn't quite pin down, he dawdled his way along until he saw the Serxner family's ancient pick-up drive past him and stop outside the Boardman home. Rowdy got out and walked up to the door. Darroll was still half a block away, but he put pace on, and by the time Boardman had let Rowdy in, he was close enough that Boardman could see him coming, and held the door open for him to come in as well.

The Boardmans lived in a pleasant ranch house, which was a lot bigger than Darroll's. Mr Boardman was inside, reading a newspaper in his undershirt. He didn't look at Rowdy and Darroll, didn't even show any sign of having noticed their arrival. Mrs Boardman did, though. She came over to them and offered them iced tea. Rowdy accepted; Darroll declined. He hated iced tea. Mrs Boardman bustled away to get Rowdy his drink. She had red hair as well; that was obviously where her son got it from. From the way she was running round, being nice to Joe Boardman's friends, she was obviously one of those pathetic women who devoted themselves entirely to their son; the sort who thought that, because now they had children to raise, their own life was effectively over. Darroll renewed his mental vow that, even if by some miracle he did ever hook up with a girl, he was never, ever going to have any kids.

Joe led them down to the basement. Chuck and Vanessa were already down there. Chuck was sitting in a lawn chair. There was another lawn chair next to it, but Vanessa wasn't in it. Darroll knew why; it was because she was too fat to get her ass into it.

"Hi, guys," Chuck said. Vanessa lifted one hand and gave a tiny little wave with two fingers, like she was the Queen of England.

A couple of minutes later Beth turned up and was shown down to the basement with iced tea. "Well, we're all here," Chuck said. He still sounded surprised when he said that. "Psychopath Club meeting is open."

Darroll was expecting Chuck to continue speaking, but he didn't, and there was an awkward silence for a long moment. Darroll gave Boardman a sidelong glance, and found Boardman was giving him one at exactly the same moment, which made them both turn away in a hurry. Thankfully, Chuck did speak again at this point.

"Well, uh," he began. "Did we all do some reading up on psychopaths?" He looked around the other five with a vague, hopeful smile.

Rowdy slid to his feet. "I have."

Everyone looked at Rowdy. It seemed that nobody had expected him to speak up. Darroll certainly hadn't.

Rowdy brandished some crumpled sheets of paper. "Jack the Ripper," he said with relish.

Rowdy, not to Darroll's surprise, was a dreadful speaker. He said "uh", a lot, and lost his place in his notes, and rambled; but somehow, Darroll found himself becoming drawn in by the big farmboy's rambling. His theory was that the most notorious murderer ever (that was what Rowdy called him) had actually been, not only a member of upper-class English society, but part of Queen Victoria's own household – her physician, Doctor Gull. Rowdy dwelt melodramatically on how he would climb into a hansom-cab (whatever they were) and be carried away from the West End of London to the East End to commit his savage crimes, then return and resume his place in Court with nobody any the wiser. Nobody except Rowdy Serxner, of course.

Darroll daydreamed a mental picture of Doctor Gull. In keeping with Gull's surname, Darroll pictured him as a tall thin figure, with a big beak of a nose, and a cloak wrapped round him. He could lift it, like a bird's wings spreading. He would lean over Queen Victoria, asking her politely whether she was quite well. Perhaps he would give her something now and again for penny-ante little ailments, like headaches or period pain (or was the Queen too old for periods by then?) Pocketing a massive salary for it. And then off into his hansom-cab; and the next day, another East End murder in the London press, newspaper vendors hawking frightful headlines at every street corner.

From there, his daydreams came homing back in, gradually and logically, to himself as murderer. He looked round the other members of the Psychopath Club, and mentally drew cross-hairs on each one of them in turn.

Rowdy would be awkward to kill because he was so burly. He could probably snap Darroll in half if it came to a fight. Chuck? He got on Darroll's nerves, sometimes, but he was still the closest he had to a friend. Chuck had a pass to staying alive.

Boardman was a possibility; Boardman was gay. He could possibly pass it off as a hate crime. His eyes lingered on Joe Boardman for a long few seconds, taking in his pale orange hair and his freckles and his open-neck shirt. He was shorter than Darroll, but Darroll was sure Boardman was fitter than him. He played a lot of sport.

The girls might be easier, because, well, they were girls. Even though Vanessa almost certainly outweighed him. Furthermore, he'd once seen a fight between Vanessa and Ann Barker. Ann Barker had gone over in ten seconds flat. Vanessa wasn't just a heavyweight, for a girl, but she wasn't afraid to use her size physically when the occasion demanded.

Beth, now. Beth was so small and fragile-looking.

Sure, Darroll was a member of this same club as her, but he had to start with someone. If he chose to murder a member of the Psychopath Club, Beth Vines was the obvious target.

Then again, Beth Vines had never done anything to piss him off, the way Ed Crowe and his cronies had. Now, there was a nice idea.

Forget about running Crowe over in a car. Use a bomb or something, blow him sky high, try and take out Crowe's entire crowd of hangers-on. Perhaps a teacher or two from Straus as well –

Rowdy was wrapping up his lecture, so Darroll reined his thoughts in.

When Rowdy fell silent at last, and began to straighten up his sheets of paper, covered with scrawled notes, Chuck began to applaud. After a second or two, Darroll joined in.

"Are we planning to do this kind of thing every meeting?" asked Vanessa. "Because I'm behind it, if we are."

Rowdy beamed. Chuck appeared pleased as well, which Darroll supposed was down to him having had the idea for the club in the first place.

"I guess it works for me," Joe Boardman said. "My folks probably won't mind us using the basement. They'll be pleased to see me hanging out with people," he added with a wry expression.

"Who's gonna speak next meeting?" Vanessa asked, and for some reason, looked straight at Darroll. Chuck looked at him, too.

"I guess I could," he found himself saying.

"You've two whole weeks to prep something," Chuck said.

"Two weeks," echoed Darroll. "A lot can happen in two weeks." He was still thinking of blowing up Ed Crowe with a bomb, and wondering how hard it would be to find out how to make one.

9

But Darroll didn't make the third meeting of the Psychopath Club, and not because of any bomb.

The radio woke him up, the last Monday before the summer vacation, talking cheerfully about how it was the coldest weather in the state for that time of year in over a decade. Darroll didn't need telling; his feet, his ridiculous feet, were sticking out from under the bedclothes, and they felt as though someone had dunked them in ice water. He slapped the button on top of his clock to silence the radio, and crawled out of bed to take a shower.

The shower restored some heat to his body. Towelling his black hair, Darroll checked his face in the mirror. He'd shaved yesterday, and though he had some stubble coming through, he could get away without it today. Shaving was a pain in the ass. Some of the boys in his class at school couldn't wait to get a full growth of facial hair. They thought it was manly. Darroll saw facial hair as one more thing that had no reason to exist, save to annoy him.

He dressed quickly, and threw a bowl of cereal and a glass of milk into his mouth, but somehow he was still running a couple of minutes late when he closed the front door and climbed into his car. Once inside the car he turned on the ignition, and then the radio. Even though he resented its age and its lack of style, he had discovered an odd equanimity in the big, lumbering old sedan; just him, inside a wall of steel and chrome, blocking out all the world for the few minutes it took to ride to school.

The road was empty. The sky above was leaden gray, and a steady rain came tumbling down, splashing in little puddles on the highway, dampening the trees on either side, till their branches sank down with the extra weight of the water clinging to their leaves. Next Monday, thought Darroll, he wouldn't have to make this drive, and the thought helped him to reach the conclusion that he was actually feeling okay for once, and that the world was a place that he could bear to live in.

Maybe that was why he put his foot down on the gas pedal a little harder, as the houses at the side of the road grew closer together and he came nearer to town and to school. Maybe that was why he turned the volume up on his radio, and hit the controls to turn it from the chatter of a news station to the booming beat of FM rock.

For about fifteen seconds he enjoyed the music. Then the radio let out a great, blaring blast of static. Darroll took his eyes off the road for a second to look at the dial and make sure that the radio, as decrepit as the rest of the car, hadn't lost the station.

When he looked back at the road, there was someone in his path who hadn't been there two seconds previously.

Instinct made him jerk at the wheel with a sudden muscle spasm, and the Oldsmobile veered sideways. Too fast, he knew immediately, and he cursed himself for letting his instincts dictate his actions. If he'd had time to think about it, he'd have just knocked over the idiot who had appeared in his way –

Then he got his first proper look at the idiot who had appeared in his way, and for a moment time ratcheted down into slow motion. Only for a moment, as he fought to regain control, realising that, instead of gripping the pavement, his tires were struggling to find purchase on the muddy puddles at the road's edge.

He saw a burly figure, at the upper level of human height and broadness, standing perfectly casually, making no effort to get out of his way. And although he only saw it for so brief a second, he could tell – it was impossible not to notice, with absolute clarity, so astonishing a feature – that the figure didn't have a normal human head, but that of a horse.

For a heartbeat Darroll questioned the evidence of his own eyes, but he didn't find any answers in his mind. He hauled frantically at the wheel, trying to regain control, but the car underneath him was losing more and more grip, going more and more sideways. He knew he was in trouble, big trouble, and that the heartbeat he had wasted in amazement might be one of very few he had left.

The car started to spin, and he realised how big his trouble was. Realised he was going to die here. Realised he was going to die without having so much as kissed a girl (never mind having sex with one), or travelled abroad, or seen New York or the sea, or carried out a single one of the murders he'd planned.

The last thought that passed through his head as the car hit the fence was that it seemed so very unfair, and yet so very typical of life, that he should die just before summer vacation started.

And then there was an impact, and he didn't have any more thoughts, not for a long time.

* * *

Time no longer meant anything. He was aware of his own breathing, but it was beyond his capability to know whether he was taking one breath a minute, or a hundred, or a thousand. He was aware that he was horizontal, and that his body still possessed all its extremities, but where he was, he did not know. It seemed unimportant. He wasn't hungry, nor did he need the bathroom. He didn't need to think; and so he did not think.

He existed.

He kept on existing.

Every now and again he heard a voice, but the words that it spoke failed to connect with whatever part of his mind was tasked with deciphering sounds. He had no way of knowing if the voice was a familiar one; he no longer cared. He knew, somewhere tucked away in a corner of his mind, that there were people in his life; his mother, his father (no, wait, not his father), his teachers, Chuck and the Psychopath Club. At present he had no use for that knowledge, and it sat there, unused, like an ornament on a shelf, growing ever so slightly dusty, yet still perfect beneath its covering of grime.

He still existed.

From time to time someone came to move his body around. He saw no reason to prevent them doing so, and therefore he allowed them to.

The next day, a million years later, a voice came back. For some reason, this one stirred more of a response in him than the others. The voice's words trickled through his head like rainwater. Rain? It was raining that morning. The radio had said so.

It was his mother's voice. What was she doing here, talking to him?

"...Darroll? Honey? Are you there?" His eyes were closed. It didn't occur to him to open them. There was a touch on his right hand.

A male voice spoke too. One he didn't know. "You must be prepared. It may take him a long time to respond, even with sedation levels dropped. Brain injuries are... well, they're hard to predict."

"Darroll." His mom again. "It's me. Do you remember me?"

Well, what a stupid question. Of course he remembered her. She was his mother, not the grocery store clerk. He tried to say so, but somehow the syllables that came out of his mouth were "Cuh-cuh plff mrr yrr."

She gripped his hand more tightly. "He can hear me!" His mom sounded like she'd won ten bucks in the state lottery.

A familiar sensation was settling over him, like atmospheric mist. Frustration. His mother was nothing but a collection of platitudes. She had nothing original in her, not a thought, not a word. She sickened him with her cheap, artificial manner. Of course he could hear her. That was what his ears were for.

"Snrsh grp," he said, trying to fill the words with the scorn he felt.

But of course, being his mother, she didn't understand. She just squeezed his hand tighter.

10

Darroll was astonished when he was allowed to eat solids again.

He hadn't missed eating real food; he'd just forgotten that his mouth existed for other reasons than talking. But when he took a bite of potato, the whole experience of eating came rushing back into his memory, like an avalanche down a mountainside. It was just an ordinary small piece of boiled potato (and boiled without salt at that), but he sat up in bed and damn near shouted out loud for the sheer bliss of it; the taste, the texture, the heat it radiated onto his tongue and his gums. Finally it started to dissolve in his saliva and he swallowed it, but that was almost equally astonishing for him, to feel it sliding past his throat and downward into his stomach.

He'd read that the acid in the human stomach could burn a hole in a carpet. How long had he been without solid food? What did that mean for his stomach? Had it been working away inside him, churning out more and more acid that wasn't being used to digest his dinner? Was it building up until he was one big, sloshing reservoir of corrosive juices inside? It hardly seemed likely. Maybe his stomach figured out it hadn't been used for a while, and shut down the acid production, like a factory laying off its workers when it was slow season.

At around the same time, they started to let him use the can, rather than have to keep lying in bed and piss into a bedpan, which was a major annoyance. Apart from the embarrassment factor of having to give it to the nurse afterwards, the hospital used disposable cardboard bedpans. They felt and looked cheap, and he hated having to touch them even with his hands, never mind slide them down under the bedclothes and onto his dick. And what if he had to piss so much that he filled the bedpan up and it splashed everywhere? What if he dropped it after he used it, or the nurse did?

It never happened, but after a while he almost wished it would because, after all, how gross could it be? They'd just give him another bed bath, and change his sheets, and it'd be fine, he tried to tell himself. But his mind wasn't about to listen to reason on that one, and kept insisting that even a few drops of spilled urine would be as big a disaster as a chemical plant going off bang and spraying chemicals over half of India. Yeah, right. Between the acid in his stomach and the urine in his bladder, he was just full of gross liquids.

So when he was allowed to shuffle to the head (as they called it in the hospital for some reason, like they were on board a damn Navy frigate) it was slow and irksome, but still a big improvement.

The next development was that he got to see a couple of doctors. Darroll guessed they were big cheeses, because they weren't wearing white coats like the other doctors who came around his ward; they were wearing fancy suits. He now knew, though he'd already surmised, that he must be downstate rather than in Muldoon's tiny hospital. Doctors in Muldoon General didn't wear suits like that.

"Well, young Darroll, it's nice to meet you," said the older one, which immediately rubbed Darroll the wrong way. Even his mother didn't call him 'young Darroll' any more, because he sulked so much when she did.

"I suppose you know something of what happened to you?" asked the younger one. Darroll didn't dislike the look of him so much; he was younger, wore a bow tie instead of a normal one, and had round glasses perched slightly askew on his nose. Darroll had to suppress the urge to reach up to him and straighten them.

"I smashed my automobile up," Darroll said. He tried to sound contrite.

"Well, yes," said the young doctor, "though oddly enough it wasn't all that badly damaged, from what I heard. Nothing like as badly damaged as you were yourself."

"Yes," the older one took over. "Darroll, you've suffered a traumatic brain injury."

Yeah, thought Darroll. Like there was ever going to be any brain injury that wasn't traumatic.

The younger one piped up again, as though he'd read Darroll's unspoken thoughts. "By traumatic, here," he explained, "we mean in the medical sense of the word. You know that when doctors use a word sometimes, it doesn't mean quite the same as when you or your friends at school might use it? So when I say 'traumatic', I don't mean that it gave you a fright... though I'm sure it must have. Traumatic, in the medical sense, means an injury that's caused by a blow or an impact from an outside force. You follow me?"

Darroll did follow the younger doctor. With his bow tie and glasses he looked like some kind of 1970s comedian, but he could tell that he was making a definite attempt to meet Darroll on his own level, without talking down to him. Whereas the older doctor didn't look like he gave a shit.

"So if I were to take an axe and cut your head off," Bow Tie went on, "when we wrote out your death certificate, we'd have to put 'traumatic decapitation' on the form as cause of death." And he chuckled quietly. Darroll found himself smiling too, for some reason. It wasn't often you found some dude who could go around making jokes about cutting your head off with an axe. He was starting to warm to Bow Tie.

"I know a guy who lost a finger chopping wood for the furnace," Darroll said, making an effort to do his part in the conversation. "Would that be a traumatic decapitation too?"

"Traumatic amputation," corrected Bow Tie. "Amputation covers any part of your body being... uh... removed. Decapitation strictly refers to your head."

The older doctor began to shuffle papers in the folder he was holding. Darroll hated people who did that. If you were bored by a conversation, you should either have the frankness to say so, or better still, go find a different conversation. Not stand there rustling papers and getting on everyone's nerves.

"By the way, I haven't introduced myself, have I?" said Bow Tie. "My name's Vickery, and this is Dr. Schwartz."

"Hello, Dr Vickery," Darroll said.

Vickery shook his head. "I'm not Dr Vickery. I'm merely plain and simple Louis Vickery. I don't hold a medical or a doctoral degree; I'm a therapist. Dr Schwartz here is the Doctor. He's a neurosurgeon, to be precise. A very experienced one at that."

Schwartz smiled thinly, making a show of being modest about his skills. Shame he couldn't be bothered to make it look even halfway realistic.

"Did you operate on me, Dr Schwartz?"

"I did," Schwartz said. "And I'm pleased to say that I found a brain inside your skull, right where it should be."

Darroll guessed that was medical humour. He figured he'd stick with Saturday Night Live.

"You can either think of yourself as very lucky, or as very unlucky," Dr Schwartz went on. "It was most unlucky that when you came off the road, you collided with a fence. One of the fence posts was snapped in half, and the top half came right through your windshield and straight at your head."

"What are the odds, huh?" said Darroll, since Schwartz seemed to have paused for a reply.

As Darroll expected, Schwartz didn't actually care what Darroll said, as long as he made some response. "The impact of the post fractured your skull; what we call a depressed fracture. The force was enough to bend the bone inward slightly. In itself, that isn't too disastrous, because the human skull is pretty solid. The real problem was this." And with the air of a conjuror plucking a rabbit out of a top hat, he reached into his suit's outside pocket, and withdrew a small plastic zip-lock bag. Darroll leaned over to look at it; there was something inside it, but he couldn't make it out.

"The fence post had a nail protruding," Schwartz went on, "attaching some barbed wire to the post. The angle of impact was such that the nail was facing you when the collision occurred, and, I'm afraid to say, the nail penetrated your skull and into your brain beneath."

Darroll reached out a hand, silently, as he listened to the neurologist. It didn't sound good for him. But, he reminded himself, he was still sitting here with what seemed like a working body. His mind appeared to be working too. Seven nines were sixty-three. Pierre is the capital of South Dakota. George Eliot wrote *Silas Marner*, only not really, because George Eliot wasn't her real name...

Dr Schwartz placed the baggie in Darroll's hand. He lifted it closer to his eyes; he could see what was in it, now, though given what Schwartz had said, he wasn't surprised. It was a nail. Not a nice new shiny one, fresh from the hardware store; it was bent halfway along, and tarnished with something that looked like rust. But Darroll presumed it wasn't rust.

Schwartz was evidently waiting for him again, so he dropped his hand with the baggie still in it. "I'm brain damaged? Hell. That's gonna make for a good range of insults when I get back to… Am I gonna be going back to school? I'm not going to have to live in a special unit, am I?"

Schwartz smiled what was evidently meant to be a reassuring smile. Vickery smiled too; Darroll much preferred Vickery's.

"We're going to have to monitor you for a spell longer," Schwartz said. "You may have some cognitive difficulties, or some functional ones; but so far things are looking pretty bright." He looked around as if about to make a confession that he didn't want overheard, and Darroll was suddenly put in mind of Chuck Milne. "See, the human brain is a mighty complex thing. I've studied it all my life and, just between you and me, there's a million and one things that I don't know about it."

Darroll figured that was meant to sound light-hearted, put him on Schwartz's side. To Darroll, the immediate effect was that it made Schwartz sound like he was licensed to poke blithely around the inside of people's heads, without knowing what the hell he was looking for in there.

Schwartz was still talking. "When someone presents with brain trauma," he said, "the general rule is that you stop the brain bleeding, remove any foreign objects or fragments of bone, and hope for the best. Don't ask me to quote statistics." Darroll hadn't asked. "In this field, every case is unique. But I can say that I've seen several patients with injuries to the brain more severe than yours, who have made a complete recovery, or almost complete."

Darroll didn't like that 'almost', but what could he do? "How long before I know if I'm gonna be one of them?"

"Well, that's Mr Vickery's department," said Schwartz. "My role in your recovery is essentially complete; I've done the hard part, now he gets to do the easy part. He will be giving you therapy, physical and mental, both to get you back up to full speed again, and to assess the likelihood of you being left with any ill effects. I shall be keeping an eye on you too, to make sure your recovery is going according to plan, and if Louis wants me to look at anything specific, I will, of course."

"This sounds... expensive," Darroll said.

Schwartz and Vickery looked at one another, then both looked back at him. "Fortunately," Vickery said, "you're out of the woods on that one. Your father's healthcare policy also covers you since you're under eighteen."

"Even though I don't live with him?"

"Even though," Vickery confirmed. "The policy doesn't specify that you have to. So his healthcare will be picking up the tab."

Darroll began to sink back into a helpless, angry resentment. His father had paid for the car he'd nearly killed himself in; his father was going to pay for the medical care to fix him back up again. Was he ever going to be able to cut himself away from his father's bankroll, actually live his own life? The thought of going on for year after year like his mother, leeching off a man who paid for her to spend all day in front of the television, because the divorce court forced him to, made him feel ill.

"You all right, Darroll?" Apparently Vickery had noticed his sudden fit of emotion.

He forced it back down. "I'm fine... I think," he said. "It's a lot to take on board, you know?" He looked back at Schwartz. "How long did it take to fix my head, Dr Schwartz?"

Schwartz raised an eyebrow; he hadn't been expecting that question. "Hmm. A few hours, as I recall. Longer than I wanted, quicker than I feared. Some of it was trying to fit pieces of your skull back together. You have a bunch of teeny-tiny little screws in your head now, by the way. Nothing to be concerned about!" he went on, seeing Darroll's startled reaction. "You might be surprised if you knew how many people live perfectly normal lives with bits of metal holding their head together. Steel mesh, some of them, or plates. All sorts."

"I must have one doozy of a scar."

"You do," Schwartz agreed; "but if your hair grows back the way it's been growing so far it'll cover it up nicely. Nobody will see it unless you go bald, and by that time, you'll be happily married, settled down and raising kids."

Oh, you have no idea, thought Darroll.

"Right," Schwartz said, closing the folder of notes he was carrying and shaking it once or twice, to make the contents fall neatly into place, the way he'd made the fragments of Darroll's skull fit back together. "Unless you have any more questions, I shall leave you with Mr Vickery. Do you want to keep that nail as a memento?"

Darroll looked at it again. "Yeah... Yes, I think I will."

"Why not?" Schwartz agreed. "Loads of kids have teeth as souvenirs from the dentist, but how many of them have a nail that they can say has been inside their brain? That should trump everyone else at show-and-tell."

Show-and-tell? He was sixteen. Darroll wanted to fling the nail into Schwartz's face. Or better still, get a hammer and pound it into his skull, see how he liked it. Who was going to pull the nail out of the neurosurgeon's head, eh? Physician, heal thyself.

Vickery coughed quietly and his eyes caught Darroll's. For an instant there was a flash of recognition between them, which removed a percentage of Darroll's anger. Vickery, at least, evidently remembered his schooldays well enough to know show-and-tell was far behind Darroll.

Oblivious, Schwartz turned away. It wasn't until he was gone that Darroll reminded himself, uneasily, that this man had saved his life.

11

Over the next few days Vickery ran Darroll through a medley of tests; everything from spatial reasoning, through general knowledge, to being able to walk along a straight line while touching his nose with one hand, as if he were a drunk driver hauled over by a cop. Although Darroll reflected, after that one, perhaps it wasn't all that unreasonable, given how he wound up in hospital. He hadn't been drunk when he came off the road, of course; he'd never been drunk in his life.

As each test was about to begin, Darroll wondered uneasily whether this would be the one that revealed just what part of his brain the nail had decided to spear itself into. But every time, he came out the other side feeling that he'd done about as well as he would have done before the accident; no better, no worse. He couldn't play the piano, but as he said to Louis Vickery, "I couldn't before." And Vickery had groaned at the ancient joke, and pretended to hit him, and Darroll figured that he might actually come through all right. All right for a guy with screws in his head, anyway.

It was three weeks before Christmas when Vickery told him that he was going home. He seemed surprised by how unenthusiastic Darroll was.

"Why don't you want to go home, champ? You're better than anyone who's had a nail pounded into his head has a right to be. Christmas is coming up. Don't you want your Christmas presents? Hell, you slept right through Thanksgiving."

Darroll hadn't meant to explain, but there was something about Louis Vickery and that damn bow tie of his. Something that made him actually want to talk to the man.

"Uh, well, home isn't exactly ideal," he said, and as he said it he knew how inadequate an explanation that was.

But to his surprise, Vickery nodded understandingly. "Yeah, I can see where you're coming from. Your Dad lives down in Georgia, no brothers or sisters, it's just you and your Mom, right? And – if you breathe a word of this I will take that nail from your bedside drawer and hammer it back into your head – having met your Mom a few times I can see why you don't relish the thought of going back to her."

Vickery took a few steps, then turned to look at Darroll again. "Darroll, you're a smart kid, and like a lot of smart kids, you're a misfit. And living in a little place like Muldoon isn't ideal for you. You don't belong there. I don't rightly know where you do belong; it could be New York, or the army, or an Antarctic expedition – but you weren't born to be a small town boy all your life."

"Muldoon fucking sucks," said Darroll simply. "And everyone in Muldoon fucking sucks too."

"I ought to wag my finger at you for using that word," said Vickery, "but I'm not going to, because I'm enough of a realist to know that there are kids half your age who know that word, these days. And when I was sixteen I used it too, so I couldn't call you on it without being a hypocrite, and I don't like hypocrisy." He gave a long sigh. "I'm not going to try to say you're exactly like I was when I was sixteen, but I grew up in a small town in New Hampshire, and I was a bright inquisitive kid, and I hated it too. I used to pray at night, literally pray, that my parents would move to somewhere bigger. Somewhere big enough to have someone else who knew how to play chess, or even a whole club of them, and a library where I hadn't read every book on every shelf. But they didn't. So I finally got away, and went to college, and escaped. I've never lived in a small town since. I couldn't cope with Muldoon, or any of those little tiny burgs in your part of upstate."

He straightened his glasses on his nose, or tried to; in actual fact all he did was set them askew in the opposite direction. "I resented it, and it came pretty close to making me resent the whole human race. If you want my honest opinion, Darroll, I'm more worried about seeing that in you, than I am about that stupid little no-account hole in your head."

"I don't hate everyone," Darroll said. "Only most people. Say ninety-nine percent?" He delivered that verdict carefully, putting just enough humour and spin on the statement to have it bounce right on the line between being a flat statement and being a joke.

Vickery chose to take it as a joke; or at least, to laugh at it. "Sounds about like me at your age," he said. "But if you want my advice, here it is; it's not on a professional basis, you're not paying a cent for this, and neither is your father's insurance. You believe that the world's put one over on you, and you want to put one over back on the world. That's fine. But the best way to do that, is to show that you can overcome the problems you've had – including this accident – and go on to be a success. I don't know what kind of success you have in mind, and you likely don't know yourself. But if you play your cards right, you'll be one. You'll make a mark, and you'll show everyone that a kid from Muldoon can be just as big a deal as a kid from New York or L.A. In fact," he added, looking over the top of his glasses, "you could put Muldoon on the map. Everyone already heard of L.A. and New York, but whoever heard of Muldoon before? Give it a few years, though, and they'll say 'Oh, Muldoon! That's where Darroll Martock came from.'"

He adjusted his glasses again. "There, I've said my piece. You can get out of my hospital now."

"Isn't Dr Schwartz going to see me again first?" asked Darroll.

"I don't believe he needs to," Vickery said, in a careful voice that set Darroll's alarm bells ringing.

"Oh? Why not?"

"Because you're fine, as far as we can tell. You have no complications to worry about, no relapses, no impairment."

"And I guess that makes me boring," Darroll concluded. He had meant that as a joke, but the look on Vickery's face showed him that he'd hit a target he hadn't even been aiming at.

"A lot of surgeons, especially older and successful specialists," Vickery said, still in that careful tone, "find themselves starting to see people as a collection of symptoms rather than an actual person. The rarer the symptom, the more interesting the person. Someone who's staged a full recovery may be a success story in one sense, but in another..."

"You mean Schwartz hoped I'd need a bunch more work doing?"

Darroll shot back at Vickery. "He wanted the excuse to poke round in my brain some more?"

"I didn't say that, Darroll, and I didn't imply it," Vickery replied, in a voice which made it quite clear that he wasn't arguing with it, either. "Just be glad you're going home."

There didn't seem anything Darroll could say to that, so he sat back down, and Vickery went away, and in a couple of hours his mother turned up and took him home, and the car journey back to Muldoon was just as grim an ordeal as he'd expected.

12

Darroll had longed to be out of hospital, but when he got home, it was so miserable, so depressing, that he almost wished himself back downstate with Vickery and Schwartz.

He'd missed nearly the whole semester, as well as all his summer vacation, lying in his hospital bed. "You'll have one week back at school," Vickery had said. "Hopefully that'll give you a chance to get back into the habit without overwhelming you. Don't beat yourself up if you find it tough. You've been through a lot. And be prepared for the decent kids to be embarrassingly nice to you, and the jerks to be even more annoying than usual. You're going to get jokes."

"I can stand jokes," he'd said, and Vickery had nodded and said something about how he could believe that.

And yes, there were jokes. At lunch recess, on Darroll's first day back, Kirk Mondschein had held him while Ed Crowe shoved his dirty, stinking jockstrap into his face. "Welcome back, Matt Kenseth," Crowe had jeered. Sarcasm, of course, but in point of fact, it did seem unexpectedly like coming home, to have Crowe and his buddies acting like dicks to him, as though nothing had changed since the accident.

Vickery was right about something else, too; the people who were nice to him were almost harder to deal with. A couple of the teaching staff – Mr Spears, Miss Leland – sought him out to tell him how glad they were to see him back and how they hoped he'd be able to get back up to academic speed. Principal Tidmarsh didn't speak to him, but at the end of the first day, as he was going down the big stone steps at the front of the school, Tidmarsh was coming up them. Their eyes met, and Tidmarsh smiled. Darroll couldn't remember ever seeing Tidmarsh smile, and he couldn't tell if the expression was meant to be genuine or a sign of menace, like the smile on the face of the proverbial tiger.

He didn't worry about Tidmarsh, though. He had been worrying about the other Psychopaths, and whether he'd find that they had moved on and left him, or worse still, replaced him with somebody without brain damage. But after he got away from Crowe and Mondschein at lunch, Chuck Milne and Rowdy Serxner had found him and practically walked him arm-in-arm to their table, where Beth Vines and Vanessa Murchison were already sitting.

"So is it true you got a hole in the head?" Rowdy asked, peering at Darroll's hairline.

"Only literally," Darroll said, pulling his chair up to the table and prodding his lunch with his fork. Dr Schwartz had warned him that he might find his senses of taste and smell affected, but school cafeteria food had smelled and tasted like shit before, and it smelled and tasted like shit now.

Chuck, on the other side of Darroll, eyed his head too. "How's it held on? Screws?"

"Screws. Right through the bone."

Opposite Darroll, Vanessa smiled to herself.

Chuck's eyes widened. "Shit. Did it hurt?"

"I wasn't conscious when they put it in."

"Better watch out if you see Ed Crowe coming for you with a screwdriver," Rowdy quipped.

"Anyhoo," Chuck said, cutting Rowdy off with a look, "you still interested in the Club? We've been meeting while you've been out of it. Turned it into quite a little regular session. Generally we get together either at Celebration Burger, or in Boardman's basement."

"Oh, I'm interested," Darroll said. "I can get to either of those easy enough. Still got my car."

"What? The one you...?"

"The one I nearly killed myself in," Darroll said, "yeah. The accident didn't wreck it completely, can you believe it? Just dinged a few panels and scraped the paint. What put me in hospital was a fence-post with a nail in it coming through the windshield and whacking me on the head."

He fumbled in his pocket for the plastic baggie, then placed it carefully on the table midway between himself and Vanessa. Four heads craned over it, regularly spaced, like a compass rose, with the nail Dr Schwartz had given him serving as the magnetic needle.

"That was in your head?" Rowdy said, eyes wide.

"Mmhm." Darroll found that he liked the awe-struck looks he was getting from the rest of the club. He could get used to those. Vanessa was staring at the nail as though it mesmerised her. As though she wanted to take it out and fondle it, or lick it, or something. Darroll retrieved the baggy and popped it back into his pocket.

Beth Vines opened her mouth, and the others at the table fell quiet. "Well, Darroll," she said, "Boardman's doing Ed Gein this Saturday. Should be good. Come join us."

"I'll be there."

"I can't believe you still drive that car." Chuck was looking at Darroll's head again. "If I nearly died in a car accident, I'd have that car taken to a scrapyard and melted down to make barbed wire."

"Yes, well," Vanessa said, "not everyone's family has enough money to afford to scrap a working car, Hawaii boy."

Chuck flushed. It was last year that his family had taken their summer vacation in Hawaii, and he'd come back suntanned, prone to expounding on the awesome joys of surfing. Within a month or so, half the school were singing Beach Boys songs at him, or asking him when he was going surfing on Lake Muldoon, a small and mundane body of water with swampy edges.

"It's a car," Darroll said simply. "Why should I stop driving it because I had one accident? That'd be like Vanessa never drawing anything again, just because she broke a pencil."

The bell sounded the end of recess, and the dinner party broke up, with Darroll promising again to be at the Psychopath Club meeting on Saturday.

13

There were six chairs in Joe Boardman's basement. Two of them were lawn chairs in white plastic, incongruous on the bare concrete floor. Two were wooden, dissimilar from each other, both looking old. One was an old armchair, stuffing bursting through splits in the worn leather, which must have been almost impossible to get down the stairs, Darroll thought. Plainly it was never going to get up them again in one piece. Joe Boardman had already claimed that seat; Darroll guessed that was his prerogative as host. He sat in the sixth chair, also leather, an easy chair so low to the floor that his legs stretched out ahead of him, all the way under the table in the middle of the chairs, and out the other side.

Soon all six of the Club were there, sitting with drinks on the table between them, in a variety of containers as mismatched as the chairs they were sitting in.

"Darroll," Beth Vines said, from the seat next to him, "that car of yours? It's really safe to drive after that smash?"

"Sure it is. Mom had it fixed up while I was in the hospital." He didn't add that his father had covered the repair bill. "And I got my licence restored, too."

"How would you feel about going for a long ride in it?"

"How long?"

"How about Chicago?"

Darroll frowned. He'd been to Chicago once, two years ago, for school, not long after he and his mother had moved to Muldoon. He'd still been too stunned, then, by the recent changes in his life to fully take in the experience of the big city.

"I suppose I could," he began. "Tell me more?"

But Joe Boardman caught Beth's eye and she shook her head. "After," she said. "I wanna hear about Ed Gein." And she shut up and sat back, looking at Joe as though he was a pastor about to deliver a Sunday sermon.

Darroll already knew about Ed Gein, of course. He'd been the inspiration for *Psycho*, and he'd eaten his morning cereal out of someone's skull. Joe Boardman had a slightly annoying way of speaking, as though he assumed none of the other Psychopaths knew anything, and he was, by god, the one who was going to enlighten them. Darroll found his attention drifting.

Toward the end of Joe's presentation, Darroll realised that his attention was doing more than drift. He couldn't focus. Panic started to bubble up inside him. Was this some effect of that goddamn hole in his head? The more he tried to concentrate, the more he couldn't, and the more the world refused to stay still around him.

He climbed to his feet, aware that the other Club members were looking at him.

"You okay, Darroll?" asked Chuck.

"I'm fine," he insisted, knowing it was a lie, hoping it wasn't obvious. "I, uh, need the restroom."

"There's one right down here," Boardman said, and pointed at the far corner of the basement.

Darroll didn't like the look of the door Boardman was indicating, which looked as though nobody had been inside it in years. But the world was starting to become more and more overlaid with multi-coloured, pulsing swirls, and he wasn't at all sure he could make it up the basement steps any more. He gave a grunt, and lurched in the direction of Boardman's finger.

As he'd expected, the little cubicle was cold and dark, and everything inside was dusty. Even though there was a lavatory inside, it didn't smell as though it had been used in a long, long time. This suited Darroll fine; his head felt as if it were, not exploding, but slowly coming apart and drifting into segments, an orange being peeled and divided by a big, invisible hand. Shakily he sat down on the seat, or rather collapsed onto it, not stopping to lift the lid or drop his pants.

What would the others in the basement think of this weakness he was showing? What would he be able to say, when he had to face them? Perhaps he wouldn't have to. Perhaps he was dying. Perhaps some little tiny piece of metal from that rotten, accursed, fucking

Oldsmobile had dug into his brain in the accident. They hadn't noticed it when they were putting his head back together, and now it had decided to come out and play, and he was going to die there, on the floor of a dusty disused john, all dignity fled.

Shaking, he leaned to one side and rested his face against the wall for support. The surface of the wall was rough, concrete blocks with a thin layer of paint, cool against his cheek. A few inches in front of his eye, he blearily noticed that a spider had spun its web; he could see its fat little form, short legs and big abdomen, quietly sitting in the middle. Waiting for some little insect to come along and make a pot-luck dinner of itself. He was certain, now, that he was about to die, and he resented the spider for being alive and not having a head injury. He willed his arm to come up, to smash the web apart and squash the spider. But his arm wouldn't move. Nothing about him would move. The only part of him that would move was his eyelids, and it took all his strength to close them so that his last vision wouldn't be that spider.

When consciousness returned to Darroll, it did so slowly rather than all at once. He wasn't certain for a while whether his hearing had yet to kick back in, or whether it was just very quiet there in the basement. He would have expected to be able to hear some noise from the rest of the club members, only a few yards outside the door. Conversation, or movement. Rowdy Serxner kicking his chair legs in that way that drove him mad, and drove all his teachers mad, too. But there was nothing.

There was nothing in front of his eyes, either, except the wall. For a few moments he didn't realise why this should come as a surprise to him, and then he remembered the spider. There had been a spider and a spider's web right there in front of his eyes when he blacked out.

There was no spider now. There was no sign that there had ever been a spider.

Darroll suddenly wondered, with growing unease, how long he'd been passed out for, slumped on top of the can like some dirty old drunk who couldn't even make it to his own bed and get undressed before passing out. How fast did spiders move? Who knew?

And if he'd been in there for a long time, why hadn't anyone at least come to check on him? They must have been able to tell he was looking ill when he staggered into the cubicle. They all knew about his accident, and his head, and how he'd nearly died.

The callous, miserable bastards. They hadn't even –

Or perhaps they'd come and knocked on the door while he was flake-out unconscious. How would he know?

Darroll took a deep breath. His head felt... well, no different from how it normally did; the sensation of it being pulled apart into segments had passed, and he was pretty damn relieved about that. He didn't actually feel too bad; bit shaky, perhaps. He cautiously rose to his feet, and found he could stand normally.

Well, he was going to damn well go out and tell those guys what he thought of them for letting him sit in that crapper like that. He jerked the door open, and marched out, ready to berate them for their disloyalty, their disregard for his well-being.

Except that they weren't there. None of them were there. The table they'd been sitting round had been pushed back from the middle of the basement, to the edge. The chairs they'd been using had been put away, too, neatly in the corner. The basement was empty of everything except the Boardman family's junk; the rusty barbecue, the box full of old LP records, the shelf with a row of empty flowerpots.

Not only had the rest of the Psychopath Club not come to make sure he was okay, they hadn't even waited in the basement for him. They'd all cleared off, gone who knew where to do who knew what.

Darroll was proud of being a cynic. Hell, it was a central pillar of his self-identity. None of the shit the world threw at him came as a surprise, none of the thoughtless, inconsiderate, cruel deeds which human beings did could shock him. But he found himself actually boggling at the callous way that his... well, not his friends exactly, but people who came closer to being friends than anyone else in this rotten broken world... could simply walk off and leave him there, flaked out in someone else's basement. Dying, for all they knew.

Turning these thoughts over in his mind, he walked slowly to the steps up to the house. Climbing them, he wondered whether Mrs Boardman would still be there, or if she and her ugly husband had gone off too. Right now, he suddenly realised, he really wanted to see another human being, someone he could talk to about the fit he'd just had. Someone who could tell him whether he ought to dial 911 and be whisked away in an ambulance, or if he was worrying about nothing. Right now, he'd talk to Mrs Boardman as if she actually merited his conversation. He'd even drink her iced tea.

Except when Darroll made it upstairs to the kitchen, and said "Uh, hi," to Mrs Boardman, what happened was that Mrs Boardman span around, dropped her iced tea on the floor, took a quick but very deep breath, and screamed with all the power of her lungs.

14

Darroll was so astonished that he just stood and stared at Mrs Boardman for a couple of moments. And a couple of moments was all that it took for her to dive for the screen door that led out onto the back porch, jerk it open, and vanish through it. Her speed would have cinched her a place on the track and field team at Straus High.

He looked at the spreading puddle of tea on the kitchen floor. For a second he wondered vaguely whether he ought to clean it up, then decided not to be so stupid; he hadn't spilled it. He went through to the lounge. Mr Boardman wasn't there, which surprised him for a second. Then he realised he was once more being stupid; Mrs Boardman's scream had been loud enough to wake the dead. It would have brought Mr Boardman out of his chair like a nuke out of its silo.

He was alone in the house, it appeared.

He pondered going up to Joe Boardman's room and rummaging through it to see whether the guy had anything juicy hidden away in there, but more important was why Mrs Boardman had run away from him screaming. Could there be something wrong with him? Had his fainting fit been caused by him bursting a blood vessel in his face or something, and was he wandering around like something out of a zombie movie? There was a mirror on the kitchen wall; it had a Jack Daniels logo in the middle, but it was functional enough for him to check his face. As ever, no prizewinner, but nothing about it that Mrs Boardman hadn't seen countless times. He stuck his tongue out at his reflection and turned away.

He followed Mrs Boardman's path through the back door and onto the porch. There was no sign of her, no sign of anybody out there. He wandered out into the back garden, as far as the rusty swing set, then turned aside. A narrow path led along the side of the Boardmans' garage to a tall wooden door, beyond which lay the street.

As he reached the door, he heard voices. Mrs Boardman, shrill and loud. Darroll had never had any qualms about eavesdropping, but he would have been hard put not to hear every word that she spoke.

"I tell you it was him, large as life. Oh, my lord, Mark! He came up out of the basement, with his face all shining and ghastly..."

"Julie, Julie!" A male voice. Darroll recognised it; Mr Tolliver, who owned the launderette on Third. He lived next to the Boardmans. "It's not possible. You imagined it."

"I did not so imagine it!" squealed Mrs Boardman's voice. "It was Darroll Martock and he came straight for me, with his arms lifted up. If I hadn't run for my life he'd have been upon me and whisked me off to Hell or worse. I am not setting foot in my house again, I swear. I'm gonna move clean out of this town."

Darroll had been on the verge of opening the gate, but his hand dropped to his side. What the fuck was this crazy woman talking about? He hadn't raised his hands to her, or even his voice. He decided that he might do better to remain hidden, for the moment.

"Okay, okay, Julie," Mr Tolliver said. "I'll go inside and look. But I sure as hell won't find any spooks in your house. There ain't no such thing as ghosts, and if you were thinking straight, you'd know that."

Darroll was still trying to figure the conversation the hell out when he heard the noise of the front door opening and closing. A few moments later, it opened again. "Like I said," Mr Tolliver called out to Mrs Boardman, "no ghosts, no nothing. Now you come along inside and have a nice drink of water and sit down, Julie Boardman, and I'll go tell your man you need him home from his fishing."

Mrs Boardman's voice, less shrill now but still querulous, died away as the front door closed again, behind her. Darroll sat tight, and in a couple of minutes, the door opened for a third time. There was no more conversation, but he could hear the footsteps of Mr Tolliver crossing the area of hardtop in front of the garage, and Tolliver breathing a little heavily. Still Darroll lurked by the side of the garage, and in a few moments more, a car engine coughed into life and drove away down the street, towards town.

Then, finally, Darroll ventured to open the door and slip out onto the street. He scarcely knew what to think. Had Mrs Boardman lost her marbles? She seemed to think not only that he'd been about to attack her, or rape her, or whatever (like he'd want to put his dick within a five foot radius of Julie Boardman), but she thought he was some kind of ghostly apparition. Which was complete lunacy, as far as he could see.

He decided the best thing would be simply to go home.

The quick way back from the Boardman house to the Martock house was to cut across, rather than go by the streets. There was an open area of ground you could walk into at the top of Joe's street, and come out the other side at the top of Darroll's. The city called it James Gruber Memorial Park. The sum total of the city's involvement beyond naming it was to put a few signs up warning against 'unruly or riotous behavior' (Darroll didn't know what that meant) and telling you that you had to pick up your dog's shit if you took it for walkies there. Which everyone ignored. Darroll had trodden in dogshit in that park a dozen times since moving to Muldoon. There was as much dogshit around the James Gruber Memorial Park as there was cowshit in most other places in this state.

He crossed the park. There was nobody else around. He stuck his hands in his pockets against the cold; somehow it felt a lot colder now than it had been when he set out for the meeting earlier. He was still spooked by the way that the rest of the club had run off and left him, and by Julie Boardman's weird behaviour. He walked slowly, trying to puzzle it out, and was still turning it over and over mentally when he reached home.

He was about to go up to the door and inside when he realised that his car wasn't there, where it ought to be, where he had left it. What the hell? Nobody would have stolen it; this wasn't Chicago, and anyway, nobody could possibly think his old heap of shit car was worth stealing.

Maybe his mom had borrowed it to run to the store? But that made no sense either. She would have gone in her own Ford if she was going anyplace.

He checked his watch. It was half past five. She'd be watching reruns of Jeopardy. She always watched reruns of Jeopardy at half past five. Ever since he could remember she'd sat there, shouting out the answers. And getting them wrong, usually. Darroll knew that you had to give the answer like you were asking a question of your own. The contestants on the show sometimes forgot that, in their excitement. His mother always forgot it.

Shrugging mentally, he pulled his keys out of his pocket. There was his car key, next to his house key and his school locker key and the padlock key for his box. Of course his mom could always have taken the spare key out of the kitchen drawer. Well, one more weirdness in a weird day.

The front door was locked. That wasn't a huge surprise; a lot of people round here kept their doors unlocked (that was how small and remote this city was, one more thing that made him despise it), but his mother had never picked that habit up. She was used to living in civilised places where, if you left your front door unlocked, someone would be inside and stealing your valuables within minutes, and they'd probably shank you if you interrupted them.

He turned his key in the lock, and walked inside. The familiar sound of the television came from the main room. "Hey, Mom," he called. "You seen my car?"

There was no reply, but the television cut off suddenly. Why had his mother turned the television off? She never turned it off. You could touch that thing and it'd burn your fingers, it'd been on so long, working up heat. It was a miracle it didn't set fire to the whole damn place.

As he came through to the main room his mother met him halfway, hurrying as if she'd jumped out of her chair as soon as she heard him. Her eyes were wide, like Mrs Boardman's had been.

"Darroll? Oh my sweet little boy... Darroll...?"

Darroll took a step backwards by sheer instinct as she rushed up toward him. It was years since she'd called him her sweet little boy, and he'd never liked the glutinous sentimentality attached to it.

"Mom? What the hell, Mom?"

As he took another step back and bumped into the wall, his mother reached him and threw her arms around him, gasping incoherently.

There was a moment where Darroll felt nothing but weirded-out confusion. He tried to struggle free from his mother's embrace, but somehow he didn't seem able to move his arms and legs properly all of a sudden, and that strange swimming feeling began to assail his senses again as it had earlier. He tried to protest – against his mother? against the feeling? – but his lips were no longer obeying his commands, either. The room tilted at a sudden angle and he felt himself falling, the rushing of air in his ears growing louder, overwhelming his other senses. He heard, more than felt, the thud of an impact with the ground.

The ground.

The ground was cold beneath his cheek.

It shouldn't be cold. Heaven knew everything in this state was cold, but he should be feeling carpet against his face as he lay there. It wasn't carpet. It was hard and cold and rough.

He found he could open his eyes (which he didn't realise he had closed), so he did.

He wasn't lying on the carpet in his front room, looking at the worn patches where his mother had trodden countless circuits from the easy chair to the kitchen and back. He was looking at concrete. Cold, grey, unadorned. A twist of his head revealed more of his surroundings; he wasn't at home at all. He was lying on the floor of the tiny cubicle in the corner of the Boardman house's basement.

He felt shaky as all hell, but managed to get to his hands and knees, then used the lavatory to climb further upward till he was back on his feet. He took a deep breath or two, and as he did so, realised he could hear voices from outside the door. His fingers scrabbled at the handle. Suddenly he felt an urgent need to get out of the claustrophobic space, back into the rest of the world.

When he jerked the door open, there were five people sitting round the table in the basement. The other five members of the Psychopath Club, exactly as they'd been earlier on, in the same order and the same clothes. He stared at them, wondering what the hell to say.

"You okay, Darroll?" It was Vanessa who broke the silence. "You're not looking yourself."

"I'm fine," he ventured. "What the hell happened to you guys?"

Joe looked at Rowdy and vice versa. Beth and Chuck looked confused.

"Nothing happened to us," Vanessa said. "We were waiting for you to come out of the bathroom."

"Waiting… for me…?"

"Uh, yeah?" Joe actually sounded worried. "You are white as a sheet, man. Are you okay?"

Darroll looked down at himself, suddenly unsure whether he was okay. He didn't see anything out of the ordinary. There were his feet, or rather his shoes, on the ground, at the end of his legs. Thank goodness he was wearing shoes. He didn't want to think about the weirdness of feet, not at the moment. His jeans, his t-shirt, his arms sticking out of the sleeves. His wristwatch on his wrist. He glanced at it, wondering how long he'd been in the can. Had to be an hour or more.

But the watch said five minutes after three. The exact time he'd gone in.

There was a sudden feeling in his stomach that he'd felt only once before in his life, when he was seven and his mom and dad had still been together. They'd taken him to Six Flags one summer and he'd been on the big rollercoaster, stretching at the entrance, praying he could force himself tall enough to be allowed on. They'd nodded him through and onto the ride, with his father (his mother wouldn't go near the thing) and it had climbed up into the sky, until the people below were the size of little beetles, and over the brink at the top, and WHAM, down it went.

He'd screamed, and his father had screamed, and half the other riders had screamed too, and the ride had plummeted back down so fast that it left his innards at the top for a few seconds, until the rollercoaster reached the bottom of the incline and shot round like a corkscrew, and his guts caught up with him. It had been dreadful and wonderful, horrible and awesome, all at once, and when the ride finally came to an end his father had helped him off because his legs had gone shaky, and held his hand as they walked back to meet his mother. He couldn't remember any other times his father had held his hand. "You okay? Was that fun, sonny?" his father had murmured. "I sure as hell thought so."

He wished for a moment that someone would hold his hand and ask him if he was okay, but unsurprisingly, nobody did so. He dropped heavily back into the chair he'd vacated a few hours ago. Or a few seconds ago, if he believed what his wristwatch was telling him. He looked at it again. It still said five after three.

"Any of you guys have the right time?" he asked in a voice that cracked in its attempt to carry off an air of nonchalance.

"About six, seven after three," said Rowdy Serxner.

"Seven minutes and forty seconds after three... now," said Joe Boardman, who had a fancy digital watch that told you not only the time but the date, and the phase of the moon, and what the fishing would be like if you were to go out fishing. Boardman's dad had bought it a couple of Christmases ago. Boardman was entirely uninterested in fishing.

Darroll took a second or two to form his next question. "I wasn't in there long, then?"

A couple of headshakes, and a couple of wordless noises of agreement. "Five minutes max," Vanessa said. "Look, Darroll, are you absolutely sure you're okay?"

Rowdy leaned over the table toward Darroll and held a finger in his face. "How many fingers am I holding up?"

"One, jerkass," Darroll said with a sudden flash of annoyance. "This many." He held a finger up of his own. Rowdy's was a forefinger. Darroll's wasn't.

Oddly enough, that seemed to make the rest of the Psychopath Club look less worried about him. Rowdy sat back down with a grunt. "Just checking in, Darroll," said Chuck soothingly. "That whack on the head you took in your car wreck... you know."

"Nothing wrong with my head," Darroll said firmly, wishing he believed it.

"They say I am mad, but I am not mad –" Joe Boardman broke in, in an exaggerated mad scientist voice.

Chuck poked Joe in the ribs. "Quit it, jerk." And Joe actually looked guilty. "No offence, Darroll, man," he muttered.

Darroll really didn't know what to think, so he changed the subject. Luckily, there was another topic outstanding that needed attention, anyway.

"What was this about driving to Chicago?" he said to Beth.

"Oh! Yes. Well," Beth began, sitting up in her chair and looking businesslike. "Do you guys like live music?"

Some question that was. Darroll couldn't remember there ever having been any live music in Muldoon. There certainly wasn't anywhere for live music to happen, unless you counted places like the gymnasium at Straus High, or the ugly VFW post in the centre of town.

From the general looks of blankness around the table, Darroll figured that the rest of the Club were live music virgins like him.

"Todd Krank is playing there the first weekend in January," Beth explained.

Darroll had never heard of Todd Krank. Vanessa, it seemed, had.

"Yeah? Where?" she asked.

"Some record store out to the west of town, one of the suburbs. Player Heights, I think it's called."

"Are you trying to get me to drive you all the way to Chicago just to see this guy?" Darroll asked. He was still trying to figure out what the hell he'd undergone, and he wasn't inclined to waste any energy on formality or politeness.

"Well," Beth said, "there's a lot we could do in Chicago. Make a whole day of it."

Joe and Chuck were starting to look interested, now.

"I'd never fit all six of us into my Olds," Darroll pointed out.

"Five of us. I'm not riding in that thing," said Chuck. "You nearly killed yourself in it, or had you forgotten?"

"I got my bike."

"You can't ride a bicycle to Chicago, Rowdy, you retard."

"My motor-bike. Could even have Chuck pillion behind me, if he won't ride with Martock," Rowdy declared, giving Darroll a hurt look. "He could borrow my brother's crash helmet."

"Would your mom let you drive to Chicago, Darroll?" asked Vanessa. "With your head and all?"

"Sure she will, and if not, I'll go anyway. They said I was fine to drive when they kicked me out of hospital, and I got my licence right here," Darroll said, absently. His mind was engaged on analysing his experience from just now. He still hadn't been able to figure it out when the meeting broke up a few minutes later.

He headed home, through Gruber Park, which looked exactly as it always did, to his house, which looked just as normal, and his mother. He was a little wary that she might leap on him again, but she didn't seem to think there was anything abnormal about her son, either.

That evening Darroll asked his mother, phrasing it carefully, whether it was okay for him and his friends to drive to Illinois. "To Player Heights," he said, expecting his mother not to know where that was. He knew, now, because he'd looked it up. Out on the west of Chicago, along with a clump of other little suburbs that somehow all had their own city names.

"Are you sure you'll be all right?" His mother gave him a look which he immediately interpreted as meaning "I don't want you to go but I'm not going to say you can't, because I don't have the guts," and he knew he was home and dry. He was quite ready to defy her and go anyway if she'd said no, but it would be simpler if he could wheedle permission from her.

"Mooooom," he said, drawing the monosyllable out into a long, resigned noise. "I'll be okay. There are six of us going. And at least I'll be in my car. Rowdy Serxner is going on his motorbike."

"It's just... you had that horrible accident, and it's such a long way to Illinois," she fretted, "and you've never been to a big city without me."

"They'd have pulled my license if I wasn't okay to drive." Darroll had been astonished that they hadn't, given the injury he'd suffered. Most likely, he concluded, they'd forgotten; in which case why should he remind them?

"I checked the long range forecast and there's no freeze coming. I have to learn to stand on my own two feet someday, Mom," he pointed out. He suppressed an urge to throw his plate at her. He could win the argument without a tantrum. "What happens when I go off to college?"

She clicked her tongue a couple of times. "Well, you make sure to call me as soon as you get there. Who are these other kids you're going with?"

He suppressed the urge a second time, at her choice of words. "Vanessa Murchison," he said. "You know her, the one who wears black always. And Beth Vines, and Joe Boardman."

"Oh, that Boardman boy," Mrs Martock said vaguely. "So is it a double date?"

For the third, and most difficult, time, Darroll suppressed his temper. "No, Mom. I'm not dating anyone. And Boardman doesn't like girls... you know."

His mother gave him another look. "But you do...don't you?"

"Yes, mom," he sighed. "But not those two freaks. When I find a girl it'll be someone normal looking."

For a second there was silence as his mother looked at him, digesting that claim, and he wondered whether she knew he was lying, and whether she could tell how much he despised most women. Including her.

"Well, all right," she finally said, "but you drive good and careful."

Next Monday, a parcel arrived in the mailbox for Darroll. At first he assumed it would be his father's Christmas present, but then he noticed that the stamp had been franked with an in-state postmark, not a Georgia one. When he tore it open, he found a fat paperback book, one that he'd heard of vaguely but never read, called *Catch-22*. Inside the front cover a message was written:

"To Darroll Martock,

"Merry Christmas and I hope your return to school has been triumphant.

"I thought you might like this. It meant a lot to me when I was your age – still does. I'll leave you to decide what message you take from it, if any. And even if it holds nothing deep and meaningful I hope you enjoy it."

The signature at the end was almost illegible, but he knew what it surely must read, even before he could puzzle out the scrawl as that of Louis Vickery.

15

Christmas was depressing. It always was. Other people had festive Christmases with decorations and holly and carol singing and bullshit. Darroll didn't. His mother didn't bother with decorations, or even a tree, and Darroll didn't see why he should go to the trouble of putting them up if his mother couldn't find the inspiration. He was still a kid and it was the parents' job, not the kids', to put up decorations and make with the festivity.

He didn't get any presents worth shit either. His father put some money into his bank account, just as he did most Christmases. His mother bought him cheap candy and some new jeans. The only other present he received was Vickery's book, which sat on his nightstand on top of his comics, keeping them from blowing about. He kept meaning to at least crack *Catch-22* open, but somehow every night when he read in bed, he ended up choosing one of the comics from underneath it instead.

The morning after Christmas dawned cold, of course, because it was always cold. Darroll awoke early, and found his feet sticking out from under the bedclothes again. He groaned and rolled out of bed. Even though he'd kept his socks on during the night, his feet were still – surprise! – cold.

He kicked his socks off and put a fresh pair on, then set himself his usual tricky task of getting the old socks into the laundry basket without using his hands. One of them had scrunched up into a vaguely ball-shaped mass, and he managed to get his toe under the ball and send it up in the air with a little kick. The sock bounced on the edge of the basket and fell inside. Darroll punched the air and acknowledged the silent applause of an imaginary crowd. He could do this, and yet they wouldn't consider him for any of the school sports teams?

The second sock was in a more awkward position, but he snagged it between his big toe and the ball of his foot, and balancing carefully on the other leg, lifted the foot and the sock upward until they were over the basket, like a crane on a construction site. He opened his toes, and sock two dropped into the basket as well.

He turned to get clean clothes out, looking at his body, naked but for the clean socks, in the mirror above his clothes drawers. There were more hairs on his chest than the last time he'd looked, a scatter around each nipple, and a few on the otherwise pale, bare patch of skin between them. They reminded him of two armies. British and German, or US and Russia, both of them surrounding a base, preventing the enemy from capturing the flag. And the ones in the middle were the unlucky ones, the ones who'd gotten caught in no man's land, stranded. Easy targets. They wouldn't be going home, except in a casket. And probably in pieces.

It only helped him to imagine his body as World War One that he had a few zits on his chest as well. Shell craters, yeah. One of them had a hair growing right out of the middle, a soldier who was trying to take shelter in the shell hole, until night fell and he could try to make a break for home base.

He pulled a shirt on over the battlefield of his chest, and went out to the kitchen where he had cereal, and a glass of milk over and above the milk on the cereal, and wondered what to do with the day before the Psychopath Club meeting. Somehow he didn't feel like doing anything, but he didn't feel like simply sitting still, either. He ended up going out and walking around the division, hands in his pockets, his breath making visible puffs of steam whenever he exhaled. A couple of little kids were running around on their front lawn, and a fat middle-aged man down the road was mowing his, never mind that it was December and there was snow on the grass. Nobody looked at Darroll. He reached the end of his street and turned onto the next one.

Halfway along, a house was having a yard sale. Darroll liked yard sales. You got to poke through other people's stuff with their actual blessing, try and figure out what made them tick. Even if they had nothing you wanted, it gave him a smug inner sensation to know he'd had his hands all over their belongings.

When he went to see what was on offer, he realised that he knew whose house it was, even though he'd never been to it. It was the Wallis family place. There were three Wallis kids, two boys and a girl. None of them in his grade at school, but he knew them to look at. He knew Mrs Wallis too, and there she was, standing in the yard looking hopeful. Darroll wondered if he was the first person who'd stopped by the sale.

"Hello there!" she trilled to him. He brought his polite smile out of cold storage for her. "Did you see our signs?"

Darroll shook his head. "Just walking round the neighbourhood and saw your tables out."

"Oh, that's a shame." The look of concern on Mrs Wallis's face was out of all proportion to the significance of the question. Once again Darroll found himself loathing this punk-ass town, where people got bent all out of shape just because nobody came to their damn yard sale. Anyone would think it was an auction of fine art, and Mrs Wallis was an Ivy League heiress who had to sell her heirlooms to pay off her taxes.

There sure as hell weren't any heirlooms on offer in the Wallis collection. Clothes that were too small for the growing Wallises, a few kitchen utensils, a box of worn paperback books. On top of the books was a stack of comics. Darroll picked them up, and Mrs Wallis pounced like a big cat stalking prey.

"You want those comic books?"

Darroll didn't know whether he wanted them or not, yet, because he'd only had the chance to look at the top one in the heap (a five-year-old Spiderman).

"I guess I might," he prevaricated.

"I want them out of my house," said Mrs Wallis with a rueful smile. "All of this has to go. We're moving to New York in a month. I'll take fifty cents for that whole heap of comics, now how's that?"

Well, fifty cents wasn't bad, there had to be fifty comics there. One cent an issue? Yeah, he could go for that. Besides, if he bought them, he'd have an excuse to get off Mrs Wallis's driveway and out of her sight. He really didn't want to be talking to her with her phony affability. And if she started telling him about her husband and his job in New York, which seemed entirely too likely, he might die of boredom. Or of jealousy, at her getting to live in New York instead of this dump.

He found two quarters, handed them over, and Mrs Wallis insisted on giving him an old leather briefcase to carry the comics in. "Tell your friends," she implored him. "And your folks."

Given this town, the yard sale might well be the most exciting thing going on within the whole city limits that day. Darroll still couldn't see himself going to call on Vanessa or Chuck Milne, urging them to get out of their houses and live it up in the bright lights of Mrs Wallis's yard. He strolled back home, his long thin legs retracing the route he'd taken, and holed up in his room to examine the comics.

16

Of course, it was typical of Darroll's luck that in his trove, there were half a dozen Spiderman comics, actual readable or tradable issues, and almost all of the rest were Archie and Jughead trash. Maybe they'd belonged to Mrs Wallis's daughter, or maybe Mrs Wallis's sons were the sort of all-American whitebread idiots who lapped up shit like Archie Andrews.

He opened one out of sheer boredom, and read it, then another, and another. He was coming to the last page of his third Archie (Moose Mason was practicing for field sports and threw a discus so far it went through Mr Weatherbee's car windshield) when his closet door opened abruptly, and someone stepped out of it into his room. For the barest of split seconds, Darroll didn't know who it was.

Then there was a lurch that came from both his mind and his heart at once.

"Oh! Hi," said the newcomer, as though it were a perfectly everyday and unremarkable thing for a second copy of Darroll to appear in his own closet, step out, and greet his own doppelganger.

Darroll – the original Darroll – was at a loss for words. All he could do was stare. The interloper wasn't an exact double of Darroll, he saw immediately. He was wearing a different shirt, which Darroll didn't recognise, and there was an ugly scar on the side of his face that looked like a knife cut.

The new Darroll closed the closet door and came over toward the bed. "This is a surprise to you, yeah?" he said. "I'm guessing you haven't been through this before."

Darroll wondered whether his voice sounded like that to other people. So nasal and unimpressive. He shook his head.

Darroll Two sat on the bed, as casually as though he owned it himself. Darroll could see the scar better now. It ran from his cheek to the back of his neck, across his earlobe. It made the newcomer look dangerous in a way he found himself envying.

The doppelganger Darroll turned to look more closely at him. "Looking at my scar? Oh, hey, you don't have one... Wait." Up until now the interloper's facial expression had been casual and relaxed, but now he frowned. "Hold still and let me look at you... You don't have a scar of your own?"

Darroll turned his head to show his own cheek, devoid of any mark save a zit or two.

"Were you... ever in an auto wreck?" Darroll Two seemed to be treading more carefully.

"Hell, yes I was," Darroll said. "Nearly killed myself. Why do you want to know, and what the hell are you doing in my closet?"

"You didn't slice your face open on the windshield?"

"No," said Darroll, then asked the obvious question. "Did you?"

"Sure did," said Darroll Two. "Wasn't the worst thing I did to myself in that, but it's the one everyone sees because of where it is. Got a metal plate in my head too –"

"I got that," Darroll One said, touching it.

Darroll Two nodded. "Okay, I think I get the picture. Only other time this happened to me, you had the scar as well." He rubbed his chin. "How the hell do I ask this next question?"

"Just ask it?" Darroll One was starting to suspect that Darroll Two lacked his own ability to speak as quickly as he could think.

"Right. Since the accident, have you had weird experiences of being, uh, lost in alternate worlds?"

"Once," said Darroll One. "But I didn't meet myself. I – "

He paused, and his twin looked expectant. His mind was starting to assemble jigsaw pieces like it was against the clock. The picture that the jigsaw made was breathtaking. Unbelievable. But short of actual insanity and hallucination, he couldn't make the pieces fit together any other way.

"I think," Darroll finally continued, "what must have happened was, I wound up in a world where I died in the crash. Got taken for a ghost. Does that sound possible?"

"Yeah, more than possible. That happened to me twice," said Darroll Two. "Blows your mind, doesn't it? How much have you figured out about it?"

"Not much."

Darroll Two rubbed his chin again. "You want to know a few things about it?"

"Sure. Have you figured out how to do it whenever you like?"

"Nope," said Darroll Two. "Far as I can tell it's random. The other time I met myself, he said the same. But I know how to get back, pretty much."

"Yeah?"

"The more change you make in the world you don't belong in," said the scarfaced Darroll, "the more likely you get jerked back. I guess it's like eating some bad food. If you just take a tiny little bite you can keep it down. But the more you eat, the more likely it is your stomach gets sick and vomits the whole lot right out. You following?"

"Nicely put," said Darroll One.

"Of course it is," said Darroll Two. "You're me. Or at least ninety-nine percent of you is. Give or take a scar, or a zit or two in different places. We're going to like the same things. Hey, where'd you get those comics?"

"Yard sale. The Wallises are moving out of state."

"Sweet. I'll check that out when I get back. And that shirt? You still have it?"

"Why shouldn't I still have it?"

"Well," said Darroll Two, "the reason I don't still have it is I was wearing it when I smashed the car up and they cut it off me, I expect. Never saw it after that day, anyways."

"So the difference between your universe and mine," said Darroll One, "is that you wore a different shirt the day of your accident, and hit your head on the windshield at a different angle and picked up a scar?"

"I'm sure there are other differences too," said scarfaced Darroll. "South American butterflies flapping their wings in a different pattern. A guy in Connecticut buying Pepsi instead of Coke to drink with his lunch. The only real differences I've found so far between universes are with myself... ourselves. Sometimes we died in that crash, sometimes we didn't."

Darroll tried to digest what he was learning. Like his mother's cooking; it took a lot of getting down. Unlike it, once it was inside, it didn't just sit as an inert lump.

"Freaky, isn't it?" said Darroll Two, evidently observing his mental contortions. "Christ alone knows how it works or why it happens to us. My money's on what happened to our head in the accident."

"You haven't tried to get it checked out?"

"Hell, no," Darroll Two said with a thin smile. "Stop and think for a moment. What would they do? Either they wouldn't believe you, and they'd drag your ass back into hospital and probably never let you out. Or if they did believe you, it'd be worse. Scientists wanting to dissect our brain, probably. Men in suits and sunglasses from the government, trying to figure out a way to use it to make money, exploit other universes... steal their oil or their crops. In fact," he went on, a solemn look on his face, "listen up to this."

Darroll One listened up.

"Me and another of us had a talk the first time I met one of myself," Darroll Two continued. "We decided some ground rules. Oh, don't roll your eyes like that, it looks stupid. Ground rules. Rule one is, you don't tell anyone else about this. Secrecy means safety."

Darroll One nodded, seeing the point of rule one.

"And rule two, you don't fuck over another one of yourself. This ability of ours is a free ticket to cause absolute fucking mayhem if we want to, in another universe, and then get away scot free because when they come looking for you, you've gone back to where you came from, and won't ever hit that particular universe again. The odds against it must be astronomical. Makes winning the state lottery look like a cakewalk."

"So...?"

"So if we wanted, we could do some way bad shit, and then leave the Darroll Martock in the universe where we did that bad shit to carry the can for us. You know what we're like; at least I assume you do. We have some grudges we'd just love to pay off, against various people. It's cool to do that if we get the chance, but you gotta do it in a way that doesn't leave one of ourselves in the frame for doing whatever. Like, for instance," said Darroll Two, with a knowing look, "I have some ideas for what I'd like to do while I'm in your universe. But I'm not going to let you get into shit for it, because there is only one person in this world or any other who I give a flying fuck for, and that is Darroll Martock. Who is me, but who is also you. Are you following me, here, Other Darroll? This is actually important."

Darroll One did follow him, and did see why it was actually important.

"So when we're done chatting," Darroll Two went on, "I'm going to sit around here for an hour, and you... you are going to go meet up with the Psychopath Club, assuming it exists here. Does it?"

"Yeah. Yeah, we have the Club," Darroll One confirmed.

"Right. Get your ass over to those guys, and stay there for a while. You may be needing an alibi this afternoon." The side of Darroll Two's face creased into a smile, making his scar pucker slightly. "Hey, you still got those cans of paint going to waste in the garage here?"

"Uh... I guess so," said Darroll One.

"You not got any immediate plans for them? Wouldn't mind if one or two of them were to vanish for a worthy purpose?"

Darroll One shook his head. "If you can use them they're all yours."

"Okay, thanks, dude. See, old Tidmarsh has been fucking around with me this week. I'm figuring this is a good time to teach him a lesson."

"Tidmarsh? He hasn't been fucking around with me, though. Not any more than normal."

"Oh, do use your brain, Darroll," said Darroll Two irascibly. "How big of a hole did you get knocked in it? I'm in your world, and your Tidmarsh is the only Tidmarsh I can hit back at by being in two different places at once. It's not like they're not all the same old sarcastic bastard at heart."

Darroll One shrugged. "Okay, go ahead. So long as I don't have to carry the can."

"Oh, I shall be the one carrying the can. The can of paint," Darroll Two said with a sly grin. "You'd better get out of here and over to... is it the Boardmans' that the Club meets at, here?"

"Yeah."

"Okay. Get yourself off to the Boardmans'. I'll wait here for an hour, if that's okay? Mind if I read those comics?"

"I guess not," said Darroll One, and slid off the bed, looking at Darroll Two still sitting on its foot. "My god, this is beyond mind blowing."

"Isn't it?" said Darroll Two. "You – I mean, we – we have the golden ticket here. Forget guided tours of a chocolate factory. We have the ability to fuck around with the entire universe."

"With multiple entire universes," corrected Darroll One.

"Yeah, better still. Right... wish me luck. And be prepared for shit to happen in two or three hours. Remember, you're as innocent as the babe unborn, and you were in the Boardmans' basement all along, right?"

"Right." Darroll looked at his doppelganger one more time. "Uh... Darroll?"

"Yeah?"

"I'm not gonna see you again, am I?"

"Not this particular me," agreed Darroll Two. "Odds against it are something unspeakably remote."

"Can we shake hands on this, then? Or will it make us both explode in a cloud of anti-matter?"

Darroll Two looked suddenly thoughtful. "That's a good question." He examined the palms of his hands, as though a small, portable nuclear device might suddenly have materialised in either one. Then he looked up again. "I guess there's one way to find out."

"If it makes the world blow up," Darroll One said, "we'll never know it."

"It would be the ultimate in awesome, though," mused Darroll Two, "To blow up an entire world. Do you think the bang would be big enough for that?"

"No idea."

"Shall we do it anyway?"

"Let's."

Darroll One approached his twin, hand outstretched. Darroll Two remained sitting on the bed, but extended his own arm. Their palms made contact; their fingers gripped one another's, briefly; their hands squeezed, and relaxed. Contact was broken.

The world around them remained exactly as it always had.

"Well, that was disappointing."

"Not really. You just shook hands with yourself, how cool is that?"

"So did you."

"Yeah, true."

"Okay. I'm outa here, I guess. You gonna be okay to get into the garage for the paint?"

"Sure I am. I know where everything is. I live in the same house as you, remember?"

"Point taken."

As Darroll One was about to leave, his twin stopped him at the door. "Hey, wait, one more question. Do you know anything about a guy with a horse's head?"

Darroll One's initial instinct was to lie and say no. Something about the subject rang alarm bells. But his curiosity won out. "He was what made me crash my car."

"Me, too. And I've seen him a couple of times since. Know anything else?" Darroll Two was trying to sound casual, and he might have damn well known that Darroll One would know that, because Darroll One used exactly the same body language when he was trying to sound casual.

"Not really. Creepy, yeah? Do you know anything?"

"No, and I want to," said Darroll Two, and this time Darroll One figured he was telling a straight truth.

Leaving his visitor to enjoy Archie and Jughead, Darroll One made his way to the Boardman house in a daze. It all sounded so far-fetched; and yet everything that the other Darroll had said fitted his own experiences neatly. More to the point, he still couldn't think of anything else, other than madness, that explained them. Madness, or brain injury. Could he be dreaming all this, lying in a coma in his hospital bed with his mother clucking over him? He stood for several minutes thinking it through, but the only answer he came up with was that there was no way of proving or disproving that, and so he might as well go ahead. Act as though this whole mother of all weirdnesses was plain old reality.

He was a lot quieter than normal during the meeting of the Psychopath Club, and let Vanessa Murchison get away with two or three factual errors in her presentation about the life and misdeeds of John Wayne Gacy.

Vanessa was coming to the conclusion of the saga by explaining how the cops found his refrigerator full of body parts (Darroll was pretty sure that part of the story actually belonged to Jeffrey Dahmer, but hey) when the door at the top of the basement stairs opened. Mr Boardman called them all upstairs with a grave expression, because there was a police officer who wanted to see them.

They all filed up and stood in a row, wearing expressions ranging from the blank to the hangdog to the insolent, according to their own individual habits when confronted by authority.

"You're Darroll Martock, aren't you?" said the cop, coming to a halt opposite Darroll.

"Yes, sir," said Darroll meekly.

"Would you happen to know anything about a criminal damage incident at the home of Mr Alvin Tidmarsh this afternoon?"

"Me?" Darroll reminded himself that he was innocent. "Oh, certainly not, sir."

"What happened?" asked Chuck Milne.

"Mr Tidmarsh has had paint tipped over his expensive automobile," said the cop, "which will certainly cost several hundred dollars to have remedied."

Rowdy Serxner gave a snort of laughter. The cop turned and glared daggers at him, and Rowdy's amusement was cut abruptly short.

"When did this happen, officer?" asked Mr Boardman.

The cop consulted his notebook. "Call logged at fifteen-oh-five hours. Perp identified at scene of crime, but fled upon sight of victim emerging from house, leaving can of paint behind."

"Well, officer, I don't see how young Darroll can have had anything to do with this, then. He's been over here since two o'clock at least, hasn't he?"

There was a general murmur of assent from Mrs Boardman and from the rest of the Psychopath Club.

"I see," said the cop.

No you don't, Darroll thought. You so don't.

"Yeah," he said aloud. "I've been here most all afternoon, and I haven't been out of the basement for like, two hours. I don't know a thing about Mr Tidmarsh and his automobile." Which was a lie, but not one that there was an atom's chance of being found out in. "It could be any number of people," he went on helpfully. "Straus High is full of students who hate the principal. If you want to check out everyone with a motive, you'll have to go through the whole school."

The cop snapped his notebook shut with a click and gave Darroll a hard look. "Don't get fresh with me."

"It's true," Chuck said. "Mr Tidmarsh isn't one of those principals who goes out of their way to be a friend to the whole student body."

"I take it you don't know anything, Mr...?"

"Milne. Charles Randolph Milne. I've been in the basement here as long as Darroll."

The cop grunted at Chuck, and after a few more inconsequential questions to the Club and to the Boardman family, he departed.

"Well, well," said Vanessa, looking round at the other Club members once they had retaken their seats in the basement. "Looks like someone finally grew a backbone. I take it that it definitely wasn't any of us?"

Darroll didn't like the way her eye lingered on him as it went round the group.

"How could it have been?" asked Boardman. "Like Darroll said, we were all down here when it happened."

"Might have been Ed Crowe?" suggested Rowdy.

"More likely Ed got Kirk Mondschein or Dig Doyle to do it," said Chuck. "Ed wouldn't get his own hands dirty any more than Al

Capone would stab another gangster himself. There are henchmen for that kind of job."

"Yeah. That's the thing," said Boardman. "Literally anyone could have done it, like Martock said. There's no shortage of people who think Tidmarsh is a douche. Hey, wouldn't it be something if it turned out one of the other teachers did it?"

There were general sounds of amusement made, and to Darroll's relief, the subject was dropped.

Darroll was on his guard for the next few days, preparing mentally to make a statement if the cops came back to pressure him again. That Saturday, he saw Tidmarsh's car in the parking lot near Celebration Burger. He was impressed. Darroll Two had obviously done a calculated job on it; instead of just hurling the paint and running, he'd gone all around it, splashing paint on every separate panel. Probably gonna take a whole respray. He felt a brief surge of respect for Darroll Two, then had to remind himself that he was only feeling okay about himself.

And that felt surprisingly good.

17

The wind blew Darroll's hair into his eyes.

He'd been standing at the top of a cliff, looking out to sea, listening to the waves crash on the rocks. The sky above him was as cold and grey as the sea below, and a chill breeze was in the air. His mother would have called it a lazy wind; it was too lazy to go around you, it simply blew straight through you, clothes and skin and bones and all, and made you just as cold as it was. It was a wind that would have been right at home back in Muldoon. But he knew this wasn't Muldoon, wasn't within a thousand miles of it.

There was a savage beauty to the scene, but there was also a wrongness. At first he didn't know why. Then it became clear in his mind, though he didn't know how, that there was a presence there with him at the top of the cliff.

His heart pounded. He didn't want to turn around, but he did anyway.

Standing a few feet inland from him, trapping him between the cliff's edge and safety, stood a man in a neat dark suit, with a clean shirt and black tie, and a horse's head in place of a regular human head. This didn't stop him from speaking, or from sounding completely human when he did.

"Hello, Darroll."

"Who are you?" Darroll realised there was a waver in his voice. "Why are you here?"

By way of a response, the man with the horse's head reached into his pocket and brought out a small folding mirror. He unlatched it; a small, precise clicking noise, audible somehow above the gusts of wind. Holding it up, he gestured with his head for Darroll to look into it.

Although Darroll could guess what was coming, he leaned forward anyway. As he'd expected, a horse's head looked back out of the mirror.

"Hello, Darroll. I'm here to show you the truth. Welcome to the real Psychopath Club."

"No."

"Yes." Horsehead didn't make any threatening moves, didn't raise his voice. He simply kept speaking, smoothly and calmly, like a politician. "You can't deny it, and you can't escape it. So why not just be it? It's so much simpler, Darroll."

"I can escape it," Darroll countered. He turned to look at the cliff edge and the sea.

"Is that your escape, Darroll?" asked Horsehead. "Remember what you know now. You're one Darroll Martock in an infinity of universes, containing an infinity of Darroll Martocks. You're one grain of sand in a very big desert, whose edges stretch out as far as anyone can travel. What is one grain of sand more or less in that desert, Darroll?"

Darroll turned back to Horsehead. There was silence for a second, apart from the eternal gusting of the wind. Two seconds. Three, four, five –

"But what if all the grains of sand acted together?" Darroll blurted. "What if we all did this, all at the same moment, every one of us?"

He twisted around again and strode for the cliff edge. He was aware, vaguely, of Horsehead watching him, but making no move. He was three steps from the edge, two, one. And then he launched himself out.

The air rushed past his ears, louder even than the wind had been at the cliff top. His body rotated as it fell, going from face-down and staring at the jagged rocks below, to face-up, seeing the figure of Horsehead growing smaller and smaller at the top of the cliff, watching him as the rocks rushed up and –

"Shit," breathed Darroll as he jerked awake.

His heart thumped as the vertigo gradually faded. He took a few deep breaths and tried to persuade himself that he was fine. As he came back to full consciousness, though, he found himself less and less certain that he actually was.

Oh, he wasn't falling off a cliff, and there were no people with horse's heads standing by his bed making gnomic remarks to him, but he still had a disconcerting feeling that there was something amiss.

It took him a few seconds to realise that his room wasn't as he'd left it.

Darroll didn't let his room degenerate to primal chaos, like some people he knew, but he was a teenage boy, right? There was always going to be some mess in his bedroom. Comic books on his nightstand, empty cans of soda pop on his desk, candy wrappers around his wastebasket where he'd missed his aim, his deodorant spray with the lid off... Signs that this was a room where someone lived.

They were all gone. Everything in his room was in place, like a museum exhibit, false and dead.

And why was he lying on top of his bedclothes, rather than under them and warm, where he belonged?

He swung his legs around and found the floor, stood up, crossed to the window. Twitching the curtain back, he looked outside. There was the street, the front garden, the parking space in front of the garage. His mother's car was there. His car wasn't.

Had he crossed the barriers between universes in his sleep? Could he even do that?

He looked out at the street for a few seconds more. Everything seemed so normal out there. Focusing his hearing, he could just pick up the sound of his mother, in bed and snoring gently.

He picked up the clock from his bedside table and pressed the button to illuminate the dial. Nothing happened. He held it to his ear; there was no ticking coming from it. It had stopped.

Which was weird, because he'd put a new battery in the clock only a couple of weeks ago...

...or at least he had in his own universe.

The clothes that he'd taken off before bed and dropped into a heap on the floor to be sorted out in the morning were gone, too.

He walked over to the closet, putting his hand on the door knob, ready to open it. *Hey, what if there's a guy with a horse's head on the other side of the door?*

He smiled a quick, savage smile to himself, and jerked the door open. Nobody, with any kind of head, was lurking inside. He took a quick look at himself in the mirror behind the door; it was too dark to see properly, but even in that light, he could tell that the shape of the head in the mirror was human. Not equine.

He quickly sorted himself out some clothes by touch. He knew where everything was in that closet, on which hangers, which shelves. That was the great thing about wearing jeans; almost anything you could put on the top half of your body went with them.

Silent in his socks, he moved out into the hallway. He needed to take a whiz, so he stepped into the bathroom. He decided not to turn the light on, and also sat down rather than standing, to be quieter. And he didn't flush once he was done. If his suspicions were right, that would be a weird one for his mother when she next used the bathroom. If she even noticed. Hey, Mom, your son's ghost came to visit in the middle of the night and pissed in your toilet. Tell that one to the Ghostbusters. An invisible man pissing in your head.

The little clock on the bathroom windowsill told him it was twenty-five minutes before three a.m.

He was more and more convinced that he was where he didn't belong, in another universe where Darroll Martock had smashed his stupid life away by flipping his piece of shit Oldsmobile into a ditch. There had to be millions of universes where he'd done that. Probably some, as well, where he'd managed to turn himself into a quadriplegic, lying on a bed all night and day, being fed through a tube, breathing with a ventilator, like Superman after he fell off his horse. He pushed that thought away quickly.

Sliding quietly out of the bathroom, he padded to the end of the hallway, and passed through the door leading through to the garage. Once he'd closed it carefully and put an extra barrier between himself and his mother, he felt less at risk.

He found a torch in the garage, where it always was, which was a relief after the experience of his bedroom. He tested it, and unlike his clock, the batteries were fine.

So what now?

If his hypothesis was correct, he could do pretty much anything now.

Anything that didn't involve leaving Muldoon city limits, at any rate. Unless he stole a car, and Darroll wasn't very confident that he'd be able to do that without waking anyone up. He knew that car thieves could hotwire an engine to start a car, but he had no idea how you set about that. (Some criminal mastermind you are, Martock, he thought. You don't even know how to hotwire a car engine.)

He shone the torch beam around the garage, in search of inspiration. It was cluttered with junk, which was why it never served its purpose of parking cars. A box full of cassette tapes, and his old boombox there next to it. He could load up some music and go out into the street and play it at top volume, till the law came to shut it off?

He picked the top cassette out of the box and shone the torch on it. A pop punk band he used to listen to when he was twelve. He shuddered in distaste at his former self, and the tape went back into the box with its fellows. He shone the torch around again.

The beam of light fell on an object he barely recognised for a second in the gloom; a tin of paint. Of course! The paint that his alter-ego had put to good use upon Mr Tidmarsh's automobile, in his own universe. He moved closer, to examine it. Black paint. Partly used, going by the dribbles of it that had dried down the side of the tin. Probably went all the way back to the days when his parents were still together. His mother wasn't much into maintenance.

There were a couple of brushes alongside the paint, too, resting in a milk carton with its top half cut off.

Darroll wondered how this scene would look, in his own universe. Probably just a dusty round mark where the paint can had stood, before his double had used it to vandalise Principal Tidmarsh's Jaguar. Good job the cop hadn't been eager enough to go to his house and poke around for clues. More interested in donuts than detection.

He clicked the torch beam off and stood there in the dark for a moment while he pondered the possibilities of paint. He rejected immediately the possibility of vandalising Tidmarsh's car again; he wanted to be original, not to steal an idea, not even from himself.

His feet were cold (some things never changed; he couldn't imagine there being a single universe, anywhere in the continuum of multiverses, where his feet wouldn't be cold in the middle of the night in Muldoon). Somewhere in the garage there ought to be... Yes; his torch illuminated a pair of rainboots. Like the paint brushes, they hadn't been touched for a long time, going by the spider webs on them. He brushed them clean with his hand and eased his feet into them. They were too small and pinched his toes. How foolish toes were. Too short be useful, but long enough to make your shoes not fit properly.

He picked up the paint brushes and shoved them both into his jacket pocket. Luckily he was wearing his black jacket, with the little design of a shark jumping out of the sea up above his left nipple. It zipped shut and kept the heat inside, as well as anything could. And it had a big pocket on the inside too, right under the shark, only on the other side of the material, of course.

The paint pot was heavy enough for him to be sure there was some paint inside, but not so heavy he couldn't carry it easily.

He left the garage via the side door opposite the house; it was quieter than opening the main door. He didn't know how much noise he could get away with making, or how much interaction it would take with people who knew he was dead in this universe to bring his trip to an end, but it made sense to be careful. Overconfidence was dangerous. He knew that now. It was overconfidence that nearly killed him when he flipped the Oldsmobile into the fence.

As he walked, he thought again of what must have happened in this universe. Maybe his alter ego had been driving that little bit faster than he had, and instead of smacking into the fence, he'd bounced off it and into the telegraph pole a few yards down the road. Or maybe he hadn't bothered to fasten his seat belt, and had gone out through the windshield like a diver through the surface of the water, and breathed his last on the hood of the car or in the ditch by the fence, his face all cut to ribbons. Oh boy. Closed casket time.

It was as cold as a bucket of penguin shit outside. Even with the black jacket zipped all the way up, he felt it immediately. He wished he'd brought gloves, but they were back in his room… at the very least; maybe they were back in his own universe. He made do by stuffing one hand into his pocket while the other one carried the paint, and every hundred steps he pulled that hand out, transferred the paint to it, and shoved the other one into the other pocket instead. The street was deserted, because of the time of night, and the cold. At this time of night, Muldoon looked more like a one horse town than ever. The thought brought Horsehead back into his mind, and he turned around quickly in case the creature was following him. But he was completely alone.

He looked up at the sky as he walked. There was a moon as thin as a knife blade, and stars, so many stars. No clouds at all tonight; no wonder it was so cold. The stars looked cold too, like tiny ice crystals in the sky, even though Darroll knew they were actually huge balls of flaming gas pumping out as much heat as the sun; he'd learned that in science class with Mr Pezanelli a couple of years ago. "So you see," Mr Pezanelli had explained, "things aren't always what they seem at first. That's science for you."

Mr Pezanelli had retired the year after that and moved to Florida. Darroll had heard he'd sent Mr Tidmarsh a postcard, saying he played golf every day at Ponte Vedra Beach. There wasn't much science involved in golf, but Darroll couldn't blame Mr Pezanelli for his choice. A lifetime of teaching science to lunkhead kids in Muldoon would make anyone long for a state where you had the sun and beaches. Where old farts could potter round a golf course all day without eight layers of clothing, and snowdrifts filling all the bunkers.

He walked out of his home division, and onto the old highway into town. One car zipped past, breaking the speed limit for sure, but there was no sign of any cop car suddenly popping its sirens to chase it.

Within ten minutes, he could see the neon sign of Celebration

Burger ahead. It wasn't illuminated, of course, not in the middle of the night. The only place in Muldoon that stayed open all night was the gas station and that was right out of town in the other direction, past the old railroad line and down by the interstate junction. As he crossed the street, Darroll thought about the interstate briefly; the occasional late-night voyagers on its pitted concrete pavement, kept awake only by the bumps and vibrations until they realised that they were nodding off and took the next exit, directed to MUL-DOON in elderly button-signed letters. They'd reach the bottom of the off-ramp and see GAS 0.1 MILE, and follow that sign too, and reach the gas station, its canopy lit up, garish against the stark black night. They'd go in and grab a coffee, or maybe a Mountain Dew (as much caffeine as a coffee), and head out again for the interstate, east or west, and all they'd ever see of Muldoon would be that gas station. Even though the interstate junction was within city limits, there were no actual houses within half a mile of it; just the gas station, and the motel, and the Arby's that closed at nine every night, an hour before Celebration Burger.

Opposite Celebration Burger was the mural. He put the paint can down on the sidewalk, and took a moment to look either way, up and down the street. It was still deserted; he might as well be the only living boy in Muldoon. Then he took a long appraisal of the mural. The painted Indians still looked goofy, and the guy in the middle in the GI helmet with his lopsided smile still looked like a retard.

He nodded to himself, and knew he was going ahead with this.

Except he couldn't get the lid off the tin of paint.

Why was he such an idiot? He brought the brushes with him, but he hadn't brought anything to lever open the paint with, even though the garage at home had more screwdrivers than a branch of Home Depot. He patted his pockets in search of anything that might do the job. He tried a quarter, but the coin was too small to get any proper purchase on the lid, stuck down by old paint for the last five years. "A lever is the simplest machine in science," Mr Pezanelli had taught him. Was he going to wreck his plan, give himself a cold walk in the frost for nothing, because he couldn't make the simplest machine ever invented by human beings?

In a sudden fit of temper, he lifted his foot, and brought it down on the paint with a savage kick. It rolled away, and he snarled silently to himself as the pain shot through his foot.

He went to retrieve the paint (it wasn't even dented) and stood it back upright. Think, Darroll, he told himself. There must be a way, there has to be a key to this problem...

...a key.

He actually laughed out loud, not caring for a moment whether anyone heard him. Anyway, why should he care? He wasn't actually here. He was just a ghost. A ghost with a pot of paint.

He pulled his keyring from his pocket and looked at the selection. Choosing the car key, he forced it under the lip of the paint pot's lid, then shoved down with the palm of his hand. General Motors might make shitty automobiles, but at least they had the sense to put a smooth plastic top on their keys, so he didn't rip his hand to pieces when he pushed.

There was a sudden gasping noise, as if the paint pot had decided it was too much effort to stay closed, and the lid popped open. Paint fumes filled Darroll's nose.

The Indians looked much better, he thought, when he'd given them both Groucho Marx eyebrows and moustaches, and the Statue of Liberty's torch turned into a huge, unseemly sex toy with surprisingly little effort. He paused for thought, contemplating whether to paint swastikas over the GI's helmet and uniform, but decided against it; he didn't want people to think that this was the work of neo-Nazis or any kind of a political statement. Because it wasn't. This was purely and simply Darroll Martock, ghost of this town, showing it what he thought of it.

Instead, he painted a mask over the GI's face, the sort that the Lone Ranger or a superhero would wear, and then added to his handiwork by painting question marks all over him, turning him into the Riddler. The other soldier on the mural, behind the first one, got a Batman mask to accompany his GI buddy. Buddy? Not any more. Sworn enemies, now. Superhero and supervillain. Was this how supervillains' careers got started? Painting subversive images on walls? He paused for a moment, imagining himself as the Riddler or the Joker, giving Batman the runaround, then remembered that he didn't have time for gloating. Plenty of opportunity for that later.

There was still paint left. At the bottom of the mural, where the big steam train ran, he got to work again. It wasn't easy to deface a train in a subversive manner that would make the citizens of Muldoon quake in their boots. Finally he used the paint to write three big, black words atop the train, all the way across the mural, twenty feet or so, in letters you could see across the street.

DARROLL MARTOCK LIVES.

His face broke out into an unaccustomed smile as he regarded his handiwork. He might by all rights be dead in this universe, or a thousand other universes, but being dead was for ordinary people. Not for Darroll.

He up-ended the paint and let the remainder of it run out of the can and over the sidewalk at its leisure. The paint brush he hefted in his hand for a moment, then pulled his arm back and threw it up in the air, across the street. It landed on the sloping roof of the dry-cleaning store several buildings down from Celebration Burger, skittered down the slope, and came to rest wedged in the guttering at the roof's edge.

Nothing more to do here tonight. He turned and headed for home, glad to be able to put both hands in his pockets this time. He kept looking up at the sky as he walked, little clouds of steam condensing from his breath and drifting upward into his line of vision. Were the stars looking down at him? Were there hidden government satellites up there, watching, recording? He almost hoped they were. Because if they checked the footage from their spy satellites, all they'd find was that the Muldoon township mural had been defaced in the middle of the night by the ghost of a boy who died months ago.

He dropped the spare paintbrush down a drain at the top of Main Street and carried on home. A couple of cars passed, one of them with an out of state plate, for whatever reason anyone from out of state could have for being in Muldoon at four in the goddamn morning. No other pedestrians at all, but he didn't care if there were; would they even see him? He was dead. He was a ghost. Only the cold freshness of the sub-zero air in his lungs, and the pain in his foot where he'd kicked the paint can, reminded him that he was alive, even if his analogue wasn't.

When he got home, he slipped back into the garage, shucked the gumboots, and re-entered the house as quietly as he left. He wasn't sleepy at all as he lay back down on the bed in the shrine to his dead alter-ego that was his room in this universe, triumph thumping in his heart.

He wondered vaguely how long it would take him to be bounced back to his home dimension. Maybe when a few people had seen the defaced mural? Obviously they hadn't yet, and wouldn't till the morning. Or maybe his mother would come in there in the morning, to gaze upon her dead son's bedroom, permanently laid out as it had been on the day he died in this universe, except tidier, and find him there in his bed. That would be a bit of a shock for her. He grinned as he imagined that from his mother's viewpoint, the ghost of her dead son snoring happily away in his own bed just like he'd never smashed up that damn Oldsmobile, and her screaming in shock and... what would it look like to an observer? Would he blink out like a light bulb being turned off? Or fade away like the Cheshire cat? Cheshire cat – that was a good one, given how he was grinning at the moment.

He was still pondering that, and still not feeling tired, when he fell asleep quite suddenly.

* * *

When he woke up he was under the bedclothes once more, apart from his feet, which were sticking out and cold as usual; but he was glad about that, for once. It was how things always were, which meant he was home.

Or was he home? He opened his eyes and sat up, scanning his room quickly.

The piles of comic books by his bed, and the pile of clothes on the floor, told him he was home. When he looked out of the window and saw his car outside, that told him he was home too. And when he threw his dirty clothes into the laundry basket and pulled fresh ones on, then emerged from his room to grab breakfast, his mother's absence of any reaction told him he was home.

"Hi, mom," he said.

"Hi, honey. Did you sleep well?" she asked, the same as always. Which also told him he was home.

Usually he just muttered some platitude at her, but this morning he was feeling so chipper, he decided to give her a proper answer. "Yup. Like a log. All bright eyed and bushy tailed."

"Oh, good," his mother said vaguely, as if she didn't quite know how to take her son's unexpectedly positive response. "Are you all fixed up for school?"

"Yup, yup." He shot breakfast cereal into his bowl, added milk, then filled a tumbler with more milk. And for once, his mother didn't chide him for drinking milk as well as putting it on his cereal.

As soon as he was done with breakfast, he dashed out of the house. He couldn't wait to get into town and see what the mural looked like; even though he was certain there would be nothing to see, he needed to be sure. He parked the car one block down Main from the mural, and walked up to it, his heart bumping against his ribs as though it had come loose and was swinging back and forth with every footstep.

The mural was pristine and undamaged, its dull paint unexpectedly bright in the low rays of the morning sun. Darroll stood there, drinking it in, considering its implications; the implications for himself, for Muldoon, for the universe.

"And what have we here?"

His heart jerked again, as the voice from behind him interrupted his reverie. The voice was all too familiar; Mr Tidmarsh. What the hell was he doing in town? Why couldn't school principals go into hibernation over the Christmas vacation instead of wandering around being assholes?

"Wool-gathering again, eh, Martock?" said Tidmarsh as Darroll turned around. The principal was holding a styrofoam cup of coffee from Celebration Burger in one hand. "Or were you merely lost in admiration of our town's civic pride and the artistic beauty of that mural? I have seen nothing hitherto that made me suspect you took any interest either in art or in good citizenship."

Darroll didn't say anything, because there wasn't anything you could say to that. There never was anything you could say, when Mr Tidmarsh went off on one of his sarcastic tirades. You just had to nod, and let him be clever at your expense, until he got tired of it and wandered off to find another victim. Darroll would almost sooner be bullied by Ed Crowe than by Mr Tidmarsh; at least Crowe didn't make himself out to be better than you. Only bigger. Mr Tidmarsh thought he was better than every goddamn student at the goddamn high school.

"Can it be," Tidmarsh continued, "that you are making a sudden and unexpected attempt to pull yourself together, and actually take an interest in some of the many things which this world provides that have genuine worth and value? Such as paying attention in class, and not having your nose in a comic book at all hours of the day? I am an optimistic fool to think so, I know, but I cling to the hope that even Darroll Martock may derive some value from his education before I am forced, with reluctant dismay, to say farewell to him forever and send him out into the big wide world. May I hope for the pleasure of seeing your handsome face at school when classes recommence? I may? So pleased to hear it."

Darroll thought that would be the end of the principal's tirade, but Tidmarsh took a step closer to him, invading his personal space. "You enjoy a little vandalism, do you, Mr. Martock?"

Darroll flinched. How the hell did he know? Terror seized him. Was Tidmarsh able to switch back and forth between universes, too? Had he watched Darroll deface the mural?

Within a second, he understood what Tidmarsh was actually referring to, but it was too late. His guilty reaction had betrayed him, and a smile came over the principal's face.

"I see. You may have contrived to persuade law enforcement that you had nothing to do with damaging my automobile, but I know better. I know damn well you did it, Martock, and I am going to make you suffer for it. Do I make myself clear?"

Without waiting for a reply he wandered off, sipping his coffee and looking smug. Darroll glared daggers after him, daggers that shot from Darroll's eyes into Tidmarsh's back, right up to the hilt each time. Oblivious, Tidmarsh climbed into his paint-blotched Jaguar, and pulled away from the kerb. Darroll watched it dwindle into the distance, still thinking about Tidmarsh's back and daggers. A smile began to spread over his face as he climbed back into his own car, and it remained there all morning.

18

The morning of the roadtrip dawned bright and snowless over the parking lot of Celebration Burger. Vanessa was in as bad a mood as if a blizzard had hit.

"I am not riding in the back of this car," she snapped to Beth.

Beth looked back through her glasses at Vanessa. "All right. I'll go in the back, you can have shotgun if you're so fussy about it. Don't you dare ruin this trip for me."

Joe Boardman waved a hand at Vanessa and Beth. "For god's sake cool down, both of you."

Both Vanessa and Beth began to protest in fury at Boardman. Darroll was finding it hard to suppress a grin. How the hell could so trivial a subject bend people so far out of shape?

The roar of a motorcycle engine cut the argument short as Serxner chugged into the parking lot, crash helmet and leathers and all. Darroll wondered for a moment or two whether guys all in leather turned Boardman on. Sure as hell they did nothing for Darroll. Rowdy Serxner in bike leathers was still Rowdy Serxner, and still a farmboy, except he smelt a bit more than usual of cows because the leathers were making him sweat.

Clinging on behind Serxner was Chuck Milne. Serxner came to a stop, and Milne hopped right down, as if he couldn't wait to be off the bike.

"What's wrong, Chuck?" asked Darroll.

"Nothing," lied Chuck. Darroll could tell Chuck was chicken about riding on the back of Serxner's bike, but didn't want to admit it. It wouldn't do him any good if he did; there wasn't room for his fat ass in the back of Darroll's car alongside Boardman and Beth, and anyway, Chuck was scared of Darroll's driving as well.

"All right," Darroll said. "Ladies and gentlemen of the Club. We are about to hit the road to Chicago."

"Woo!" came from Serxner. Everyone else just stood there.

"We all prepared?"

"Whatcha mean, Boardman?" asked Serxner.

"Well, road trips need planning," pointed out Boardman. "They don't just happen."

"Eh? Of course they just happen. Spontaneity is part of the fun."

"In your world, perhaps, Rowdy. If you fail to prepare, be prepared to fail." Joe Boardman adopted that self-righteous expression of his, the look of a man who knows his opinion is the right one and be damned to anyone else. "Like, has everyone been to the can? We don't want to have to stop off at every gas station on the way because someone needs the restroom. And it's probably a good idea to bring some food along too. Potato chips, cookies, whatever. So we don't need to stop for food either. So we can blast right on through to Chicago."

"Like I'm gonna be able to help myself to chips when I'm riding this thing," pointed out Serxner.

"He's right about going to the restroom, though," Vanessa said. "And have you got a full gas tank, Rowdy?"

"Yeah. How about you, Martock?"

"Filled mine last night."

"I didn't need to ask *him*, Rowdy," Vanessa pointed out. "I was there." Which was true; Darroll had been in Celebration Burger with Vanessa, Beth Vines, and Joe Boardman. They'd been talking about the next day, with levels of excitement ranging from studied nonchalance (Darroll) to undisguised relish (Joe and Vanessa). And Darroll had driven Vanessa home afterward, via the gas station.

Rowdy Serxner grinned at Vanessa, and made a smacking noise with his lips. "You guys out necking?"

"If we were it's none of your gorramn business," retorted Vanessa.

"Hey, relax, relax," said Chuck, flapping his arms. "Why shouldn't Darroll and Vanessa get smoochy-woochy in an automobile? It's what automobiles were invented for. Say, Bryan Barlow and Sue Planck went all the way in the back of his Ford. I know that for a fact."

Darroll almost asked Chuck how he knew, but decided he couldn't be bothered. He looked at Serxner. Serxner looked at

Vanessa, then grinned at Darroll. A sudden hate bomb exploded in Darroll's chest. Right now, he was just about ready to kill Rowdy Serxner for his stupid leering face and his dimbulb prurience. He could do it, easy. Let them head out toward Chicago, onto the interstate, and all he'd have to do would be to pull up alongside Serxner's motorbike and drift over across the white lines into him. Crunch. The bike flipping over and over, off the road and into oblivion, and more satisfying still, Serxner and Milne flipping over and over too, arms and legs flailing. Bouncing off the road, like basketballs off the wooden floor of the Straus High gymnasium, except they'd leave little wet red patches everywhere they bounced. He smiled quietly. Another one for the mental files.

But it would spoil the road trip. Spoil Beth and Vanessa's fun. Maybe if he did it on the road back...? No.

"Well, I'm going to the little girls' room," Vanessa said. Nobody made the obvious wisecrack about Vanessa belonging in the big girl's room instead. Beth nodded silently, and turned to head into Celebration Burger as well.

Darroll was prepared for them to be in there forever, because that was what happened when girls went to the restroom, but they were out surprisingly quickly, and piled back into the Oldsmobile.

Darroll followed Rowdy's motorbike out of town, down the highway that had been a main US route years ago, before the interstate came, and across the grade crossing with the old railroad track. Like the highway, the railroad was a memento of days gone by; it owed its continued existence only to the fact that nobody could be bothered to trek all the way out to Muldoon to lift the rusty old rails and recycle them. Once it had been a major route on the rail network, carrying lumber and resin from the sawmills up to the northwest, and cattle on their way to the slaughterhouses. Passengers, too; there had been a station next to the crossing fifty years ago. Now they travelled by road instead, passengers and freight alike.

Darroll wondered idly what it would be like to ride on a train. And what it would be like to be in a railroad accident. In a car crash you at least might have some control over your actions. In a railroad crash, you could do precisely nothing. You would either live or die, and only fate knew which. He wasn't sure whether that would be more comforting than a car crash, or less so. And he hoped he wouldn't ever have to find out.

Rowdy turned into the gas station and Darroll parked alongside the store. Boardman and Vanessa went inside after Rowdy; Boardman came out with a coffee, and Vanessa with a Baby Ruth bar. By the time they emerged Rowdy had filled his tank and was ready to go.

"Next stop, Chicago," said Boardman as he opened the door to get back into the Oldsmobile.

* * *

Darroll admitted it to himself only gradually, but he found himself enjoying the trip. The tiny convoy of his Oldsmobile and Serxner's motorbike soon reached a steady speed that made a rhythmic, near-hypnotic, bump-bump over the joints in the concrete roadway. Darroll could see how accidents happened on the interstate. Some guy, travelling salesman or whatever, in the car on his own after a hard day. Bump-bump-bump-bump, over the joints, lulling the driver off to a soothing restful sleep. For about ten seconds. And then he veered off the road and smacked into a barrier, or flattened himself against the ass-end of a huge truck that was trundling along ahead of him. Darroll wondered whether you actually woke up in an accident like that, whether you actually had time to feel a split second of sudden intense, enormous pain before you blacked out again forever. Or whether you just drifted off and never woke up again, until you found yourself at the pearly gates with St. Pete glaring at you and telling you you were a selfish, stupid ass for killing yourself that way, and how do you think you made that trucker feel? No heaven for you, bozo.

"Hey," he said, conversationally, "if I went to sleep and crashed the car and killed myself, you think I'd wake up in time to experience the pain, or would I just never know about it at all?"

"What a goddamn stupid morbid question," said Boardman from the back seat.

"No stupid questions," Vanessa said from the front. "Only stupid answers. Plus, we're the Psychopath Club. That's a really interesting question. Dunno the answer though."

Beth, behind Darroll, didn't say anything. Darroll moved his head and squinted into his rear view mirror, and found out the reason; Beth was oblivious, sitting with her headphones on and staring out of the window.

Rowdy's bike moved up alongside Darroll. Rowdy raised his hand to his forehead in a salute. Milne didn't; Milne was holding on tight with both hands. Darroll couldn't make out his face, inside his helmet, but he bet himself Milne was crapping his pants. Darroll saluted back, and gave Rowdy the thumbs-up. Serxner put on a little more speed, and moved ahead of the Oldsmobile, then pulled in front of it to let a speeding pick-up go by in the passing lane.

As Chicago grew nearer, traffic grew heavier. The interstate had widened from two lanes to three, but it was still becoming more and more jammed. Serxner, on his bike, could have threaded his way through the traffic and stolen a march on the Oldsmobile; but he chose to stay in convoy with them, to keep the club together.

"That's team spirit," said Boardman. And Darroll couldn't argue with that.

Thankfully the exit they needed came before the interstate reached downtown and became solid with traffic. The bike sped up the off-ramp, with Darroll behind it. Beth slipped her headphones off. "We're nearly there?"

Vanessa looked at the list of directions she'd made in her little notebook. "Nearly there," she echoed. "Ten minutes."

Darroll checked his watch against the clock on the dashboard. Incredibly, for this piece of shit car, the two agreed. They were the better part of an hour ahead of schedule, despite the traffic.

19

"An art gallery?" Boardman looked at Darroll, astonished, scornful. "Who the hell goes all the way to Chicago and then goes to an art gallery?"

"I do," Darroll said. Boardman shrugged.

"You are genuinely nuts, I swear. Well, you can go to your art gallery if you like, but I'm going to Navy Pier with these guys."

"Actually," Chuck said, "I'll do the gallery too."

That made Boardman boggle again. "Why, Milne? Why the hell? Are you allergic to having a good time or something?"

Rowdy snorted with laughter, and Vanessa gave him a shove. "Hey, quit arguing, will ya? We don't do peer pressure in the Psychopath Club. If Chuck and Darroll want to go to an art gallery then they can go to an art gallery. I'm going to do Navy Pier, though," she added.

"I went to Navy Pier last year with my folks," Chuck explained. "It kicked ass, but I wanna do something I've not already covered. Hence, art gallery. I'm not scared of culture. Something that sets me above the dumb animals."

"Like Ed Crowe," Darroll drawled, and Rowdy laughed again.

"Also, they have American Gothic," Chuck said, with reverence in his voice. Darroll had forgotten that. He'd seen it on the school visit, and like everything else that was hyped up in advance, he'd found it a letdown. He was about to say he'd join the Navy Pier party instead, but then he remembered the gallery also had Andy Warhol's electric chair art, and he did want to see that again.

"I'll come to the gallery too," Beth Vines said quietly. As so often, whenever Beth actually spoke, it made everyone stop and look at her.

"I'm not here for Navy Pier or art galleries or the aquarium or anything else," she continued. "I'm here to see Todd Krank. And he won't be onstage till evening. An art gallery sounds more fun to me than barging around in a huge-ass crowd of tourists, and spending all your money on overpriced cotton candy and souvenirs."

"Wow," Vanessa said. "I think I just got out-gothed."

Boardman sighed. "Okay. You three sad sacks go look at your pictures while Rowdy and Vanessa and me are having the time of our lives at the pier. What time we going to meet back up? And where?"

"Here?" suggested Vanessa.

"Nah," Rowdy said. "I don't want to be sitting round a parking garage that smells of old piss for hours, if those guys are late."

"Well, where, then?"

They eventually agreed to meet at the big statue at the landward end of Navy Pier.

Chuck, Darroll and Beth set off for the gallery, walking abreast, Darroll and Chuck on either side of Beth. Darroll wondered how they looked, two guys and one girl like that, especially since Beth was so distinctive, all straight hair and glasses and so tiny. She couldn't be more than five feet high. Maybe she was self-conscious. Maybe there were rides on Navy Pier you couldn't go on unless you were tall enough, and she was worried she wouldn't be.

The gallery was surprisingly busy. Darroll could hear some foreign voices among the clusters of people at the entrance, which surprised him. In his case, he was here in Chicago because it was the biggest city he could easily reach from his home. What was their excuse? If these tourists came from France or Germany or wherever, they could have flown anywhere in the whole wide world. Why the hell did they choose Chicago where they could stand around and get in his way?

It didn't take long for them to pass through the entrance, and be able to start looking at the paintings. Chuck made a show of standing in front of each one, tilting his head from side to side and squinting, to show what a complete art connoisseur he was. He looked like a complete asshole to Darroll, but Darroll decided he didn't need to point that out to Chuck. Let the jerk enjoy himself.

Beth, meantime, moved around at a steady pace, saying not a word, and the most she did to acknowledge any of the paintings she was looking at was to adjust her glasses a fraction now and again.

It was obvious that they were approaching something special when, after a while, they found the next room in the gallery had a security guard by the door, and another one inside.

"Ah, here we go," said Chuck, and stood next to the guard, sucking in his cheeks and tilting his head as he looked at the celebrated painting. Beth and Darroll joined him, flanking him.

It was just the same as it had been when he'd been here on the school visit, and Darroll still found the painting grating on him as he regarded it. American Gothic. Everyone knew the thing. People used parodies of it, in advertisements, or just to show how clever they were. Pasting the heads of pop stars or politicians onto the bodies of the two people in the painting. And what about the guy who painted it? He must have sold it for millions. Never have to work again.

"Classic, but like so many classics," Beth said softly, "the actual thing doesn't live up to the anticipation."

Chuck looked at Beth as though she'd said something obscene. Beth returned his look, like a baseball bouncing off a wall and back to Steve McQueen in an old movie Darroll had seen that year, channel-hopping in his hospital bed. Chuck shrugged and looked back at American Gothic.

Darroll couldn't bear the sight of the thing any more. He walked on out of the room, leaving Beth and Chuck behind. For some reason he was angry; not just angry but seething mad, his heart thumping, as though it, too, were Steve McQueen's baseball. He barely took in any of the pictures in the next few areas, and when he did look at any, they seemed tawdry and pointless. Why the hell was he here and not at Navy Pier having fun? Worst decision of his life. His anger kept growing, aimed now not just at the art around him but at himself.

He was so busy being angry that at first, he didn't realise that the swirls were coming.

When he did figure what was about to happen, he didn't have much time to find a place to be inconspicuous. Heart pounding with nervousness as well as rage now, he looked around desperately, and found the current room had a bench in the middle, for people like Chuck to sit on and look at paintings and nod like an oil derrick to show how cultured they were. He dropped onto the bench in relief. The swirls rose as high as his eyes, and for a few moments, he knew nothing.

When awareness returned he was still on the bench, and nobody was paying him any heed, which suited him fine. He remained on his ass to begin with, while he assessed the situation. What kind of world was he in this time? Was there another instance of him wandering around? Were Beth and Chuck there, admiring the art, or were they at home in Muldoon in this dimension – or perhaps at Navy Pier?

He began to retrace his steps through the gallery, moving carefully, peeking into each separate room before entering it. He had no particular objection to meeting himself, but he didn't want to do so in front of dozens of people. Neither did he want to bump into Chuck and Beth twice in two separate bodies within minutes. That might have awkward consequences.

But he went all the way back as far as American Gothic without finding Chuck or Beth, and the inference he drew from that was that they weren't there, and consequently, he wasn't there either. If he even existed in this universe and hadn't died months ago in Muldoon in the wreck of the Oldsmobile.

He found another bench and sat down to think, putting his hands in his pockets. One hand found something that made him pause; his pocket knife.

He sat there for several minutes with his hands in his pockets, while he thought deeply and considered potential courses of action and their outcomes. But they all kept coming back to the same thing, as people passed by, none of them Beth or Chuck, none of them paying any heed to him sitting quietly.

Ah, well. He finally stood up, and walked slowly back into the room with American Gothic. The security guard was still in place, looking thoroughly bored. Darroll walked back up to confront the painting.

He took a minute to imprint it upon his retinas and his memory; the round rimless glasses, the pitchfork, the barn in the background. He drank every aspect of the artwork in, until he was certain he could paint it again himself, if he had only just happened to have the skill of the artist. He tilted his head on one side and squinted, as he'd seen Chuck doing earlier, acting the art connoisseur, acting normal. Or what passed for normal in this joint, anyway.

His hand slipped back into his pocket and he started a mental countdown from ten. When he reached one, he moved suddenly forward, his hand emerging from his clothing with the knife blade extended.

For a fatal second the guard was caught by surprise as Darroll reached the painting and brought the knife up to it. Then he wasted another second by yelling "Hey!", by which time the blade was already halfway across the bespectacled man's face. The canvas made a harsh tearing sound, a release of tension.

As Darroll completed the first slash, the guard finally leapt at Darroll. The second motion of the knife blade was interrupted halfway across the woman's collar, just short of her throat. Darroll dropped the knife, and it slid away across the floor as he struggled with the guard for his footing.

"What the hell?" bellowed the guard. "What the hell?"

Darroll didn't know what the hell, and he didn't know why the guard was making such a noise instead of focusing on him. He didn't much care, either, although a couple of the guard's blows landed on his face painfully. He was waiting for the swirls that he knew must be coming to reward him, for making such a difference in a world where he didn't belong, and sure enough, there they were. For a few seconds the guard's hands felt muffled and remote, as though they were gripping him through a thick blanket. Then they were gone entirely and he was sitting on the bench again; the first bench, several rooms away from American Gothic, from which the swirls had taken him away.

His heart was still thumping; he wasn't sure whether it was from the swirls, or from the adrenalin rush he'd just given himself. He felt in his pocket. His knife was gone. Oh well. It hadn't been anything fancy, but he would have liked to have the option to hold it, to think about what he'd done with it.

What had he done with it?

He stood up quickly. He knew that, in this universe, American Gothic would remain intact, just as the Muldoon mural had remained undefaced. He knew, on an intellectual level, what he'd see if he returned to that room now, but a part of him needed to go and see it anyway.

Halfway back to American Gothic, he bumped into Beth and Chuck.

"Oh, there you are," Chuck said. "We thought we'd lost you. Where are you going?"

"I want to go back through there," said Darroll. "I want to see that one painting once more before we finish here."

Chuck raised an eyebrow at him. "Really? I had the impression you found it disappointing when you saw it just now. Like Beth said, some paintings are so much a part of the human zeitgeist that you see it all the time, here there and everywhere. And then when you finally see the actual real thing…"

"Yeah," Darroll said, wishing Chuck would shut up and stop meandering on about art, "but I still want to see it again." And he headed on through to the room where it hung.

It was, of course, pristine and undamaged as it hung there on the wall, the woman looking at the man, the man looking out at the gallery. The security guard barely glanced at Darroll, uninterested. The painting he was looking at had never known the touch of a vandal's hand.

Beth moved up behind him.

"What's it say to you, Darroll?" she asked him, in a voice even quieter than her normal tone.

"You know what it says to me, Beth? It says that no matter what I do, I'll never make a difference."

"What do you mean?" Beth seemed to be surprised by his answer.

He pointed at the painting. "This is just one painting. There are millions of others like it. You're just one person, and so's that security guard, and so's Chuck. There are millions of others like us. So many millions that no one person can have more than an infinitesimal effect no matter what they do…"

"So…?"

"So," said Darroll, "from now on I'm gonna do what the hell I want and fuck it. Nothing matters, Beth. Nobody matters. Certainly not me."

Beth looked through her glasses at him, silently.

"And what I want right now is to get out of this place, go over to Navy Pier, and find the others. And then go see that gig of yours. Coming?"

Beth paused a moment, shrugged, nodded. "Okay. Let's find Chuck and move out."

20

"What're we gonna do with the time?" Darroll asked, finding a parking place at the far end of the block from the record store in Player Heights.

"I guess we go get tickets, hang out?" hazarded Boardman.

The Club piled out of the car, stretching and making little noises, once more on two legs instead of four wheels. The motorbike parked alongside them as Darroll turned off the ignition.

Milne came over to the car, helmet under one arm, his hair tousled and sweaty. Darroll wound down his window.

"Hey, you guys. That coulda been worse, huh?" chirped Milne.

Yeah, Darroll wanted to reply. I could've run you and Serxner off the road and killed you both. Car beats motorbike, like rock crushes scissors.

"There a payphone round here?" Darroll wondered. "I promised I'd call my mom sometime today to let her know I was okay."

"Not got a cellphone?" asked Milne, and Darroll shook his head. He was sure his dad had a cellphone, a big grey cellphone the same colour as his business suit, and his soul. His dad could have afforded to buy him one, same as he could have afforded to buy him a decent set of wheels instead of the Oldsmobile.

"Lucky if you find one anyplace around here that hasn't been vandalised to shit," predicted Vanessa.

But Vanessa was wrong; there was a working one nearby.

"Why'd you want to call your mother anyway? You hate her," Rowdy said.

"I said I would."

"So?"

"So I'm keeping a promise. Is that unfashionable? You guys go on ahead," Darroll suggested. "Get in line for the tickets. I won't be long." And he didn't intend to be.

He dug a dime out of his pocket, dialled, then pushed the coin into the slot. His mom squawked into his ear, in that distorted, tinny tone that you only ever got from public phones.

"Darroll, sweet pea? Are you okay? Did you make it into Chicago all right? Are you having a nice day?"

"Sure did, mom," he said, trying to sound both proud of his achievement and nonchalant, as though it were a performance he could turn in every day if he had to. "We're over at Player Heights now, by the record store."

"How about that Serxner boy? Is he all right? I don't like to think of him –"

"He's fine too," Darroll interjected. He knew that if he allowed her to, his mother would spend the rest of his dime on bending his ear about how dangerous motorbikes were, and how Rowdy Serxner was just a boy and shouldn't be riding one, never mind with that Charlie Milne hanging on behind.

"Well," his mother said after a moment, as if her thoughts had been derailed by her son's interruption. "You enjoy your concert, or gig, or whatever it is they call them now. It was concerts when I saw Neil Diamond in Devaney Park, but that was a long time ago…"

"Not that long ago," he said, dutifully, knowing she expected it of him, and she laughed.

"Well! Whatever it's called, you and your friends enjoy it. I'll hear all about it when you get home!"

"Sure you will, Mom. I'll tell you all about it." He could feel the anger welling up inside him again at the sheer, tedious banality of his mother's conversation, the conversation that was the only way she knew how to talk. And as he felt the fury, it redoubled, reinforced by anger at himself for letting her ramble on and on without calling her out, for being complicit in letting his mother be the most boring woman in the whole goddamn Midwest.

There was only one thing to do, and he did it. "G'bye, Mom."

As he replaced the phone, he remembered a cartoon he'd watched when he was younger. There was a guy who got phone calls from his boss, and every time he fucked up, his boss would – with the weird, warped style that only cartoons could exhibit – reach through the telephone handset, form a fist, and punch the protagonist. Now that would be something. Imagine if he were able to reach through the telephone, all the way along the wires and cables to his mom, and have his hand suddenly pop out of her handset and grab her by the throat. Yes. Strangle her to death, right there in her own living room. And when the cops came to investigate, he'd be all sweetness and light and innocence. Who, me, Officer? But I was in Chicago at the time. Half a dozen witnesses. Couldn't possibly have been me. Must have been a burglar who panicked when he discovered her and killed her when she tried to call the cops. That's why the phone was off the hook when she was found. Yeah.

This daydream occupied him all the way down the block, over the uneven and poorly maintained sidewalk, and to the record store.

Vanessa and the others were not in line for tickets, for the excellent reason that there was no line for tickets. There was a small wooden table by the door, and a stringy-haired, middle-aged man with denims and a pot belly behind it. On the table was a little metal box. Darroll watched as his money dropped irrevocably into the box.

"Hand," said the fat guy. Darroll blinked in confusion.

"Hand?" the fat guy repeated, and picked up a small rubber stamp. Darroll belatedly realised what he wanted, and cautiously extended his fingers towards the clerk. Thud, went the stamp on the ink pad, and then it landed on the back of Darroll's hand, leaving a smudgy purple impression of a quarter note up against his knuckles, at a skew angle. Darroll thought that if he were the doorman for this gig, he'd take better care how he stamped his customers' hands. He'd get those quarter notes straight, for sure. So straight, you could line up his customers and make them put their hands out in a line, and you could play the notes in a little tune.

He looked around the store as he walked on from the entrance. There was a raised, open area in the window; the stage, of course. Empty at the moment, with the better part of an hour to go before the gig got started; a couple of amps sitting ready, and a drum kit at the back (or at the front, if you were standing outside the store on the sidewalk looking in). A bunch of cables snaked over the floor. A couple of rows of chairs had been set up to the left of the stage, a motley collection with hardly two the same colour or design, and the corresponding space to the right of the stage was empty; standing room.

There was a cash desk in the middle of the store, with space on all four sides of it, so that the cashier could sit there, a spider in a web, and see any part of the store from that vantage point. The walls were covered in sun-faded album sleeves and equally faded posters for ancient bands' gigs. The Doors, Commander Cody and his Lost Planet Airmen, Foghat; what ludicrous names bands had. Further inside, there were racks of CDs, LPs, and singles, with signs hanging from the roof to point buyers in the right direction; soul, rock, disco, oldies, New Releases. Boardman was standing in New Releases, his fingers flipping through CDs. He didn't seem to be finding anything interesting.

"Where's the others?"

"Oh, hi, Martock. Milne and Serxner went off to get food. Vanessa's someplace at the back, I think. I don't know where Beth got to."

Peering into the gloomy rear of the store, Darroll could see Vanessa along with a couple of other people, but not Beth. He moved over to the cash desk.

"Uh, hi," he ventured to the clerk. "What time does the gig start?"

"Headliners' van just got here," said the clerk, who looked like a younger, thinner version of the guy at the door. "They'll probably be soundchecking in five, ten minutes."

Darroll didn't quite know what soundchecking was, but he didn't want to ask and make himself look clueless. "Thanks," he muttered, and headed into the depths to join Vanessa.

"Seen Beth?"

"Outside," Vanessa said. "With the Typhoids. She wants to show them how mahoosive a fan she is."

"Fucking hell," breathed Darroll.

"Oh, come on, Darroll. Let her have her fun. Not like she gets much."

Darroll was still considering which smart answer to choose to that, out of the two or three that came to his mind, when a door in the back wall opened. A tall, lean young man with the narrowest shoulders Darroll had ever seen walked through, a guitar case in one hand. He knew who it was straight away, since Beth had shown him about eight million photographs of him and the rest of the band; it was Todd Krank.

Even if he hadn't known that, he could have taken a good guess. You could have taken the guy's guitar case away from him and stood him up against a wall, like a police line-up, and anyone would have said "He looks like a musician." Furthermore the guitar case had a TODD KRANK AND THE TYPHOIDS sticker on it; TODD KRANK in big, black letters, AND THE TYPHOIDS rather smaller underneath. And furthermore still, behind Krank, like a caboose following an old-time railroad train, came Beth Vines. Darroll had never seen Beth looking quite like that before; there was a light in her eyes, where normally there was only Beth's default blank stare into infinity, and a vibrant energy about her whole body, absolutely alien to her normal style. Darroll gave Vanessa a nudge to draw her attention to it, but she'd already observed it for herself. "Wow-ee," Vanessa breathed quietly to him.

Krank came to a halt, looking about the store as if he were king of a very small and inadequate kingdom that didn't please its ruler much. Beth stopped in his wake, and seeing Vanessa and Darroll, gave them a little, nervously excited wave. Maybe Krank saw her do it; whatever, he turned to look at them, and came over to them.

"Hi," he said in a smooth, deep voice. It instantly made Darroll's mental alarm bells go off. It was too polished, too studied to be real. It was like smooth, cheap plastic. It was like his mother's voice had been on his birthday.

"Hi," muttered Darroll.

"Hi!" said Vanessa, more enthusiastically.

Beth scooted around Todd Krank and stood at right angles, Krank on her right, Darroll and Vanessa on her left. "This is him!" she told them, breathlessly. "This is Todd Krank himself."

Krank smiled a smooth cheap plastic smile. "I am he," he admitted, as though he were Mick Jagger or someone, caught hiding behind sunglasses looking like a regular guy who'd simply come to the record store to buy the new Offspring album.

"Where's the rest of the Typhoids?" Vanessa wanted to know. As if in response to her question, two more guys came through the still-open door. One held a guitar case that was a match for Krank's own, except that as well as the TODD KRANK AND THE TYPHOIDS sticker it also had one which said LIVE MUSIC IS GOOD MUSIC (non sequitur, Darroll thought to himself) and a third which said THE ESCHATON IS HERE. Darroll tried to remember what an eschaton was. Something to do with the end of the world, wasn't it? It sounded like the slogan you'd get on a religious nut's placard, warning you that the apocalypse was nigh, that God was about to consign you to hell to be roasted alive, forever and ever amen, and be jabbed at by little devils with sharp, red hot pitchforks. And serve you right for falling asleep at the wheel and hitting that truck.

The other guy was carrying no instrument, but he had a big holdall in either hand. Both of them were open at the top; one of them was full of leads, cables and musical paraphernalia. The other contained something black and fabric-looking, which Darroll realised, after a moment or two, had to be T-shirts. Band T-shirts. Darroll might not know much about music, but he did know that touring bands always had merchandise with them. Merch, they called it, because life was too short for three whole syllables in a word. T-shirts, badges, CDs, stickers. He looked over toward the cash desk; it was covered in stickers from different obscure little bands who'd played the store, or perhaps had just snuck in and slapped their stickers there, like guerilla graffiti artists on a railroad trestle.

"Hey, Mikey," said the guy with the bags. Todd gave him a fine glare.

"Uh, sorry, Todd," said Bag Guy. Darroll made a mental note of what Todd Krank's real first name evidently must be. "Where's Pascoe?"

"He went for a piss, I think," said Krank, then turned back to Vanessa with a smile. "That's life as a band. I've seen the inside of every men's room between Detroit and North Dakota. Glamorous, huh?" He touched his long, jet black hairdo as if to smooth it into place. It wasn't necessary; he had so much damn hairspray on that a single hair that dared stand out of line would have been as obvious as a drunken hobo in the middle of a West Point parade. Vanessa giggled, and Beth, evidently concerned that Todd was looking at Vanessa and not her, made a hurried response. "We came right down from the next state ourselves to see you! I made these guys go potty before we left!"

Which was a lie. That had been Boardman. Darroll knew it, and Beth knew it. How pathetic, Darroll thought. Is she that desperate to impress this posing jerk with his hair and his guitar?

"Wow," said Krank. "That's impressive loyalty, right, guys?" The other two musicians nodded, taking their cue from Krank. Darroll suddenly wondered whether these guys had been together since high school, like a musical version of the Psychopath Club. Maybe they'd sat in their local equivalent of Celebration Burger, hating the rest of the world, blobbing together out of sheer inability to get anyone else to notice them. And perhaps one day Krank had said "Wouldn't it be cool if," and they'd started playing music, and now here they were.

For a few seconds Darroll imagined himself on the stage at the front of the shop, with the rest of the Psychopath Club behind him. Serxner at the drum kit, whacking it with all the strength of his big burly bull-calf body. Beth with a bass slung over her shoulder, favouring the audience with that blank stare of hers. The audience would think she was in the zone, that she was lost in the spirit of performance. They wouldn't know she looked like that all the time.

He couldn't see any of the others playing anything, though. No guitarist for the Psychopath Club band. The fantasy evaporated.

"You been to see us before?" Krank was still talking to Vanessa rather than Beth.

"I have," Beth piped up. "I saw you when you were playing St. Paul last summer. I was staying with my aunt." She stretched up toward Krank. Darroll was struck by the disparity between the two. Tall thin Krank, shoulders so narrow you could have up-ended him and slid him into a bottle without him sticking; little Beth Vines, head at Krank's chest level, no boobs to speak of, but still more breadth to her body than the musician.

"Oh, yes," drawled Krank. "That was one cold-ass weekend, wasn't it?"

"I snuck in," Beth confided proudly. "I'm not twenty-one yet but I got in the bar anyway. Don't ask how." And she grinned at Krank. Was she trying...? Darroll realised with surprise that Beth was flirting with Krank like a groupie. He wouldn't have believed it possible, if he weren't seeing it with his own two eyes. What was she hinting? That she'd given the doorman of the bar a blowjob or something to be allowed in, even though she wasn't seventeen yet, never mind twenty-one? Darroll imagined Beth giving Krank a blowjob. It wasn't a very erotic image, especially since his mind chose to picture her being able to do it without even having to kneel down, because Krank was so much taller than her.

Vanessa moved around Darroll to stand next to Beth and be able to look at Krank. "Yeah, we come from Muldoon. Tiny little no-mark burg, middle of nowhere. Don't think we even have a bar that puts bands on. Closest we have to music is the high school marching band."

Again that plastic smile from Krank. "I was in my high school marching band. They threw me out because I got into a fight with one of the other members. I hit him with my trombone."

Trombone?

"Hit him so hard I bent it. Well, who knew how expensive trombones are? Could have broken his arm and had it fixed for less. So I was out of the marching band. Maybe but for that I'd have stayed with it and still be playing trombone instead of..." Krank lifted his guitar case a little higher and jiggled it, as the end of his sentence. He nearly hit Beth in the face with it but, disappointingly for Darroll, didn't quite.

"We gonna get soundchecked, Todd?" The other guitar-toting musician spoke for the first time. "If we don't, the local losers are gonna get in first and mess with everything."

"Like it matters," Krank said. "Not like there's even a sound guy in this place. We're just playing on amps tonight." But he still let his instrument drop back to his side, and gave Vanessa a smile. Darroll didn't like that smile. Apart from being plastic, it lasted a couple of seconds too long, and Krank looked a little bit too deep into Vanessa's eyes.

"Well, we'd better get ourselves set up. Got to sound our best for fans as loyal as you. Alan, you go find out where the merch is gonna go, while Casey and me get plugged in. How big's the stage? Jesus, two steps either way and I'll fall off that thing."

21

The support band was dreadful. There was a tall skinny boy in a lumberjack shirt who had two different guitars, neither of which he could play worth a damn, and a woman with glasses who sometimes sang into a microphone, and sometimes into a megaphone. Darroll preferred her through the megaphone, because you couldn't make out the lyrics so easily that way, and since the lyrics were rotten too...

During the support band's set, Darroll got the swirls again, for the second time that day. First time ever that he'd had them twice within twenty-four hours. Maybe it was mere chance, maybe it was being away from home that made him less rooted. He couldn't begin to speculate about the possible causes. He had his hands full coping with the symptoms.

He took a quick look around. Rowdy and Joe were leaning up against one of the shelving units, looking disenchanted; Vanessa, with the unerring accuracy of her subculture, had found the only other goth chick in the place and was having an animated conversation with her over by the door. Beth was nowhere in sight at all, but that didn't surprise Darroll; she had expressed zero interest in any musician other than Todd Krank and his bandmates, so if she'd wandered off during the support act, it hardly came as a surprise. What was more of a surprise was that Chuck was at the front of the little crowd, watching this shit as though he actually enjoyed it. Jesus. Some people were weird.

But most importantly, none of them were watching him. It didn't matter if they saw him sneak off to the restroom, but there was something about his hops and skips between universes that made him self-conscious. He preferred to be alone when they happened. He couldn't help it if he materialised on the other side of the barrier in front of someone, but he could at least try and remain clandestine on this side.

Which meant the restroom, again. Clark Kent could dive into a phone booth and reappear as Superman, but that was different, somehow.

The bathroom in the record store was a dirty old cubicle, serving all genders indiscriminately. Once inside, he found out that the musical community of Chicago also liked to write graffiti on the toilet walls, about an even mix of the musical and the scatological. There were a couple of band names he recognised, and a couple of jokes ditto, but he couldn't spend time reading them all. The swirls were getting stronger, and even though he was sure by now that they didn't portend some kind of fit or medical crisis, he still didn't think he could stay on his feet during one. So he sat down on the lavatory seat and closed his eyes.

He could still hear the faint sound of music coming from the stage outside. As well as hearing it he could feel it; every thump from the drummer travelled into the floor, along the floorboards, and up through the soles of Darroll's Hi-Tops into his legs, setting up a strange counterpoint with his heartbeat. The drums were the last thing Darroll managed to keep focus on as the swirls took over, and once again Darroll was plucked out of his place and time, the great cosmic random number generator taking another spin to determine where he'd pop out.

It seemed like no time at all when the swirls stopped, as it always did. Darroll made a vow to himself that next time, he'd look at his watch as soon as they hit, so he could see whether they actually did take no time at all – whether his transport actually went back or forth in time at all, or merely sideways.

He did look at his watch now, and it looked about the time he expected, but he couldn't be certain to within a few minutes. The drum vibrations coming through his feet, and the music coming to his ears, sounded same as they had before the swirls. Maybe this was one of the universes where the only difference between here and his home was a snowflake that had a different shape in Nepal, or the front page of the local newspaper in Butthole Springs, Arizona, that had a typo in a different word.

The only way to find out was to get out of this stinking lavatory cubicle, so he did. It opened into a dusty corridor, with cardboard boxes stacked along one wall, and another door that led back into the store. Darroll opened the second door and peeped through.

He expected to hear the same band playing, and it was; the guy with the two guitars couldn't play either of them in this world, any more than in the other one.

He hadn't known whether to expect the Psychopaths to be here. If this was a universe where he'd died in the accident, who would drive Beth and the others to Chicago for the gig? But as he scanned the crowd, whose backs were all to him because they were watching the band on the stage in the store's window, he recognised the distinctive form of Rowdy Serxner with its broad shoulders, and Boardman's red hair next to him. Okay, if they were here, the others had to be too. Yes, there was Vanessa, and there was Chuck –

He suddenly stepped back into the passageway and closed the door, keeping his hand on the handle. He was breathing hard. There was someone next to Chuck whom it had taken him a few seconds to recognise, and even though he'd experienced it before, it still freaked him for a while.

Taking a few deep breaths and willing his heart to stop bumping and thumping like a dodgem car against his ribs, Darroll opened the door a crack once more. Yes. It had to be. He took a long, careful look, impressing on his memory the appearance of the lanky guy alongside Chuck in the audience. Somehow, it seemed that it might prove useful in the future if he learned to recognise that sight that nobody normally got to see, unless they were a twin or had some freakish ability to arrange mirrors; the back of his own head.

The head didn't turn around. Darroll wondered whether his counterpart was actually enjoying this show, or whether he was only standing up there next to Chuck for lack of anything better to do. Either way, he didn't want to be seen in the same room as his double. Nor did he want to have to lurk in the lavatory until he was returned home; apart from being gross, what if Chuck or someone came to use the facility, and found Darroll inside when he'd just left him outside by the stage?

To reach the front door of the store, he'd have to run the gauntlet of the audience. That was taking a chance. What if the jerk-ass band playing thought it was okay to shout out sarcasm from the stage at someone leaving their gig partway through? That guy in the lumberjack shirt looked enough of an asshole for that. Then everyone would look at him, see him by the door, see him still in the audience too. No. Not the front door.

That left the back door. Darroll snuck a glance in its direction. It was ajar, and there was nobody by it. Hunching his shoulders up, to disguise his profile in case any of the Psychopaths glanced round, he broke from cover and took long strides toward the door. Eight steps took him to it. He jerked it open, letting in a cold gust of January air which made him realise how warm it had become inside the record store now that the live music had begun. Swiftly he slid through it, pulling it almost closed behind him, just a crack left again.

He was expecting the door to open onto another street, but it would have been an exaggeration to credit the alley outside with the name "street". The thoroughfare was blocked by two cars and a van; he squeezed alongside the van briefly, to find, not unexpectedly, that it belonged to Todd Krank and the Typhoids. They'd painted a big copy of the band's logo on the side, to prove it. Darroll smiled to himself. It was hardly the tour bus that you heard successful rock bands talk about, or write songs complaining about what a hard life it was travelling on one, week in and week out.

"Hey!"

The van window to his left had opened a little way, and someone was looking out of it. It was Todd Krank, and he sounded confrontational.

"What?" called back Darroll.

"Hey, don't scratch up the van," clarified Krank. He wound the window the rest of the way down and leaned out as far as he could, which wasn't far, because the alley was so narrow and the van was parked so close to the wall. Darroll only just fit into the tight space. Vanessa couldn't have squeezed through there.

Darroll inched his way toward the front of the van, and Krank gave a slight snort. "Oh, it's you. How's it going inside?"

The familiarity of Krank's greeting took Darroll a little aback. He reminded himself that he wasn't in Kansas any more, as it were; this was another universe, no matter how similar to his home continuum it might seem. Maybe the conversation he'd had with Krank inside the store had gone differently. Maybe Darroll and Krank had actually found something to talk about other than how far he'd come to see the band.

He squeezed up to the window; if he wanted to get out to the front of the van, he'd have to duck down and slide underneath the wing mirror, which blocked further progress at head height. It was claustrophobic, and he was glad Krank had wound his window down. Looking inside the van, he saw that alongside Krank was the guy with the guitar case covered in stickers. Darroll tried to recall his name and failed, but luckily, Krank said "You met Casey already, didn't you?"

"Hey, man," drawled Casey from the driver's seat. He had an accent that came from somewhere further west than Krank's; Darroll guessed Seattle. Every second guy aged under thirty in Seattle was a musician.

"Hey," echoed Darroll. "You guys not watching the other band?"

Krank chuckled, a little self-satisfied sound. "Pascoe and Alan are. I wouldn't touch those jerks with a ten-foot pole. They make the Purple Beehives sound like Apple Pie For Wolves."

Darroll had heard of neither of those bands (he supposed they were bands). He laughed, and then hated himself for laughing and not being honest enough to tell Krank he hadn't got the first idea what he was talking about. That was the sort of trick Chuck pulled. He ought to be above that, better than that.

"I lasted one song," Casey remarked. "I like to give everyone a fair shot. A dog's allowed one bite. But speaking of biting, they did." He picked up a cigarette and a cheap plastic lighter from the van's ashtray between the front seats, and applied the flame to the end of the cigarette.

"Good idea, man," Krank said, and Casey exhaled a cloud of smoke. Darroll hated smoking, the same as he hated all the million addictions to which human beings voluntarily subjected themselves. He decided he'd better not mention that either.

And then the scent of the smoke reached his nostrils, and he immediately realised that this wasn't tobacco smoke. He coughed, involuntarily, and would have moved back, only he was jammed up against the alley wall.

"You not a smoker?" said Krank, with a supercilious smile. "You should try it."

Casey looked dubious all of a sudden. "Todd. The boy looks about fifteen."

"Sixteen, actually," Darroll said firmly, aware as he said it how futile a distinction it must seem to two musicians atop the lofty pinnacle of their mid twenties.

"I was smoking when I was fifteen," Krank pointed out. He plucked the joint from Casey's fingers, and transferred it from his right hand to his left, resting on the windowsill of the van. "Relax, it's good stuff. Probably better than what most of Chicago's smoking at the moment... I know this one guy."

Darroll suppressed the urge to panic, to squeeze out from beside the van and hot-foot it down the alley, away from these jerks and their drugs and their superficial, supercilious world. Instead, a new urge came over him.

This wasn't his world. He could do anything he wanted here and get away with it. If he wanted to smoke a marijuana cigarette in this world, did it really, actually count? And furthermore, if he got stoned in this world, would he still be high when he resumed his proper place?

Todd evidently saw his hesitation. "If you wanna give it a shot, go on. If not, no offence. Your call entirely. What's your name, anyway, kid?" He turned back to Casey. "This dude came all the way down from Muldoon with a bunch of his buddies to see us. Least we can do is smoke him up, yeah?"

That made Casey chuckle. "Muldoon? Th' fuck's that place?"

It was strange how Darroll's hand reached out to Todd's and he took the joint. It was as if he wasn't even controlling its motions himself.

"Uh, it's a couple hundred miles away, right off the interstate," he said vaguely as he wondered what to do with the unfamiliar object. "And my name's Darroll... with an O."

Sensing his puzzlement, Todd smiled. "Hold it like that, Darroll-with-an-O, yeah. Just put it in your mouth, firm enough to hold it, close your lips on it... yeah. And you want to breathe in through your mouth now, but keep your lips closed, so it goes in through the joint – "

Darroll followed the instructions as closely as he could. An acrid tasting cloud of fumes shot out of the reefer, into his mouth, and down his throat. He coughed violently, and smacked his head on the brick wall behind him.

"Whoa, easy," Casey said. "You really haven't done this before, have you?"

"N... no," Darroll gasped. He wasn't sure if the thumping in his chest was from the cannabis, or from the coughing, or from the humiliation.

"This ain't California," said Todd suavely, primping his already-immaculate coiffure. "Not every little town in the back-end of noplace has weed plantations growing all round it, Casey. I don't suppose you get many stoners in Muldoon? Or musicians?"

"None of either," said Darroll, recovering some control.

"Too bad," Krank said. "But you're sixteen, you said? Another year or two, you can escape, you can go anywhere you like, come here to Chicago, go to New York or L.A. or any damn place."

Darroll shook his head, taken aback to find Krank talking so like Louis Vickery. "Nah... Muldoon's the sort of place you can't escape from," he said. "Even if you travel halfway round the world, Muldoon stays with you."

There was a moment's silence before Krank drawled, "Well, either you're a naturally poetic type or the weed's hit you already, because that, Darroll-with-an-O, was profound. Have another go." He plucked the lighter from Casey's hand and applied it to the end of the joint till it glowed. "Take this one easy, don't breathe it all in like you're about to swim a length underwater."

And Darroll found that the second time was easier than the first. The smoke still tasted vile, and felt weird and alien going down into his internal workings (he briefly pictured himself cut in half, like a Damien Hirst piece in a modern art display) but he didn't feel the urge to cough it straight back out again.

"Hold it inside a few, then... yeah, like that, breathe out."

Krank's fingers rescued the reefer from Darroll's fingers. They were long thin fingers. Musician's fingers, Darroll supposed. A steady jet of smoke exited between Darroll's slightly parted lips as he exhaled. It reminded him of the picture on the front of his copy of *The Hobbit*, with Smaug the dragon breathing smoke out of his nostrils. Like dragons did.

"See, you're learning," Casey said cheerfully. "Mike – uh, Todd and me, we generally have a smoke before a gig if we can."

"Does wonders for my voice," commented Todd, who was either too stoned to notice Casey's slip of nomenclature, or too mellow to care about it.

"Thanks," said Darroll. "But, uh, I don't think I'll have any more. I came out here for some air." The sudden thought had come to him – was it a genuine reasonable fear, or drug-addled paranoia? – that one of the other Psychopaths might genuinely slip out of the back door for some air, and find him here. With a marijuana cigarette in his fingers, to boot.

"No worries," drawled Todd. He checked his watch. "We're onstage in about forty-five. Get yourself a breather, try not to freeze to death, see you back inside, huh?"

"Yeah, see you in there," said Darroll, conscious of his inability to say goodbye in a snappy way. Same as always, in any universe.

He ducked down under the wing mirror and out into the alley. He could now see that it did have an exit at each end onto a street, though it was a struggle to reach the end. He had to thread his way through a maze of parked vehicles and trash cans, smelling worse even than the smoke from the joint he'd just shared.

He emerged onto a residential side street, full of identical apartment buildings, and lit by regular columns. In one direction he could see the busier street where he'd parked his car, near the main entrance to the record store. The other way, the street stretched out into gloom and infinity. A middle-aged woman came along, with a small dog on a lead, so small that its legs had to rotate like a steamboat's paddlewheel to keep up with its owner, even though she wasn't setting an Olympic pace herself. It stopped to piss against one of the lamp posts as Darroll watched, and the woman jerked it onward.

He had no intention of going back to the record store, of course, because all the cannabis in the world wouldn't get Todd Krank stoned enough that he'd overlook the sight of two separate, identical Darroll Martocks in his audience as he played. But equally he had no real aims in mind. It was too late in the evening to think of finding some big public spot like the Art Institute in which to cause a scene. He pondered finding a burger joint as he walked and going in there to wreak some mayhem, grabbing people's food, throwing it around, decorating the restaurant with the contents of the trash can. But that seemed pretty damn penny-ante stuff after slashing up American Gothic.

He decided to give everyone on the next block that he passed the finger, but the next block was devoid of anyone but himself. Okay, the next block. But the only person he passed on that block was an old guy doddering along on a walking stick. Darroll threw him the finger anyway, because he'd promised himself to, but the old guy didn't respond and Darroll wasn't sure whether he even saw the gesture. Maybe he was blind. Maybe he'd been blind for years. Maybe the only time he ever went out was in the evening, when the sidewalks were quieter, and he walked the same path every day because he knew every step of it, knew to the exact figure how many paces it took him to reach the next corner. That was depressing, and Darroll pushed the thought away. It made him disinclined to throw anyone else the finger, too.

He wandered idly on, his footsteps taking him on a spiral that wound outward and back inward again, until he found himself approaching the record store again, only from the other direction.

Was he bored enough to create some minor commotion purely to get him back to his own space and time?

As he pondered that question without coming to a decision, Darroll reached the opposite end of the alley where he'd smoked the joint with the Typhoids. He glanced down it, not expecting to see anything.

And certainly not expecting to see Beth Vines and Todd Krank locked in an embrace against the alley wall. But that was what he saw.

Just like when he'd reached out to smoke that damn joint, his body seemed to go into motion of its own accord, and he strode into the alley and towards Beth. He was seething, furious. How dare this posing bastard Krank lay his hands on Beth Vines? How dare he push her up against the wall, hold her there while she squirmed, like a butterfly being pinned to a piece of card?

He broke into a run, and the motion made both Beth and Todd turn their heads toward him. Todd had one hand behind Beth's head, and the other one on her breast. He had one leg raised, too, rubbing up against the side of Beth's thigh.

Todd's mouth opened silently. So did Beth's. Or maybe they weren't silent; the blood was roaring in Darroll's ears. He couldn't have heard a bomb going off. He didn't stop to think; what need was there to think?

He might have thought a dozen things, such as the twin facts that Todd Krank had ten years and almost as many inches on him. But he didn't.

He just smacked the singer right in the mouth, and as he did so, the soundtrack of the moment seemed to realise that it had lapsed, and kicked back in.

" – the fuck, you little turd?" snarled Todd, and aimed a kick at Darroll that connected to the side of his knee, painfully.

Beth shrieked, and Darroll smacked Todd on the mouth again, and then grabbed him by his so-carefully arranged hair and tried to swing his head into collision with the alley wall. He might have succeeded if Todd hadn't kneed him in the balls. That really hurt, and Darroll doubled up.

Todd threw a punch at him and Beth tried to grab Todd's arm, and Darroll head-butted Todd in the breadbasket. Todd fell over and dragged Darroll with him, and as the two of them rolled about in the dirt at Beth's feet, incongruous snow began to fall from the sky, lending the scene a false veneer of calm and peace.

Darroll was so busy getting thumped by the bigger, older guy that he almost didn't realise that the swirls were coming back; it was hard to tell them apart from the spinning feeling he had in his head from Todd pounding at him. For a guy with sensitive musician's fingers, he sure packed a hell of a punch.

By the time he did realise, he only had a couple of seconds to take things in before he was yanked away. The snowflakes dropping from the sky, Beth's mouth open in a scream, her tiny thin eyebrows raised so high they were lost to view behind her bangs. The stink of the garbage in the alley, the gleam of the dim light reflecting on the window of the band's van. They all impressed themselves on his mind like a polaroid. And then he was out of there.

22

Thud thud thud thud thud. Darroll's heart was pounding in time with the noise of the drums. He was back inside the lavatory cubicle in the record store. Quickly he glanced at his watch under the dim light of the unshaded bulb above him. As he'd expected, he was back to his starting point in time as well as in space.

His jaw hurt where Todd Krank had socked him a good one. Rising to his feet, he peered into the small, discoloured mirror that was installed above the equally small and discoloured basin in the corner of the lavatory. He couldn't see any marks on his face, but in that light and in that poor specimen of a mirror, it was hard to know whether there were none, or whether he just couldn't see them clearly.

He was shocked, but elated at the same time. His body was still pumping endorphins. There was a dull ache in his knuckles where he'd connected with one blow, or maybe more, on Todd Krank.

Two things worried him about the fight. One was that as he reviewed the sequence of events, he couldn't decide whether Krank had been assaulting Beth in the alley, or whether the two of them had just snuck out there for a quick necking session before the Typhoids went on stage.

The other one came immediately on the heels of the first one, and it was that even as he'd run in to attack Krank, he hadn't known whether Krank and Beth's embrace had been consensual or not. The mere sight of the two of them together had stoked him into a rage, enough to make him so crazy that he was prepared to take a pop at a guy the size of Krank. Krank could have handled a minnow like Darroll with ease, if not for the element of surprise.

He thought about those two issues for two or three minutes, and couldn't figure out a halfway decent answer to either.

A bang on the door interrupted his reverie. "Gimme a second," he shouted, and quickly checked to see that he looked okay, then unlocked the door. He had to turn sideways to squeeze past the guy who was waiting. It was all about being in tight spots tonight, he reflected as he walked out into the store once more.

Speaking of tight spots, where the hell was Beth Vines? He thought back to before the swirls came down. She hadn't been there with the rest of them, even then, had she? She'd slipped out sometime near the start of the support band's act.

Who were finally, thankfully, calling it a day. The lanky poser with the lumberjack shirt stepped up to the mic and thanked everyone for being such a vurra, vurra loyal audience, reminding them that they could get badges or CDs from them for whatever donation they thought appropriate. Darroll entertained a brief, sharp fantasy of stepping up to the guy and dropping a dog turd in his donation box.

As the band started to unplug cables and unpick the tangle of wiring on the stage, he spotted Vanessa and signalled to her. She didn't come when he signalled; instead, she signalled him to come to her, which was Vanessa all over. Stifling a flash of anger, he joined her.

"Vanessa," he said quietly. "Where's Beth gotten to?"

"She said the support band was shit and went out for a walk round the neighbourhood," Vanessa recalled.

"Well, they were shit."

"Yeah. Still. I felt sort of bad about letting her go off on her own. This is Chicago."

"No, it's not. It's Player Heights."

"Darroll, don't be a pedantic asshole, you know what I mean."

"And you know what I mean," Darroll rejoindered. "This isn't the ghetto. Do you think she's gonna find her way into a crack house, come out with pupils the size of pinpoints?" He wondered, suddenly, whether his own pupils were normal. He tried to remember whether they'd looked out of the ordinary when he checked the mirror, and couldn't.

"She'll be back in time for the Typhoids," Vanessa said. "No way she'd miss them. Right?"

"Right," Darroll said, thinking about Beth and Todd Krank, and Casey with his little nasty-smelling cigarettes. "But I'm going out to look for her."

"I'm coming too, then," said Vanessa. "I don't want you wandering off and getting lost as well as her."

Darroll was on the verge of giving Vanessa the verbal smackdown for her silly concern about his safety, but he reined himself in. It was growing later in the evening, and he didn't know the area. Besides, Vanessa was no shrinking violet. Darroll thought again of the time she had won a fistfight at school. He wouldn't have put it past Vanessa to have felled Todd Krank with one blow, and then kicked him right in the stones as he lay there in the alley, if she'd found him putting the hard moves on Beth Vines.

As it happened, they ran into Beth within two minutes of leaving the record store. She was walking calmly up the street toward them, one hand tucked into a woollen mitten, the other mitten dangling to allow her to carry a can of 7-Up. She was taking dainty sips from it.

"There you are," Darroll said. "We were wondering what happened to you. That useless abortion of a support band finally quit making a racket."

"There's gonna be like half an hour before Todd and the guys go on," Beth said with unconcern. "I had plenty of time."

"Where'd you go anyways?" asked Vanessa.

"I went round to see if the Typhoids were out back," Beth said. "Two of them were, but they were smoking dope and they told me to come back later."

That made sense, Darroll figured. Casey had been worried enough about Darroll's age, and Beth, with her skinny little form and almost invisible tits, looked even younger than she was.

"So I'm going back now. Now is later," Beth said with simplistic sarcasm, and a tone that strongly hinted she didn't need Darroll and Vanessa to chaperone her.

"No," Darroll said suddenly and stepped into Beth's path.

"Darroll, what the hell?" Which was about the strongest cussword that Darroll had ever heard Beth Vines employ.

"Beth, you don't want to be hanging out in Chicago back alleys with dope-smoking musicians," he said, and looked to Vanessa for support.

"Oh, I don't know," Vanessa said. "If they've got some decent ganja, I'm down with stealing a few tokes. I am in favour of anything that makes the utter meaninglessness of life vaguely more endurable."

Which wasn't quite the support that Darroll had been looking for, but he supposed it was better than nothing.

"I don't like the way that guy Krank was looking at you girls," Darroll said, as they began to retrace their steps together.

"Oh, relax, willya, Darroll?" Vanessa entreated him. "He's a musician. Male musicians always think they can lay the heavy charm down on the ladies and make us melt. We know better, right, Beth?"

The look Beth gave Vanessa did not suggest that she was on the same page. She turned at the corner, and headed for the alley and the back entry to the store. As they negotiated the crosswalk, the first flakes of snow began to drift down from above.

"Ahh, nuts. Yet again Mamma Nature does the dirty," sighed Vanessa. "We're gonna have to drive home through this."

"I'll be okay," Darroll said. "After ... after what happened, I'm not the sort to take any chances in the snow."

As they approached the van, Casey and Krank were standing outside it, along with a third member of the band, the one Darroll had seen carrying the bag full of power cables and shit. Casey had what looked like the roach-end of a joint in his hand, but he flicked it away into a dirty puddle as Darroll and the girls approached.

"Howdy-doody," drawled Todd.

Darroll had been holding his breath quietly, but he relaxed. Even though he knew, rationally, that Todd would have – could have – no memory of their fight in a universe far, far away, it was still a relief for him to be greeted so affably.

"You told me to come back later," Beth reminded Todd.

Krank looked at his watch. "Yeah. I'd love to hang out, Beth, but it's starting in to snow, and we're meant to be starting our set in ten minutes."

"The last lot overran," pointed out Casey.

"Support bands always overrun. It's the second law of live music."

"What's the first law?" Beth asked Krank.

"The sound guy is always up his own ass."

"And the corollary to that," Casey added, "is that the more incompetent the sound guy is, the further up his own ass he is."

"I didn't think there was a sound guy here," Darroll pointed out.

"Pascoe does setup when we're playing a gig without a sound guy from the venue."

"Yeah," Krank interrupted Casey, "and the first law still applies."

Casey laughed, and Alan said, "I'm gonna tell Pascoe you said that." But Alan laughed too. So did Beth and Vanessa. Darroll didn't laugh. He didn't think it was very funny.

23

Beth hung around the merch stand when the gig was over. Darroll didn't mind the Typhoids – they were better than the support band with that awful guitarist, at least – but no way would he have driven two hundred miles in winter to see them.

"We need to move it," Rowdy said to Darroll. "I don't know about you guys, but my folks will be expecting me to work tomorrow. Same as every day."

Darroll was so, so glad he didn't live on a farm. Living in Muldoon was bad enough. Living on a farm in Muldoon? He'd slit his wrists. Except Muldoon being Muldoon, the blood wouldn't flow properly. It'd freeze into little red icicles right there on his wrists, and then the red would turn to black like a polar explorer's toenails, and he'd still be alive and in Muldoon, just with a couple of extra scars.

"Well, you better go drag Beth away then," he said to Rowdy. "Or else she's gonna climb into Todd Krank's guitar case and go home with him."

Chuck Milne snickered. "Rowdy's right. Even this late it's gonna take us four hours to get home. Is it still snowing?"

"Stopped before the band did." Darroll had taken a look outside in between the set-closer and the inevitable encore. Darroll didn't care to admit it to the other Psychopaths, but he wasn't relishing the thought of driving home to Muldoon in a snowstorm. Luckily, the snow hadn't settled on the streets, only dampened them a shade.

Rowdy moved over to Beth, and Darroll trailed after him.

"Hey, Beth. We need to get on the road."

Beth gave Rowdy a look, as wistful as any neglected puppy.

"I know, I know, the band were great." (Casey, behind the merch table, gave Rowdy the thumbs-up.) "But it's a fuck of a long way back to Muldoon."

Beth sighed a long sigh. "Goddamnit to hell," she said, which was the second time Darroll had heard her use that word in one night. "Okay." She turned to Casey. "Are you guys staying in town? Where's Todd?"

"We've got a room at a Super 8 a few miles from here. Todd? Went off with Pascoe to load up the van, probably have a smoke," Casey said.

Before Rowdy or Darroll could stop her, Beth jammed the signed CD and T-shirt she'd bought into her purse, and was off out of the back door like a rat up a drainpipe.

"Ahh, no," moaned Rowdy. "We have to get her moving."

Darroll strode after Beth to find that outside the back door was a little circle of fans, including Beth Vines, Joe Boardman and Vanessa Murchison, plus half a dozen others. Todd was sitting on the back step of the van, with a cigarette (just a tobacco one now) in his hand, smiling at them. Even after the performance, his hair was still immaculate. Darroll wondered if he set it with fucking concrete or something. The drummer of the band was lifting kit from the alleyway into the van a piece at a time, and glaring at Todd every time he had to squeeze past him. The glares bounced off Todd's hairstyle like bullets bouncing off steel plate.

"Beth... Vanessa? We got to set off," Darroll said firmly. Beth turned her puppy eyes on him. Darroll wondered whether Beth had been trying to extract the address of their motel from Todd and Pascoe.

"Holy crap, it's nearly midnight," Boardman exclaimed. "You gonna be okay to drive us home, Martock? What about you and your bike, Rowdy?"

"I'll be fine," said Rowdy stoically, "as long as we leave right now."

"You heard your friends," said Todd to Beth. "You have a long drive home. Glad we got a room to crash out in. I don't envy you. Who's driving... you...?" He flipped his hand once or twice at Darroll, and Darroll remembered that Todd didn't know Darroll's name. Not in this universe.

"Yeah, my car and this dude's bike."

"Get y'self a coffee," Todd advised Darroll. "Hey, have these." He dug into his pocket and extracted what Darroll first thought was a handful of coins. He was about to refuse them indignantly, when he realised they were a handful of badges with the band logo on. TODD KRANK and the TYPHOIDS. He almost refused them indignantly anyway, but then he slid them into his pocket.

The snow held off as they returned to the interstate. Vanessa went straight to sleep in the back passenger seat behind Beth. Darroll cranked the window down to let cold air in and keep himself awake, but Boardman, behind him, complained so much he wound it back up. Whereupon Boardman fell asleep too.

Which left Darroll with Beth to keep him company for the entire journey.

"Enjoy yourself, huh?" he said to her, because he literally couldn't think of any better way to start the conversation, and because he needed to get a run-up to what he wanted to ask her. He couldn't just ask her from a cold start.

"Oh, they were great," Beth said, quietly but sincerely. "Even better than the other time I saw them. Todd really knows how to put on a show... well, the whole band does, I guess. But Todd's a great front man. He's got charisma."

Charisma, Darroll echoed mentally. That elusive characteristic. Undefinable, except in its absence. Not one of the Psychopath Club could summon up a single ounce of charisma.

"I guess he does," Darroll concurred. An exit on the interstate flashed by. The tall lights of the facilities at the junction shone out into the night; Subway, Burger King, Hardee's, Motel 6, Super 8. He thought of the Typhoids in their Super 8 back in Chicago (sorry, Player Heights) and wondered whether they were all going to sleep in one room. If they were, Darroll was damn sure that Todd Krank would be the one who got the best bed. Casey and Alan would toss a coin for the other one. And Pascoe would be the one who got to sleep in the bath, like John Lennon and his Norwegian wood.

"You didn't like them, did you, Darroll?"

Darroll took his time about answering that one. "I liked their music well enough," he said finally. "But I don't think I liked Todd too well. He's... all surface. He's the sort of guy who's so focused on performing, that he's forgotten how to stop. He doesn't know any way of interacting with people, other than by pretending he's a star and showing off to them, you know?"

To his surprise, Beth made a noise of assent. "I see what you mean. I think I can understand why he does it, though. It must be tough, being a performer. Having to take your stage persona on and off like a suit. Did you know Chuck Milne and Rowdy Serxner are talking about starting a band?"

Darroll didn't know that. "Wow. I know Chuck can play guitar, but what's Rowdy gonna do?"

"Drums, probably. Anyone can play drums."

Darroll wasn't at all sure that Rowdy Serxner could play drums, but it didn't seem the moment to say that.

"Chuck asked me if I wanted to be in. I don't know how to play anything, though. He said I could learn bass, but having a female bass player is such a cliché, you know? Almost as bad as having a female keyboard player who stands at the back, and plays one note at a time with a finger."

"Beth," Darroll said, ignoring Beth's implicit question for the moment, "can I ask ya something?"

"Course."

"Do you..." He paused, cleared his throat, wound the window down an inch, and began again. "Did you find Todd Krank attractive?"

He expected Beth to take her time over answering that, as he'd taken time over her question a few moments before. But she came straight back with a reply. "I find his stage persona attractive. Which is the point of his stage persona. But his stage persona isn't him. I don't know what the real Todd Krank is like. So I don't know whether I would find him attractive."

In other words, Darroll thought, neither yes nor no. He still didn't know whether Todd had been trying to force himself on Beth when he interrupted them, or whether Beth had been a willing participant. Or had even initiated the shenanigans. A hot burst of rage slashed across his mind. Why were there never any simple answers in life? Why were things always in shades of grey instead of being nice, clear, cosy black and white?

The conversation came to a halt. Darroll wound the window down all the way once more, heedless of Boardman's comfort in the seat behind him, and dug into his pocket for the handful of badges which Todd Krank had given him. He flung them out of the window, and they bounced away in the Oldsmobile's wake. Looking in the mirror, he imagined he could see them glinting faintly in the light from his tail-lamps.

But as he knew perfectly well, that was only his imagination. He couldn't really see them at all.

24

The next time it happened, he was in school. After the sideslip at the Todd Krank gig, he'd wondered what the hell he was going to do when the swirls hit him in front of people and there was no hiding place. He'd wondered, too, what it must look like from the outside. Did he just blink in and out, like a Hollywood special effect? He couldn't think how to find out.

He should have given the question more thought, he realised, when the swirls started to well up around him in class. He should have asked himself "Where is the single place you spend most time, and are unable to get under cover with ease?" and the answer would have come: "At school, Darroll, you fuckdoodle, where else?"

Panic grabbed him by the ankles, like a zombie hand bursting out of the ground to seize him. Could he stand up and run out? Would that make more of a spectacle than if he just sat there and hoped? Would he even make it to the restrooms before he was caught – or before the swirls overwhelmed him?

He'd gotten away with it on the bench in the Art Institute, and it was the memory of that which made him keep his seat. He had a desk at the side of the room, and he leant against the wall. He didn't want to fall over if he lost control.

At least it's only Mr Spears, he thought as the swirls zoomed around his head twice, plunged into his eyeballs, and raced up his optic nerves to switch the connections around in his brain.

His head was on the desk suddenly. That would attract attention... He sat up with a jerk, and hurriedly scanned the room. At least it's still Mr Spears, he thought now.

Darroll was not only against a wall, but toward the back of the room; only one empty desk behind him. The faint noise that resulted from him sitting up made Oscar Jacobic, at the desk to his left, turn his head. Oscar's eyes met Darroll's, and for a second, Jacobic stared into them.

After that, it was like watching a row of dominoes tumble over.

Oscar Jakobic took a sharp intake of breath, loud enough for Debbie Bloch, at the seat behind him, to stop doodling cartoons on her paper and look up. She saw Darroll too, and gave a little squeak, clapping her hands to her mouth. Darroll had never actually seen anyone do that before, outside the movies. It seemed Debbie, like his mother, took Hollywood as her tutor for body language.

Debbie's reaction combined with the adrenalin pumping through his body, to make Darroll burst out in sardonic laughter. The laughter made Rowdy Serxner and Vincent Mills turn and look, and Rowdy burst out with a tremendous "WHOA," and that made Mr Spears look over at that side of the room.

Darroll didn't detest Spears the way he detested Mr Tidmarsh or Miss Patterson. He was an unassuming little man, barely an inch taller than Darroll himself, and looked shorter because he was bald on top of his head, though what hair he had was still brown, running round in a semi-circle from one ear to the other via the back of his head. Mr Spears took the attitude that if you went into his class wanting to learn, he would teach you. If you went in not giving a fuck, he would leave you alone as long as you didn't actually cause chaos, and spend the time dealing with the schmucks who actually did want to learn. That suited Darroll. And so, when the revolution came and the entire staff of Straus High were lined up against the gymnasium wall, Spears would be the last one to get a bullet in the head. Or should it be the first? Would it be crueller to make him watch the other teachers executed?

Darroll filed the thought quickly away for future analysis, because Mr Spears was staring at him. The whole class, in fact, was staring at him. Nobody was saying anything. Darroll felt vilely uncomfortable at being the cynosure of attention. He held up his hands and put on what he hoped was a sheepish, 'who, me?' expression.

The movement seemed only to fascinate them more.

For a couple of seconds he resisted the realisation, then allowed it to sink in; it was too strong to fight off, however jarring. This was another universe where he was dead, and here he was sitting in his old seat in the middle of class, and they all think they're seeing a ghost –

"Oh my god," he said, partly from genuine surprise and partly for effect, "I'm dead, right?"

A ripple of gasps ran through the class. A few nods. No words. A couple of people with desks near to Darroll got up from them and retreated across the room.

"Darroll. Darroll Martock." Mr Spears' voice wavered wildly.

Darroll made the snap decision to milk the situation. If this was anything like the previous times the swirls had hit, pretty soon he'd be jerked back to where they had begun, so what did it matter? What did anything matter? "That was my name," he said. He rose to his feet, stretching out one hand towards the class.

There was sudden, instant hubbub. "Stay back!" cried Mr Spears. Two girls and one boy screamed. Several people backed right up against the far wall.

And one person stepped forward, holding a hand out toward him in return. It was Vanessa Murchison. Of course.

"Come back, Vanessa!" commanded Spears, his voice cracking. Hollywood again, Darroll thought. Vanessa shook her head slightly, and stood there, hand still reaching for him.

Well, if this was going to be Hollywood, Darroll was on board. "Ah, Vanessa," he said, "you can no longer reach me where I am."

"What's it like to be dead, Darroll?" asked Vanessa. Her eyes were fixed on him like little round, brown magnets to a fridge door. A fridge was just about what he felt like. Cold and inanimate.

"It's cold, Vanessa. So cold." Hamming it up still, but not exactly a lie. Or was it? He honestly did not know, and how could he work out the philosophy of it all at a moment like this?

"I'm sorry, Darroll." Still her hand was reaching out.

"Vanessa!" Mr Spears took a step forward, toward her, then back again.

"Don't be sorry. You'll all be dead soon," Darroll said. "You'll all be dead and cold like me, very very soon." With the last three words he took three slow paces forward, timed to match the words. "You'll all be coming with me –"

He lifted his right hand up and out, toward Vanessa. Vanessa took a couple of quick steps toward him and her hand caught hold of his.

It was warmer than his, he instantly noticed. That was the one piece of information that lodged straight in his brain and hunkered down there, while his other senses began to spin again. There were a couple more screams, and another noise that sounded something like a thunderstorm and something like the static of a radio in between stations, and his sense of balance stood on its beam-ends again, and boom, he was back at his seat with his head on the desk.

Again he sat up quickly, and glanced around. Nobody was paying him any attention. Everyone was seated properly. Mr Spears was on the other side of the room writing something on Bryan Zugorski's paper. He concluded that he was back where he belonged, and that evidently the touch of Vanessa Murchison's hand had been what sent him home.

Interesting.

There were ten minutes left of class before recess, and he was glad to sit there quietly and take advantage of Mr Spears' policy of letting you alone if you didn't want to learn. Somehow, Darroll thought that what he'd learned in this lesson was going to be worth more to him than all the English literature that Mr Spears had taught him in his entire school career.

After class, he joined up with Vanessa and Chuck, who were already in conversation by the time he got out of the door to meet them. Chuck didn't look entirely pleased to see him approach.

"What's cooking?" Darroll asked.

"Just talking band stuff," said Chuck.

"Band stuff?"

"Yeah, Darroll," Chuck said, with an air of annoyance, as Rowdy Serxner approached the three of them with his shambling gait. "Band stuff. The band you said you weren't interested in."

"That's going forward still?"

Rowdy gave a smirk. He didn't often get to be the cool kid.

"It damn well is," Vanessa told Darroll. "Rowdy and Beth are turning into quite the rhythm section."

Darroll thought back to Player Heights, and how he'd imagined Beth playing a bass. He pictured it again, the instrument slung over her little shoulders, Beth staring out through those big round glasses of hers like she was from Seattle instead of fucking Muldoon. The doubt suddenly assailed him that it was Beth and the others, after all, who were going to put Muldoon on the map, and not him, not him at all.

Then he considered plump Chuck and his dorky face, and Rowdy with his placid bovine expression, and took comfort. Beth had the look of a performer, that enigmatic, blank, thousand yard stare. But the others? Not a chance.

"Okay," he said, "I know when I'm not wanted, I'll leave you rock stars to it."

As good as his word, he went and sat on the steps out front, under the pale sunshine. It was still cold, of course, but the sun made it a little less so. He wasn't at all envious of Chuck and the band. He had something better than a band, something Chuck Milne could never have. Yeah. Let Chuck enjoy his band and his dreams of stardom. Darroll was happy with his dreams, of death and killing.

25

Darroll received an email from Beth on Friday. He read it on one of the library computers, wondering why Beth always sent emails instead of talking to people. Of course Beth didn't like talking much – Darroll didn't, himself – but it seemed crazy to send those electrons whizzing up and down cables, all the way to wherever Hotmail kept their servers, only to return to a computer in the same room they had just left.

The email had been copied to the other five members of the Psychopath Club. When he opened it, he read:

"A man died last night. Meet after school to discuss. Usual place."

At first Darroll thought that was melodramatic, but after a moment's reflection, he decided to defer judgment. It might be cool. Who was dead? What relevance did it have to the club? She could have said in the email, but she hadn't. That made Darroll immediately think there was something about this that Beth didn't want to write down.

He looked for Chuck, to ask him if he knew why Beth was being so mysterious, but he wasn't in the library as normal. He found Joe Boardman, though, when he went downstairs. Joe was sitting on the grass at the front of the school with a French textbook, staring at it and looking gloomy.

"Hey, Boardman."

Boardman looked up. "Oh. Darroll."

"What's eating you?"

"French test end of this afternoon," sighed Boardman. "I wish I didn't have to do French. I want to be a scientist."

"There are French scientists, aren't there?" Darroll pointed out. "Just think, you're working for some big important project for the government and they need someone to go to CERN and deal with the scientists there. 'Who can we send?' they say. 'Wait, what about Joe Boardman? He speaks French! We can send him!' And boom. Free trip to Europe."

"Uhm." Joe didn't look convinced.

"Anyway." Darroll sat down on the grass bank, next to Boardman. "You got an email from Beth?"

Joe looked back up from his book. "Saying what? I haven't checked email today."

"Something about a guy dying and we have to meet after school?"

"Well, if a guy died, I guess she'd know," Boardman remarked.

"Why?"

"Because Beth's dad runs the funeral home, Darroll, why else you think?"

Darroll had forgotten that. He was annoyed at his forgetfulness. The local mortician's identity was one thing a psychopath into murder and dead bodies should know. His annoyance made him bark a reply to Boardman. "So what are we meant to do about it? Bring him back to life, like Jesus Christ, or ET?"

"Well, I don't know," said Boardman, closing the book on his finger and looking up at Darroll with irritation. "But if she wants to meet us after school, maybe we ought to go and find out, rather than sitting here speculating when we have zero evidence and I have a French test to revise for? If I don't get a pass mark in this one, I won't be there after school, because Mrs Krukowski will murder me."

"You should murder her first," said Darroll with a dry laugh. "Then you wouldn't have to worry about any French test."

Boardman gave Darroll another stare. "I worry about you sometimes, Martock. I worry about you. Look, I'll be there, you be there, we'll worry about it then. Right now, I don't care if it's the President who's lying dead in the mortician's. I've got French verb conjugations to worry about." And he opened the book again.

Darroll was about to take the hint when Boardman was interrupted again. "Hey!" came a bellow from behind him, and a hand reached round Boardman's head. Startled, Boardman dropped his textbook, the pages flipping in the breeze as he was pulled backward with one hand, while his assailant's other hand jammed something white and fabric into his face.

"Hey! Boardman! Does this smell like chloroform to you?"

Ed Crowe, of course. That least endearing of combinations ever, a bully who thought he was also a stand-up comic. As a bully he was a lousy comedian, but unfortunately, as a comedian he was an effective bully. Patsy Young was behind him. She giggled, which was pretty much all she ever did. Go round with Crowe, simpering at him and giggling at his jokes. The received wisdom at the school was that Ed and Patsy were fucking. Darroll wasn't so sure. Darroll wouldn't be surprised to learn that Crowe was too stupid to know how to fuck, or too much in love with himself to want to.

Boardman tore himself away and rolled over onto his hands and knees. As he tried to get up, Crowe gave him a shove. It knocked Boardman sideways, but he was agile and managed to twist out of it and regain his feet. Darroll took a couple of steps to stand by him, and immediately realised that he'd made a mistake; he'd drawn Crowe's attention to him as well.

"Oh hey, Joey-boy, you got your lover to protect you too?" snorted Crowe. A few more people began to gather, the way they always gathered when it looked like there might be a fight. Vultures. They wouldn't fight themselves, but they wanted to see blood.

"Too bad I couldn't have you, Crowe," snapped back Boardman. "Martock's too much of a pencilneck for me. I just adore big muscular fellows like you." And he puckered up his lips.

Christ, thought Darroll. There is going to be murder done. Murder right here in the yard of Isidor Straus High School, and oh the irony, I won't be the murderer. I thought if there was ever a murder in this goddamn school it would be me –

For once Crowe was lost for a witticism. He opened his mouth once or twice and nothing came out. Nobody else said anything either; it was as quiet as a funeral. The funeral that Joe Boardman was going to attend in the star role. The funeral he'd just dug his own grave for.

"You fucking little faggot," Crowe finally gasped, and swung at Boardman.

Crowe was big and beefy and a good fighter on pure weight, but he was so angry that he was even less subtle than usual. Boardman was a lot quicker than him, being smaller, and naturally agile besides. He darted to one side and Crowe's punch missed by a mile. So did his second and his third.

"What's up, Crowe?" taunted Boardman. "You so desperate to get your hands on me? In front of Patsy? Aren't you scared of hurting her feelings?" He dodged a fourth blow. "Hey Patsy, I'm sorry you had to find out about Ed this way."

Patsy Young's eyes bulged a little and she strode forward at just the wrong moment, as Crowe aimed another punch at Boardman that was never going to connect in a million years. The swing missed Boardman all right, but it got Patsy right on the ear. She folded up like a deckchair at the end of a day at the beach, went over and bit the dust. There were gasps; one of them came from Darroll himself, which he only realised after he exhaled it.

Crowe, being Crowe, didn't bother stopping to check on Patsy. He jumped at Boardman, literally jumped, and got him round the waist. Boardman smacked him on the head with his own fists, three or four times, but Crowe didn't seem to notice it. "You're dead, Boardman, you're dead," he kept repeating as he held Joe Boardman with one hand and smacked him back and forth round the face with the other. Little drops of blood sprayed out from Boardman's nose.

Darroll dropped down to the ground by Patsy and put his head up against her chest. She was still breathing, at least. He realised after a second that he had his ear pushed up against her boob. He suppressed a reflex urge to jerk his head away before anyone saw, and instead found a rising temptation to replace his ear with his hand and give her tit a grope. This was probably the best chance he'd ever get to cop a feel. A feel from Patsy Young, anyway. A memory of the alley in Player Heights, Todd Krank's hand on Beth Vines, flashed across his mind and distracted him.

Between the two urges and the jolt from his memory, he did nothing, and within a couple of seconds, Mr Tidmarsh strode up.

"What the hell is going on here?" he bellowed as he grabbed Ed Crowe by the scruff of the neck. Crowe dropped Boardman, who staggered. He was bleeding all down his shirt. Darroll realised his chance to get up to anything with Patsy was gone. He couldn't decide whether he was relieved or disappointed. Surely a real psychopath would have just gone straight for the sexual assault?

"Joe Boardman hit Patsy Young," said Digby Doyle. Doyle was a thin-faced, stoop-shouldered kid whose father was night clerk at the motel by the interstate. He hung round with Crowe a lot and told him he was so funny, he was gonna be on television in a few years. He hated his real name; he told everyone to call him Conan, for some reason, like the barbarian, but nobody else did except for Crowe and Patsy Young. Most people just called him Dig.

Mr Tidmarsh loomed up over Darroll and Patsy, who was starting to make little feeble noises. "And you, Martock? Were you involved in this outrageous assault upon a girl half your size?"

"Sure he was," said Doyle before Darroll could say anything.

Tidmarsh turned to Doyle. "Go fetch Miss Joyner. Run, boy, run!"

Doyle sprinted off to fetch the school nurse while Tidmarsh stooped down to examine Patsy.

"I didn't hit her," Darroll began, standing up to give the principal space next to Patsy. "She got in the way –"

"In the way? Did she now? Well, boy, you've put yourself in the way," breathed Tidmarsh at him venomously. "In the way of some very serious trouble. Quit that!" He jumped back to his feet as Ed Crowe tried to give Boardman another punch behind his back.

"Crowe. Get out of my sight before I do something I may regret. Boardman, Martock... you are going to come along with me." Mr Tidmarsh's voice had lost its timbre of worry, and now it was almost a purr of contentment. Darroll knew it was no good to protest his innocence. Tidmarsh had been looking for an excuse to wreak revenge on him, and now he had it.

Patsy Young was sitting up before Miss Joyner even reached her. "I don't need no nurse, I'm okay," she protested.

"Patsy. Did Boardman strike a blow against you?" Tidmarsh was still purring, like a big lion who knew damn well that he was king of the jungle and could do what the hell he liked. Including toying with his prey before he devoured it.

Patsy just looked blank, which was nothing new. "I don't know, Mr Tidmarsh."

Darroll scuffed his toe against the ground, wishing they'd get on with it. He knew he was screwed and Boardman was screwed worse. His toe caught something white and fabric, the dirty jockstrap that Crowe had shoved in Boardman's face.

He stooped and picked the cheese-bag up, then jammed it into his pocket. Ed Crowe would have to buy another damn jockstrap if he wanted to go round pulling that trick in future.

As he straightened up, he found Tidmarsh's index finger in his face. "Mr Martock, Mr Boardman. With me."

So Mr Martock and Mr Boardman trailed off after Tidmarsh, leaving Miss Joyner to coo over Patsy Young along with Dig Doyle.

Afterward, Darroll tried not to think of the fifteen minutes that followed. He found it much more pleasant to recollect himself kneeling over the motionless body of Patsy Young, sprawled on the ground, and to fantasise about what would have happened to Ed Crowe if he'd hit her hard enough to have done any permanent damage to her. He wouldn't have gotten the chair – there was no death penalty in this state – but Darroll found the thought of Ed Crowe locked up in jail, probably getting his virgin ass raped, a strangely fascinating one.

26

After school, Darroll waited for Beth to appear. Boardman turned up first. "I passed," he said. "But I'm never gonna be able to talk science to real French people."

Vanessa came up to them, which saved Darroll from having to think of something to say to Boardman. "I take it you guys got the email?"

"We did," Darroll said.

"So. Death." Vanessa looked heavenward, one hand on her ample bosom. A faint scent of her patchouli tickled Darroll's nose. "Some of us run from him, some of us embrace him, none of us can escape him."

"I take it you embrace him?" Darroll drawled.

"You ever embrace anyone? You should try it someday," retorted Vanessa, and a snort came from behind Darroll. It was Rowdy. How the hell could a big guy like Rowdy move as quietly as he did? Darroll never could figure it out.

Darroll yawned extravagantly, to show the contempt he felt for Rowdy.

"Oh, do knock it off, you guys," Vanessa said. "We have to put up with the likes of Ed Crowe and Dig Doyle making our lives hell, and that's bad enough. Do we gotta bicker with each other as well?"

Darroll was tempted to yawn once again, but she did have a point, he supposed. And Rowdy spoke up, before he could think of anything else to say. "Yeah, point. No offence, Martock? You're a mensch."

Darroll didn't know anyone else in the entire school who would call him a mensch. In fact, the rest of the school probably didn't know what it even meant. He wasn't one hundred per cent certain himself, but he did know it was a compliment, so he wasn't going to knock it. He nodded to Rowdy, to show that there were no hard feelings. But he filed that snort of amusement Rowdy had given in his memory of grudges.

"You know what Beth wanted, Rowdy?" he asked.

"I got a good idea," drawled Rowdy. "You know Eddie Inniss, that old fart who lived out to the north of town? Drove a car even older than yours, Martock?"

So much for no hard feelings. Didn't Serxner know that to insult a man's automobile was to insult his manhood? Not that the Oldsmobile was much of a manhood… Darroll shut that thought straight down; he didn't like the way it was going.

"Never heard of him," Boardman said.

"Ehh. Well. He died yesterday. He had cancer, I think. But yeah, main thing is, he's dead. And the smart money," Rowdy concluded, "is that he's lying there right now, in the Vines funeral home, waiting to be buried or burned, or whatever the hell they're gonna do to him. The smart money says, Beth's gonna sneak us in to check him out."

"Thought you said he already checked out," Darroll remarked. It was a feeble joke, he knew, but Vanessa laughed anyway.

"Check him out?" Boardman didn't sound happy.

"Well, have you ever seen a corpse, Boardman? Outside of movies and computer games, I mean, of course."

Joe Boardman had to shake his head.

"Nor me," said Rowdy. "I've been there when they slaughtered hogs and such, of course, but they're animals. This is a real live dead human being."

Darroll gave Rowdy a look to see whether the big farm boy was trying to perpetrate a wordplay of his own, but there was no sign of it on his features. It was just like Rowdy Serxner to say something that ought to have been funny, but not to realise it and deliver it so as to lose the joke.

"Rrrrreally," breathed Vanessa. Darroll could swear that her voice travelled up a whole octave during that one word. "I saw my grandfather when he was laid out, but I'm on board with seeing more dead bodies, if that's what's on the menu."

"I could be wrong," Rowdy added. His tone of voice showed that he was certain he was right.

"Are there laws against that?" asked Boardman.

"What, against dying?" asked Darroll.

"There's laws against interfering with a corpse," Rowdy said. "I don't rightly know what that means. I suppose necrophilia. Or cannibalism."

Darroll might be a psychopath, but neither of those held much appeal for him. Not where the corpse concerned was a butt-ugly, scrawny old guy. Would it be any different if it was someone younger, and female? He thought back to Patsy Young, lying there motionless where Ed Crowe had laid her out unconscious, and tried to imagine her as a corpse, naked on a cold marble slab, him running his hands over her cold naked body... Nah. That was sick. No, not even sick; it didn't arouse any emotion in him at all, positive or negative. A corpse was a corpse.

What if it was Vanessa? He conjured the slab back up in his mind, and laid Vanessa's lifeless body upon it in place of Patsy's. It took more room up on the slab, of course. He imagined Vanessa's plump breasts sagging downward on the table, him climbing on top of her...

Again, no. He was almost disappointed that he didn't crack a boner from thinking about committing necrophilia upon Vanessa Murchison. If he was going to be a psychopath, a real true proper psychopath, he ought to be able to get a hard-on from that mental image in no time.

"I think interfering with a corpse just means preventing it from being buried," Joe Boardman said. "Necrophilia and cannibalism have their own laws."

"Do they really have laws on the books about that?" Rowdy seemed surprised. "Do they need them?"

"You'd be surprised what atrocities the human mind is capable of when it plumbs its darkest and most sinister depths," Vanessa intoned, her eyes half closed. Striking a pose, the pose she usually struck when she was going to go off on one of her Gothic bursts. Fortunately, before she could build a full head of steam, Chuck and Beth came hurrying up.

"Hey, guys. Beth's asked me to say this, because she's not much into the talking thing," Chuck began. Darroll looked at Beth, lurking at Chuck's flank, silent as the grave that Mr Inniss was shortly due to be shovelled into. Beth met his gaze for about two seconds, then looked away.

"The thing is this," Chuck went on. "Beth's father's got a stiff on his books. First time in weeks." He glanced about him, checking that there were no eavesdroppers around. As if anyone would ever be interested in trying to overhear what a bunch of no-account losers like them were saying to each other, Darroll thought.

"So as we're pursuing our interest in the dark side of human nature and... and all that jazz..." Chuck was beginning to falter a little. Darroll suspected him of having prepared this speech in advance, and losing track of what he'd prepared at this point.

"...well, Beth thinks she can sneak us into her dad's place and we can get a look up close at a dead body," Chuck finally concluded. Darroll looked over at Rowdy, who was grinning in satisfaction at having predicted the position so accurately.

"I'm in," Vanessa said before Chuck could even ask the Club whether they were down with the idea.

"Yeah," Rowdy concurred.

"It's hardly *Stand By Me*, is it?" Boardman shoved his hands into his pocket and rocked back and forth on his heels.

"No, it's not, and you're not Wil Wheaton," drawled Chuck. "And we're not going crawling through any leech-infested swamps."

"Leeches suck," Rowdy muttered, and Darroll gave his impassive face another suspicious look.

"You in, Boardman?" Chuck didn't deliver the question as a challenge, but as a gentle enquiry, with an encouraging look. He was trying to be nice to Joe. Darroll guessed Chuck knew about what had happened with Ed Crowe. The whole school probably knew by now.

"I'm in if you guys are." That was about as close to a 'yes' as Joe was going to come up with, Darroll thought.

"That's all of us, yeah... no, wait, you aboard too, Darroll?" Chuck corrected himself.

Darroll thought again of Vanessa naked and cold and motionless on a marble slab, and then of the scrawny, ugly old corpse of Mr

Inniss. Did they actually have marble slabs in a funeral home, or was that only in a hospital when they were doing an autopsy?

"Is he gonna be on a marble slab?" he asked Beth suddenly, out loud, and all the others looked at him curiously.

Beth spoke for the first time in her little voice. "It's called a table, and it's stainless steel."

Darroll shrugged, hoping he hadn't made a fool of himself. "Whatev. I'm in. We going now, or later?"

"I say now," Rowdy suggested, "if Beth's down with it. Better not do it after we eat, in case any of us lose our lunches over him."

"That'd be a hoot," Darroll said. "Imagine spewing up right there in the coffin, and fastening the lid back on. Then when the funeral came, everyone'd be smelling your puke and saying to each other, "Wow, Mr Vines sure didn't do much of a job embalming that body.""

Joe Boardman put his hands on his hips and gave Darroll a look. "You have the imagination of a sick, sick man, Martock."

"Oh, I don't know," Vanessa said. "This society has so many taboos and cultural barriers around death. We'd be much healthier if we got rid of them all. No reason that death can't be a subject for comedy the same as anything else."

"We can go now," Beth said. "The funeral home is separate from my actual home, but it's only next door. We just need to slip inside when Mom and Dad aren't watching us. Rowdy, you live outside town, will your folks worry if you don't come straight home after school?"

"Nah," said Rowdy. "Long as I'm home in time for last milking."

So Rowdy got on his bike, and the other five crammed into Darroll's Oldsmobile, and they left the school lot to head the half-mile into Muldoon proper where the Vines Funeral Home was located.

27

As Beth had suggested, it wasn't difficult for them. They snuck around the family house quietly, making sure that Beth's parents didn't spot them, and then Beth led the Club into the yard behind the house. She paused for a second to make sure her parents were still clear of the scene, and then beckoned them over toward a big, solid wooden door in the side of the adjacent building, which was the funeral home, evidently. "Quick, quick, quick," she whispered as they disappeared through the door one after another, like paratroopers leaping out of a plane in sequence, Darroll thought, except Beth Vines didn't exactly resemble any sergeant he ever heard of.

Inside the funeral home it was cool and dim and completely quiet.

"Where do we go?" Joe whispered. His voice had dropped to as soft a level as Beth's normal tone.

"This way."

They came to a staircase, broad and wooden, leading up and down. Beth took them down it. "The stiffs are down here," she told them. "I think because it's cooler under the ground, so we keep them in the cellar."

"If this was a film," Joe said, still in that whisper, "this is where the zombies would come bursting through that door and kill the first one of us, and the rest of us would have to hole up someplace in this house."

"And get killed off one by one," Darroll said. He'd seen that kind of movie too.

Chuck rolled his eyes. "Quit it, both of you."

"We'd have to use improvised weapons," Joe went on, regardless. "Like scissors and... and... what else? Do they have spades in here, for digging the graves with?"

"Nobody is hitting anyone with a fucking shovel!" Chuck was the first one to speak above a whisper since the Club had entered the funeral home.

The door was made of wood and had a plate screwed to it that said NO ADMITTANCE. It locked with an old-fashioned mortise lock. Beth reached out and turned the key. In the silence, the click of the lock operating sounded unnaturally loud.

"Here we go," Beth said, turning the handle and letting the door swing open. It was dark inside, apart from the small area where light from the stairs spilled inside.

"What was that?" Chuck's head jerked suddenly round to look behind him.

"What was what?"

"I heard a noise."

"No you didn't, you big wuss." Darroll hadn't heard any noise.

"Yes I did." Chuck was back to whispering, but somehow managed to get a pitch of indignation into his whisper.

"Come on, guys," breathed Vanessa. "We doing this or not?"

Beth led the way into the room and turned on the light.

The mortuary was more modern than the door giving access to it would suggest. There was one central feature which was impossible to ignore, and that was the table in the centre of the room. To Darroll it looked like a slab, no matter what Beth called it.

All six of them crowded around it. Darroll noticed little grooves in its surface. For blood, he supposed. He wondered where the blood ended up, after it ran into the grooves. Was there a huge reservoir of congealed blood beneath the floor of the room? Or did it just run into the sewers for the rats to feed on?

"Where's old Inniss?" asked Rowdy. "He ain't here."

"Well, of course not." Beth gave Rowdy a scornful look. "We don't just leave corpses lying out here when they aren't being worked on." Darroll liked that 'we'. "We put them in these drawers." She indicated the far wall from the door, where there were rows of handles which Darroll had initially taken for filing cabinets or something.

"Goddamn, my father never labels them," Beth complained. "You're meant to tag a drawer when you put someone inside it, but he never bothers." She jerked at one handle and a drawer slid open. It was surprisingly deep, even though Darroll knew it had to be long enough to fit a corpse inside. A faint miasma of antiseptic came out of the empty unit.

"Where are you, dead man?" Beth crooned quietly, and tried the next drawer, which was equally empty.

Chuck started. "I'm fucking certain I heard a noise," he said, turning to look back through the door at the stairs.

"Actually I thought I did too." Joe moved as far as the door and peeked through, though he displayed no sign of wanting to go any further away from the others than that.

"Quit imagining things," Vanessa told them. "Here's old Inniss."

Here, indeed, was old Inniss, inside the third drawer Beth tried. The Psychopath Club crowded around it, and stared at him.

"He's no prettier dead than he was alive, is he?" commented Rowdy.

Inniss's face was lined and creased with age. His eyebrows were bushy and mostly white, with a few black hairs among them, and his face had sprouted some two days' worth of stubble. Darroll didn't know whether that meant he'd died unshaven, or whether it was true that your beard kept growing after you died. His skin was chalky pale, and he looked as if he hadn't eaten for a month.

"He looks weird," said Chuck, gesturing to the hollow concavity that was Inniss's abdomen.

"Skinny old dead people always look like that." Beth was almost as cool as the corpse. "Dad will give him a going over tomorrow," she said. "Make him look all neat and tidy before he goes in the casket for people to get a good look at."

"Will people be coming to see him? His wife died years ago, didn't she?"

"I heard Dad tell Mom that he's got a son in Kentucky or someplace. He'll come up and make sure he's safely planted, so he can take all Dad's money and belongings."

"Belongings, yeah. Probably a coffee can under his bed with fifty dollars in."

"Oh, fuck you, Joe. You're such a cynic."

"Fuck you back, Milne, you know I'm right –"

The incipient argument was cut short by a crash that had all six of the Club jumping out of their skins.

"Aaarg!"

"What the fuck, man?"

"Oh my god! The door!"

Vanessa was the first one to recover the power of movement. She strode back over to the door, which had slammed shut, and jerked at the handle.

"It won't open."

"It has to."

Rowdy joined Vanessa at the door. He gave it a heave, then twisted the handle strenuously, but the door remained firmly closed.

"Hey, you losers!" came from the other side of the door.

Fear on Vanessa's face was replaced by fury. Like Darroll, she recognised the voice of Ed Crowe.

"Crowe, you motherfucker, let us out of here," she snarled at the door. The only response was a medley of laughs from the other side. Darroll could discern Patsy Young's giggle among them; it sounded as though there were three or four more there, as well.

"Or what?" shouted Ed Crowe triumphantly through the door.

"Or I will fucking kill you."

"You couldn't fucking kill a white mouse. None of you jerkass goth losers are worth horse shit."

"Let me out, you bastard!" growled Rowdy Serxner.

"Go fuck one of your dad's cows, Serxner." That voice was Dig Doyle's.

"Come on, let's get out of here or they'll make enough noise to bring people."

Feet ran upstairs, then silence fell on the other side of the door.

"Well, that's us well and truly screwed," remarked Chuck Milne.

"Bastards. Those bastards. They must have followed us in," Rowdy mumbled.

"There's no other way out of this room," Beth said, in answer to a question yet unspoken.

Darroll stared at the door in thought. There was something he'd read once, something –

"Paper," he said aloud. "We need some paper. As big a sheet as we can. Or anything flat. X-rays! X-rays would do."

"There aren't any X-rays in here," Beth pointed out. "This is a funeral home, not a hospital mortuary."

"There has to be some paper somewhere," Darroll repeated, eyes wandering around the room. "That'll do!" He strode over to the far corner of the mortuary where, sitting on a small table, he saw a magazine open to its centerfold. "My god, undertakers have their own magazine?" he added, as he picked it up. "I bet that makes for some gripping late night reading, yes sir."

"Darroll," said Chuck, putting on his most reasonable voice, "mind telling us what the hell you are talking about here?"

A surge of self-satisfaction pumped through Darroll's veins.

"I," he said, "am going to get us out of this place. Let me through to the door."

The other club members moved back and Darroll knelt down by the door with his magazine. He opened it at the centerfold again, and pushed it as flat against the floor as he could. Then he examined the bottom of the door. There was a gap; not a huge one, but large enough.

"That's not going to work, Darroll," said Joe.

"Sure it is."

"No it's not. That only works in books. In fact, it only works in dreadful old kids' books. Like the Hardy Boys or the Three Investigators."

And Archie comics, Darroll almost said, but he somehow didn't want to admit to the group that he read those.

"The reason it's in those books is that it does work," Darroll grunted, easing the magazine under the door, until all but an inch of it was on the far side. "Now, we need a pen or something to poke the key out of the lock and onto the magazine."

Vanessa bent over to examine the lock. "That would be a genius scheme," she said, eye to the keyhole, "if the key was still in the lock."

"What?"

"Crowe and his mob have taken the key away with them."

"Ahh... you're joking."

"I told you that only worked in books," Joe said, smugly. Darroll leapt to his feet.

"You looking for a fat lip, Boardman?"

Chuck Milne pushed his way between them. "Dudes, dudes, dudes. Notwithstanding the cool factor inherent in holding a fist fight in a mortuary, we need to keep focus here."

"He's right," said Joe. "We have to figure out how to get out of this place. Apart from anything else I need the bathroom."

Beth leapt to her knees. It was a strange movement; for a second she seemed to go up in the air, instead of straight down, before she landed by the door. She strained to force her fingers under it.

"No room," she said, and looked up at the others.

Darroll got back to his feet, and looked around the room, counting with his finger.

"Six. Inniss is in that one, so there's five –"

"Five what?"

"Five drawers to hide in."

Boardman's eyes bulged as Darroll grasped the handle and slid the drawer alongside Inniss open.

"Come on, guys, no time to lose here," he said.

"I'm not hiding in there!" hooted Rowdy.

"Where else you gonna hide?" Darroll lifted one leg over the side of the drawer.

"What fucking good will that do?" Chuck sounded barely less shocked than Rowdy.

Darroll climbed into the drawer and sat upright, his upper back against cold metal. "Use your brains, will you? We get caught here, we get hell to pay from Beth's folks. If us five hide in the drawers, Beth can holler for her old man, then she just leaves the door open behind her and we can all scram."

"And what," said Vanessa, "if Mr Vines locks the door behind him?"

"I'm not getting into one of those drawers either." Boardman shoved his hands into his pockets resolutely. "I really do need the bathroom."

Darroll lay down, frustration covering him like flea bites. "Someone shut the fucking drawer."

It was Vanessa who pushed it closed, leaving Darroll's world cold and dark apart from little lines of light where the drawer didn't quite fit its housing. He took a cautious breath. The smell of antiseptic was stronger now he was shut inside, and the chill of it tickled his nose.

Then the drawer jerked open again.

"You could suffocate in there," said Beth quietly, and Darroll, deflated, climbed back out.

Beth moved over to the desk where Darroll had picked up the magazine. "If there's no other way," she said reluctantly, "there's this." She picked up a telephone handset.

"Oh my god, Beth. We can't call the cops."

"No, we can't, not on this phone, even if we wanted to. This line goes to Dad and Mom's house. Dad uses it to tell Mom if he needs anything bringing over. Sometimes he calls her to say what he's got a mind to eat for supper."

"Your parents will tear us all a new one if they find we've been sneaking in here to eyeball corpses," Darroll objected.

"I've been grounded before," Beth said philosophically. "And if we don't get out before Joe ends up taking a whiz in here, the trouble we're in will go up exponentially."

Nobody had anything to say in response to that, and Beth picked the phone up and pressed something on it. After a couple of seconds she spoke. "Dad? Hey, Dad, it's me. Yeah. Yeah, you aren't gonna believe this –"

* * *

The group was subdued when Mr Vines arrived to free them from their prison. Beth had slid the drawer containing Mr Inniss closed, but it didn't deter Vines from giving them a five-minute lecture on how tempted he was to call the cops and have them all thrown in jail for trespassing, interfering with a dead body, and wasting his goddamn time. Then he disappeared with a snort and with Beth in tow behind him, back into his house.

Rowdy climbed onto his bike and sat there looking dejected without starting the motor. Darroll leaned against the side of the Oldsmobile.

"We gonna go looking for Crowe and his gang of idiots?" asked Joe.

"Nah," Chuck said, "they'll be long gone. And anyway we can't take them on mano a mano. We all know that. If we want to get our own back on those jerks, we're gonna have to use what we have a decent amount of and what they totally lack."

"Brains?"

"I was gonna say subtlety, Darroll, but brains too, yeah. Let's all give some thought to how we can score back off Ed Crowe."

Darroll smiled quietly to himself.

"What you grinning at, Martock?" asked Rowdy.

"Nothing," he lied. "Nothing really."

28

The Club were in a new venue; the Serxner family farm. Not the main farmstead, or any of the smaller buildings that lurked around it like autograph hunters around a TV star; down to the south of the actual farmhouse, where the Serxners lived, was what had once been another farm. The Serxner family had bought that farm in the 1970s, amalgamating its land into theirs. Having no use for a second farmhouse, they had let it sit there and decay. Which made it the perfect spot for the Psychopath Club.

Darroll and Chuck had arrived there early and Rowdy gave them a guided tour. The farmer who had owned it previously, Rowdy told them, had dropped dead in his own barn one day and lain there for a week before anyone found him. As with Eddie Inniss, the farmer's only relatives lived far away – in California, this time – and were eager to sell up and pocket the old guy's estate (which wasn't worth much, because the farm had been increasingly neglected as the farmer had grown older and more doddery).

So the building was full of junk from thirty years before. Darroll was astonished that Rowdy had it sitting right on his own property, and had never bothered mentioning it or searching through the contents for anything of value. Darroll didn't know anything about antiques or memorabilia, per se, but he did at least know that there were some things collectors would pay for.

"Jesus, look at these," Chuck said, picking up a stack of 8-track cartridges. "Are they, like, what they had before CDs? I thought they had vinyl before CDs."

"They did," Rowdy said. "I think these came before vinyl."

"I thought that was wax cylinders," Darroll said.

"I think these come between vinyl and wax cylinders," Rowdy said, but he didn't sound at all sure. Chuck put the stack down, then picked the top one up again for closer examination. "God, look at the hair on this guy," he laughed. "And the open neck shirt!

And the medallion! He must have been a swingin', groovy dude back in nineteen seventy fuck."

Darroll had found a heap of books and picked a few up. One was a James Bond novel. Darroll liked James Bond films. There was always plenty of fighting and blood, even if Bond was fatally obsessed with sex. He gave it a quick, cautious sniff; there was no overwhelming stink of mildew, and the pages weren't stuck together. "I'm grabbing this one, Rowdy. It might even be readable."

"Mmhm," said Rowdy, absently. He was looking at the plastic case that Chuck was holding. Chuck flipped it over to examine the other side. "Program One: Something's Happening, Doobie Wah... I don't get it. What's the difference between a track and a program? If these are called eight tracks, how come there's only four programs on them?"

"Don't ask me," Rowdy said. "Hey, Jumping Jack Flash! That was by the Rolling Stones, surely?"

"So this dude covered it," shrugged Chuck. "They did that a lot back then. All those wrinkly old rock stars would buy a song from a songwriter, and all the different record companies would have their bands record it, and hope they got the one that sold the most. And then the Beatles and Bob Dylan came along and started writing their own songs, and changed the whole thing."

Darroll stuffed *Moonraker* into his pocket. "You guys still trying to write songs?" he asked the other two.

"Not trying, Darroll," said Chuck, looking a little hurt. "We are writing songs. Well, I am."

"I'm not," Rowdy said firmly, as though the thought of being taken for a songwriter filled him with dismay.

"We've played a few practice sessions. Beth's doing real well on bass. You should see her. She looks awesome."

"Maybe I'll come by some night when you're rehearsing," Darroll said, which was a complete lie, and he was pretty sure that Chuck knew it was a lie, too. But it was the sort of lie you told someone because you didn't want to hurt their feelings by saying 'No'. Even though the person you just lied to probably knew it was a lie, the same as you did, they also knew you said it because you didn't like to hurt their feelings. So nobody minded. It was so weird how they always told you never to tell a lie, but if you tried to actually tell the truth, people got all on edge and upset. It was this kind of thing, he figured, that made Vanessa sound off about how society was sick.

"Helloooo?" came a shout from the front of the house. Chuck dropped the 8-track and he and Rowdy went out to collect the new arrival. Darroll, not knowing quite why, picked the cartridge up and put it in his jacket pocket alongside the paperback book. There was just room for them both to slide in there; it made his pocket bulge a bit, but he wasn't James Bond, about to enter the casino at Monte Carlo and worried that the cut of his suit wasn't symmetrical.

Beth, Vanessa and Joe had arrived together. Despite the chill in the air, Vanessa was sweaty. "Jesus, Rowdy," she said, "could we not meet someplace where we didn't have to walk halfway across the county?" And she plumped her ass down into an armchair, the only good one in the house. There was another one, but as well as being a repository for thirty years of dust, the same as everything else round here, it had pointy springs coming through the seat that would spike a hole in your ass if you sat down without extreme caution. Darroll had had enough of sharp metal poking into his body, so he sat on the floor. So did Beth. Rowdy picked up a square piece of hardwood and put that on the dubious chair so he could sit in it safely. Chuck occupied the stool in front of the ancient upright piano, and played a couple of notes experimentally. One didn't sound at all, and the others were out of tune.

"Lay off that noise, willya," said Joe Boardman, who was left standing upright, as though this were a game of musical chairs at a party and he'd been the slowpoke when the music stopped. There was a staircase that led upward, coming straight up out of the living room, and he sat on the bottom step.

"Are we in session?" Vanessa asked.

Chuck looked around, as if he needed to count heads before giving an answer, even though there were only six of them, same as always. "We are in session," he confirmed. "It's your turn in the witness box today, right, Darroll?"

Darroll arose from the floor, and moved forward to occupy a space in the middle of the gathering. Because they were sitting all around, he couldn't face them all, so he chose Joe Boardman to focus on, since he was sitting furthest away.

"Yeah," Darroll said. "Now I hope you guys aren't going to get fussy at me here because the subject I'm planning to talk about isn't an individual psychopath, not strictly speaking. But it's relevant, I reckon. Very relevant."

Nobody objected; not that Darroll would have been deterred much if they had. For one thing, he had no backup topic. He hadn't prepared anything else to talk about other than this.

"I'm guessing that you guys were all brought up on the usual kids' stories. Fairy tales. Snow White, Cinderella, all that Walt Disney type of bullshit. All part of the Great American Way of Life, right? Well, firstly," he said, holding up one finger, "most of those stories aren't American. They go way back to before there were even any white people in America. Most of them were German. The brothers Grimm were German. I had no idea. See, my mother used to read them to me, out of this big old book that her mother probably read to her out of, before I could read at all."

There was a slight frown on Joe's face. He didn't know where this was going, which suited Darroll. He wanted to come out of left field on this one.

"That book was about yay big," Darroll went on, "and yay tall. Quite a hefty volume. But after a while I figured that my mother only ever read me the same few stories over and over. And after a while more, I came to realise that... well, that words had lengths. Do any of you guys remember not being able to read? And finding out that the same set of marks on paper meant the same thing, every time?"

Joe still looked blank. Darroll took a quick glance around and was pleased to see that Vanessa, at least, was nodding quite firmly.

"After that I understood that that book had a lot more words in it than my mother was ever reading out to me," Darroll recalled. "Once I knew the size of a word on a printed page I realised that there had to be more stories in there than my mother was reading to me. Had to be. I guess," he said with a self-deprecating smile, "that that laid the foundations for me to be a nerdy kid. Mom was way pleased with how quick I learned to read and count. A lot of that was down to wanting to be able to get inside that book and find out what else was in it."

Somehow although he'd meant to use Joe Boardman as his focus for his delivery, he'd rotated on his axis a bit and was facing Vanessa, there in the big old armchair, deep between its arms, looking like a trapdoor spider peeping out.

"Eventually I gave it a shot. The book was so big I couldn't even hold it very easily. I had to lay it down on my bed to read instead of keeping it in my hands. I don't remember all the stories I found that my mom never read to me, but one of the first ones was... Hey, Rowdy. You slaughter animals on your farm, right?"

Rowdy blinked in surprise as Darroll suddenly turned his head and addressed him. "Well, yeah, sometimes. My dad does it, not me. He says I'd only screw it up if I tried. Honestly, I'm glad. I guess I could do it if I had to, but I'm glad I don't."

"Well," Darroll said with a thin smile, "let's be grateful for small mercies. Because this story went something like this. Once upon a time, there was a family with three little boys, and one day their father slaughtered a hog, and he let them all watch. After he was done, he went off to work someplace else on the farm, and the kids' mother took the youngest child off to give him a bath. So then the oldest child said 'That was fun! Let's play at slaughtering.' And he took the knife, and stabbed his brother with it, just like that."

Darroll clicked his fingers, and the sound echoed around the semi-derelict room, seeming louder than it had a right to. The audience was silent. Vanessa was leaning forward in the chair, her eyes fixed on Darroll, whilst Beth's eyes had gone very wide in her small, round face. They looked out of proportion, Darroll noticed, like the eyes of someone with a much bigger face like, say, Rowdy Serxner's.

"So his brother screamed – no surprise there," Darroll said, looking up for a moment with studied nonchalance. "His mother heard the scream, and came rushing down to see what had happened, and there's this boy lying dead with knife holes in him and his brother stabbing away at him cheerfully. The mother pitches a fit, grabs the knife, the boy fights for it, and next thing, whaddya-know, the mother's stabbed him. So he expires right there on the floor next to his brother."

Beth's eyes were getting wider still. Darroll was amazed they could go so wide while the rest of her face was frozen in one expression.

"So the mother freaks out for a few moments, and then she realises she's left the youngest child in the bath," Darroll went on. "She rushes back up, but guess what? She's too late, I guess this youngest one must only have been a toddler, and by the time she gets back to him, he's drowned in the bath water. Three dead kids out of three. The mother is so distraught she can't bear it, gets a piece of rope, and hangs herself right then and there. And when the father comes back from working in the fields, what does he find but three dead children, one dead wife, blood and… and stuff everywhere. So, well, you probably guessed this, he takes the knife and cuts his own throat. The end." Darroll shrugged. "Happily ever after."

"Wow," said Chuck Milne softly. "That's kind of fucked up."

"That's what happens when you don't have proper safety procedures on farms," Rowdy said, earning himself an eyeroll from Chuck.

Darroll ignored both of them. He was looking at Beth, who was still sitting there huge-eyed and open-mouthed like a grotesque baby bird, and Vanessa, who was staring at him intently in a way he couldn't decide whether he liked or not.

"And that was the story," he said. "I was, what? Three years old? Four at the most. I had nightmares for weeks after that, and every time my mother tried to read me a story out of that book, I'd scream. I'd throw a complete fit. She couldn't understand it. 'But you love these stories,' she said. And what was I going to say? That I'd snuck into the book without telling her and read all this bloodthirsty shit? No way. I was old enough even then to figure I probably didn't want to fess up to having pulled that trick."

Vanessa tried to move in her chair, but she was such a tight fit in it she had to wriggle around before she could free her ass. "Death is all around us every day," she said, grunting a little from her exertion, "and pretending to kids that it isn't, is doing them no favors. They have to learn sooner or later."

"Oh, what?" exclaimed Chuck. "You think it's cool to scare little kids shitless by reading bloodthirsty stuff like that to them when they're hardly out of diapers?"

Beth suddenly spoke. "That depends," she said in her usual hushed voice, "on what you think of the effect it had on Darroll. Either he's screwed up, or he's saner than most of this town, including the rest of us."

That silenced both Darroll and Vanessa.

"I'm not trying to dis you, Martock," Chuck said firmly, "but the way I see it your outlook on life isn't exactly happy and outgoing. And now you've shared that story with us, I guess I can figure how you took that turn in your life. Sorry, Vanessa, but it's morbid and it's icky and whoever put that in a kids' story book wants their ass kicked from here to hockeysticks."

"But that's the thing," Darroll said. "I looked it up, years after. Turns out that story, and a whole bunch of other ones, were in the original German collection by the Grimms. They were feeding that kind of gruesomeness to little German kids from two hundred years ago, right up to... well, I guess they must have taken some of the worst ones out of modern editions, I don't know exactly when. Dig this, though; Hitler and the Nazis really went for this shit. Old Adolf said they were pure Aryan folk tales that showed how strong and creative a culture they were, or some old horseshit like that, but it's my belief that he just dug the blood and violence. Probably jerked off to them at night, him and his one ball. The irony there," he added, as an afterthought struck him, "is that old Hitler used to burn books he didn't like. Well, a few years later, Mom took me to the Hallowe'en festival in the town where we lived then, with a nice big bonfire, right? I snuck that book out under my coat, and while we were watching the bonfire I was holding onto it, waiting for my chance. And when Mom took her eye off me a moment to talk to some people, I grabbed that book out from inside my coat and I threw it right onto that fucking bonfire and watched it burn up like an Indian widow."

"Like a what?" Rowdy. Of course.

"An Indian widow. They used to jump onto their husband's funeral pyres. In India. The country."

Joe Boardman spoke for the first time in a good while. "So how's it make you feel, Martock, talking about this? Did you ever tell anyone else?"

"No. No, I didn't." Darroll hadn't been expecting that question and didn't know how to answer the first part of it. "I guess I'm glad I got it off my chest." He looked away from Boardman, not wanting to see how he'd take that answer, and found himself looking at Vanessa instead. She was staring at Darroll again, and her eyes looked hungry. What was it with girls' eyes today? Vanessa's were as weird as Beth's. He wasn't sure whether he liked that look.

"Are you feeling vulnerable, Darroll?" Vanessa said, and Darroll wasn't sure whether he liked that question, either. Because he was. He'd intended to tell the tale in order to show the Club how twisted he was, how he'd been full of dark thoughts and desires right from his cradle. But at the same time, he'd given them an opening into himself. That was a mistake. A bad one. He mustn't leave an opening like that again. He had to shore up this one.

"Vulnerable? Why should I be?" And he turned away from Vanessa, as well.

But when he turned away, there, standing in the kitchen door, no, actually he was leaning casually against it, was the man with the horse's head. That head was turned to one side, just enough to show he was relaxed, but not enough to stop him looking at Darroll with both eyes. His arms were folded.

29

Darroll's mouth went from normal to dry in the space of a heartbeat. His tongue rasped against the inside of his cheek. He shot a quick glance around the room. None of the others had noticed anything, but they were mostly sitting with their backs to the kitchen door, apart from Joe on the stairstep, and he couldn't see around the corner of the stairs to where Horsehead was standing.

Darroll's initial instinct was to shout out and draw everyone's attention to it, but he suppressed it with such force that his fists clenched involuntarily. What if he shouted, and pointed, and they all looked at the kitchen door, and nobody but himself could see anything? That would be disastrous. Not only embarrassing, but it would prove he was mad. Well, he knew he was mad, anyway, but then the whole club would know he was mad. And that was something Darroll really wanted to avoid, even if he was pretty sure that Chuck and Vanessa and perhaps Beth had their suspicions about him.

So he conquered his surprise, and forced himself into an air of nonchalance once more. As he did so, Horsehead bobbed his head in a nod, and gave him an approving look. Darroll had no idea how a horse's face could look approving, or indeed disapproving, but somehow he knew that that was the expression on the long, chestnut face. Next, Horsehead unfolded his arms and beckoned Darroll over with one finger.

Darroll worked his mouth for a second, to get some saliva back into it and moisten his throat so that his voice wouldn't crack when he spoke, then addressed Rowdy. "There's a bathroom behind the kitchen here, yeah?"

"Yeah," Rowdy confirmed. "It's kind of old and gross, but it should work."

Darroll stepped between Beth and Rowdy toward the kitchen door, and as he did so, Horsehead quietly retreated into the kitchen to make way for him. He preceded Darroll all the way through the big old kitchen with its ancient rusty stove and 1960s plastic fitments, and down towards the door out onto the back porch. Opposite that there was another door, which was the bathroom.

Horsehead paused by the door and gestured to Darroll to enter.

No, signalled Darroll with a shake of the head. *You first.* He remembered that the bathroom was long but narrow, and he didn't like the idea of Horsehead being between him and the door.

Horsehead held both hands out, his body language portraying frankness and openness. You have nothing to fear from me, he seemed to be saying.

Darroll gave Horsehead a look which said something like, all right, but I still don't trust you, and stepped inside. Horsehead followed him in, and closed the door, shutting the world out and leaving the two of them inside the bathroom. Looking at each other.

Darroll broke eye contact after a few seconds, by sitting down on the closed lid of the lavatory, which he didn't need to use. He wondered for a second whether he ought to try to piss in case the others, outside, were listening out for the sound of it; then he dismissed that as overly paranoid. Horsehead, in turn, sat down on the edge of the stained, superannuated bath.

"What do you want?" asked Darroll in a low voice.

"Want? I don't want anything," responded Horsehead, at an equally hushed level.

"Everyone wants something," fired back Darroll.

"I'm not everyone."

"You're certainly not. Everyone else doesn't go around wearing a horse's head."

Horsehead looked slightly hurt by that remark. "I expected you of all people, Darroll, not to make personal remarks based purely on somebody looking a little unusual."

Which was a fair point, Darroll supposed. "Okay... no offence meant. But having a horse's head isn't the same as having a wall-eye or a scar, is it?"

"Would you prefer me to look like this?" asked Horsehead, and with a faint blip the horse's head vanished and was replaced by something Darroll definitely didn't prefer.

"Christ! No," said Darroll, squeezing his eyes shut. After a second he opened one of them cautiously, and was relieved to find the horse's head was back again. "Why can't you just look like me? After all," he pointed out with some feeling, "most likely you're simply a part of my deranged, brain-damaged imagination."

"Perhaps I am," said Horsehead, "but whether I'm real or imaginary, the human form is not one that I would be willing to take. I am not human, nor would I wish to be mistaken for one."

Again, Darroll found himself unable to argue. "Yeah, I take your point. But what are you doing here? What do you want? Do you want me, is that it?"

Horsehead shook his head a couple of times, and the hair on his mane drifted gently back and forth in the eddies that the motion created in the air around it. "I don't want you, Darroll, because I already have you."

"What?"

"You heard me perfectly well. And if you look within yourself, you will find that you know it perfectly well too." Horsehead crossed his legs over. The neatly pressed legs of his suit ended at a pair of polished shoes, rather than hooves.

Darroll looked within himself, or tried to. Horsehead sat patiently on the bath while he did so. After a few moments Darroll abandoned the attempt. "I don't know what the hell you mean," he said, forcing himself to keep his voice from rising, "and you don't have me. Nobody has me."

"That only means that you don't understand yet," Horsehead said. "There will come a time when you understand perfectly, and welcome your partnership with me. No hurry, kid. We have all the time in the world. And all the time in all the worlds."

"Yeah," muttered Darroll, "of course you know all about that."

Horsehead rose to his feet. "You will understand more when you return to this house and meet me here again, alone."

"Oh, yeah? What if I never come back here again? What if I come here with a bulldozer and flatten the place?"

"You will return," said Horsehead calmly, stepping into the bath. "Until then, may the road you walk upon be smooth." And with those words, he dissolved into a sudden mass of dirty, opaque water, the colour of a river flooding in winter, full of earth and manure and run-off from the land, and probably the bloated bodies of a few dead animals. The water hung there for a split second, then dropped into the bath with a splash. It swirled around, and ran away down the waste pipe, leaving Darroll covered with dots of the unpleasant fluid.

He looked for a towel, but of course there wasn't one. It had to have been twenty years since anyone washed their hands in this joint. There was some toilet paper, and he pressed that into service to dry himself before opening the door and stalking back outside.

"What the hell were you doing in there, Martock?" asked Rowdy as he rejoined the other Psychopaths. "Sounded like you poured about ten gallons of water down the drain. And there's water all over you."

"Yeah, well," Darroll drawled, "the pipes in this place aren't what they were, I guess."

He flopped back down onto the floor, facing the kitchen doorway, trying not to think of Horsehead, or of the splashes of fluid on his clothes and body. Trying not to imagine them as acid, slowly dissolving him.

Chuck spoke. "Well, if we're done with Darroll and his... his revelations, we have a bit of band business to deal with. If Joe and Darroll don't mind," he added, in the sort of throwaway manner that made it clear he assumed they wouldn't, and tempted Darroll to object on sheer principle alone.

"The name?" said Vanessa.

"The name," agreed Chuck.

Joe Boardman looked up from examining his fingernails. "For the band? You guys not picked a name yet?"

"That's the trouble," said Chuck. "I've thought of a dozen names myself, and everyone else hates all of them. Even I hate some of them."

"So I suggested that we put all the choices of name in a hat," Vanessa said, "and pick one out at random."

Cliched, thought Darroll, but he kept quiet.

"It's fair," said Rowdy with an air of deliberation.

"I guess so," said Joe. ""Who's gonna pull out the winner? Me or Martock, I suppose. We don't have anything at stake."

"Oh," Darroll said, "I've got a name for the hat, if you guys don't mind me buying a ticket for the lottery."

"You're not in the band," said Chuck, giving Darroll a suspicious look.

"So what?" interjected Vanessa. "None of our suggestions have stuck, or we wouldn't be going through this ritual. I don't mind if Darroll or Joe want to put a suggestion into the hat."

"That's a good point," said Beth Vines, and Rowdy nodded slowly. Chuck shrugged. "Fine, Martock gets a name in the hat. Boardman, you want in as well?"

Joe shook his head. "I'm happy just to be the guy who draws the winner out."

Vanessa took her sketchbook out of her bag and with a quick jerky movement tore out the last page before the back cover. "Okay," she said, folding the sheet of paper over and over, and then neatly tearing along the folds to separate it into five slips. "Does it have to be an actual hat? Because none of us has one except for that damn beanie of Chuck's and, no offence, Chuck, I don't think that's quite what we need."

"Jesus, Vanessa," Chuck grumbled. "You're a fine one to judge anyone else by their choice of clothing."

Darroll thought she had a point, since Chuck's beanie was hardly a thing of beauty any more than the head of lank hair that it covered, and he wouldn't have liked to put his hand inside it, still warm and greasy from Chuck's head.

"I know," Beth said. She rose and walked through to the kitchen. A few seconds later she returned, holding a saucepan in front of her, its lid slightly askew.

"We're going to draw it out of a saucepan?" Rowdy said, eyeing Beth as though he thought she was trying to put something over on him.

"Jeez, guys, it doesn't matter what the hell you draw it out of as long as it's random," Joe commented. He took the saucepan from

Beth, removed the lid and looked inside, then held it up at an angle to show how empty it was.

Vanessa passed out the slips of paper and some pens from her collection of art implements. Darroll watched the others as they received them. Beth wrote something on her slip without any time for thought. Vanessa herself sucked the end of her pen for a moment, then wrote something down. Rowdy looked blank and didn't write anything. Chuck wrote, scowled, then scratched it out and substituted something else as Joe held the saucepan out to Beth and Vanessa to receive their offerings.

Darroll wrote down one word on his slip of paper and looked at it for a second or two, waiting for second thoughts. They didn't come, so he put a full stop after the word and underlined it lightly, then folded the slip in half and dropped it into the saucepan. As he did so, Chuck scowled at his paper again, wrote something else on it, and tossed it into the saucepan quickly. His indecision was obvious as he jerked the beanie off his head, shook his hair into a semblance of shape, then replaced the woollen hat and looked expectantly at Rowdy, who was still contemplating his blank slip of paper.

Christ help them if Joe draws out Rowdy's slip, thought Darroll.

"Today if possible?" hinted Vanessa.

"Mmhm," was all Rowdy said. But he did finally write something.

Once Rowdy's paper had joined the others inside the saucepan, Joe stood in the middle of the circle, hefting the pan aloft. "Okay," he said, with a smile that Darroll took to mean Joe could see how ridiculous this whole thing was. "Ladies, gentlemen, boys and girls, the name of your band is…" He reached in, selected a piece of paper and unfolded it. "Horsehead."

It was odd how Darroll had known that it would be his selection that was pulled out of the saucepan. Sure, sure, there was a twenty per cent chance it would be his, and that was a damn sight better odds than the state lottery. But he had known with complete confidence, somehow. He just had.

Chuck was frowning again. "What the hell? Was that yours, Rowdy?"

"Nope," said Rowdy.

"It works," Beth said with an air of finality. "It was better than my suggestion anyway." She looked at Darroll. "That was yours, wasn't it?"

"How did you know?"

"Saw it in your face," Beth said laconically.

"There've been worse band names, for sure," Vanessa said. "Also, gives plenty of scope for graphic design. Logos, T-shirts." She had flipped her sketchpad back to the middle and was scribbling something in it.

"So I'm in a band called Horsehead," Chuck said. He didn't seem to think as much of the name as Beth and Vanessa.

"We're in a band called Horsehead," Rowdy corrected him, and Chuck flipped his hands in the air.

"Fine, fine, the band is called Horsehead. I think it sounds like something you'd put in your enemy's bed."

"Are you guys that bad?" said Darroll mischievously, and Chuck gave him the finger.

Joe put the saucepan down on top of the piano. He had to reach past Chuck, on the piano stool, to do so, and nearly dropped the utensil in doing so. One slip of paper fluttered out of the pan. Darroll caught it neatly in mid-air and glanced at it.

It read KENNY CANCER AND THE BLASTOMAS. The handwriting was Chuck's. Darroll could guess who Kenny Cancer would have been, if that slip had come out of the hat. Suddenly, Horsehead seemed an excellent name for a band.

30

It was three weeks later when Darroll saw that Mr Otway's store was open again. Mr Otway had a barn filled with what he called antiques, and what Darroll called junk, out to the north of town. He sold things out of it, usually in the summer, to tourists who were 'getting away from it all' by driving out into the wilds around Muldoon. Some of them were positively eager to buy rusty old pieces of farm machinery and yard ornaments to take back to their city homes and use as decorations. Darroll was never, ever going to do that. If he lived long enough to escape Muldoon and go live in a city, the last thing he wanted was to fill his living space with reminders of the country.

Eric Otway also had a moderately steady income from selling the same antiques, or junk if you preferred, to restaurants and bars. Darroll was no fan of bars anyway, because he was no fan of alcohol, but he disapproved still more strongly of the sort of bars he saw all the time on TV. The sort where they made the place up to look like a 1950s gas station, with vintage pumps and metal signs advertising oil and Free Air, and reproduction maps on the walls. Most of them were brands that Darroll had never seen on an actual gas station. They probably went out of business decades before he was born. Why the hell would anyone want a bar to look like a gas station, anyway? Sometimes Darroll thought that if he made it to twenty-one and went into a bar, and found it all dolled up like a vintage gas station, he would march right up to the barkeeper and ask for a glass of premium. And laugh.

Otway also rented a store in Muldoon itself. He didn't keep regular hours, or regular anything, there. He opened it when he felt like it, and sometimes weeks would go by when it remained locked. Other times he'd open every day for a week or more. June Otway had died not long after Darroll and his mother had moved to Muldoon, and everyone said that Eric Otway had gone kind of nuts for a while from grief. Darroll couldn't understand how you could be so close to another human being that you could lose your mind just because they died.

Darroll thought Mr Otway was creepy. He had majorly bushy eyebrows that met in the middle, and his hair was longer than an old guy's hair ought to be. Either he was so relaxed about his appearance that he couldn't be bothered to keep it cut, or he was trying to look like a much younger man than he was, and either way Darroll didn't think that was good. But on the other hand, Mr Otway's store was always a surprise. Going into it was buying a lottery ticket; you could get nothing for several weeks, or you could find something that would blow you right away. Chuck Milne's guitar had come from Otway's store, and Chuck always said he only paid ten dollars for it and it was worth hundreds. Darroll's belief was that Chuck was exaggerating, but there was no doubt Chuck dug that guitar. Even having to play in a band named by Darroll didn't seem to be deterring him.

And Darroll was bored with nothing to do, yet again. So he looked at the junk in the window for a moment or two, then pushed the door open.

The store had been a diner once upon a time, in the days before the interstate had usurped the role of Main Street as the major highway through the region. It still had the counter running the length of the store, and a row of little round seats along the counter. Every one of the seats had a box of junk sitting on top of it, and there were more on the counter, plus a good amount of stuff that had either spilled out of boxes or had never been inside them.

Otway was sitting behind the counter at the top of the store, and he grunted a greeting to Darroll as he came in. Darroll made an indeterminate noise himself, and quickly headed for the nearest box, before Otway could start anything more formal in the conversational line. Even though that particular box was full of unloved toys and held nothing of interest to Darroll, he dug through it for a few moments, until he was sure Otway's attention was off him. He was the only other person in the store. Darroll had never seen more than one person at once in the Otway store.

Halfway up the counter, Darroll struck paydirt. A stack of comic books. Much bigger than the stack he'd found at the yard sale, and older comics, too. From the 1980s. He didn't know the price guide values for every comic book ever (he wasn't that much of a geek) but he knew old comic books cost money. Everyone knew that, though. That was the trouble, thanks to that fat prick on the Simpsons. Now, there was a show Darroll despised, even more than situation comedies set in bars that were made up to look like old gas stations.

So he didn't just snatch the heap of comics up and run up to old Otway with them. That would have been a tactical error. No, Darroll thought. We play this one nice and cool.

He left the comics right there, while he browsed on through old utensils and unfashionable clothes made out of nylon, and useless novelties such as souvenirs of trips to Meramec Caverns or mugs saying WORLD'S BEST DAD. He allowed himself a brief fantasy of buying the mug, smashing it, and mailing the pieces to his father. He was counting in his head meanwhile, and only when he reached five hundred did he return to the comics, pick a few up from the top of the heap and head over to Eric Otway.

"How much would these be, Mr Otway?" Pleasant, polite, well bred. Darroll had little or no respect for the niceties of good manners or honouring one's elders, but he wasn't above playing along with them when he wanted to create a good impression.

Otway plucked them out of his hands and looked at them, each in turn, as if he had memorised a price guide, and was mentally checking each issue off against it. Darroll shuddered inwardly. Surely the old fart couldn't be as savvy as that –

"Dollar gets you four," Otway said abruptly. "Or if you want the whole stack, call it thirty bucks. Got to be a couple hundred there."

That had been Darroll's own estimate of the number of comics. Otway apparently knew everything in his store, even if he didn't know the price of old comics. Or did he? Was a quarter a good price for a 1980s issue of *Punisher*?

He knew without checking that he had three dollars in bills in his jeans pocket. Probably another buck or so in coins. Sixteen comics. How the hell could he choose just sixteen comic books out of a stack of two hundred? Going home wouldn't help. He had an emergency ten-spot in one of his bedroom drawers, and that was the net total of his financial resources at the moment. The Chicago trip at new year had cleaned him right out, even though he'd borrowed in advance on his pocket money from his mother. He still owed twenty bucks on that. He'd tried asking her for it anyway a couple times, when she was drunk, but she never got quite drunk enough to forget the debt.

He felt in his pockets nonetheless, in case by some miracle he had any more money. He didn't, but he did find something hard and unfamiliar inside his jacket, on the left. It took him a few seconds to remember what it was. When he did, an idea struck him, and he pulled the 8-track cassette out.

"Hey, Mr Otway. Would this be worth anything? It's old."

Otway, of course, was also old; old enough to remember 8-tracks. He made a 'hmmmm' noise and took it off Darroll, holding it up to the light (it was pretty dark inside the store, due to the dust on all the lights and the piles of junk half-blocking the windows).

"Your mother's? I bet she dug this guy when she was a girl," Otway said with what seemed to Darroll like an unpleasant and gratuitous smile, tapping a long dirty fingernail on the flowing-haired guy whose picture adorned the cartridge. Darroll gave a little laugh, because he guessed that was what was expected of him.

"Some guys collect these," remarked Otway thoughtfully. "You don't hardly see them round these days." He pursed his lips; Darroll realised that Otway was weighing him up, the same way he'd weighed Otway up just now. "You got any more of these?"

Darroll thought of the heap of the old cartridges back at the semi-derelict farmhouse. "I can do," he said.

"Well, how's about a deal, then?" Otway suggested to Darroll. To his own surprise, Darroll liked the way that by simply offering Otway the old cartridge, Otway was now treating him as not simply a customer, but someone with whom he could negotiate a deal. A deal from which they could mutually benefit.

Darroll raised an eyebrow to invite Otway to elucidate.

"Get me a dozen of these," Otway said, "and you can have that whole stack of magazines."

Comic books, Darroll wanted to say. They're not magazines, you old fool, they're comics.

But instead Darroll just said "That sounds fair." He suspected that the deal he'd been offered meant that the cartridges were worth more, but what did he care? The cartridges were no damn use to him, and furthermore they didn't even belong to him. They were... well, they belonged to Rowdy Serxner's father, he guessed. So he supposed he was about to become guilty of theft and of fencing stolen goods. He didn't care about that, either; if anything it made him feel like a real daredevil scofflaw. "You around later today?"

"Can be," Otway said laconically, "if you need to go fetch them?"

Darroll nodded. "Give me an hour, two hours max."

He strode out of the store and into his car. Reason told him that the comics would still be there when he got back, but a small irrational voice kept insisting that he had to race to the farmhouse as quickly as he could, and back again as well. He consciously shut that voice out. He didn't appreciate being dictated to by his own subconscious, especially about something as unimportant in the grand scheme of things as a heap of fucking comic books.

For that reason he didn't slam his foot down on the gas pedal, either. That was wasteful of gas, as the teachers kept telling them. He didn't give much of a rat's ass about gasoline shortages or global warming, but he didn't want to get hauled over by a cop. Knowing his luck, the one time a cop would actually be in Muldoon with a radar gun would be the time he was in a hurry to get those comic books. No, he corrected himself. The time he was in a hurry to get those comic books by exchanging them for a bag of stolen 8-track cartridges. Imagine being slung into juvenile prison for that, full of gang members and rapists. What did you do, then, dude? You shank someone, you attack a woman? No, I stole a bunch of antique 8-track cassettes. God, his ass would be grass within a day.

And so he drove at a steady twenty-five all the way down to the farmhouse, and signalled carefully before he turned off the highway and onto the rutted track that led to it. The track hadn't been maintained for years, and the Oldsmobile's shocks protested every time he bumped one wheel through a rut or pothole.

The afternoon was getting along as he slid quietly out of the car. Even though the farmhouse wasn't in sight of the Serxners' own farm, he moved carefully, and as quietly as he could. For the same reason, he didn't close the car door once he was outside the automobile. He stood there for a moment, listening. He could just hear the occasional faint sound of a car passing on the interstate, away in the distance. Other than that, not a thing, not even a bird squawking.

He would have liked to enjoy the silence for a while, but he was on a mission, he reminded himself.

The door of the farmhouse, as he'd expected, was unlocked. He entered without any difficulty. It was cool and dull inside, and the smell of decay and neglect that he had noticed on his previous visit still prevailed.

He wished he'd had the thought to bring some sort of bag with him. The cartridges weren't heavy, but they were larger than CDs, and awkward to carry. They didn't stack properly.

He'd tucked about half a dozen under one arm, and was calculating how many trips to and from the car he would have to make before he had the entire collection in his possession, when something alerted him to the fact that he was no longer alone.

He didn't believe all that nonsense about the hairs on the back of your neck standing up when something from the supernatural realm impinged upon you, but the sensation he felt at that moment was as similar to that as made no matter. He couldn't hear breathing – he couldn't hear anything – but he knew someone else was in the room with him, and he had a damn good idea who.

"Hello again," he said, trying to make the greeting sound casual. Distant, without being outright hostile.

"Hello," echoed Horsehead from behind him. "You're getting good. How did you know I was here?"

"I felt you."

"They can't arrest you for that," Horsehead quipped, with some emphasis on the word 'that', which Darroll picked up on.

"Oh? And what can they arrest me for?"

"Stealing 8-track cartridges? Gonna sell them on to an international cartel of outdated musical format collectors, no doubt." The voice behind him snickered in a way that was both human and not, at the same time. It prompted Darroll to turn around, at last.

There he stood. Horsehead wasn't wearing a suit this time; he was dressed in leather trousers and boots, fastened by a belt with a big metal buckle, and all he was wearing above the belt was a waistcoat that hung open to reveal his chest, which was hairy, muscular, and indubitably human. Darroll's eyes examined Horsehead's neck. There wasn't a line that he could point at and say, that's where the human ends and the horse begins. The two species blended into one another between his shoulders and his chin. Darroll could see a vein that went from one to the other, without any interruption or diversion.

Horsehead snickered again, and struck a pose as he saw Darroll eyeing him. "Funny. I didn't think I was your physical type at all."

"Don't flatter yourself," Darroll rejoindered. "My interest in you is purely academic."

"So you think," Horsehead said smoothly, "so you think. You may learn someday that there is much more to it than that. Much more."

"Oh, may I?" Darroll said in annoyance. He didn't like the way that Horsehead kept spinning those cryptic clues at him, like a pitcher throwing a curveball. Quite apart from the fact that he came into Darroll's dreams and caused him to fall off cliffs. "Look. I want some answers from you. You haven't paid me a visit just to lay a smackdown on me for stealing a bunch of fucking cassettes, have you? What do I even call you, anyway?"

"What do you think of me as?" That was typical. He asked a question, he got an answer in the form of another question.

"I dunno." A lie, and he quickly corrected it. "Horsehead."

"Then Horsehead is my name," said Horsehead.

"What were you called before Horsehead?" asked Darroll slyly.

"I didn't need a name before," Horsehead said. "I knew who I was, and nobody else needed to. Hmm. Horsehead. Simple, accurate, concise. It suits me. Thank you, Darroll."

Darroll couldn't work out whether Horsehead was genuinely grateful or whether he was taking the mickey out of him.

"Okay, I'll ask you again what you're doing here," he said.

"Keeping a promise," Horsehead said. "I like to keep my promises."

"A promise?"

"Don't you remember? I promised you I'd see you again when you returned to this house. You returned, ergo, I am here to see you again. Cause, effect." Horsehead held up his left hand with the word 'cause', and his right one on 'effect'. Then he brought them together to form a ball.

"Why did you make that promise?"

"Now you're moving the goalposts. You didn't like the answer I gave your last question even though it was accurate and complete, so you ask me another one. It would have saved us both time if you had asked that question first."

"And it'd save us both time if you answered it," snapped Darroll, "instead of lecturing me on grammar and debating technique. I get enough of that at school."

"Very well," sighed Horsehead, who seemed to have been enjoying that exchange. "I am here to show you something."

"Well, go ahead and show me," Darroll said. "But if the reason you're dressed up like you were going to a gay club is that you want to expose yourself to me, or some shit –"

"Darroll, Darroll." Horsehead's big equine eyes were full of sadness. "You are the only friend I have, and I am the only friend you have, and yet you talk to me like that?"

"I'm not your friend."

"You are. You may not know it, but I am the best friend you have ever had or ever will have."

Darroll sighed, unimpressed, and wanting to show Horsehead he was unimpressed. "Fine, we're best buddies. Pardners even. Now where's this thing you want to show me?"

"There is no hurry. Why not fill your car with your loot, first?"

Darroll didn't like the word 'loot' but he felt he could hardly protest it. "Right, sure. Give me a hand?"

The last suggestion was made mostly in jest, but to Darroll's surprise, Horsehead stepped forward and started to pile his muscular arms with the cartridges. Between the two of them, they collected up the entire heap. They went out to the car together, and dumped them all on the back seat of the Oldsmobile.

"Right," Darroll said. "Get in, and tell me where to go. But don't be too long. I want to get these back to old Otway this afternoon, before someone else gets to those comic books."

Horsehead shook his head. "What I have to show you is inside the farm. There is something there more valuable to you than these cartridges. Much more valuable in both financial terms, and in terms of its worth to you… to us."

That was another riddle, but Darroll followed Horsehead back inside, to the kitchen. Horsehead lifted one leg and tapped his foot against a cupboard door. "In there, Darroll."

Darroll squatted down, jerked the door open and looked inside. "This is valuable?" He pulled out a china plate, undecorated, with a chip at one edge. "Stealing a dead man's 8-tracks is bad enough. I'm not going back to Otway with a stack of his crocks and pans, even if I thought for a second he'd give me a red cent for them."

Sorrow in Horsehead's eyes again. "Take a second look, Darroll. Always take a second look at everything."

Darroll looked at the plate suspiciously, as if he expected it to suddenly burst forth with glowing letters round the edge, telling him that it was the one plate to rule them all. The plate remained unchanged, so he put it down on the floor and looked back inside the cupboard. There were more plates, and a few thick plastic containers with sealable lids. Tupperware, they were called, weren't they? He pulled those out too, but they were empty.

Putting them down on top of the plate, he reached way deep into the cupboard, putting his whole head inside, heedless of spiders and dust. There was another box at the very back, this one made of wood rather than cardboard, with a hinged lid that closed onto a hasp. He grasped the box, and pulled it out.

"Always take a second look," Horsehead repeated.

The hasp was shut, but there was no lock. Darroll flipped it back, and looked inside. He looked at the box's contents for a long moment, then glanced back up at Horsehead.

"That's a gun."

"That," said Horsehead, "is a .45 Colt Commander semi-automatic pistol, with an aluminum frame, manufactured in 1960 in their factory in Hartford, Connecticut, and with a magazine holding seven rounds. In other words, yes. It is a gun."

Darroll's fingers touched the weapon. It was cold. There were some smaller cardboard boxes beside it in the larger wooden box; ammunition.

"Has this thing been sitting here ever since that old farmer turned his toes up?" Darroll wondered aloud. He brought the box up for a closer look. He was hardly an expert on guns. Boardman was. Boardman's father would hunt anything that he could bring home on his truck and a good many things that he couldn't (not to mention fish). Boardman had shown Darroll his father's gun cabinet one time; "I've fired that one, and that one, and that one, not that one..." he'd said. He might have been standing in front of a bookshelf showing Darroll which books he'd read.

"How else would it be there?" asked Horsehead.

"You could have put it there." Darroll's eyes dropped back to the Colt for a moment. "I mean, look at it. It's clean. You're telling me that this revolver..."

"It's a pistol, Darroll. Its chamber does not revolve."

"...this fucking *gun* has been in a box under the kitchen sink in this place for twenty-five years? No. I do not fucking buy it." Darroll slammed the lid of the wooden box shut and sprang back to his feet, holding the box out to Horsehead. "You say it's valuable. Take it. Sell it, get rid of it, whatever."

Horsehead did not take the box from Darroll. "You surprise me, sometimes," he said. "I would have thought you would immediately have seen the possibilities that possession of this weapon would bring to you."

"Like the possibility of getting caught with it, and slammed into jail for years?" Darroll said, but his heart wasn't in the argument any more; he was only arguing with Horsehead because it was the only way he knew how to hold a conversation with the guy, with all his questions and oblique statements.

Because he had to admit, there were possibilities. An awful lot of possibilities, and some of them made Darroll's toes curl up inside his shoes to think of.

Of course, Horsehead could tell. "Second thoughts are as important as second looks," he said, stooping to pick up the Tupperware boxes and tossing them back inside the cupboard, followed by the chipped plates.

"You still didn't answer me," Darroll said. "You didn't say whether this... this pistol has been under that sink for decades, or if you planted it there for me to find."

"Why would I do that?"

"Maybe you want me to kill someone with it?" Darroll said. His voice had suddenly dropped down to a low mutter; the same level that it had been at the last time he was in this house, having a conversation with Horsehead.

"I already told you, Darroll, I don't want anything. But I know that you want things. A number of different things. You do, don't you?"

Darroll nodded, slowly, thinking of some of the things he wanted, and trying not to think of some of the others.

"Well. Give some thought to which things you want most, how you can achieve them, and whether the ownership of this weapon will assist you in any of them. That is my suggestion. In the meantime," Horsehead went on, "one of the things you want quite badly is that stack of comic books in Eric Otway's store. None of them are especially valuable, as it happens, despite your suspicions earlier; but they are certainly worth more than thirty dollars in resale value, to the right purchaser. And since you have a load of 8-track cartridges in your back seat for which Eric Otway is happy to barter comics, since Eric Otway serves as agent for a man in Minneapolis who collects 8-tracks and will pay him five dollars apiece for any he does not own... everyone comes out of this little transaction a winner, do they not, Darroll?"

"What about you?" asked Darroll shrewdly.

"Me? I am the house at Las Vegas. I am a baseball team with Billy Bonds on. I always win," Horsehead responded. Not a boast, a statement of simple fact.

"That must be nice for you," said Darroll sarcastically. "How about if I turned this gun on you right now, and shot you with it? Would you still call that a win?"

"Is that what you want?"

Darroll jerked the box open, and brandished the gun – not pointing it at Horsehead, he knew well enough not to point a gun at someone unless you were planning to shoot them, but holding it up and waving it to add emphasis to his argument. "And there you go again! Answering a question with a question. You never give me a straight answer. You should be in fucking politics."

"Are you sure I'm not?" Horsehead answered, and smiled. Darroll couldn't help but be amused too. The thought of Congress, full of Horseheads in suits, all of them answering questions only with another question. It probably wasn't so damn far from what actually went on there, at that. He lowered the gun again and Horsehead acknowledged it with a bob of the head.

"Jesting apart, Darroll," he said, "I strongly advise against shooting me. The act itself would be unpleasant for me, and the consequences would be unpleasant for you. In any case, I stress once more that I am on your side, as you are mine, and we are very useful to each other in many ways, some of which may not yet be apparent to you."

"Okay." Darroll placed the gun back inside the box carefully, and closed it once more. "I promise I won't shoot you, dude."

"Thank you," said Horsehead, with elegant simplicity and apparent genuine gratitude. "Now, were you not eager before this little... diversion... to carry out a trade with Mr. Otway in town?"

"Yeah."

"Run along," Horsehead said. "I shall see you again soon, friend." He walked nonchalantly through the kitchen door and out of the farm.

Darroll picked up the wooden box with the weapon inside and followed him. He was only ten seconds behind Horsehead, but by the time Darroll was through the door, Horsehead was nowhere to be seen. Darroll looked around; there were no obvious hiding places outside the farm, not for someone the size of Horsehead.

He shrugged, placed the box carefully in the trunk of the Oldsmobile, then on second thoughts wrapped the box up in a ratty old blanket that had been inside the car since he'd owned it. He believed Horsehead. He would see him again soon. But for now, there were comics.

31

The next time Darroll got the swirls, he was at home. The symptoms never grew any more bearable; they were still as unpleasant as they had been the first time. He always wanted to vomit, but never quite could; he always felt as though the world was not only spinning around him, but growing larger. Or else he was growing smaller. Either way, the sensation was what he imagined water must feel like in a vortex around the plughole, before being sucked down and out, into the filthy germ-infested pipe on the other side of the plug. It was all thoroughly metaphorical, except that the world he had been born in, on the right side of the plughole, was as shitty as any of the dimensions he'd met beyond the plughole.

He had shifted enough times now that he had a routine. First step was to ascertain whether or not he was dead in the world he had landed in. If he was at home, and if he didn't run straight into his own counterpart to make the answer to his question obvious, this meant checking to see whether the Oldsmobile was parked out front, and whether the little shrine existed in the lounge with his photograph as the centrepiece. If the automobile was absent, or the shrine was present, then this was a world where Darroll did not belong, where he had died stupidly and needlessly in the highway wreck.

This time, his mother was nowhere to be seen. The house was empty. The flowers and black ribbon were there on his photograph, and there was no sign of either his mother's car or his own in front of the house. Which all added up to one thing.

He returned to his bedroom, mentally rubbing his hands in anticipation, and walked over to the closet. His clothes were all inside, of course, because once again his mother had tidied his room up when he died, and then left it exactly as it was. Never setting foot in it again, like that song said. He dropped to his knees and looked for the box containing the gun he had taken from the old farm.

It wasn't there.

Frowning, he crawled all the way inside the closet, looking for the box, in case it had somehow been pushed further inside or had something else placed on top of it. No sign. And then he realised why, and also realised why Horsehead had laughed when he had removed the gun from the farm.

In this universe, Darroll had died months ago. He had never been to the old farm with Rowdy and the rest. Never been back to it on his own, to steal the eight-tracks and exchange them for comic books. Never picked up the gun from the kitchen cupboard, and never heard Horsehead laugh. Horsehead knew, of course. Any universe where Darroll was a walking ghost, such as this one, that gun would still be right where it had always been. Back at the farm.

He sat back on his heels, and thought.

If he had never taken the gun, then the gun was still at the farm. And if the Psychopath Club hadn't been to the farm, which was more than feasible if he was dead in this world, then the farm was very likely deserted and unused. He could just go and collect it. Of course, he didn't have an automobile to drive there in this world either, but he had legs. He just had to make certain that nobody saw him on the way.

That wasn't difficult. The hardest part was getting away from the house, checking to make sure nobody on the street was watching. Not only was this the most likely place for him to be seen, but any eyes that saw him here would most likely belong to someone who knew he didn't belong here. They'd set up a hue and cry that Darroll Martock's ghost was walking down the street where he had lived during his life. Darroll didn't mind playing ghost – he had done it enough times to have worked up a basic routine for that, now – but it would probably lead to enough of a scene for it to trigger his being yanked back to his home dimension. Wasting his efforts.

But he slunk away from the house without being observed, and down to the highway. He felt easier, now. Anyone who saw him on the highway from a moving vehicle would only glimpse him for a second or two. Not enough to recognise him, even if they were familiar with him. The highway had no sidewalk alongside, but there was enough of a grassy verge that he could walk along it without having to dodge traffic.

The next setback came when he reached the track that led from the highway up to the wreck of the farm. Something was wrong, he instantly knew. Instead of the rutted, bumpy dirt track that led to the farmhouse in his world, there was now an actual metalled driveway, smooth hardtop in good repair, leading up from the road to the farm. And the farm itself was no longer derelict. Even from this distance he could see it was in decent repair and inhabited.

It didn't take a genius to figure out that in this present reality, not only had Darroll managed to kill himself in the accident, but the old farm was not abandoned. Perhaps Rowdy's family had decided to fix it up instead of letting it fall apart, or perhaps someone else had bought it instead of the Serxners.

Either way, there was unlikely to be a forgotten gun at the back of the kitchen cupboard, and Darroll didn't feel like trying to get inside to find out.

He was at a loss, now. He had no transport to get anywhere in the wide world beyond Muldoon, and no obvious way of acquiring any. He pondered the idea of walking down as far as the interstate and standing at the on-ramp, with his thumb held out, but he wasn't sure people actually did that any more, or whether it was even legal. He didn't give a damn for the law, of course, but to be hauled in by the fat, useless local cops for so petty an infringement as illegal hitch-hiking would be a real kick in his dignity.

Instead he turned back toward town. He passed the street leading into his home division, and instead, took the turning to Muldoon's small graveyard. It wasn't far from the highway, a roughly square enclosure half filled with memorial stones from the last forty years, when the graveyard behind the church had grown too full of bones for any more burials. There was a stainless steel arch over the entrance which reminded him of the photographs he had seen of Auschwitz, although the letters on this one read MULDOON CEMETERY rather than ARBEIT MACHT FREI.

As he'd hoped and expected, the cemetery was small enough for him to have little difficulty finding what he sought. It was in the back row, the area beyond it undisturbed by graves as far as the fence at the far side. The topmost letters were large enough to be obvious from a distance. MARTOCK.

He walked up to his grave, suddenly aware of how silent everything was. No birds, no insects, not even any sound of traffic from the highway behind him. Nature had reached out to her volume knob and twisted it down to zero. Just as she had the last time he'd been at the farm, before he met Horsehead again.

The grave was larger than most of those around it, and grander. As well as the main stone, there was a second smaller stone in front of it, like a chicken next to a mother hen.

The big stone had his full name, Darroll Rolf Martock, and his dates of birth and death. The little stone bore a memorial verse:

> *A loving soul with a mind so sharp,*
> *A smiling face and a generous heart.*
> *All too soon you were taken away*
> *But we'll see you again in heaven one day.*

The stones were black and the writing on them was silver. Darroll knew instantly that it was not a cheap memorial, and he also knew instantly who had paid for it. "We" will see you again in heaven one day? Yeah, that "we" meant "I", and the "I" meant his father. He was filled with an urge to kick the stone over, but it was too heavy and well-planted for him to bother even trying. He stood glowering at the stone and its inscription for a moment longer. Christ, the poem didn't even rhyme properly. And what was that bullshit about his smiling face? He gave the monument a hideous leer, trying to put on a face like the Joker out of Batman. That was the only smiling face he ever wanted to show anyone. Ever.

Then he pulled down the zip on his pants, and relieved his feelings over the stone.

Zipping himself back up, he strode out of the cemetery, hate bubbling away inside him, a pot of sour soup on a stove. He was imagining going back to the freeway, hitching that ride, getting all the way down to Georgia somehow, and paying his father a little visit. Hello, dad! You thought you'd see me again in heaven one day, did you? Got news for you. There's no such place, and if there were, you wouldn't be going there. You're going the other way, right now. Ka-blam! Bye bye, world's worst dad.

He paused by the entrance to the cemetery to catch his breath, and also to regain some perspective. World's worst dad, just because he divorced Darroll's mother and never came to visit, and bought him a shitty old car? There were fathers out there who killed their kids. Or raped them. Or killed them then raped them.

He shrugged mentally, and headed on into town. He no longer cared if anyone saw him, but nobody paid him any heed as he turned left onto Main Street and walked on past the launderette, past the liquor store, and onto the cross street that led toward Muldoon's library.

The library was a surprisingly lavish establishment for a town the size of Muldoon. A few decades ago, some local farmer had left his estate to the town, and they had spent the windfall on what had then been a real state-of-the-art library. Now, of course, it was aging quickly, and it was no longer open every day because they couldn't afford to pay the staff, but it was still there, and still large. He climbed the steps in front of it, and walked through the revolving door with its brass push-plate.

The library was quiet. Well, it's a library, he reminded himself. There were only a couple of people inside, plus one young woman behind the issue desk who looked at him without curiosity as he entered, and then returned to whatever job she was doing, gluing books back together or putting anti-theft tags inside.

Instead of turning right for the fiction section, as he normally did, he turned left and entered the non-fiction section. That part of the library was deserted, which didn't surprise him.

He'd never used the microfiche readers before, but he knew they were there, and he was going to need them. Some libraries had internet and computers, like the ones at Straus High, but not Muldoon's public library.

There was a filing cabinet right alongside the microfiches, and a plastic stand with a "how to" guide standing on top, which he took a glance at. You were encouraged to just dig into the microfilms in the cabinet and take a good old look at whatever info they contained. Great.

He opened one of the drawers and started to flip through the contents. He soon found what he was looking for; it was new enough that it was in the frontmost folder of its section. Extracting the fiche from its fellows, he clicked the reader's switch on, sat down, and inserted the little plastic sheet.

Muldoon no longer had its own newspaper; that had closed down for lack of circulation while Darroll was barely out of diapers, and long before he'd found himself marooned in the damned place. Instead, the local newspaper was the county's gazette. There were vending machines in town where you could buy it, though Darroll had never seen anyone doing so; certainly not from the one outside Celebration Burger.

Darroll hit paydirt first time, and smiled slightly. He'd made the front page. Well, whoopee, although the amount of news that happened out here, he'd have been more surprised if he hadn't made the front page.

LOCAL YOUTH DIES IN AUTO SMASH

They'd really gone to town on the story. First there was a quote from the sheriff, who confirmed that the Oldsmobile had been in good mechanical repair, and hinted that Darroll himself had been to blame for excessive speed in poor road conditions. Next came some words from Alvin Tidmarsh, who said that Darroll had been "a quiet but intelligent and very promising" student who had had a potentially star-studded future cut short. That made Darroll want to laugh, but being in a library, he suppressed the urge; not because he cared about any damn library rules, or social norms, but because he wanted to avoid drawing attention to himself.

Because he'd already decided what he was going to do after he finished with the microfiche.

He read on. There were details of his funeral plans (closed casket, no surprise there; at the Vines funeral home, again, scarcely a surprise). What did interest him was the third interview quoted in the article, whose source was credited only as "a fellow student at

Isidor Straus High School in Muldoon". Whoever that might have been, they'd said, "Darroll was average, but not in a bad way. He was pretty much the quintessential, pure all-American boy."

Darroll kicked the leg of his chair gently, and mulled that one over. He didn't know who could have said that. He didn't know anyone at school who even knew the word "quintessential", and even setting that aside, where the hell did anyone get off on calling him an all-American boy? That was the last thing he wanted. The very last thing. Nobody called him that and lived.

More than likely the reporter had just found he needed another inch of space, and made that quote up straight out of his head. He looked back up at the top of the article, and then down to the end, but he couldn't see any credit or byline for the writer.

Not that it mattered. He'd seen all that he needed to, or cared to.

He retrieved the microfiche from the reader, not bothering to turn the machine off, and dug inside his pocket for the cigarette lighter that he had carried around ever since the trip to Chicago, the one that Todd Krank had lent him and that he'd never given back. He jerked the drawer of the filing cabinet containing the microfilms open again. Holding the one with the story of his death over the open drawer, he clicked the lighter and applied the flame to the corner of it. It caught in an instant, faster than he'd expected. He dropped the flaming plastic onto the top of the folders in the drawer, and in only a second or two, they too began to burn.

Turning away from the cabinet, he held the lighter, flame still burning, against a row of encyclopedias on the shelf behind where he'd been sitting. They were leather-bound and didn't want to burn immediately, so instead he found a pile of leaflets on how to use the reference library and set fire to them instead. As they started to burn along one side, he picked them up quickly, two at a time, and jammed them in between reference volumes. The last few were too well ablaze for him to move by the time he reached them, so he left them to set fire to the tabletop where they sat, and headed for the door out of the reference library.

As he reached it, fire alarms started to ring. He wondered if the library had sprinklers. Probably not. Fucking cheapskate town.

Gets what it deserves. Now and in every universe.

He was first person out of the building, but before he reached the bottom of the steps outside, the swirls were upon him again.

32

Darroll had known from the start that the Horsehead gig was going to be a disaster.

There was nothing he could do about it; nothing any of them could have done. Nothing they did do that they shouldn't have done, either. It was just that this was the Psychopath Club, and things didn't go right for them, ever. If there wasn't someone eager to step in and sabotage their plans, then bad luck alone would suffice to leave those plans floating, belly-up and bloated, in the muddiest and most polluted creek in the county.

So when Chuck Milne had given him a stack of photocopied flyers at the start of the week, he hadn't bothered to tell Chuck not to waste his time, but had taken them and promised to give them out. Darroll, of course, had no friends whom he didn't share with Chuck, not one. Chuck had to know this as well as he did. But that was how you were meant to do it. You started playing little local gigs and within a year or two you were filling stadiums, and driving cars that cost a million bucks, and abusing drugs and journalists and chat show hosts. And then you died, aged twenty-seven, leaving a good looking corpse like Cobain. Which should please Vanessa. Darroll wondered whether she'd had just that outcome in mind when she joined Horsehead, the band.

Darroll accepted the flyers, then, and took them home with him. That Monday he had a check-up scheduled with Vickery, his therapist, so he escaped school at lunchtime. Arriving home, he gave one flyer to his mother, who looked at it as though it were a demand from a little green alien to take it to her leader. "What's this, honey?"

"Horsehead are playing their first gig. Chuck and Vanessa and those guys. At the VFW, this Saturday. You do know what a gig is, Mom?" he asked with crushing irony.

"Of course I do," she replied, turning back to the television.

She wasn't angry; she just sounded vague. Darroll might not have despised her so much if she responded to his barbs with some kind of genuine annoyance. But she never did.

So that got rid of one flyer. The other forty-nine that Chuck gave him were in his bedroom. He stuck one on the wall to the left of his door, where it looked undersized and pathetic, and not at all like a real poster. Chuck (or more likely Vanessa) had taken a blurry photocopy of a decrepit old man in a raincoat and plastered lettering on top of it, punk style, with details of the gig. Derivative. "Be there or be a duodecahedron," it said at the bottom.

He took one more flyer, folded it in half, and put it in his pocket, which left forty-seven to gather dust on top of the comics on his nightstand for the rest of the week.

"Mom!" he shouted. "Are we going to see Vickery or not?"

His mother reluctantly turned the television set off, and they took her car to the hospital. Instead of the new, modern building where he had seen Schwartz while under his care, his appointments with Vickery were in a smaller and older building, round the back of the main hospital site.

"Good afternoon, Darroll," said Vickery as they walked in. "Good afternoon, Mrs Martock. Anything to report?" Vickery was wearing a bow tie as usual, this time pale green in place of the scarlet one which he generally preferred.

"Not really, doctor," said his mother. Darroll winced. He knew that Vickery wasn't a doctor. Vickery saw the wince, and his eyes met Darroll's momentarily. "Darroll seems pretty normal, still."

The words jabbed at Darroll like a knife, and for another second his eyes locked with Vickery's once more.

"No news is good news," said Vickery cheerfully. "I'll still run through the standard tests, though, just to make certain Darroll's reflexes and senses are all as they should be, and see how they correlate with his scores from last time. Probably a formality, but since insurance is paying for them we may as well make sure, mmm? If you'd prefer to wait outside, Mrs Martock, that would be fine."

For once in his life, his mother took a hint and went to wait outside. The door closed, and Darroll and Vickery were left together.

"I'm ready for the tests, Mr Vickery," said Darroll, emphasising the 'Mr' enough to show that he knew better than his mother. Vickery gave him a smile, in turn, to show he'd picked up on it.

The tests were as dull as ever. Darroll had to walk in straight lines, show he had depth perception, connect dots on a sheet of paper with a pencil, and so on. But it was an afternoon out of school, at least. Furthermore, Vickery was still the only adult in Darroll's life to treat Darroll himself as an adult.

"I think we're done," Vickery said at last. He folded his hands with his elbows resting on the desk, and looked at Darroll over the top of them. "We've made good time. Fifteen minutes to my next appointment. How have things been going for you, Darroll? I don't mean in medical terms, necessarily. I mean generally."

Darroll gave Vickery a suspicious look. "They're okay."

"Really okay, or is your 'okay' shorthand for 'I don't want to talk about it'?"

For a second Darroll kept up the suspicious look, then he gave a half-laugh. "The second one."

"Well, don't let me pry into your life if I'm not welcome."

"It's okay," said Darroll, "and that time I did mean it. Life's shit, but life always is, yeah?"

"Certainly life is very rarely perfect," agreed Vickery. "In my experience, the best way to deal with it is to remember that everyone else's life has moments of sucking rocks too. That book I sent you, *Catch-22*? I always found that helped to remind me of that. Dare I ask what you made of it?"

"I haven't actually read it," Darroll said, surprising himself for a moment with his own honesty. There was something about Louis Vickery that made him disinclined to indulge in easy lies. "But I will do, I really promise."

Vickery didn't appear surprised or disappointed by the confession. "A good book's like a good bottle of wine," he said. "Once you have it, it's there when you feel in the correct mood to crack it open and enjoy it, and it doesn't matter if that time doesn't come for a month, or a year, or longer. How's your campaign to put Muldoon on the map looking?"

Darroll gave a vague shrug. "Nothing too spectacular. Some of my friends are doing better than me." He reached into his pocket and pulled out the handbill for the Horsehead gig that Saturday. "They started up a band."

Vickery took the handbill and looked at it. "Horsehead, huh? Is Muldoon beginning to develop a cultural scene?"

"I wish," said Darroll. "This is their first gig."

Vickery picked up a desk diary and opened it up. "Sadly I have a prior engagement this Saturday," he said. He turned the book around and showed it to Darroll, as though he knew that if he didn't, Darroll would suspect him of telling an easy lie himself. The whole of Saturday evening in Vickery's diary was blocked out with the one word BRANDY. Darroll hoped that that was the name of Vickery's girlfriend, rather than meaning he had an alcoholic weekend planned.

"Well," Vickery said, "is there anything else you want to raise, any questions before we finish?"

"Yeah," said Darroll, "Why do you wear bow ties?"

Louis Vickery's eyes narrowed for an instant at the question, then he gave Darroll a smile. "I shouldn't have been surprised by that, having seen as much of you as I have. Recent research has suggested that a significant factor in hospital-acquired infections is the neckties worn by male doctors. That's the answer I'd give most people, at least."

"No shit?"

"No shit. You can imagine it, can't you? Doctor X bends over a patient in bed, his tie dangles down, maybe brushes against the patient. Then off he goes on his rounds, and every other patient he bends over gets the same tie and the germs that it picked up from that first patient, right in the face."

Darroll laughed a little. He couldn't help himself.

"Yes," Vickery agreed, "it sounds a bit crazy, and I'm sure it's not a huge factor, but where health and hygiene are concerned there's no point in taking even small risks if you don't have to. So even though I'm very rarely called to deal with a patient who has anything infectious, I prefer not to wear a traditional tie. That's the answer I'd give most people, as I said."

He paused, and unfolded his fingers, before refolding them in exactly the same pattern once more.

"For you, though, Darroll, I'll also confess that I like to wear a bow tie because it immediately shows that I like to set myself apart from normal, male, professional human beings. I like to fool myself, God help me, that there's enough wriggle room in my position and my lifestyle for me to be the myself who isn't quite like anyone else." He reached up to his throat, and tweaked the pale green bow tie. "Not every act of rebellion is an obvious one, right? It may be a small rebellion, but it's my damn rebellion."

"Right," said Darroll. But what he was thinking was, you poor bastard. You think you're rebelling against society by wearing a green bow tie. You're part of the establishment, and you know it, but you're too chickenshit to face up to it like an honest man, so you kid yourself that you're striking a blow for freedom. The world's smallest rebellion ever. Darroll actually found himself feeling sorry for Vickery, quite deeply so. It was a feeling so rare that he had to examine it cautiously to be certain it was genuine, actual pity.

Vickery closed his diary with a snap, and stood up. "One more visit on the monthly schedule," he said, "and if that's like today, then I don't think I need to see you again more than once every six months. Not unless there's anything that gives you or your mother cause for concern. This is a shame," he added, "because I enjoy seeing you."

"I enjoy seeing you too," said Darroll.

"And part of the reason I enjoy seeing you," went on Vickery, "is that you're one of the few people I know who wouldn't say that simply as a pleasantry, but only if you meant it. So thank you." He opened the door. "Mrs Martock? You can take this young rogue out of my sight. He's disgustingly healthy, and his physical symptoms are well within parameters. My secretary will arrange another appointment in a month."

"Oh, thank you, Doctor," his mother said.

"He isn't a doctor," Darroll grunted. His mother looked vague once more; Vickery gave Darroll a knowing look. Darroll remembered that look all the way home to Muldoon. He really ought to crack open that book, *Catch-22*, he thought to himself.

Back to school on Tuesday. The rest of the band had not been idle. "Chuck and me stuck a flyer to every lamp post in town, last night," Rowdy Serxner boasted that morning.

Tuesday afternoon, Darroll parked the Oldsmobile in the lot at Celebration Burger, and set out to walk round the block. Plenty of the handbills had been ripped down already; on one or two poles, a torn fragment or corner could still be seen. A couple more had been defaced. LOSERS, big black letters said over one. Another one had the old guy in the raincoat crudely amended to have him holding an enormous, deformed, equine penis jutting out of his pants. The band name had been amended from Horsehead to Horsedick. Darroll tore that one down himself. He didn't put another one up in its place.

Wednesday, Vanessa joined Darroll at lunch, looking sullen. She did sullen very well, even when she was at school and out of her heavy make-up.

"That scumsucking bastard Tidmarsh won't put a flyer up on the notice board," she snorted as she sat down opposite Darroll and jabbed her spoon clean through the foil on top of her yoghurt pot.

"Why not?"

"He says the notice board is for school activities only. We all go to this useless school, though, don't we? It's no different from all those sport team notices that go on the board, and they stay there for weeks after they're obsolete."

"Well, what do you expect?" Darroll said. "Tidmarsh is a jerk, and if he's paid enough attention to know who's in the band, it's all people he despises, people like you."

"Favouritism," scowled Vanessa. "Nepotism."

Darroll had to go and look up what nepotism meant in the dictionary after lunch.

Thursday, Ed Crowe started a fight with Chuck Milne right in class. Darroll missed it; he wasn't in that class with Chuck. Vanessa told him afterwards. "That bastard Crowe ripped one of our handbills up. Right in his face. And said he was gonna beat tar out of him on Saturday night. Said if he wanted to be rock and roll, he'd give him rock and roll all right."

"Jealousy," Darroll said to Vanessa airily. He was growing more and more glad that he wasn't part of the band. Who wanted to rub their fingers raw on guitar strings and sing till they were hoarse, only for Ed Crowe to show up and cause a riot? "He's just mad with you guys because you had the idea of starting a band and he didn't."

When Darroll saw Chuck later, he bore the marks of Ed Crowe's fists.

"You okay, Chuck, man?"

"I'm okay," said Chuck, not looking it. "Least, Crowe smacked me about some, but luckily it was in Ms Leland's class, and Leland knows just how Crowe likes to operate. So when Crowe said I started it, she didn't even bother asking me if he was lying. She just made those big sorrowful eyes at him, and said he needed to figure out how to deal with situations with appropriate mechanisms. So Crowe said 'what?' and Ms Leland said, 'Not with your fists, Edward.' Which shut him up." He rubbed his jaw contemplatively; it was red, and looked ready to darken into a bruise. "We're gonna have to be careful Saturday though. I'm sure Crowe and his usual sycophants are gonna come and cause trouble."

"Don't look at me," Darroll said. "I don't mind playing roadie for you and helping you set your gear up, but do I look like a security guard?"

Chuck had to concede that Darroll didn't.

That was four bad days out of four that week so far, but Friday brought the jackpot. Rowdy Serxner showed up at school in his mother's car rather than on his motorbike. She got out and opened the door for him. When he emerged, he was wearing a bandage round his wrist.

Chuck and Darroll both saw him at the same moment and looked at each other. Neither of them said anything. They didn't need to; they both saw the resignation and dismay in the other one's face, and knew it was a simple reflection of the expression on their own.

"Uh. Guys. I got some bad news for you." Rowdy came up to them, looking even more hangdog than usual.

"No kidding," drawled Chuck, exasperated. "Rowdy, what the hell have you done to yourself? Have you fucked up your hand?"

"I came off my bike last night," Rowdy said. "I was coming back from the gas station, and a squirrel ran out onto the road."

"A squirrel? Jesus Christ, Serxner," Chuck hooted. "A deer or a badger or something big, I could understand, but you fell off your stupid bike avoiding a squirrel? You could have gone straight over it and never felt the bump."

Serxner backed off a step.

"How bad is it?" Darroll enquired, as Chuck paused for breath.

"Sprained wrist," Serxner said. "Not broken, but the doctor strapped it up. I'm not gonna be able to play Saturday. I'm... I'm sorry, Chuck."

Chuck had clapped his hand theatrically over his eyes. "Oh my god. This is the last straw. We are fucked. We are royally, regally fucked." His hand dropped down and he peered at Rowdy hopefully. "Can't you play with one hand? Like that English guy in that band?"

"He's a professional musician," Rowdy pointed out in his usual stolid manner. "And I think he has a special kit for it, doesn't he?"

"Well, what else are we going to do?" Chuck's hand went back to his head, this time to let his fingers go through his hair. Darroll wondered if he was actually going to see Chuck tear his hair. He'd read about that in books, but never seen anyone actually do it. But Chuck didn't; and before anyone else could contribute further to the conversation, the school bell sounded.

"Christ," Chuck said again. "Okay. I'll see you at recess, Rowdy. Tell Beth and Vanessa and... and we'll think of something. We'll have to think of something."

Before Darroll could even set both feet outside the classroom door at recess, they grabbed him, Vanessa on one side of him (using both hands), Rowdy on the other (using only one).

"I'm coming, I'm coming," he protested as they tugged at him. The rest of the Club were waiting for them. Chuck was looking fraught, Joe morose. Beth's expression, as ever, was unreadable. She ought to be a poker player, Darroll thought.

For a few seconds they all looked at each other, nobody wanting to be the first to break the silence. It was Chuck who finally took point on that. "Okay, guys. What the... fuck are we going to do?"

"There's no way you can play?" Vanessa asked Rowdy. "Not if we strapped you up tight as hell, and filled you full of morphine?"

Rowdy shook his head glumly. He looked about to reply, but Joe got in first. "Morphine?"

"Painkiller," said Vanessa witheringly. "It's not a drug."

"Yes it is!" said Rowdy.

"No it isn't. Not a drug drug."

"What the hell is a drug drug? Are you crazy? It's a drug, end of."

"Shut the hell up!" growled Chuck. "That doesn't matter. What matters is the gig tomorrow!"

"I guess we're gonna have to cancel it?" Rowdy said.

"Can't play without a drummer," said Beth. It was so weird how even though she had such a little girl voice, the softest of any of them – Vanessa talked as loud as any of the guys, louder than Boardman – everyone shut up the moment Beth spoke, and she could be heard clearly.

"We're screwed," said Rowdy, eyes downcast. "I'm so sorry, you guys –"

"One of you can do it," Vanessa said decisively. Both her arms came up from her sides, fingers pointing, like a Wild West gunman drawing his twin Colts. One of them pointed at Joe Boardman and the other one at Darroll.

"No," said Darroll.

"No way," said Joe.

"Yes way," said Chuck. He tilted his head upward a bit, and Darroll knew that Chuck thought he was squaring his jaw, ready to impose his will on Joe and himself. Well, Darroll was wise to his game, and Darroll wasn't about to be imposed upon.

"Oh. Please." Beth again. "You... have to."

"No we don't," Darroll corrected her. "Who says we have to? Why?"

Chuck's brow furrowed in annoyance, but it was Beth who spoke again, so of course Chuck didn't interrupt. Beth's tonguetip flickered out to moisten her lips. "I wasn't going to tell you guys this," she said, not looking anyone in the eye. "I emailed Todd Krank and he's gonna be coming. All the way here to see us. It was... I was gonna surprise you guys with it when he showed up."

Darroll figured he was supposed to be impressed by that, and treat it like a bombshell. He couldn't decide whether to play along with that or ignore it. Chuck and Vanessa both reacted as if it were a bombshell; and so, a second or so too late to ring true, Darroll followed their lead.

"Wow... But couldn't he come along anyway, if we reschedule?" asked Rowdy diffidently.

"Todd Krank is a professional gigging musician," Beth said, her voice actually becoming a shade less soft for a moment. "The odds of us finding another night when he isn't playing himself are pretty long."

Darroll again felt a twinge of skepticism at that claim. He wouldn't have given much for the chances of the Typhoids getting a rebooking at any venue where they'd already inflicted themselves on the public.

"Please, guys," Vanessa said. "This is a chance we can't miss. If Horsehead gets the nod from Todd, we could actually pick up some fans that way."

Once more Darroll experienced deep skepticism. Somehow, though, he found it hard to give Vanessa a flat refusal.

"Are you guys scared?" Chuck blurted suddenly.

"No," snapped Darroll.

"Yes," said Joe with an air of sincerity.

"Yeah? You think I'm not scared too," Chuck went on, "having to stand up in front of people and perform? I'm scared, Vanessa's scared, Beth is scared out of her fucking pants."

"I wasn't scared," Rowdy muttered.

Ed Crowe and Kirk Mondschein were approaching, and Ed gave them a scornful look. Darroll decided that the conversation needed curtailing, before any more trouble broke loose. A random thought came to him, and he voiced it before he could think better of it.

"Okay, okay," he groaned. "Let's be rock and roll about this. Let's toss a coin for it."

Chuck and Vanessa both looked blank at that suggestion. Rowdy snickered. "You have such weird ideas, Darroll."

But Joe Boardman shrugged, and then nodded. "What the hell, it's as good an idea as anything." He fished a quarter out of his pocket. "Ready?"

"Ready."

The coin spun in the air. If this were a movie, Darroll thought, they'd run the camera in slow motion here, and make sure the coin was lit up with care, so that it would gleam in the sunlight as it spun through the air. All Hollywood, all unsubtle.

Joe snatched the quarter out of the air and slapped it onto the back of his other hand. "Call it."

"Tails," said Darroll. He always said tails in any coin toss.

It was heads. Everyone looked at Darroll.

For a few seconds Darroll was sorely tempted to give the rest of the Club the finger, turn on his heel, and walk away without looking back. Then he spent a few more seconds in the even more pleasant fantasy of dragging a machine-gun out of his pocket and spraying them all with bullets until they went down into bloody heaps of shredded flesh, Chuck's arm here and Beth's leg there and Vanessa's tits –

"Sure, I'll do the fucking gig," said Darroll, closing down the last image in his mind like a steel bar descending across it. "I'll be no fucking good, but I'll do it. Rowdy, can you at least show me the barest fucking rudiments of drumming tonight?"

"We'll have a whole band rehearsal," Chuck said.

"Yeah," Vanessa agreed. "You'll be awesome in no time, Darroll."

It was rare for Vanessa to be caught out in overt optimism, but after half an hour behind the drum kit, Darroll knew his original doubts were justified. More than justified.

Darroll had never paid much heed to drummers. They were there, just there, at the back, quietly (well, not exactly quietly, but hey) getting on with things. They didn't perform antics or play to the crowd – at least, not during gigs. You never saw a drummer do a power slide. After half an hour, Darroll knew why. It was because it took drummers every atom of their concentration and every fibre of their muscle to do what they did.

He soon found out that the little stool he had to sit on was most uncomfortable on his skinny ass, and he couldn't move an inch in any direction without feeling as if he was going to go over sideways or on his back. It didn't help, either, that the ground in Rowdy's barn wasn't flat, so if Darroll put any force into playing, not only the stool but the whole drum kit wobbled around.

Then came the problem of the kick pedal. He had never given any thought to kick pedals, and he wasn't prepared for the necessity of co-ordinating his feet as well as his hands. Rowdy was a patient instructor, but Chuck and Vanessa soon started to grow irked at Darroll's inability to maintain rhythm for more than four bars at a time.

In fact, Darroll was also getting impatient with himself. Drums were a simple instrument, pretty much the simplest of all, they'd been around for thousands of years – so why couldn't he keep up with the "One AND two AND three AND four" that Rowdy kept repeating, like a Hare Krishna chant?

"I thought they had drum machines nowadays," Darroll grunted.

"They do," Chuck said, "but we don't have one, can't afford one, and don't know anyone we can borrow one from, so."

"Couldn't her best buddy Todd bring one with him?" Darroll jerked his head in Beth's direction.

"They don't need one," Beth said. "They have an actual drummer."

"Who doesn't break his fucking arm right before a gig," Darroll added.

"I didn't do it on purpose," Rowdy protested, like a cow mooing in surprise when someone shot it in the ass with an air gun.

"Didn't say you did, dude. Darroll… please." Chuck used the tip of his guitar pick to point to the drum kits. "You can do this. And when you do this, you will go down in the annals of the Psychopath Club."

Like that meant anything. Like that meant a single, solitary atom. But Darroll picked the sticks up again, and jammed his foot against the kick pedal.

"Okay, one AND two AND three AND four..."

Darroll went to bed that night with sore hands, sore knees, a sore head, and a deep sense of gloom. They'd spent three whole hours in Rowdy's barn, with Rowdy trying grimly to install a sense of rhythm in Darroll's head, and glue the sticks to his hands in the right places and at the correct angles. By the end, he had begun to grasp the first principles by sheer force of repetition, but it was too little, he knew. There wasn't enough time. It didn't help that most of the songs they expected him to play were Chuck Milne's own compositions, and hence completely unfamiliar to him.

No, it was too little and too late, and tomorrow night was going to be a disaster of lameness. It was going to suck even by the normal, nerdy standards of the Psychopath Club. He lay on his bed flicking through an anodyne escapade of Archie and Jughead, wishing the swirls would come for him, but as he already knew, they never did come when he wanted them most. Eventually he found sleep, or sleep found him.

33

When he woke, he had a disconcerting feeling that Horsehead had been in his dreams again. But no memory of the dream remained intact, and within a few minutes, the worry faded away, followed shortly afterwards by the memory of his apprehension. He didn't miss it; his head was full enough of concern about the gig that evening.

The VFW post was an ugly, functional building on one of the short cross streets that linked the two longer main streets of Muldoon. An American flag flew limply outside it, and the big parking lot was long unrepaired, huge gaping holes marring the hardtop surface. There was a board at the front of the building, sun-faded, its movable letters warped and damaged by years of use. It advertised NEXT SATRDAY – DANCE – DREW VILJOEN AND HIS POLKA POODLS. No mention of this Satrday. For a moment Darroll was surprised at that; then he remembered that the caretaker and handyman at the VFW was Lucas Crowe, Ed Crowe's uncle.

The Serxner family truck already sat in the parking lot. Rowdy's father was helping unload his drum kit, while Rowdy himself stood by looking out of place and embarrassed, his wrist still bandaged up. Darroll could sympathise with Rowdy, for once. He felt out of place and embarrassed himself, and the urge to get back into the Oldsmobile and drive away again, very fast, almost overwhelmed him for a moment.

Instead, Darroll walked over to the truck. "Howdy, Mr Serxner."

"Howdy yourself, young Darroll." Oscar Serxner set down a drum next to a water-filled pothole, and reached out a hand. Darroll, knowing what was expected of him, shook it. He hated shaking hands. It was so artificial. Everyone's hand was always either too hot or too cold or too clammy or too limp, or else they grabbed your fingers so hard, you thought they were going to break them. Darroll hated that kind most of all.

Of course, being a farmer, Mr Serxner was a finger-breaker. The wild thought came to Darroll that if Oscar Serxner broke all his fingers, he wouldn't have to play drums tonight.

"You filling in for my boy tonight?" Serxner said with a chuckle. "Clumsy young fool, to get himself crocked."

"Aw, Dad," said Rowdy wearily, as if he was used to his father belittling him in front of his friends. "I didn't do it on purpose."

Maybe. Maybe he had done it on purpose to get out of the gig. Darroll shot Rowdy a quick, sharp look, but all he received in return was the standard, slow, bovine response from his pale grey eyes.

"That's the plan, Mr Serxner," Darroll responded.

"Well, good luck to you, boy," said Serxner senior. "I've lived in Muldoon most all my life, and we ain't never had a rock and roll band here. Not in forty years. Maybe you guys will have fans showing up here in ten years, just to see where you went to school and played your first gig." He chuckled, as if he knew how slim the chances of that were. Darroll certainly knew it.

"Well, this is our first time playing live. Anything can happen," Darroll said. He was annoyed at himself as he spoke for voicing such platitudes, but Oscar Serxner's entire life was made up of platitudes. He was that kind of man. If you spoke an original thought to him, he'd shy away from it, like a horse pecking at an obstacle in the road. It was simpler to descend to his level, simpler to just use platitudes rather than trying to drag his thoughts upward.

Luckily, Beth and Vanessa came out of the building at that point and gave Darroll the excuse to dodge away from Oscar Serxner. He picked up the kick-pedal for the bass drum and walked over. "Hey guys. How's it looking?"

"Grim," Vanessa said gloomily, "but did you expect anything else? Come on, get your ass inside and set up."

The inside of the VFW was as ugly and functional as the outside. The stage was at one end of the main room, with a bar (closed and shuttered) at the other. It wasn't even a permanent stage; it was made up of wooden segments, which could be moved and stacked up when the stage wasn't needed. The sound system consisted of precisely one microphone and one rickety-looking stand. Evidently Beth and Chuck were going to play through their amps.

Chuck was tuning his guitar on stage, and making a long job of it, frustration in his face. The other two occupants of the room were Chuck's little brother, Hal Milne, and another kid that Darroll didn't know. Presumably a friend of Hal's, given that the two of them were engaged in an animated argument.

"Where's Boardman?" Darroll asked Vanessa.

"I think he's on his way," she said. "We don't need him anyway, not yet."

Oscar Serxner strode past them, drum stool under one arm, hi-hat under the other, carrying them both as though they weighed no more than a couple of drumsticks.

"My mom's going to be here," Darroll said.

"That's a bad thing?" Vanessa picked up on the tone of Darroll's voice.

Darroll just nodded and gave her what he hoped was an expressive look.

"My folks won't be," Vanessa said. "None of their business what I do, and it's not like they care." She sounded quite cheerful about her parents' absence. Darroll envied her.

"Come on." Rowdy had approached them from behind as they talked. "Let's get the drums set up. If we hurry we can have a last practice as part of the soundcheck, before people get here."

Darroll couldn't even remember how the drums were set up, and had to get Rowdy to show him. Chuck watched, with growing resignation on his face. Beth plugged her bass in, and slung it over her shoulder. It was enormous, compared to her tiny frame. It looked as if it ought to drag her over with its weight, like a backhoe trying to lift too heavy a load. She plucked a few notes, and the low twangs echoed through the hall. Hal Milne and his friend stopped arguing, and looked up in anticipation.

Darroll pumped his foot on the pedal a couple of times, experimentally. Thump, thump, came the sound of the bass drum.

"Shut your noise up a few, guys," Chuck asked. "I'm still tuning."

Any guitarist who took as long to tune up as Chuck Milne

couldn't know his job very well, Darroll thought. He rose from the stool and walked forward, jumping off the stage.

"I need to piss," he grunted to Rowdy as he passed.

It wasn't all he needed. He needed to be away from the Club. They might be the closest he had to friends, but just now, he could scarcely bear the sight of them. They all revolted him. Fat Vanessa and her wobbling bosom, Beth's oversized glasses, Rowdy's hulking clumsy body.

At the back of the hall there were two doors, marked RESTROOMS and NO ADMITTANCE. He chose RESTROOMS, and then MEN as opposed to WOMEN. No DISABLED here, of course. If you were disabled in Muldoon, tough titty. Perhaps the VFW had been built before disabled people were invented. Although, Darroll reasoned, you'd have thought foreign wars were a good source of –

The thought broke off as he pushed open the door labelled MEN. Horsehead was in there, sitting on the shelf between two washbasins, swinging his legs casually, and reading a James Bond novel. The same edition that Darroll had picked up at the old farm. Could it be the same actual copy? Darroll tried to remember what he'd done with it. He couldn't.

"I told you I'd be here," Horsehead said, not looking up from his book.

"Did you?"

"Yes. Last night." He finally turned his head towards Darroll, one large inhuman eye studying him. "Oh, you forgot. Dear, dear. You need to focus upon your dreams more. If you forget your dreams, you will miss out on a great many things."

"Very philosophical," drawled Darroll.

"I mean it!" Horsehead swung his legs one last time, then slid down to a standing position. "I can't always advise you directly. Meeting in bathrooms all the time is less than dignified."

"So you got something to say to me?"

"Only this," Horsehead said. "Tonight is a turning point. Not just for you but for others. Even I don't know everything that's going to happen tonight, or as a consequence of tonight. But it's going to be a wild ride, Darroll, my friend. Such a shame, wasn't it, that your friend Rowdy came off his motorcycle? Such a shame."

He leaned down. Darroll had never been so close to Horsehead before. The brown colour of his head darkened to black around his mouth and huge nostrils, and his teeth were unexpectedly large and dangerous-looking. Also, there was a little crop of hair all over his muzzle, which Darroll had never noticed before. Darroll took a step backwards.

"Sorry," Horsehead said quickly, stepping back himself. "I didn't mean to loom. Easy for me to forget that you're shorter than me, in this dimension."

"You what?"

Horsehead waved one hand. To Darroll, it seemed an unnecessarily patronising gesture. "How matters appear to you is often different to how they truly are. Surely you must have realised that by now?"

"Well, yes. I think..."

"In a very real way, Darroll," Horsehead said quietly, "you are a giant among men. In some regards, you even dwarf me."

Darroll didn't know how to respond to that, so he said nothing.

"Anyway," Horsehead went on, "I shall be there tonight to watch you."

"Well," Darroll said drily, "it's a dollar to get in." He dug into his pocket and pulled out one of Chuck's flyers, handing it to Horsehead. The creature took it, and folded it in half with careful precision. Then he tucked it away in one of his own pockets, and pulled out a dollar bill, equally crisp, and also folded once.

"Uh, no. You pay Joe Boardman on the door. When he gets here."

"But I am already inside," smiled Horsehead. Darroll shrugged, and took the bill from him. A dollar was a dollar, he supposed.

As soon as the banknote left Horsehead's grasp, he turned toward one of the cubicles. "Enough for now. Until later, my friend."

He stepped inside and the door closed. The lock rattled, then rattled again.

Darroll stood, uncertain. There was no sound of anyone using the cubicle for its avowed purpose. After a few seconds, he stepped forward and pushed the door gingerly. It swung open. The lavatory was empty.

Stepping inside, Darroll verified that Horsehead was gone, then closed and locked the door again. He reached for the zip on his pants, then paused, opened the door, and chose the other cubicle instead. Somehow he didn't care to remain inside that first one.

When he emerged from the restroom, Beth Vines had left the stage and was standing by the door looking out, alongside Rowdy. Darroll joined them.

"Waiting for your friend Todd?" he asked, not bothering to keep contempt from his voice.

"Yeah. He said he'd be here. He promised."

"You know," Darroll went on, "staring into the street like a lost soul won't make him suddenly appear out of nowhere. He won't be coming. Why would he drive a hundred miles or more here, and a hundred back, to see four high school kids making fools of ourselves, in a concrete block building, in the dullest town in the Midwest?"

Beth stared up at him through her glasses. Darroll knew he'd hurt her. He had meant to. Cruel to be kind. Better for her to lose her dream now, than during the actual gig.

"I'm not saying he was right to promise he'd come, and get your hopes up. Sometimes... sometimes I guess it's easier to tell someone what they want to hear, even if you know they're going to have to find out the truth later on. That sucks. And Todd Krank sucks for not being better than that. I know you want him to be better than that; I know you think he's awesome. But he's just a guy with a guitar, who eats his dinner and brushes his hair and changes his boxers the same as anyone else, Beth. Right, Rowdy?"

Rowdy didn't say anything. He was too busy looking sorry for himself.

"Of course," Darroll added, one corner of his mouth twisting into an involuntary smile, "if this was television, Todd would drive up and turn into the parking lot right... about... now." He turned to face the street, and lifted one finger, ready to point it at the vehicle that would bring Todd Krank to the gig, that would prove Beth right and himself utterly wrong.

But no vehicle came, because this wasn't television, and after a few seconds Darroll let his hand drop back to his side.

"Darroll," Beth said in her quiet little voice, "lots of times I hate people for being wrong. But you? Right now I hate you for being right." She turned away and walked back inside, leaving Darroll there with Rowdy, and with a feeling that he hadn't exactly handled that situation well.

"Jeez, I was just saying," he muttered to Rowdy.

"She's a girl," Rowdy pointed out unnecessarily. "You have to be careful how you talk to them."

"Careful," growled Darroll, angry because he knew he'd been right about Todd and had put himself into the wrong by talking to Beth like an enormous jerk. "You're a fine one to talk about being careful. If you hadn't fallen off your bike – Hang on."

Darroll swung round, away from the door, and looked Rowdy in the eye, staring him down.

"You said you came off your bike because you were trying not to hit a squirrel, right?"

"Yeah." Rowdy's reply was guarded; too guarded.

"Definitely a squirrel?"

"Well, I didn't stop to take a photograph," Rowdy retorted.

"You sure it wasn't anything... larger?"

"What do you mean, Martock?" Definitely too guarded, now, and Darroll knew.

"You have to tell me this, Rowdy. Did you get knocked off your bike by – by a weird guy with a... a horse's head instead of a human one?"

The flash of fear in Rowdy's eyes was unmistakable. "What the hell are you talking about?" he blurted.

"Rowdy, you have to tell me. I won't tell anyone else, I won't breathe a word, but you have –"

Darroll's entreaty was cut short by the arrival of a vehicle in the parking lot. It turned in from the street too quickly, making a squeal of tyres, and then a scraping noise as its wheels traversed the loose gravel. Two more followed it. They pulled up in a loose row, and people started to emerge. The first one Darroll recognised was Ed Crowe; Patsy Young was there too, and Dig Doyle and Kirk Mondschein and three or four more of that crew.

"Aw, shit," breathed Rowdy, and dived back through the door. Crowe saw him retreat, and grinned sarcastically.

Darroll was half tempted to follow Rowdy, but two things stopped him. One was that he was frantically trying to analyse the expression he'd seen in Rowdy's face before Ed Crowe's arrival interrupted them. He was scared, all right, but was it fear due to learning that Darroll knew what had really made him fall off his bike? Or had Rowdy genuinely taken a tumble due to a squirrel in the road? Was Rowdy afraid that Darroll, talking about people with horse's heads, had suddenly flipped, lost his reason?

The other thing that stopped Darroll retreating after Rowdy was that he was tired of slinking and hiding. He hadn't realised it until now, but he was. So what if Ed Crowe had more muscle than him, and more money, and more friends? Ed Crowe couldn't do what Darroll could do. Ed Crowe couldn't travel between dimensions. Ed Crowe didn't have a friend with a horse's head who could... Darroll didn't know quite what Horsehead could or couldn't do; but he was pretty certain that he could stomp Ed Crowe into a grease spot, if he wanted. A smile spread over his face at the thought.

"What are you fucking grinning at, Martock, you retard?" Crowe swaggered up to him and performed his usual trick of invading his target's personal space, standing six inches too near and leaning toward them.

"Nothing," Darroll muttered, discarding six separate smartass retorts that would get his ass pounded by Crowe, until all he was fit for was filling potholes in the parking lot. Not yet, he told himself. Soon, but not yet.

Crowe gave him a shove – not enough of one to send him flying, or even to signify the start of a fight; more of a perfunctory gesture, as if he knew it was expected of him. Dig Doyle snickered on cue, and the whole party shouldered their way past Darroll and into the building.

"Dollar to get in," Darroll heard Joe Boardman say from inside.

"Fuck off, faggot." Ed Crowe's reply was equally audible.

Darroll took a deep breath and went back inside. Joe Boardman was sitting behind the table at the door, wearing a frown. The box into which Ed Crowe's bunch ought to have put a buck each remained almost empty.

"Well, shoot," Boardman remarked with faux cheerfulness to Darroll. "What do I do? They just pushed straight past me. Haven't paid a dime."

Darroll looked over to where Crowe's brigade was milling around in front of the stage, grinning at Chuck and Vanessa ominously. "The way I figure this," he added, quietly so that only Boardman could hear, "they're here to bust the gig up. Not getting a dollar out of them is gonna be the least of our problems."

Boardman turned to look too, and nodded slowly. "Shit... this is gonna mean trouble."

"Whose parents are coming?" Darroll asked. "I know Vanessa's aren't. My mother will be here in a moment, but she's completely useless."

"I think Beth's might," Joe said. "Chuck's folks definitely are. That's his kid brother over there."

"And Rowdy's father's here somewhere. Shit, I wish Rowdy hadn't screwed his wrist up. He's the only one of us who can fight worth a damn."

"If he'd been on the door, we might at least have gotten a few bucks out of those jerks," Joe said.

Darroll shook his head. "I need him at the front when we start playing. If he doesn't give me the signal, I won't have any idea when we're getting to the end of a song, and I'll just keep playing and sound fucking awful."

Speaking of Rowdy, he was gesturing at Darroll. When Darroll didn't move, Rowdy came over to him instead.

"Ten minutes, Chuck says."

"Okay. You sure you're good to warn me when we hit the last verse of a song?"

"Yeah, yeah," Rowdy promised.

* * *

Fifteen minutes later the four of them were on stage. Darroll was deeply glad that the drummer sat at the back, where it was harder for people to look at him, and also harder for him to look out and see Ed Crowe and Patsy Young's sneering faces. He had a drumstick in each hand, he had a sheet of paper with the setlist and crib-notes in Rowdy's big scrawly handwriting taped to the floor, and he would still sooner have been anywhere else in the entire universe.

The first song was one of Chuck's, and Chuck had moved that to be the opening number purely because it began with four bars of bass solo from Beth Vines. Beth was standing sideways on to Darroll, the neck of her bass pointing out into the audience; pointing straight at Patsy Young's head, as a matter of fact. A number of others were out there, now, as well as Ed Crowe's group. A few kids from the grade below Darroll at Straus High, Chuck Milne's parents looking completely out of their element, and his mother, looking, God help him, proud, as though the charade they were about to go through was anything to make a mother proud of her son. Beth's lips moved, counting silently, one two three four, plunk plunk ker-plunk, plunk plunk ker-plunk. "Come in on 2nd beat 4th bar," the instructions on the sheet read. Darroll drew in a deep breath.

Plunk plunk plunk, went Beth's bass, and Darroll came in on what he hoped was his cue, two three fo-our. Chuck's guitar chimed in on the first beat of the next bar, and Darroll flailed away, multiples of four stacking up in his head, like the chairs stacked up at the side of the room. He caught a quick glimpse of his mother again, pride gleaming upon her face, as Vanessa's vocals began, singing something about how no matter how hard she tried she couldn't live and she couldn't die.

Three minutes passed glacially. Darroll almost dropped a stick, somehow retrieved it, missed half a bar in surprise at his own deftness in not dropping it, and found the beat again. He suddenly realised that he'd forgotten to use his foot pedal all through the song, and had just been playing on the snare and the tom. Too late now, he decided. Next song.

Rowdy was making increasingly wild gestures at him from the side of the audience and Darroll realised, from what little he could hear of Vanessa's singing, that they were approaching the end of the song at perilous speed, like Thelma and Louise thundering towards the edge of the Grand Canyon. He caught Rowdy's eye, and mentally crossed his fingers. Time to wrap up... now...

Chuck smacked a last chord from the guitar. Beth's arm dropped to her side. Vanessa's voice held a last long note. And Darroll let go a breath that he hadn't realised he'd been holding. No matter what else, they'd at least reached the end of the song in unison. He wished he had the confidence and skill to have done a little drum fill at the end there, but what the hell.

There was some desultory applause, mostly from Chuck's parents. Ed Crowe and Patsy Young were laughing. Kirk Mondschein was exaggeratedly miming vomiting.

"Hey there, Muldoon," Vanessa said into the vocal mike. Darroll had to admit she sounded confident, whether or not she actually was. "It's forty years late but who gives a fuck? Rock and roll finally made it to this city. We're Horsehead!"

One isolated cheer came from Hal Milne. It tailed off into an embarrassed giggle.

"Next song's our take on a PJ Harvey number," Vanessa went on. Darroll looked down at his cribsheet and gripped his sticks tighter.

Two lines into the song, the power went out.

For a second, the only sound was the faint twang of unamplified electric guitars, and the contralto growl of Vanessa Murchison's voice. Next moment the guitars died away, Vanessa changed the lyrics of the line she was singing to "...what the fuck?", and Ed Crowe leapt up onto the stage shrieking wildly, and tried to grab Chuck's guitar out of his hands.

Of course. Darroll had been getting ready to curse their lousy luck that a power cut should strike their first ever gig, but it made far more sense that that bastard Ed Crowe had just cut them off at the fuse-box.

Crowe almost succeeded in his attack by sheer surprise; Chuck Milne let go of his guitar as Crowe grabbed at it. Crowe tried to hop back off the stage with his stolen trophy, but was foiled by the strap that held the instrument round Chuck's neck. Chuck gasped as the strap pulled tight, and Crowe stumbled.

Vanessa hurled the microphone down, with a force that would have deafened everyone in the room had the mike still been live, and jumped off the stage to confront gangling, blond, stupid Kirk Mondschein, who was readying for a run-up to join Crowe. It was like watching an apple square off against a stalk of corn. Down came Vanessa and she smacked straight into Kirk, nullifying his own momentum, and sending him spinning aside to land in a gasping heap. A second later the heap gasped some more. Vanessa threw herself on top of him, spitting in fury, and began to pummel him with her fists.

Darroll didn't like to think what it must be like to have Vanessa Murchison punch you.

Alongside him, Beth Vines was somehow still playing, staring rigidly through her glasses, fingers plucking the bass with worryingly precise timing. Hell with this, Darroll decided. I need to be out of this shit.

He hopped up from his stool, shoved the hi-hat cymbal over in his haste to escape, and vamoosed off the side of the stage.

Faces loomed in front of him and were gone as he ran and dived between bodies. Somehow, there seemed to be more people in here, now that the lights were off, than there had been when they were playing. He saw Rowdy Serxner staring around in disbelief, or more likely incomprehension, and Chuck Milne's mother with her face screwed up trying to make sense of the darkness and her surroundings, and then his own mother, her hand clapped to her mouth in a frozen expression of dismay. Darroll didn't know anyone else who did that. It looked so fake. He was convinced that his mom had picked the habit up from watching television.

He dodged her, thinking he was headed for the door, but realised he'd lost his bearings in the dark when he almost stumbled over Vanessa. She was still sitting astride Kirk Mondschein, who wasn't moving any more. Darroll wondered if he was even breathing any more. He grabbed Vanessa's arm. "Let's get the fuck out," he yelled at her as loud as he could, hoping she could discern his voice.

She half-stood up, half-let Darroll heave her to her feet. She didn't weigh as much as Darroll had imagined. Dig Doyle swung a fist at him; Darroll swung one back, with the arm that wasn't holding Vanessa, and only as he made contact with Doyle did he realise he was still clutching his drumsticks in that hand. The sticks jabbed at the side of Doyle's face and he yelped with pain, allowing Darroll to evade him and drag Vanessa past him.

As he looked around, a beam of light came from a suddenly opened door; Darroll saw someone run out through it. He tugged Vanessa's arm, and the two of them squeezed outside and into the parking lot.

After the darkness inside, the light made him blink. "Are you okay?" Darroll gasped to Vanessa, and she nodded. Rowdy ran past them, yelling wordlessly, headed for his father's truck. Darroll suddenly realised that Rowdy's dad was sitting in the truck, head back, asleep; he hadn't been in the hall.

Rowdy came within an ace of being hit by another truck turning into the parking lot from the street; it honked its horn, Rowdy stumbled aside, and the truck pulled up with a squeal.

At least it wasn't a cop car, Darroll thought, and then someone hit him from behind and made him stagger. It was Ed Crowe, with Chuck Milne's guitar clutched in his hands. Vanessa grabbed at him, but he shoved her aside and broke into a run.

The run lasted for exactly two steps. Then somebody tall loomed up in front of Crowe, and formed a solid barrier into which he charged, full tilt.

"Whoof," panted Ed Crowe.

"Shall I take that?" asked Todd Krank.

He plucked the guitar from Crowe's suddenly loose grip, and in a seamless movement lifted it away from Crowe, around his own body, and out to an angle of ninety degrees sideways. As he completed the movement, Casey stepped up from behind Todd, and took the guitar, leaving Todd's hands empty. He brought them both up in front of him as fists, in case Ed Crowe had any fight left in him.

Crowe didn't. He sat down on his ass, unfortunately avoiding all the puddles around him, and looked to have no further interest in anything except holding his own midriff and gasping.

The lights inside the hall flickered on again. Krank and Casey exchanged a glance, then stepped forward into the building. Darroll followed. As they entered, the plunk-booming sound of a solo electric bass echoed out of the door.

Above the milling chaos on the dance floor, Beth Vines was still playing methodically on stage. She had sat down cross-legged on her amplifier, and was hunched over the instrument, almost hugging it. For a second she stared straight at Krank and Casey. She had to see them, Darroll thought, she had to know who they were; but she didn't stop until she reached the end of the song's bass part. Then she finally put her bass aside carefully on a stand, hopped down from the stage (a big jump, for so small a woman), and walked over to the door, looking neither left nor right.

"Thanks for coming," she said, her small voice cutting through the surrounding noise like a descending blade.

"I said I would," Todd said simply, as though it went without saying that any promise made by Todd Krank would permit no force in the universe to break it.

"Would this be your friend's?" Casey said politely, holding out the guitar to Beth.

"It's Chuck's," said Beth. Darroll looked around and saw Chuck approaching them, limping slowly and painfully.

"Where's Joe?" asked Vanessa. Then she gasped as she saw Joe lying on the floor by the door. He wasn't moving. She ran over to him. Darroll followed, more slowly.

"Oh my god, Joe!" cried out Vanessa as she dropped to her knees and stared at him, curled in a ball, holding his stomach, eyes closed. "Joe? Are you okay? Did they stab you?"

Joe didn't open his eyes, but he did open his mouth. "Don't be clueless, Vanessa. This isn't Detroit."

34

Half an hour later, Darroll stood with his hands in his pockets, watching Horsehead play the balance of their debut live gig. Their audience comprised nine people, five of whom were the band members' families. Todd Krank cut a suave figure sitting on Rowdy's drum stool. "Well, I don't really play drums," he'd said with a studied smile as Rowdy Serxner explained what had happened, "but given how determined you guys have been to rock..."

And Beth had almost swooned on the spot.

Of course Vanessa and Chuck tumbled over each other to say yes, yes, if the great Todd Krank would deign to sit in on drums with such unworthy acolytes...

The fact that Darroll had already substituted for Rowdy, and played one song and one-tenth, wasn't even mentioned. So Darroll didn't mention it either. He just stood at the back, and stared at Todd as he played.

He was only distracted when someone plucked at his sleeve alongside him. It was Casey.

"Wanna come outside, dude? Wanna smoke?" Casey's voice was barely audible over the music. He illustrated the words by holding two fingers up to his mouth. Miming a cigarette.

Why not.

Outside the sun had finished setting, leaving only a faint red glow in the west, and stars were coming out. It was starting to grow cold, the way it always did in Muldoon as soon as the sun set. Casey leaned on the side of the Typhoids' truck, and took a battered metal case out of his pocket, followed by a small and thoroughly functional-looking little pipe. Darroll leaned on the van alongside Casey and watched him at work.

"So Todd brought you along, huh?" Darroll said after a few seconds, to break the silence. He preferred silence himself, but he figured he ought to make some effort to be sociable, if Casey was going to let him smoke his dope.

"'Myeah," said Casey. "I go around with him. All the time, I mean. Some people think I'm his boyfriend. I'm not," he added, "we're both straight. I just hang out." He returned the metal case to his pocket and pulled out a lighter instead, clicking it into action. "Interesting things happen around Todd. He's that sort of guy."

He drew on the pipe. Darroll watched. After what seemed to Darroll a longer time than it probably was, Casey exhaled, and offered Darroll the pipe and lighter.

Darroll took one in each hand and looked at Casey. "I'm a newbie," he said, hating himself for confessing it; and yet there was something about Casey that made the confession feel comparatively easy, almost safe. He had to remind himself that this was a guy he'd met only once before. He didn't even know if Casey was his first or his last name.

"Oh yeah, course you are. Okay, you light the lighter, hold it over the bowl till the payload glows orange. Keep your thumb over that little hole, and breathe air in through the bowl. Then when you're running out of lung space, let your thumb go from the hole, and that lets air through. Easy after you've done it a few times," Casey promised.

Darroll stuck the pipe into his mouth, over to one side so that he could talk out of the other. He felt like Popeye the Sailor. "Go on," Casey encouraged, seeing him hesitate.

After a couple of false starts, Darroll produced a flame from the lighter, and managed to inhale a lungful. He just about managed to conquer a fit of coughs that jumped on him from ambush, and breathed out in a hurry.

"Spot on, bo," Casey said. Darroll undertook a quick stock-take of his body. It seemed much as it ought, save for his lungs still grumbling about the unusual duties they'd been put to.

"Hey, Casey, what's your name? I mean, is it Something Casey, or Casey Something?"

"Would you believe," Casey said, with a wry look, "that I was actually christened Casey Jones?"

There was something in his look that gave him away. "No," Darroll said.

"Quite right, because I wasn't. John Casey's the actual name. But everyone calls me Casey, because who the hell is called John? It's the stupidest, blandest, white-breadest name you can give a boy. Only people with no imagination call their son John."

"I think your parents would like my mom," Darroll remarked, and Casey gave him a look of sympathy.

"Yours too, huh? Tough breaks, kid. Of course if you put the name the other way around, like in public records – Casey, John – it sounds like Casey Jones, so I get all the jokes anyway. Any more questions for me, while you're here?"

"Is it possible to simultaneously hate someone, and want to be them?"

Darroll didn't know why he asked that. The words just came out of his mouth on their own, with no conscious volition behind them.

Casey claimed back the pipe and lighter, and held them motionless, still leaning against the van, his head turned toward Darroll.

"Now that's an interesting question," Casey drawled. "Is my stash hitting your philosophy button? Sativa will do that."

"Guess it must be that," Darroll said, pondering the question himself.

"Todd, right?"

"Todd." Darroll nodded. "He – Look, can I say this? You're his best friend, yeah?"

"Oh, believe me," Casey said, "I can understand. Some folks don't like Todd, and the ones who don't, tend to really not like him. He's a guy it's hard to feel neutral toward. Do I take it there's jealousy involved?"

"Or envy. I don't know whether I want him to be less of a poser, or whether I want the... uh, the sheer nerve to go round like he does all the time. He never even seems to think he's doing anything unusual."

Casey lit the pipe again. After taking his hit, he said, "You still at school, right? Would you not be having the greatest time there ever, am I correct?"

"Pretty much."

"Thought so. Let me give you the history. I'm from Washington state originally, but we moved east, and I wound up at high school with Todd. He wasn't called Todd then. We were both pretty unpopular. Too many brain cells, not enough muscle. Helped rescue each others' bikes from trees more than once, yeah?"

Darroll nodded.

"Well, you might not want to let Todd know that you know this, but it's as much my story as it is his so I'm damned if I don't tell you," Casey said with frankness. "One day we were hanging out together and making death lists... we used to do that, fantasise about becoming superheroes or dictators, about being In Control somehow, anyway. And then we'd debate how to kill everyone who ever made our lives miserable, and the order we'd rub them all out in. Sick, huh?"

Darroll didn't think that sounded sick at all. Darroll did that himself.

"Anyhoo, one day we decided we'd had as much as we could stand of being the bottom of the hierarchy. Even the goddamn handbell team beat us up! We decided that from that moment, we were going to change. Not be victims any more. Be people who had a right to be who we were, where we were, when we were. Well," he went on, "I don't think the new me lasted a week. With me, you get pretty much exactly what you see, yeah? But Todd... Todd's change stuck. Todd is the same person now that he became that day. He literally rethought himself. I don't know how the hell he pulled it off," Casey said, turning the pipe round and round in his hand. His fingers had calluses on the end, from his guitar strings. "Perhaps Todd, the Todd who everyone sees now, the Todd who goes round acting the rock star and the alpha male, was inside Mike Rugeley all along. Perhaps he just came out all ready formed, like an airbag out of your steering wheel. Or perhaps his spirit was floating round the atmosphere all ready formed and looking for a host, and saw its chance with Todd. Either way, that's who Todd is, and that's why."

Darroll couldn't decide whether he was impressed or not.

"Did it work?" he said. "I mean, did people start to respect you?"

"Sorta," said Casey. "At least, they respected Todd within days.

And soon after, when Todd made it plain I was still his number one friend, I picked up the side effects from it. I finished high school under Todd's umbrella. It didn't do vast amounts for my own self esteem, but it sure made life easier."

"Wow," Darroll said. "This stuff makes you spill the beans, doesn't it?"

"Don't worry, dude," said Casey reassuringly. "Anything either of us says here goes no further, right?"

"Right," promised Darroll. It felt strange to be taken into Casey's confidence. It reminded Darroll of something, but his buzzed brain took a few seconds to work out what; Vickery. Here was a second adult, like Vickery, who was treating him as another adult. Okay, Casey was younger than Vickery, only a few years Darroll's senior, but what did that matter?

"Oh, and within a month," Casey added as an afterthought, interrupting Darroll's musings, "Todd was playing guitar and writing songs. Sure, he'd played trombone before, but guitar, never. And within another month he had me learning too. When he started, somehow there was no way I wasn't going to follow suit. And after that – "

Casey broke off as both of them became suddenly aware of a figure, looming up at them out of the darkness. The pipe and lighter disappeared into Casey's palms, and his hands slipped into his pockets. For a moment, Darroll had a deep, unreasoning panic that it was Horsehead, but a second sufficed to dispel that worry; it was only Rowdy Serxner. He sniffed, twice, and a frown formed on his face.

"Have you two been... smoking drugs?"

Just like Rowdy. In Rowdy's world, there were cigarettes and tobacco and things it was legal to own and smoke, and there were drugs. Rowdy would exhibit the same knee-jerk moral indignation towards cannabis as he would if he'd come upon Casey injecting heroin into Darroll's veins, right there in the parking lot. And he'd probably describe both as "smoking drugs". Darroll wanted to be angry with Rowdy, but when he tried, he found he was so relaxed, so empty of negative feelings, that he could find nothing more than mild pity for him. Very strange. Was it down to the recent tumult of events, or just Casey's pipe?

"Relax, mister straight edge," Casey told Rowdy. "I thought you were meant to be a drummer? Can't be a proper drummer if you don't enjoy a little recreation now and again."

Rowdy looked as disapproving as it was possible for his big, square face to look, which wasn't very.

"You'll get into trouble, Darroll."

"No, I won't, because I'm not a complete fucking imbecile. Anyway, I only smoked it because Casey was here." Darroll found it was easier to be angry at himself, for taking the trouble to defend himself against Rowdy's simplistic morality, than it was to feel anger against Rowdy himself.

"Yeah, with your mother only just inside? Not cool," said Rowdy. "Anyway, they finished playing, and I need to wake my dad up, so we can shift all the kit back out of the building."

"Okey-dokey-doo," drawled Casey. "Playtime's over, kids. Time to find out what being a musician is all about. It's spending two hours moving heavy shit around and playing cat's cradle with cables, so you can play for twenty minutes to a bunch of pencil necks who write bad reviews of you on their Livejournals, because you didn't play any covers of what few songs they know."

But Casey pitched in and played roadie, despite his cynicism. So did Todd. Darroll again wanted to be angry – why else would Todd be helping out, except because he wanted to impress Beth Vines? – but he couldn't summon up the anger. The reservoir of rage inside him, that normally brimmed over, dark and deep enough for sea-serpents to swim in its depths, had run dry. It was giving out the sort of bubbling, coughing noises that the school water fountain did when its tank was empty and nobody had remembered to change it. A few dribbles of annoyance came out when he worked at it, but the comforting reserves of hatred he normally would have called upon? Gone.

It worried Darroll to have no anger to call upon. It felt wrong, something missing. It was that pipe of Casey's. He decided he wasn't going to smoke anything, any more, ever again. Then he recalled that, if he adopted that resolution, he'd be following Rowdy Serxner's advice, and that was scarcely what he wanted on any subject.

He was still turning the matter over in his mind by the time the loading was finished. Rowdy drove away with his father, the Milnes left, and Joe Boardman slipped quietly away as he always did. All of a sudden it was just Vanessa and Beth, and Todd and Casey, and Darroll himself and his mother, all standing in the parking lot outside the closed and locked building.

Beth was looking at Todd, clutching her guitar case as though she wished it too had a perfect hairstyle and a languid pose. Vanessa was standing by Beth, clearly ready to intercede if Beth did make a sudden grab for Todd.

But she didn't. She just stood there, silently, as time ticked by. And eventually Todd spoke.

"Lively evening, huh?"

Casey smiled, loyally, but said nothing. And Beth still didn't speak, so Vanessa did.

"Yeah. Thanks for helping us out, Mr Krank."

"Mr Krank is my father," said Todd, which made Casey snort with laughter. Todd corrected himself. "Okay, he's not called that, but please don't call me Mister. It grates so." His hand went up to straighten his hair yet again. "In any case, the pleasure was mine, I assure you."

Darroll narrowed his eyes, trying to decide whether Todd was being genuine or sarcastic. It was so hard to tell with Todd.

"But Casey and I really need to move. We've a long drive in the dark ahead, and my lights aren't one hundred percent reliable. That's band vans. It's a law of nature that there's always something wrong with them. You'll find out."

Darroll's mother made a move, as if to speak, and Darroll suddenly worried that she was going to invite Todd and Casey to stay overnight, to sleep on the sofa or something.

"Come on, mom," he said quickly, before she could say whatever she was going to say. "I'm way tired."

He turned his back on Casey and Todd, and began to walk towards his car. As he did so he realised someone was following him. He looked over his shoulder expecting to see Casey, but instead, it was Vanessa.

"Hey, Darroll," she said, more quietly than her usual voice, "thanks for getting me out of there earlier."

Darroll hardly knew how to respond. He had no objection to taking credit for it, but really, he hadn't put any conscious thought into it.

"I didn't put any conscious thought into it," he repeated aloud to Vanessa.

"So?" Vanessa didn't seem discouraged. "Life isn't about what you think, it's about what you do. Didn't you ever do the right thing without thinking before?"

Darroll shook his head cautiously.

Vanessa stepped up to him, and before he could retreat, threw both arms round him and drew him close against her. Darroll tensed. He could smell her weird gothic perfume, and since he'd closed his eyes the moment she touched him, that was the only sensory input his head could work with, until she released him and he opened them again.

Vanessa giggled a little, a girlish sound very different from her usual studied cynicism. "I didn't think about that," she said, and she turned to beat a retreat.

A horn honked; Casey at the wheel of the Typhoids' truck, on its way out of the lot. Todd sitting beyond him in the shotgun seat, like a king on his throne. Casey had the window down and one elbow resting on the ledge. The hand corresponding to the elbow was holding the pipe. "Later, man," called out Casey as the vehicle plunged forwards. Darroll raised his hand in silent farewell as it turned onto the street and was lost to sight.

On Darroll's way home, in the passenger seat of his mother's car, he thought back to the first meeting of the Psychopath Club. God, how things had changed. Not just for him, of course. Look at Rowdy, playing in a band and everything. He'd never have had the courage when Darroll first knew him, making stumbling speeches about Jack the Ripper.

Thinking of Jack the Ripper reminded him of Horsehead, and of his words earlier that evening.

The next time he saw Horsehead, he ought to ask him whether he knew who Jack the Ripper was, the mysterious guy who'd slid his knife between the ribs of Whitechapel prostitutes like a key sliding into the ignition of a car. It seemed like the sort of thing that Horsehead might know.

Then he decided that he didn't want to ask Horsehead, after all.

Because if Horsehead didn't know, he'd only be disappointed. And if Horsehead did know? Then he'd be terrified.

And he had a wild, unreasoning, but growing conviction that Horsehead knew; that he knew more about death and dead people than anyone else, ever.

Also, he had a suspicion verging on certainty that when the lights had gone out earlier, and the brawl had started, Horsehead had been in that hall.

35

It was a Saturday morning when Darroll got the swirls in his car for the first time. It was March, and it was cold like every March in Muldoon, like every month in Muldoon.

He had remained in bed for a long time after waking, intermittently drowsing and looking at comics, until the need to visit the bathroom had driven him forth. The bathroom floor was cold as he pissed into the bowl; it was like standing on an iceberg. Little clouds of steam rose from his urine. He held his breath until he was done. He didn't want to be inhaling the tainted vapor of his own piss.

He considered going back to bed, but it was a clear day outside, the first after four grey wet ones, and he was hungry as well. So he dressed, breakfasted hastily, and picked up his car keys. There would be nothing to do in Muldoon, of course, but he might as well do nothing out in the cold air and sunshine. It beat doing nothing at home.

And then, two blocks from Celebration Burger, he felt the swirls coming on. For a second he felt only panic; what the hell should he do now? He could imagine all too clearly being jerked from one universe to the next while travelling at thirty miles an hour, and he couldn't think of any positive outcome.

Thankfully, there was plenty of space at the roadside for him to park quickly. He stumbled out, slamming the door, and tottered into the entrance of one of the boarded-up buildings that were common in this part of town. He crouched down. He could smell piss. Not his own. Probably some drunk guy had relieved himself here in the last few days, on his way home from a bar. Needing to piss was like the swirls. When the need came upon you, you had to do something about it.

That was the last thought Darroll had before the swirls became the deep, solid blackness between dimensions, and for a couple of seconds, he knew nothing.

Returning to awareness, the first thing he noticed was that the smell of urine had gone. Like the spider that vanished in the basement, it was the little things that signalled that he'd transferred from one world to another. In this world, the guy going home from the bar had visited the restroom in the bar before leaving, or waited till he made it home, or relieved his bladder in one of the other doorways along the street. Or perhaps he'd decided, fuck it, I'm not going to the bar tonight, I'm just going to stay home and drink beer here instead.

The second thing that he noticed was missing, which he spotted a few moments after, was his car. It was no longer parked next to him; he had a clear view right across the street. Evidently, whatever he'd done this day in this universe – if he was even alive here – he hadn't driven the Oldsmobile downtown. A prickle ran down his spine. What would have happened if the swirls had shunted him between worlds in the car? Would he have appeared in mid-air in this world, with no car and no support, to crash to the ground and roll down the street at bone-breaking speed, perhaps to be hit by another car?

He finally rose to his feet from the crouch he'd fallen into in the doorway, and stepped onto the sidewalk, looking up and down the street. There was nobody in sight in either direction. Not unusual for this part of town, but it meant there was no easy way to tell what status Darroll held in this world; ghost, doppelganger or Normal All American Kid. Shrugging, he walked toward the center of Muldoon. He would find out soon enough. He rehearsed a few lines mentally which he could use if he ran into anyone who treated him as a revenant.

As it happened, he met nobody until he was in front of Celebration Burger. He glanced through the window, and there inside was Vanessa Murchison, dressed in a purple velvet blouse the size of a tent, with braid and sequins decorating it, pushing french fries into her mouth like logs going into a sawmill. He hesitated for a couple of seconds, then jerked the door open and stepped inside. The warm smell of grilled meat drove the last remaining hints of the shop doorway from his nostrils.

Vanessa turned to look at him, and her face registered surprise. Darroll quickly rehearsed again what he, in the role of ghost, could say to Vanessa. He already knew she wasn't scared of him as a spirit; it would be fruitless to tell her he'd come to take her away to the afterlife, or any bullshit like that. The urge came over him, instead, to give her some piece of profound wisdom from the grave. Except he couldn't think of anything.

Luckily, he didn't have to. Vanessa spoke.

"Darroll? What the hell are you doing here? You told me you were down in Georgia, visiting your father." She rose from her seat, strode over to him, and without any warning, enveloped him in a firm embrace, her warm lips seeking his.

Whatever else Darroll had expected, it wasn't that. He was too taken aback to resist, or even to turn his head, as Vanessa planted a smacker squarely on his mouth.

After a couple of seconds, she ended the kiss, released the embrace, and took one step back. "Well, what happened?" she asked. "Did the trip get cancelled or something?"

Okay, Darroll thought. This is a world in which Vanessa Murchison kisses me routinely. We must be dating. Christ, what the hell was this world's Darroll thinking? Although this world's Vanessa knew how to kiss. He licked his lips surreptitiously. There was a faint aftertaste of Vanessa on them. Even though it was mingled with the aftertaste of Celebration Burger's fries, he didn't find it unpleasant.

"Yeah," he said, with studied vagueness. "Yeah, Dad had to go to Miami, with his business." He named a city half at random. "So I'm, uh, here."

"Well, how about that?" Vanessa beamed at him. "I thought this weekend was gonna be a total bust. Things just started looking so much better."

Darroll assessed the position quickly. Presumably, the Darroll who belonged in this universe was indeed in Georgia, visiting his father. Vanessa had kindly dropped that info in his lap. And if that were so, the coast would be clear, up here in Muldoon, for him to fill his twin's shoes.

He could agree with Vanessa's conclusion. Instead of being a busted weekend, things had, indeed, just gotten so much better.

He hoped that down in Georgia, right about now, the Darroll Martock who called this universe home was punching his father right on the snoot.

"There isn't a club meeting, is there?" he asked, with the air of someone temporarily forgetting a minor social engagement.

"Well, of course not, idiot," Vanessa said. The last word was spoken, not with scorn, but with indulgent amusement. "You weren't gonna be here for it, were you? So we held it over to next week. Did you forget?"

Darroll took his cue from Horsehead, and didn't answer that question, asking one of his own instead. "Do you want to just hang out?"

"Of course," Vanessa smiled, and gave him another hug; this one not a full-face double-arm affair, but one arm around him, side to side, her left ear bumping gently against his right one. She scooped up a handful of fries. "Come on, let's go."

And they went.

* * *

Darroll had never spent so long in the company of one single person of his own age before, far less a girl. He was surprised to find himself enjoying the hell out of it, even though – or perhaps because – they were essentially just wasting time together. First they wandered aimlessly around the streets of Muldoon, talking; then, at Vanessa's suggestion, they walked out of town and down the road to the town's burial ground. The space occupied, in another universe, by Darroll's own gravestone was empty, devoid of any marker. Looked like his twin from this world really was alive and well, down in Georgia.

Vanessa wandered round the stones for a spell, reading out names and inscriptions. Then she sat on a grass bank at the back of the cemetery, and beckoned Darroll to join her. When he did, she started making out with him.

Darroll tensed up as soon as she started. His twin in this dimension might be a man of the world, but Darroll wasn't. More worrying still, he had a suspicion that the more intimate Vanessa became with him, the more likely she'd realise everything was not as it seemed.

Sure enough, after a couple of minutes, Vanessa sat back and looked at Darroll. "What's wrong?" she asked, matter of factly. "Don't tell me you're upset at not being in Georgia. You've told me often enough how much you despise your father. Aren't you over the moon at not having to go visit the old bastard?"

"Yeah," Darroll said, mind looking for an excuse frantically. "Only now, I'm gonna have to go visit again soon, and it's gonna be hanging over me instead of being over and done with."

He could tell from the look on Vanessa's face that his response was plausible enough to satisfy her. "Oh, honey," she said, and leaned back in to kiss him again. "You always see the darkness and never the light, don't you? It's no wonder we're such soulmates, sitting here in the middle of death's domain."

Darroll's initial reaction to that statement was amusement, but he kept a straight face. And he had to admit there was something not unattractive in this situation. Sitting in a burial ground, on a cold, sunny day, looking out over the graves with a woman who kept kissing him, unprompted? Yeah. He was going to have to spend some time analysing this afterwards.

But meantime, he let Vanessa kiss him some more, and tried to relax, though that wasn't easy when she started using her tongue, and he found himself getting an erection. He wasn't sure whether she knew it, and luckily, she didn't seem inclined to send her hands exploring below his waist. After some time, she sat back again, and took out a pack of menthol cigarettes. "Sure I can't tempt you?" she said, selecting one from the packet.

What the hell, Darroll suddenly thought. "What the hell," he said aloud. "Lemme try one."

"Whoa," Vanessa exclaimed. "I finally corrupted you, huh? Is this what they mean by taking a relationship to the next level?" She extracted a second cigarette from the packet and passed it to him.

Once lit, it tasted very different to the dope he'd smoked with Casey and Todd, and he wasn't at all sure that he liked it. He tried to conceal his doubts, but Vanessa's eyes were sharp enough to see through him.

"Not so keen, Darroll?"

He took another draw on it, and exhaled. "I could maybe get used to it," he prevaricated.

"Well, don't do it just because I do," Vanessa warned him. "It's not healthy, and it costs big bucks when you add it all up."

But he smoked the whole cigarette down to a stub, and then crushed it out in the long grass where they were sitting.

"Darroll?" she said, looking not at him but into the middle distance, contemplatively. Darroll suspected that she had stolen that look from television, and practised it assiduously. Like his mother. Except that when Vanessa pulled that trick, the thought amused him more than it annoyed him.

"Mmm?" Non-committal.

She reached inside her outer garment; her jacket, or drape, or whatever you called those things fat girls wore, that went over their arms but didn't fasten in the middle. They looked like the icing on top of a cupcake.

"I created something for you," she said, and pulled out a folded sheet of paper. Not just ordinary paper; it looked like expensive artist's paper, which also made it look as though folding it in quarters, which Vanessa had, was disrespectful to it.

Created, thought Darroll. Not 'did', not 'made'. Vanessa created things.

He unfolded the paper. He had to admit it was good. A sharp-fanged vampire, stereotyped in looks but not in dress, his widow's peak half hidden behind a blue work-cap and wearing overalls, was gleefully biting the neck of a beautiful, screaming woman. Behind them was a rental truck. On the side of it, TRUCK HIRE had been painted over, graffiti-style, so that it read TRUCK VAMPIRE. Overhead a full moon bulged in the sky, and three bats, each with cute little vampire fangs and grins, flapped around.

"You did this?"

Nod.

"For me?"

"Yeah."

He looked at the drawing again. The thought came to him that perhaps she meant the vampire to be him and the victim her.

"Can you keep hold of it for now?" he asked. "I'd have to put it in my jeans pocket, and it'd get creased to hell."

"Sure," she said, returning it to the mysterious holding area, somewhere inside her clothing. She stood up, and he followed suit.

"You know last week I said that I might want to go further with you, Darroll?" she said, not quite looking him in the face.

"Yeah?"

"I'm pretty sure I do."

Oh, shit. Ohhh, shit.

Darroll turned around for a second, staring into the long tangle of grass that grew high against the back fence of the cemetery.

"Darroll?"

Finding no inspiration in the grass, he turned back around.

"I think I do too," he said. "But I'm not sure I want it to be today."

He hadn't known whether he would have the strength to say that, until the words actually came out. Well, he thought, I've done my equivalent in this world the biggest favor I ever did anyone. Let's hope someone, in some dimension, pays it forward for me.

Vanessa looked disappointed for a second or two, then shrugged and smiled. "Wow. I am officially the only high school girl in history to get turned down by a boy for sex."

"If you're that bothered about it," said Darroll, "you could always ask Ed Crowe. He goes round like he's the first high school boy to be accepted by a girl for sex."

She laughed. "Ed Crowe hates everyone who is cleverer than him, which is every student in our grade, and his friends are only his friends because they use him to boss around people they couldn't boss around themselves."

"What about Patsy Young?"

"I wouldn't soil my lips with what I think about Patsy Young. I have to kiss my mother when I get home."

This time they both laughed and Darroll reached out to her, awkwardly. She looked down at his hand a moment, then smiled and took it in her own. It was warmer than his, and dry. He'd always imagined Vanessa's hand would be sweaty-palmed.

"Come on," she said, and they walked out of the cemetery, hand in hand.

"Where shall we go?" he asked.

"Do you actually want to be with me?"

At first he thought that was sarcasm, but then he figured it was a genuine question.

"Yeah. Yes, I do." Repetition for emphasis.

"Okay. Shall we go down towards the freeway?"

"Hell, why not."

Dusk was starting to fall. There was no sidewalk, but traffic down the road in and out of Muldoon was never heavy enough to worry about.

"You know, Darroll," she said, "that's one reason I like you so much."

He looked across at her, to indicate he was listening.

"Not a lot of guys turn down sex. Not even with a fat chick, never mind what they claim to their friends. Not at our age anyway."

He took that as meaning she'd already boffed more than one guy. Was he surprised? No. Was he disappointed? He wasn't quite sure.

"I never met anyone else like you, Darroll. You're so unique."

He stopped dead, and looked at her.

"What's wrong? That's a compliment, honey."

Darroll looked down at himself, at the hand holding hers. What the hell was he going to say? What could he say? How could he even think of starting to try to explain to Vanessa that he had seventy billion duplicates floating around in quasi-parallel fucking continuums, and so did she?

She spoke again. "Being unique is awesome, Darroll. Anyone who can be completely their own self is automatically an incredible person. God knows, I wish I was unique myself. I get so tired of being a generic fat Goth chick who wears too much black and smokes cigarettes and shows off her fat cleavage."

He knew this was his cue to tell her she was unique, but the lie stuck in his throat, like the prayer of that evil old murdering king in Macbeth, who Joe had been telling the Club about last week.

"You're incredible anyway," he said instead, which stretched the truth a lot less. "You don't need to be cool in a unique way, to be cool."

"Wish I believed you."

"Wish I believed myself."

They started walking again. Soon they came to the old grade crossing, where the freight railroad had crossed the road with its loads of logs.

"Shall we walk up the railroad?" he suggested.

"It's dark," Vanessa said. Then she added, "If we go up there, there'll be nobody else around."

"Yeah?" he said. She had to be leading him on. Part of him suddenly, urgently wanted to follow where she led. But he thought again of his duplicate in Georgia. What would happen when he came back to Muldoon, and found that Vanessa thought she'd been with him that Saturday night?

If he had sex with Vanessa, it would screw over his duplicate even more cruelly than just hanging out with her would. He didn't mind breaking promises to ordinary people, but this was a promise he'd made to himself; we don't screw our own selves over.

Very well. He wasn't going to have sex with her.

But damned if he wasn't going to at least try for first base, if she let him.

Vanessa looked up the railroad dubiously. "I'm not sure we ought to do this."

"It'll be okay," Darroll assured her.

They turned to their right, and began to walk along the railroad line. Ballast crunched under their feet in the dark, and the moonlight gleamed faintly off the parallel metal rails. For a minute or two, neither of them spoke. Darroll became increasingly aware that the silence was awkward. His first instinct was to break it with some vapid pleasantry, but he decided against it. Instead, he waited to see how long it would take Vanessa to find the silence too uncomfortable.

Vanessa didn't seem to mind the quietness, though. They walked on. Somewhere over to one side, the faint smell of a skunk came to Darroll's nose. Funny how at this distance they didn't smell all that unpleasant. It was only when they landed their spray directly that the scent threw a rock in your face.

Finally it was Darroll who did speak.

"It's not easy to be unique," he said.

"How do you mean?"

"It's not just 'being yourself'." He wiggled his fingers in the air, to demonstrate the quote marks around those words. "Being yourself is fine, but there are always other people who are enough like you that the difference is infinitesimal."

"You think?"

"Well, do you think you're unique, Vanessa?"

"I already told you, you jerk," she said. "I wish I was unique but I know I'm not."

"I met another girl, kind of like you. Really like you in fact. But I don't think she liked me. Maybe I was wrong..."

"Maybe she didn't see through your act."

"My act?"

"You put on this act, Darroll. Like you despise the world and everyone in it, including yourself. You use it like a shield. Any time anyone tries to get through to you, you swivel that shield around, and they bounce right off of it. Is that shield to keep other people out, Darroll, or to keep you in?"

He roughened his voice deliberately. "I don't know what you're talking about."

"Yes you do. You don't need to pretend, Darroll. Not with me. Not here."

And she slipped an arm around him. He was silent.

"You don't know what to do, do you?" she said. "You've been keeping people out for so long that you don't know what to do when someone gets behind your defences, Darroll. Relax. I'm not here to hurt you. I'm here because I want to be close to you. That's why I drew you this. Because I wanted to. Because I like you."

She pulled out the drawing of the rental truck vampire again, as if he needed reminding of it. As if he could see it, by the faint light of the moon.

"No," he said. "You think it's an act, Vanessa. You think I'm putting it on. I'm not. I swear I am not. I genuinely despise everyone and everything. This world's full of shit, Vanessa. The world is full of shit. People are full of shit. When you kissed me, earlier, you know what you were doing? You were sucking on the end of a thirty foot long tube, most of which is full of shit."

Vanessa took a step away from him. He kept on.

"You've been honest with me, I'm being honest with you. I hate you less than I hate the rest of the world. I probably hate you less than I hate myself. In comparative terms that's a massive compliment. But all I am, Vanessa, is a big black hole full of hate."

He never did figure out why saying that made Vanessa step forward again and kiss him. A long kiss.

"That's all anybody is, Darroll," she said after she'd taken a breath. "It's easy not to realise but pretty much everyone is that way. Hollow. Some of us are honest about confronting it and owning up to it. Like us."

A pregnant silence followed. Again it was Darroll who broke it.

"Do you want to go sit over there in the grass?"

"Sure thing," she said. "Oww... Hang on a moment, I've gotten my foot stuck. Nnng." She fidgeted about, trying to dislodge it.

Darroll felt it before he saw it, and felt it before Vanessa did; a faint, low vibration, like the start of an earthquake. Which it couldn't be, of course. That was about the one thing that could be said for this state; it didn't get earthquakes.

"Can you feel –"

He turned around, and then he saw the lights.

"Christ! Vanessa! Move your ass, there's a train!"

He grabbed her and pulled. She let out a yelp of pain as her jammed leg twisted.

"I can't move!"

"You have to!"

"I can't –"

"Take your shoe off!" he yelled, and dropped to his knees to assist her. A sharp pain shot through both joints as he landed on rough-edged ballast. The lights on the front of the train were close enough, now, that he could see she was wearing the world's stupidest, most inconvenient goth boots, with laces that criss-crossed all the way up to her knee.

Why were feet so stupid?

The sound and light increased. There was no horn or siren from the locomotive, just a throbbing, grinding vibration as it grew closer to them.

He sprang back to his feet and again tried to heave Vanessa free from the rail.

"Get out!" she snarled at him, like a wild animal spitting, and she gave him a sudden violent shove. He was already half off balance, and the push sent him stumbling backward, away from the rails. He would have fallen on his back, but somebody caught him around the waist and elbows. He cried out, but the sound was lost in the shriek from Vanessa, the roar of the engines, the scream of the rails.

The shriek was cut abruptly short and something warm splashed over his face, his hands, his clothes –

"I'm sorry, Darroll."

Somehow those words were clearly audible over the noise of the train. He twisted around, but he already knew whom he would see holding him.

"Sorry?" he howled at Horsehead.

Today Horsehead was wearing a formal white shirt. He could not have chosen a better designed garment to highlight the splashes of Vanessa Murchison's blood.

"You... you killed –"

"I did not kill her," Horsehead broke in firmly. "Despite my existence, accidents happen. No – don't look –"

But of course Darroll looked anyway. The train was still moving, wagons loaded with lumber processing past, calm, methodical, inexorable, like the chariots of Jagganatha. He realised that he, as well as Horsehead, had Vanessa's blood on his face and hands, and on the crumpled sheet of paper that he was somehow still holding. He tried to speak to Horsehead again, but as he fumbled for words, the swirls leapt out of the darkness and enveloped him, eddying around him like the wheels of the lumber waggons. He was glad enough to surrender himself to them.

He was glad enough, too, to smell the piss of the doorway again. It was infinitely preferable to what he had smelled a few moments before. He remained in the doorway for several minutes, eyes closed, panting quietly like a dog.

When he finally stood upright, he caught sight of his own reflection in the glass of the door, and he shuddered.

The piece of paper in his hand was creased half into a ball. He unfolded it. The vampire and his victim were marked by streaks of dark red, their creator's blood soaked into the paper and drying. He looked at it for a long moment before refolding it again, neatly, into quarters. Then he climbed back into his car and drove home, where he headed straight for the garden tap. Underneath it sat a neatly coiled snake-spiral of hose.

The water was as cold as everything else in the state, as cold as his own mind and heart. Before today he would have resented the coldness. Now he accepted it, welcomed it, as he cleaned Vanessa's blood from himself as best he could.

When he was done, he went inside, stripped off his clothes, and threw them all into the laundry basket, then headed straight for the shower. When the water came through hot, he turned the control to make it cold instead, and stood there under its icy blanket for a length of time he afterwards realised he had no idea of; it could have been a minute, or an hour.

He finally emerged from the shower, dressed in clean clothes, and put the bloodstained drawing carefully away in his desk drawer. Then he lay on his bed, hands folded behind his head, looking at the ceiling.

He was wondering what the odds were of his landing in a universe where almost everything was the same as what he knew, but where the abandoned logging railroad was not abandoned. He was also wondering whether he could believe Horsehead when he claimed Vanessa's death was an accident.

If he believed it, the obvious conclusion to draw was that Horsehead had some means – he couldn't start to speculate what – of showing up when violence was about to break.

He spent so much time thinking about those things that it was only several hours later that he thought about his twin in that universe, away in Georgia for the weekend. His twin, who would arrive back in Muldoon to find Vanessa Murchison suddenly and obscenely dead in his absence. A closed casket ceremony, for sure.

He tried to find some sorrow for his double, but there was none in him. No sorrow, no remorse, no human feeling at all. Only the red memory of Vanessa's blood on Horsehead's face and clothes.

36

He awoke abruptly the next morning. One moment asleep, the next, pow, open eyes, fully awake and aware.

Had he been dreaming? He couldn't remember. He thought he'd read somewhere that we all dream every night, it's just that we don't always manage to remember the dreams. Or maybe it was only a theory.

He threw off the bedclothes, swung his legs out of bed, and his feet (which were cold) touched the floor (which was colder). As he hit ground, the thought occurred to him. He'd figured before that he was a psychopath. He'd been wrong, then, quite wrong. But now? Now, he was.

He stood naked for a moment, digesting that thought, then dressed, went through to the kitchen and drank half a pint of milk straight out of the container.

The Club had agreed to meet in Celebration Burger after lunch that Sunday. "For milkshakes and massacres," Chuck had said, straight-faced. Darroll arrived a few minutes late, breathing hard and trying not to show it. He knew what he expected to see, he was even pretty sure of what he expected, but he couldn't be one hundred per cent certain until he arrived.

He pushed open the front door, like a cowboy stepping into a saloon, and surveyed the interior. There were only four figures, not five, in the corner booth with the round table that the Club had informally made their own, and Darroll's heart gave a little sideways lurch before he realised that one of the four was Vanessa, wearing too much eyeshadow as always, indubitably alive.

"Boardman's running late," Chuck started to say, but Darroll paid no heed. Instead he addressed himself direct to Vanessa.

"Vanessa? Come out here for a second, will ya?" He tried to make it sound both flippant and firm. The sort of request she couldn't resist. Psychopaths are charismatic, Martock, he reminded himself. Be charismatic. It's all a massive put-on.

Vanessa arched her fiercely plucked eyebrows and shuffled round the table on the bench, until she could squeeze out and rise to her feet. "What do you want?"

Charisma, charisma. "Well, what I really want is to kiss you," he said, and looked her in the eye.

Vanessa didn't say anything for a second or two, then she reached out to him, wrapped her arms round his shoulders, and planted an enthusiastic smacker on Darroll's lips.

Charisma. Feel something. Why can't I feel something? I ought to be feeling something. Agh. Charisma.

Rowdy Serxner was the first onlooker to react, making a sound like a police siren approaching. The second reaction came from across the restaurant. Two girls from Straus High came scurrying over. One of them was Olivia Hobsbaum, a tall skinny creature who irritated Darroll intensely. The other, he had to actually think to remember her name. Sahara something. Like the desert. Sahara. Dry, sandy and barren of any human intellect.

"Oh my god! Vanessa! Did I see you do that?" squealed Olivia.

"Duh. Yes. Unless you're out of your skull on crack, and you think you saw me fire pancakes out of my pussy."

"But you kissed Darroll Martock! He's creepy."

"Your testimonial is appreciated," Darroll drawled. "You only think we're creepy because your stupid little minds can't take in what life is really like, and ours can."

Sahara, meantime, was staring at Beth Vines. "Beth?" she broke in. "What are you doing here with the losers?"

That set off a general hubbub, and for a couple of seconds Darroll couldn't make out what a single person was saying. Then, as if by magic, they all broke off in unison apart from one, and Darroll heard Beth's unraised voice saying " – and finally, they amuse me, and you guys do not. End of."

Olivia grunted and turned to Sahara. "Come on. We don't have to stay here and talk to these jerkasses. We might catch the goth cooties." She turned and strode out of Celebration Burger, with Sahara in tow behind. Darroll gave them his middle finger as they departed.

"I think we won that one." Vanessa smiled a dangerous, triumphant smile at the Club.

"You guys." Chuck struggled for words. "Are you guys... Have you done that before? Kiss?"

Yes, thought Darroll.

"No," said Vanessa. "But I think we maybe should have."

Chuck rubbed his chin. Darroll rejoiced inwardly. He'd put a real dent in Chuck today, if his psychopathic spider-senses were reliable. Chuck might be the founder of the Club, might see himself as the leader, but Chuck didn't have the charisma to do what Darroll had just done.

* * *

Over the next few days, Darroll found himself coming dangerously close to being happy. Which was nice in many ways, of course, but it was a state of mind he wasn't used to. He kept worrying it wasn't appropriate for a young hate-filled sociopath like him.

To begin with, the swirls left him alone for almost a month. All he had to do during that time was survive school, and even that took a lot less energy, now that he had Vanessa in his life. Ed Crowe and his buddies were always a thorn in his side, of course, but even they receded into the distance, a dull persistent ache instead of a continual, stabbing pain. His mother continued to be oblivious, even though Vanessa became a regular visitor to his house, and he to hers.

After two weeks, they began to have sex. To his surprise, he found he enjoyed it quite a lot. By mutual agreement, they decided not to do it in either the Martock house or the Murchison one. That would court trouble.

So they dallied with one another in the open air. They avoided all the usual necking spots in town. Apart from anything else, the thought of stumbling over Ed Crowe and Patsy Young, locked in grunting, sweaty coitus, made Darroll shudder.

Instead they slipped down to the long grass at the back of the burial ground, where they'd sat and talked the day the other

Vanessa had met her violent and bloody death.

Afterwards, Vanessa methodically began to button her clothes up again. She was wearing a velveteen goth jacket, so there were a lot of buttons. "Do you go to hell for fucking in a graveyard?" she asked Darroll.

"You go to hell for just saying 'fuck' in a graveyard," he said, poker-faced, and Vanessa snorted with laughter.

As if in response to the sudden influx of warmth into Darroll's eternally frozen soul, the weather brightened up and an early summer hit Muldoon, making alfresco romance an attractive proposition all around. The second time they did it, Vanessa bit him on the neck. Darroll was startled for a second, then he bit her back, to which Vanessa responded with surprising fervor. Next day at school they both had hickies. A few people sniggered, and Chuck Milne gave Darroll an expressive look, which Darroll met with a modest smile.

"You need to be careful, Martock," Chuck warned him. For a moment Darroll thought Chuck was making a threat, but there seemed no menace in his words or his expression.

"I bought some rubbers from the gas station," Darroll said.

"I didn't mean that. I meant Tidmarsh and his goons. They'll throw your ass in the cooler if they find you've been copping off with Vanessa."

"How they gonna prove it?" Darroll rejoindered.

"Dude, you both have hickeys the size of a planet."

This was true, as Darroll appreciated, but there hardly seemed much they could do about it so late in the day. He made a vow to rein in that part of his sex life with Vanessa. But that evening, somehow, they both acquired more, Vanessa sinking her teeth into his neck like the vampire in her drawing while he played with her breasts. God, how could he have thought they were oversized or ugly?

Chuck Milne's warning was not misplaced. That Friday, Mr Tidmarsh bore down on him at lunchtime, cleaving his way through other students, a destroyer's prow slicing through the sea.

"Mr Martock? I hope you're well," Tidmarsh began in his usual sarcastic way. Darroll still hadn't found a way of countering this verbal martial art, and could only stonewall.

"Very well, thanks," he said blandly.

"Oh, I'm pleased to hear it. I was afraid that you might have contracted some hideous and rare sickness."

"Who, me?"

"Yes, you. In light of the ugly and inappropriate discoloration of the skin on your neck." Tidmarsh leaned in closer to Darroll, disgust in his face. "My office, Martock. Now."

Darroll trailed away after Tidmarsh. Dig Doyle's lips made an exaggerated kissing noise in Darroll's direction, and Patsy Young giggled like a tray of crockery being dropped downstairs.

The interview in the principal's office was relatively brief, but that was all that could be said in its favour. Tidmarsh tore Darroll a new asshole. It was inappropriate for any student of Straus High to be sexually active at all, Darroll was informed. It was less appropriate still to flaunt one's pretensions to adulthood by strolling around the school displaying love-bites like a guttersnipe. That was the actual word Tidmarsh used. He also remarked scathingly on the example it set to other students. As though anyone in school would see Darroll as a role model.

"You do not only set a bad example," Tidmarsh went on, gunning himself up to a crescendo, "but you bring shame upon me as your principal, not to mention yourself and your family. Oh, but wait. You don't have a family, do you, Mr Martock? Except your mother."

Darroll had been prepared to let Tidmarsh's sarcasm and scorn wash over him, but that blow struck home, and Tidmarsh saw that it struck home. He moved in for the kill.

"It saddens me that, with no father to serve as your role model, you have run off the rails in this way. If you came from a normal family unit, no doubt you would have been a useful and valuable student to this academy, rather than the feckless, reckless, waste of space and time that you are. You need to think about where you are going, Martock. You need to think very hard. If I see you with any more... disfigurations... of this nature, you will be out of this school so quickly you will still be wondering what hit you when your ass lands on the far side of town. Now get out of my sight and out of my office, you worthless, fatherless object."

Tidmarsh dropped into his chair and began to shuffle the paperwork in his in-tray, as a signal to Darroll that the interview was over. Darroll sidled out of the door and closed it, then leant against the wall outside, taking in deep whooping breaths. The rage that usually filled him had died away for a few weeks. Now it was back, and like wine bottles hidden away in a cellar, seemed only to have become more powerful and more seductive with age.

Think very hard? Oh, he was going to think very hard, all right. His imagination felt as though it was bursting clean out of his brain. He pressed his face against the wall, its dull paint cool on his cheek, and images paraded past him in a mental zoetrope.

37

It was more than a week before the swirls finally remembered Darroll, but that was all right; it gave him more time to make plans. He had expected to have to rein in his sex life with Vanessa, and he had expected it to suck.

But while Vanessa had also had to suffer a similar Tidmarshian tirade, she had a copious make-up collection – she amassed it the way Darroll amassed comic books – and she put it to use, not only to conceal her own signs of feral love-making, but also to hide Darroll's. She would meet him before classes in the morning and sneak behind the bleachers. There, she would daub his neck with concealing foundation, while Joe Boardman or Chuck Milne kept lookout, until only close inspection would reveal anything out of the ordinary.

When he did finally find himself being jerked free from his home continuum again, it was early in the morning, a Tuesday. As usual when the swirls came for him at home, he snuck quickly into his own closet for privacy, and once they died away and left him elsewhere, he peeked out to check the lie of the land.

His bedroom was empty, and resembled a museum, the sign that he had arrived in a world where Darroll Martock was no longer numbered among the living. Creeping out of his room, he ascertained firstly that his mother was still asleep, and secondly that his portrait in the lounge had the black fabric band and the floral accompaniment. That put it beyond doubt. In this universe, he was a ghost. A walking, talking, tangible ghost, with a free rein to do whatever he pleased.

He knew what would please him more than anything else. Sure, it would take some legwork, since he had no Oldsmobile to drive around in this world; but nothing good ever came easy, right? Darroll was sure that Tidmarsh would say exactly that, if he was asked.

He let himself out of the house quietly and ran up the street into the park at the edge of town, then crossed it, heading overland for the old farm building. His heart was pounding from more than mere exercise. If this universe differed sufficiently from his own, it might sink his whole plan before it started. But then he turned his head, as if sensing a sound from the distance, though he heard nothing.

Silhouetted against the early morning horizon, watching him, was Horsehead. Neither of them acknowledged the other. But Darroll had seen what he had seen, and he was pretty sure Horsehead had seen, and recognised, him. And now he wasn't worried any more. Somehow, he knew he would achieve what he was after.

And he did. There was the Colt, under the sink, where he knew it would be. He pulled out and opened the box containing the gun and the ammunition, then paused for a moment, scrutinising it. He couldn't put his finger upon it, but there seemed to be something different about the weapon.

He glanced behind him quickly, half expecting to see Horsehead, but there was nobody else in the ruined farm.

He turned his focus to the gun again. He wasn't enough of an expert to pinpoint what the difference was, or even whether there really was one. It might just be his imagination. In any case, it hardly mattered. As long as the weapon did the job he wanted it for, that was all he cared about.

He left the wrecked farm, with the Colt loaded and tucked inside his windcheater, and set out across country again. He didn't want to be seen going through Muldoon. He was pretty certain nothing bad could happen to him, but if he set off an encounter, it might force him back to his home continuum before he was ready, and that would mean an end to his plan.

He crossed round behind the burial ground, hopped over the road that led east out of town (no cars in sight), and traversed farmland again until he came out on the next road, a mile north-east of Muldoon, with Straus High between him and the town.

He checked his watch. School had already started. Perfect.

The next part involved risk, but that couldn't be helped. He set out down the road toward Straus High, keeping his head down on the rare occasions that traffic passed. Nobody stopped. Nobody seemed to heed the presence of a grain of sand in the oyster of this dimension. He smiled to himself at the concept. Sand became pearls, and damned if he wasn't going to come out of this trip with a big, luscious, shimmering gem.

Nobody was in sight at the school gate. He darted inside and across the parking lot, holing up temporarily in the little metal bicycle shed at its edge. He reached inside his jacket, checked the gun, and took a few moments to compose himself.

He looked inside his mind and asked himself whether he wanted to push onward, to cross the boundary he was approaching. The answer was yes, and it made his heart sing. It felt like when he and Vanessa were about to make love, only somehow even more intense and thrilling.

He peeped out of the shed, waiting for the coast to be clear. Part of him expected to see Horsehead there, watching him take this next step on his journey, but he was still alone.

He decided he couldn't wait around for Horsehead. He crept out of the shed and up to the school building, then around to the building's northern end, where the school offices were. Bent over, to stay out of sight from inside, he counted the windows as he passed underneath them. One, two, three... four. The window he crouched under was open, allowing the summer breeze inside. That was just perfect. It wasn't only the breeze that would be sneaking inside that room.

His head popped up to take a swift look through the window. Tidmarsh sat reading a magazine, behind his desk, sideways on to the desk itself, and hence with his back to the window.

Zero hour, here we go. Darroll quickly jerked the window fully open, crouched for a moment with his hands on the windowsill, then vaulted up.

Tidmarsh swung his chair around and saw Darroll, perched on the sill and halfway into the room.

"How dare you – " he began to bluster, then he realised who he was looking at, and his ugly, pink face paled visibly. Wow, thought Darroll. I always thought that was another Hollywood trope. He jerked his leg out from underneath him and onto the floor inside.

Then the rest of him followed suit, gasping a little for breath. Tidmarsh was gasping too.

"Martock. Darroll Martock. You – you're dead," Tidmarsh panted, his eyes bulging out, the magazine falling forgotten to the floor.

Darroll realised that he'd omitted one thing. He hadn't prepared a speech for the occasion. Damn it! Oh well, when at a loss, improvise.

"Yeah," he said, reaching into his jacket. "And guess what?" Out came the Colt. "You are, too."

For a second he had the sudden worry that he'd forgotten to disengage the safety catch, and that his words would be followed by a faint, disappointing click. Instead, the gun fired.

Darroll's wrist jerked as the force of the discharge pulled at him. He hadn't expected the weapon to pack such power. It actually hurt his arm. And the sound! It was like a cannon going off, and it made his ears ring.

For a couple of seconds he stood there, amazed. Amazed not only at the unexpected force of the gunfire, but also at the fact that he had truly just done what he had done. Then he let his arm, still holding the Colt, drop to his side, and for the first time since pulling the trigger, he thought to take a look at Tidmarsh.

Disappointingly, the principal had not been blown half-way through his office wall. Nor had he even been propelled back into it, to slide down it leaving a messy trail of blood behind him. Hollywood, Darroll guessed, was wrong yet again.

But he must have scored some kind of a hit, because Alvin Tidmarsh was lying on the floor of his office, bent double. His mouth was open, as if to cry out, but no sound escaped him; or if it did, the echoes of the gunshot drowned it.

There had to be an alarm, Darroll thought. That was so loud, people must be coming. But maybe there's time –

Pushing the gun back inside his clothing, he knelt down by Tidmarsh's head. Bending over him, Darroll sank his teeth into the principal's fat, wattly neck. It felt vile in his mouth, almost dusty. Certainly nothing like the warm, soft, living skin of Vanessa Murchison. But he sucked on Tidmarsh's neck for a few seconds, until he was sure that he'd left the principal with the mother of all hickeys.

Then he dived for the window again, climbing out hurriedly. Had he fatally wounded Tidmarsh with his attack? What if he didn't die? What if he was alive and – Oh, what the hell does it matter? What's he going to say? Yes, Officer, I saw who did it. It was Darroll Martock's ghost. Dig his body up and arrest him.

He landed on the ground outside the window, missed his footing slightly, and dropped onto his hands and knees. And as he stared at the blades of grass underneath him, the swirls started to bubble up.

He was going where no law, no retribution, could find him or punish him for his crime. He was going home.

He rolled over onto his back, staring up at the sun with a glorious grin on his face. And the sun was the last thing he saw, as the swirls rose higher and higher and took him away from the scene of his murder.

38

The previous time that Darroll had gone to Vickery's office downstate for tests, he had reached the point of such frustration with his mother and her endless fretting and clueless questions, he'd suggested it might no longer be necessary for her to sit around and wait while Vickery tested him. Vickery had fiddled with his bow tie, and said that he didn't mind Darroll being alone with him, so long as his mother okayed it, and came back at the end of his session to pick him up and be notified of any news.

So now his mother had dropped him off at Vickery's clinic and had gone on into the city. Clothes shopping, coffee, alcohol – Darroll didn't care. It meant he was free from her for an hour, and even an hour away from his mother was an hour of his life improved. Also, it meant he could talk to Vickery without worrying that his mother was eavesdropping.

About Vanessa, for instance. Darroll wasn't about to tell Vickery about the swirls, but he did want to tell him about Vanessa; not so much as a boast, but because he was curious to see how Vickery would react.

How he reacted was to grin a little patronisingly at Darroll, congratulate him, and say that it was further proof of how Darroll was developing into a perfectly normal teenager, head injury or no head injury. Darroll didn't challenge that opinion, even though he knew Vickery was one hundred per cent in error.

Then, after a little more small talk, Vickery pulled a few medical implements out of a desk drawer, and ran through what he called some routine tests. Routine they plainly were; Darroll suspected that Vickery wouldn't even bother with them, if it weren't for the fact that they were being billed to his father's insurance company ("To running little spiked wheel over patient to test reflexes: $500.00.") The one Darroll liked best was the little hammer with which Vickery tapped him on the knee and made his leg jerk. He was fascinated by how a touch in the right place could make his leg move so pronouncedly without any input from Darroll himself. It made him imagine taking a much larger hammer to Ed Crowe's knee. A sledgehammer, maybe. A sledgehammer to the knee would put paid to Ed Crowe sneaking up on people and making them smell his jockstrap for a good long while.

He was just starting to enjoy that daydream when he realised that the swirls were about to hit him again. He jumped to his feet abruptly, making Vickery blink.

"Is everything all right, Darroll?"

"Uh, yes," he lied. "I just really need the can. Ate something bad..."

Vickery waved at the door to the corridor. "Just along to the right, outside."

Darroll strode out of Vickery's office and into the washroom wishing, not for the first time, that he didn't keep having to hide in lavatories when the swirls came down upon him. It wasn't dignified. He didn't want to wind up like Joe Boardman. Boardman couldn't even visit the restroom at high school without jeers from Ed Crowe or Dig Doyle. They affected to believe that he was going in there for an assignation with a lover. Darroll couldn't understand why gay guys should fuck in a restroom. Especially a public restroom, grimy and stinking of piss.

Luckily, there were no guys making out in the clinic restroom. There was nobody else there at all as he ducked into the first cubicle and, without bothering to lift the seat, sat down, waiting for the swirls to rise up above eye level, carry him away, and dump him like dead seaweed at tide level on a beach.

He sometimes worried what would happen if he landed in a universe where the building he was in didn't exist. Especially if he was above ground level. What if he got swirled in a skyscraper in Chicago, that had never been built in the dimension where he arrived? Would he crash to the ground and die horribly?

It hadn't happened yet, and it didn't happen this time. The restroom looked identical to the one he had departed from. He took a quick look about him for spiders, but didn't see any. Well, after all, this was a hospital, and presumably they kept it cleaner than the Boardman house basement.

For a moment he stood undecided, then stepped back to Vickery's office door and took hold of its handle. And now he found the first change; the door, in this universe, was locked.

He released the handle, and looked left and right. Nobody else was in sight. With no plan in mind, he wandered up the passage toward the reception desk and the front door of the unit. As he opened the double doors at the end of the corridor, he froze; there, leaning on the front desk, was Vickery, chatting relaxedly to the receptionist. He looked up at the double doors, and his eyes met Darroll's.

For a second, Darroll's legs felt wobbly, as though Vickery really had used a lumphammer to test his reflexes. But after a second, Vickery looked away and began chatting to the receptionist again. He showed no sign of recognising Darroll.

Darroll took a deep breath and walked across the foyer to the doors. They slid open for him, detecting his presence as though he belonged in this universe. Which he plainly did not; for if Vickery didn't recognise Darroll, the inference had to be that Darroll had never been his patient here, and the inference from that was that this was another universe where he was dead.

Outside, there were the same amount of clouds in the sky, the same trees in the hospital grounds. Unsure what to do, Darroll walked slowly along the path leading to the parking lot. He knew his mother wouldn't be there in this universe, because Darroll was dead in this universe.

"Hello, Darroll."

Darroll jumped. Lost in his own thoughts, he hadn't seen the figure lurking in the ornamental bushes at the side of the path.

"I might have known you'd be here."

Horsehead stepped out of the bushes, brushing away a couple of stray leaves.

"Might have known? Why?"

"You like to be around when I..." Darroll looked for the right word. "Travel."

"I like to keep an eye on you because you are my friend. I am concerned for your welfare."

"More than you are most people's," Darroll rejoindered.

"Of course. Most people are not my friends like you."

"Most people can't even see you," Darroll challenged Horsehead. He didn't really expect Horsehead to make a satisfactory answer to that, and indeed, the creature merely looked into the middle distance, neither confirming nor denying Darroll's statement.

"So what am I gonna do now?" Darroll said. "Throw rocks through the hospital windows till I get sent home?"

"You have free will," said Horsehead mildly, again neither affirmative or positive.

"I'm open to suggestions."

Horsehead lifted one arm, and pointed back at the door to the clinic.

"Have you ever wondered about the learned and solicitous Louis Vickery?"

Darroll gave Horsehead a long look. "What do you mean?" He wasn't quite sure of the definition of 'solicitous', in all truth.

Horsehead's arm remained outstretched. "He will be coming this way very shortly."

Darroll turned to regard the door. When he looked back, Horsehead had gone. He took a glance in the bushes; no sign of life. Then the clinic door opened, and Louis Vickery did indeed emerge.

Darroll thought of hiding in the bushes himself, but he disdained to show such cowardice, and just loitered on the path. Vickery passed him, paying no heed, heading for the parking lot.

"You could follow him," said Horsehead, who was all of a sudden standing there again.

"I'd lose him as soon as he got into his car."

"Perhaps not."

Darroll looked at Vickery again, and when he turned back, Horsehead had vanished once more.

Instead of climbing into a car, Vickery walked straight through the parking lot and along another path at the far side, which led to the main campus of the hospital. Darroll followed him as far as the main hospital gate, where Vickery joined a few other people under a plastic shelter. A bus stop. Why the hell was Vickery riding a bus? He had to be able to afford a car. Perhaps it had broken down, or he didn't have a parking space, or it was more ecological to take the bus.

There was a flat fare of one dollar. Darroll followed Vickery onto the bus, and paid it.

They headed towards the heart of the city, but Vickery rose from his seat well before they reached it. Darroll arose, too, and left the bus in Vickery's wake. His head was held up and his steps jaunty. He walks like a guy in a good mood, thought Darroll, a happy man. Must be nice to be Louis Vickery.

They crossed one intersection, turned down the next side street, and then Vickery strode up the path alongside a small, neat house with flower beds out front. Darroll dawdled till the front door had opened and Vickery had disappeared inside the house.

Darroll looked around him, half expecting Horsehead to have rejoined him silently, but there was no sign of company.

He left the sidewalk and took the path up to Vickery's house. A movement startled him, but it was only a cat trotting across his path, a black and white animal. It gave him a disdainful look.

Darroll edged round to the back of the house, where he couldn't be seen from the sidewalk at the front. Behind the house were a neat lawn and a tree. Nothing of any real interest behind the house, so Darroll eyed the building itself. Then, still not really sure what he had in mind, he stood beside the nearest window, twisted his head to the side, and carefully peeped through. The laundry room. It was every bit as interesting as the laundry room at his own house, which was not at all.

He rested his hands on the windowsill, thinking. He had never longed to commit housebreaking in the same way as he had murder, but what was there to stop him? Even if he was caught in the act, he wouldn't be in trouble. The worst that could happen to him would be that he'd be jerked back to his own dimension. He could get used to this immunity.

Grinning, he flexed his fingers, and tested the window. It was laughably simple; it came open a crack before the latch stopped it opening further, but the crack was easily wide enough for Darroll to push a key through the crack and trip the latch. Useful things, keys, he thought as he pushed the window wide open and landed silently on the floor of the laundry room.

Somewhere inside the house, obviously, was Louis Vickery. What would Darroll do if they came face to face? He could hit him with impunity, because a scuffle would send him home. But Darroll realised he didn't actually want to punch Vickery out. The thought worried him. Surely a real psychopath would just attack anyone, given the opportunity, no matter who?

He was still pondering as he walked out of the utility room and into the kitchen, which was tidy and equally empty. The front room was empty, too. Where the hell had Vickery gone?

He had to be upstairs. Darroll climbed the stairs slowly, trying not to make a sound. At the top, he picked a door at random, and pushed it open. And there he found Vickery.

Vickery wasn't wearing his bow tie any more; he wasn't wearing anything. Neither was the blond-haired man with him. They were doing something that made Darroll stand, wide-eyed. Vickery's eyes went wide, too, and for a second or two, there was actual silence in the room, because everybody was too astonished to speak.

Vickery was the first one to recover. He dropped what he was holding and bounced from the bed to his feet, confronting Darroll. "Get the fuck out of my house!" he snapped.

"Don't shoot!" called out the other guy, trying and failing to hide his nakedness with both hands.

"I ain't gonna – " began Darroll, but Vickery was advancing on him. Darroll had always assumed that Vickery was a wimp, but even buck naked, he looked dangerous right now. Perhaps the wimpy style came off with the bow tie, like Clark Kent taking off his glasses and becoming Superman.

Darroll backed out of the bedroom, which he instantly realised was a mistake. Retreating only encouraged Vickery to move further forward.

"Look," he began, "I'm sorry –"

Vickery was still bearing down on him. Darroll took another step backward, and that was an even bigger mistake, because there wasn't any floor behind him now; only the stairs.

"Jesus!" he heard Vickery exclaim, just the one word.

Darroll tumbled downwards, his arms flailing vainly for purchase. Then things were vague for a few seconds, but they involved the world turning upside down in confusion, and a great deal of pain. Darroll closed his eyes, and when he opened them again, he wasn't in Vickery's house any more; he was back in the restroom at the clinic.

He was still gasping for breath.

Leaping to his feet, he unlocked the cubicle door and shoved it open. It hit something, and when Darroll came out of the toilet, he realised that the something was Horsehead.

"What the fuck, man?" he hissed as he confronted the being.

"I might ask you the same," said Horsehead, stepping out of the way of the door.

"You did that deliberately," accused Darroll. "You sent me off after Vickery because – because you wanted –"

"I wanted you to die? Why would I wish my friend dead?"

"No! Because you wanted me to see him and that other guy doing... doing that!"

Horsehead lifted one hand and stroked his long chin in thought. "Do you mean to tell me that you find the sight of homosexual activity more of an ordeal than dying in pain?"

Darroll's thoughts caught up with his anger. "Wait, what? I just... died?"

"If you will fall backwards down a flight of stairs," Horsehead said evenly, "you must expect to suffer more or less serious injury."

"I... I... Oh, God," Darroll blurted. He looked Horsehead in the eyes, those large and deceptively placid eyes, for a second, before he turned and almost ran out of the restroom and back into Vickery's office.

Vickery was still sitting behind the desk, of course, and he looked up as Darroll came tumbling into the room. "Hello! Are you okay?"

he asked, observing Darroll's state as he sank back into the chair opposite.

Darroll forced himself to control his breathing, and brushed his hair into place. "I'm fine," he lied. "Just wanted to make sure I didn't overrun my time with you." He looked at Vickery, who seemed genuinely concerned. He reminded himself that this was not the same Vickery who had just encountered Darroll in his own bedroom, not the Vickery who had watched him fall downstairs and… kill himself?

Also, this was not the same Vickery whom Darroll had just seen without any clothes on. That was a relief. His Vickery had a diary with BRANDY written in it. His Vickery was straight. Presumably.

He sat as passively as he could through the remaining tests, and was glad to escape when his time was up and his mother took him away again.

39

Back in his room in Muldoon, he was about to pick up a comic when a thought hit him. Instead of the comic book, he picked up the paperback which Vickery had sent him at Christmas. He read the cover blurb for the fifth or sixth time, scowled, and dropped it in the trash can.

But less than five minutes passed before he guiltily retrieved the book, jumped onto his bed, and finally began to read it.

About twenty pages into *Catch-22*, the telephone rang. He let his mom answer it, hoping it was nothing to do with him, but she came and pushed his door open. She never knocked. He had no fucking privacy.

"Your friend Joseph is on the phone," she said. It took Darroll a second to figure that she must mean Joe Boardman. "He says, do you want to go round to his and play on his... his box, is it?"

"X-Box," said Darroll. The correction was pointless. She would never remember it.

He suppressed the urge to throw *Catch-22* at his mother's head, and dropped it on his nightstand.

"Joe?" he said into the phone in the hall.

"Hey, man," said Joe. "Why don't you come round? Chuck's here. We're playing Halo."

Darroll almost said no, but the thought of his experience with Vickery today combined with his eternal desire to be away from his mother to tilt him into assenting.

Joe's bedroom suited the obsessive Joe, but it was too tidy for Chuck, who always looked as if he'd thrown his clothes on in pitch darkness inside a dumpster. Chuck sat on the corner of Joe's bed like a garbage sack, next to Joe with his neatly combed red hair and spotless shirt. Overhead, the musician Alex Atrox glowered down over the room from a nearly full-size poster. The poster would have been a misfit in Darroll's room, but Joe's bedroom was larger, the poster more proportionate to the room's size.

Darroll mumbled a greeting as he came in.

"How was your day off?" said Joe.

"Okay," Darroll lied. "How was school?"

Joe just rolled his eyes. "Crowe still can't handle the way I am."

"You'd think he'd be glad there was one guy who's not gonna make eyes at his best girl," commented Chuck.

Normally Darroll was good at Halo, but not today. He struggled even to match Chuck, and Joe kept handing his ass to him, with more holes neatly drilled in it than Nature had ever provided it with. He couldn't focus; the events of today kept buzzing around his head. He couldn't decide whether he was more unsettled by the sight of Vickery and his boyfriend in flagrante, or the suspicion that he had killed himself in that tumble downstairs and somehow been restored to life, as well as to his proper dimension.

Finally, Darroll pleaded that his hands were aching, and threw down his controller. Joe hit pause.

"What's biting you?" he said. "You can't hit a barn door tonight."

"Thinking," said Darroll curtly.

"Does it hurt?" asked Chuck, and Darroll gave him the finger.

"What's on your mind, dude?" said Joe.

There was no easy way to say what Darroll wanted to say, so he just said it.

"Joe. You're gay. Why?"

Joe didn't answer for a moment or two. He sat, looking ahead of him at the wall, chewing his lip. Then he spoke.

"Why do you ask?"

Great. Answering a question with a question. As though he didn't get enough of that trick from Horsehead. But then Joe spoke again.

"Don't tell me that dating Vanessa has made you come out, Darroll."

Darroll laughed at the incongruity of it.

"Well, you can laugh," said Joe, "but there's something odd about you and I've always thought it. Don't worry about me, if that's what you're thinking. You're not my type."

"I'm straight, for sure," Darroll said, relieved that he was on truthful ground. "But I found out someone else I know is gay, and it kind of threw me."

"If I knew what made people gay," said Joe, "I'd never be short of invitations for after dinner speeches. I don't know. Nobody knows. But one thing's for sure, which is that it's not a choice. I didn't pick it, and whoever you're talking about didn't, either."

Darroll could find no way of asking how Louis Vickery could be probably straight in this world, and definitely gay in another. Not without giving away a secret compared to which being gay was the most trivial thing in the world. He decided to take his cue from Horsehead and Joe, and ask another question.

"If I'm not your type," he said to Joe, "who is?"

"I don't know that either," said Joe, "not exactly. I figure I'll know when I meet him. I hope so, otherwise I'm not in for much of a love life."

"Not Alex Atrox, then?" said Darroll, smiling to show the suggestion wasn't serious.

"Of course not," broke in Chuck. "Joe's gay, remember?"

This was enough of a non sequitur that Darroll was thrown off his train of thought.

"What does that have to do with anything?" said Joe.

"Well, look at her." Chuck gestured at the poster of Alex, and Darroll finally figured what Chuck meant. He exchanged a look with Joe.

"Chuck, you dingbat," said Joe, "Alex Atrox is a man. Have you ever actually listened to anything of his?"

Chuck froze in the very act of reaching under his beanie to scratch his lank hair.

"You fuckin' what?" The words had a veneer of scornful confidence, but Darroll knew Chuck well enough to hear the subtext, the subtext that meant a horrible dawning.

Joe gave a little laugh, more surprised than amused.

"Gospel truth, Chuck. Look at that crotch."

Alex Atrox's crotch, up on the wall, looked down on them,

impassive in its asexual latex smoothness.

"No shit?" Chuck was on the defensive now, and Darroll moved in for the kill.

"Of course no shit, duhhh. Why's that freak you so much, Milne? You like to jerk off to Alex Atrox or something?"

Chuck's reaction showed that the 'or something' was wasted verbiage. He leapt to his feet, his beanie crooked from the sudden motion.

"Dude –" began Joe, but Chuck was already halfway to the door. He swept through it, and closed it behind him quite hard. Hard enough to show emotion, but not hard enough to be called a slam, because Chuck didn't have the guts to slam it properly in someone else's house.

Joe sat back on his bed and puffed out his cheeks. His face was normally thin, angular; when his cheeks came out like that, they widened it till it was approaching the plump softness of Chuck's features. Darroll figured he was expressing mild surprise, but to Darroll it just made Joe look like a hungry hamster.

"That wasn't nice," said Joe after a few seconds.

"I'm not nice."

Joe's eyes were steady on Darroll's face. "If it was Ed Crowe… Darroll, Chuck needs his friends. And he needs them not to be shitty to him."

Darroll tried to tell himself that he didn't care what Joe or Chuck said, the pair of them, but the lie wouldn't take. The reproach in Joe's eyes was too strong.

"He shouldn't be such an ignorant jerk then, should he?" he muttered, but he said it in a tone that showed Joe he accepted the rebuke.

"Nobody knows everything." Joe sat forward again. His upper body came closer to Darroll's. "I help you with your science homework, you help me with languages –"

"Yeah, yeah." Darroll swallowed his pride and got to his feet.

"Don't you run out too."

"I was going to go find him. Apologise."

"He'll be gone by now. Talk to him tomorrow."

Darroll sat back down.

"Do you jerk off to Alex Atrox?" he said.

Joe's eyebrows rose.

"Rather a personal question… No, I don't. I like his music, I don't like his style. Can you imagine me in a latex catsuit?"

Darroll tried, and succeeded. Then he wished he'd failed.

"By the way," Joe went on, "Chuck isn't gay. I can tell these things. Gaydar." He tapped a bony finger against his forehead. "Plus I'm a good judge of people generally."

That was splendid. A good judge of people who didn't know one of his best friends was a murderous psychopath. A sudden rush of confidence came over Darroll.

"You're a savvy guy," he lied. "Come on, let's stop sitting round clucking about sex and shit, like old hens. Let's get some Halo on."

They got some Halo on, and Darroll shot Joe in the head eight straight times in a row.

40

"Strike three!" Darroll whooped.

"Goddamn," Joe Boardman said, dropping his bat, "you've gotten good this year, Darroll. You ought to be on the team."

"Maybe," Darroll drawled, walking up to Joe and reaching out to pluck the ball out of the air as the catcher threw it back.

"Maybe, nothing. We need pitchers. I'm going to tell coach you're one." Joe dropped the bat on the ground, and looked at Darroll as if daring him to argue the point.

"Whatev," Darroll said, and Joe looked at him again, and walked past him out of the batting cage, leaving Darroll with Kirk Mondschein, who'd been catching for them.

Darroll was about to turn and follow in Joe's wake, when Kirk surprised him by saying, "He's right."

"Yeah?" Darroll arched an eyebrow at Kirk.

Kirk picked up the bat and leaned on it. He was so damn blond, and his skin was so pink, you could hardly see his eyebrows in the pale April sunshine.

"What's it to you, anyway, Moonshine?" Darroll continued.

"What the gay boy said. You're good," Mondschein repeated. "You could make the team if you gave a damn."

"Like you give a damn about anything," Darroll retorted. "All you care about is following Ed Crowe around and wagging your tail when he pats you on the fucking head." For as long as Darroll had known Kirk Mondschein, he couldn't remember another time when he'd actually had a conversation alone with him, without Ed Crowe being there to butt in and make himself unpleasant. Darroll bet Kirk had been following Ed around since they were in kindergarten.

"Ed Crowe's a good guy really," Kirk said loyally. "People don't see what he's like out of school, when he's kicking back. People make him nervous, you know? On edge."

That was a good one. Nervous? Ed Crowe didn't have any nerves to be nervous with.

"Well, you know him better than me," said Darroll, "but all I know is Ed Crowe and his gang of goons, which includes *you*, Moonshine, have made my life a misery ever since I moved to this town. Made my friends' lives miserable, too. You guys bust up Vanessa's band's first fucking gig. That was a pretty shitty thing to do." He hefted the baseball in his hand, eyes narrowing, and Kirk lifted the bat, ready to strike at the ball if Darroll carried out his unspoken threat of slinging it right at Kirk's dumb blond head.

"That wasn't even Ed's idea," Kirk blurted.

"Oh yeah? Was it yours?"

"Christ, no!" yelped Kirk.

"Digby Doyle then?"

"No way. It was Patsy."

"You're shitting me."

"Cross my heart, Martock. It was Patsy Young. She was bent out of shape about Vanessa Murchison and Beth Vines being in a band. She thinks she can sing. She really can't," Kirk added conspiratorially, and Darroll smiled slightly.

"Not like Vanessa can either," Darroll yawned. "Typical high school band. Twenty percent talent, eighty percent pose. Why do you think I stayed out of it?"

"Stayed out of it? I thought you were the drummer."

"That was strictly one night only, Kirk. Rowdy Serxner's the drummer, only the great dumb fuck fell off his bike and busted up his wrist, the week of the first gig. They talked me into sitting in for him."

"What? No way!" Kirk gave an open-mouthed goofy smile. Darroll felt like pinching himself. What the hell was Kirk Mondschein doing, treating him as an equal? For a second, he wondered if the psychopathic murderer within him was shining through, making Kirk respond to him with respect. Then he reasoned that it was more likely that Kirk was impressed with him because he was dating Vanessa Murchison. You have to be a cool dude to get a steady date in high school; ergo, if you have a steady date in high school, you must be a cool dude. That was logic. Well, it was teenage logic, at least.

"Yes way," he said to Kirk. "Bet you guys could make a band that wasn't any worse than ours."

Kirk shook his head, looking slightly wistful. "Nah. I think we really just knew we couldn't do it, so we didn't want you to have it either. Are you still playing? Gonna be gigging down at the VFW again?"

"Yeah, they're still at it," Darroll said. "They're not gonna get me in again though. In fact," he said, fuelled by a sudden urge to cement the newly found détente between himself and Mondschein, "I was sort of glad you guys stopped the gig. I was only one song in, and I already wanted to throw the sticks down and walk out. Drumming is hard fucking work, you know? It looks like you just sit at the back and whack away in rhythm, but it's way difficult, and tires your arms out. Way more than baseball."

"Who knew?" said Kirk, in wonderment. Darroll reflected that there were a great many things that Moonshine didn't know. Most of them, he never would.

"Well, listen, Kirk. I'm not a guy who bears grudges," Darroll said, lying right through his teeth, because bearing grudges was what Darroll did better than almost anything. Bearing grudges was what made Darroll who he was. "If Ed Crowe stops acting like a jerk towards me, I'm prepared to give the guy a shot."

Ha ha. A shot. Straight between the eyes with Horsehead's gun. That was the kind of shot Darroll wanted to give Ed Crowe.

For a moment Darroll thought he'd overplayed his hand; that his casual offer would just make Kirk Mondschein laugh, and remind Darroll that Ed Crowe was the king of this school, and that Darroll was a mere peasant toiling in the fields to raise the king's crops. But Kirk looked thoughtful for a moment. He was plainly taking the suggestion seriously.

"Hey, look," he said after a few seconds, "I'll talk to Ed later. Tell him I was speaking to you. You know, I always thought you were kind of a jerk, hanging out with people like Joe Boardman and Chuck Milne –"

Darroll smiled a worldly smile at Moonshine.

"Joe Boardman and Chuck Milne are just like you and me." Another huge lie, but who cared? Todd Krank had thrown away his entire stock of truth and remade his life as one huge enormous lie, and not only did he have everyone fooled, but he looked ecstatic about it. "They're just trying to survive in this... this breadcrumb of a town, this cesspit of a school. Trying to last without being killed, or killing themselves. Then they can go away to college, and start actually living, rather than just existing." He took a step closer to Kirk, body language carefully calculated to include Kirk in what he'd said. "Don't tell me you're not doing that, Moon. You want to get the fuck out of Muldoon. Everyone does. And that happy day will come a hell of a lot quicker for all of us – you, me, Ed Crowe, Joe Boardman, Patsy, Vanessa – if we all make an effort to get along."

The speech was straight out of the Archie Andrews Big Book of Platitudes, of course, but Darroll knew Kirk would be impressed by it, for just that reason. And indeed he was. "Shit, Martock," Kirk said, shaking his head, "I hadn't thought of it that way."

A seed had been planted in the unpromising, dry earth of Kirk Mondschein's head, slowly struggling its way to germination, sucking up what few drops of intellectual water landed on it. Perhaps it might actually grow. Perhaps even Mondschein might make it out of this town one day. Jesus Christ, had he just done Kirk Mondschein a favour? Darroll tossed the baseball away.

"Think it over some more, Moonshine," he said as he walked away, taking long measured strides like a Hollywood action hero. Radiating charisma.

41

Over the next few days, Ed Crowe and his friends left the Psychopath Club more or less alone. Sometimes Darroll found Kirk Mondschein looking at him, as if he was still trying to make sense out of that conversation they'd had out in the batting cage. It was kind of creepy, especially given Moonshine's pink complexion and lack of discernible eyebrows, but it certainly beat having Ed Crowe's jockstrap shoved in his face.

He asked Vanessa one evening whether she'd noticed anything similar.

"I guess," she said. "Patsy Young is still a bitch, but she just ignores me now. I get more grief from Olivia. Anyone would think, the way she sneers at me for dating you, that she wanted you for her ugly, freckly little self."

Darroll hadn't considered that possibility. Could his stock really have risen so high in the market that two girls were getting ready to square off over him? If they were, his money would be on Vanessa every time. He remembered how she'd taken Kirk Mondschein down, during the VFW rumble.

He let the memory of that replay in his mind. He was in his room with Vanessa, watching television; or at least, Darroll was half-watching an episode of the Simpsons. It was far less interesting than the memory of Vanessa socking Moonshine. He was lying on his bed with his legs apart so he could see the television screen between his feet, while Vanessa sat in his desk chair, at forty-five degrees to the screen, idly poking through the contents of his desk. Darroll approved of her disdain for the Simpsons. That Bart Simpson, carrying on like he was such a rebel. He was as solid a pillar of the establishment as the President.

"Oh, wow," Vanessa suddenly exclaimed, jerking Darroll's attention away from Bart Simpson inviting the fat comic book guy to eat his shorts for the one millionth time.

"What?"

"Never knew you read these." Vanessa swivelled around in the chair, to show Darroll that she'd pulled one of those goddamned Archie comics out of the stack on his desk. Darroll rolled his eyes involuntarily. If Bart Simpson was an establishment figure, Archie Andrews was a million times more so.

"I thought you were only into the superheroes," Vanessa said. She'd found the whole cache of Archie comics, hidden away in the middle of the much bigger pile of actual readable comics that he'd traded from old Otway.

"I read Archie, years ago," Vanessa went on, flicking through the pages with a nostalgic smile. "Who do you root for? Betty or Veronica? I was always for Veronica."

"Far as I'm concerned, they can both suck my dick," Darroll said laconically. "I never read those things. I only picked that bunch up by accident."

"By accident? There must be twenty issues here."

"There was a yard sale, a few months back. I bought a whole stack of comic books, thinking they were superhero Marvels, and most of them turned out to be this heap of crap." Darroll climbed off the bed and took the comic from Vanessa's hands. "This comic makes me so mad," he said, smacking its front cover with his index finger to underline his point. "Year after year it goes on and on and on, and nothing ever changes. And the characters in it! You can't tell me that Archie and his white-bread pals bear any resemblance to any high school in the United States today. Hell, they bore no resemblance in nineteen-fifty, never mind today. This publication is worthless, Vanessa. No, it's worse than worthless. It's pernicious. It's unrealistic lies, from cover to cover." Darroll concluded his tirade by ripping a page clean out of the comic as he reached his crescendo.

For a moment, Vanessa looked startled at Darroll's outburst. Then she laughed, grabbed the book back from him, and tore a second page out, followed by a third. That made Darroll laugh too. He liked Vanessa's laugh. It wasn't a silly, shrill giggle; she knew how to deliver a laugh that was real and unrestrained.

"Hey, you know what?" Vanessa exclaimed, holding up the

last page she'd ripped from its place. "If you don't want these, we should totally make something out of them."

"What the hell can you make out of Archie comics? A bonfire?"

Vanessa was looking around for her bag. Like her, it was oversized, and big enough to hold a good many surprising things. Including the sketchbook which she pulled out of it.

"Art, Darroll," she said with a gleam in her eyes. "I can make art. We can make art."

Darroll raised one eyebrow. "We?"

"Get back on the bed," she invited him. Darroll shrugged, and obeyed, as Vanessa wheeled the chair away from his desk and turned it to face the bed.

"No, don't just lie down," she said as Darroll lay back. "I want you... Do you mind me sketching you?"

"I'm fine."

"Well, I want you to lie like... like a murder victim."

Darroll turned his head sharply to face Vanessa. For a guilty second he feared that she knew something that she could not know, that she had no possible means of knowing.

"How does a murder victim lie?" he asked guardedly.

"Well, uh... can you sprawl? Put your arms and legs out... yeah, like that." Vanessa had selected a pencil and was already at work as Darroll rearranged himself. "That's great! Just lie like that, try not to move."

Darroll closed his eyes and imagined himself as a corpse. How had he met his death? A bullet, a blade, murder, suicide, accident? Was this what he would have looked like if he'd died in the wreck of the Oldsmobile, and been laid out by Beth Vines' father?

He felt oddly calm and peaceable for a while. Then, to his own surprise, he found himself growing aroused at the thought of himself, cold and lifeless, young and forever pure, tucked neatly and permanently away inside the sliding drawer unit in the mortuary. The antiseptic smell and the darkness that he had found inside the drawer, the day Crowe's mob had locked him down there, called out to him from his memory.

He drifted into a state of neither sleep nor wakefulness, in which time became an irrelevancy, and it was only when Vanessa said "There... I think that's good," that he opened one eye to look at her.

"You all right, Darroll?" she asked, looking at him. "You enjoy that, huh?" Then she frowned, and without warning, reached over to him and felt his crotch.

"Wow. You did enjoy that." Her hand rested on his erection for a second or two before withdrawing.

"I never had a beautiful girl want to sketch me before," Darroll said. Which was true, but a long way from the whole truth. The look Vanessa gave him suggested that she knew it wasn't the whole truth, too.

But she didn't press the subject further. "Do you have any paste?" she asked him, instead.

He opened the other eye and leaned up on his elbows, his arousal dissipating. "There should be a glue stick in the top desk drawer," he said.

There was. Vanessa found a pair of scissors, too, and used them to attack the comic book. Then she went to work with the glue stick for a minute or two, before holding the results of her work up for Darroll to inspect. "There! Whaddya think of that, huh?"

Darroll looked at Vanessa's work. The pencil sketch showed a sprawled figure, laid out on his back, clothes torn and body pierced by multiple slashes from a knife. Blood, shaded dark grey in heavy pencil, flowed from the wounds and into pools on the floor in the foreground. Where the dead man's head should have been, the incongruously grinning features of Archie Andrews had been pasted into the picture.

Darroll's eyes moved away from the picture and back to Vanessa, meeting her own eyes. She was smiling; the smile of a talented person who knows she's used her talent to create something valid, something worthwhile. Something that did not exist before she made it.

"You're good," he said to Vanessa, and he meant it. Then he added, "You should do some more."

She did some more. Over the next few hours Vanessa created

half a dozen further sketches, all dark and savage, filled with death, doom and mayhem, and all of them featuring Archie's pals. A skeletal figure, crucified on an ornate frame with daggers driven into its hands, wore the face of Reggie Mantle. In the original comic panel Reggie's mouth had been open in laughter; now it resembled a frozen rictus of agony.

Another sketch captured a helpless pedestrian being mown down by an automobile whose grille and headlights had been drawn to resemble a wickedly grinning face; the pedestrian was Jughead Jones, eyes closed nonchalantly, unaware that his jaywalking had given him a split second left to live before a violent demise. A third sketch featured a young woman looking into her vanity mirror only to see a hideous, rotting zombie looking back out at her. The woman bore the head of Betty Cooper, and this one had a speech balloon too: "But – but Archie! I only did my hair this way because I thought you'd like it!"

"Wow, it's late," Vanessa said. "I need to get home. Anyway, I think I'm all drawn out."

"You going to show anyone these?" Darroll said, gathering the bits of scissored-up comic book and shooting them into his wastebasket.

"Might do. You know I want to go to art college. I might put these in my portfolio, if I still like them in a week. I never know whether something I've drawn is any good straight away, you know?"

Darroll didn't know. "I didn't realise. They look good to me, but I can't draw worth a damn."

"Bet you can," Vanessa said. "Bet you could if someone actually showed you how. Would you like me to?"

Darroll realised that he would, and nodded.

Vanessa laughed. "You'd like to be able to draw dead, grotesque things, wouldn't you? You cracked a boner just lying there playing dead. You ought to be a goth, you really ought. You see the beauty in the dark side."

You have no idea, Darroll thought. No idea at all.

And then the urge suddenly filled him to try to tell her, to try to explain the inexplicable to her, to make her believe the unbelievable. He knew he had to do it quickly if he was going to do it at all, or else he would think better of it.

"It's not so much the dark side," he said, his eyes watching hers warily to evaluate her reaction. "It's more that... well, everything is so insignificant, in the big picture."

"Go on." Vanessa's eyes met his, inviting him to elaborate. He could tell that she knew something meaningful was coming.

"You at all familiar with the parallel universe theory?" he said. His heart was thumping, as it had just before he shot Tidmarsh.

"Yes, I heard of it," Vanessa replied. "It's a stupid name. It should be called the branching universe theory. If universes were parallel they wouldn't meet at all. Parallel things don't meet. Like railroad lines."

God, always with railroads and Vanessa, Darroll thought.

"Whatever it's called, you get the idea," he said. "Right?"

"Sure." Vanessa reached out to Darroll's desk, where an open packet of candy sat, and picked one piece out of the bag. "Open wide," she instructed him, and when he did, she popped the candy into his mouth.

"There's a universe," she said as he swallowed it, "where instead of my feeding you that, I ate it myself. And another universe where, instead of M&Ms, that was a packet of Reese's Pieces. Is that what you mean?"

"Yes," he said, having disposed of the candy. "Now... just think how many different universes there are. All of them essentially similar, one tiny difference perhaps. You and I are the same in probably more than ninety-nine percent of those universes. Ninety-nine point nine nine nine percent," he corrected himself.

"You're gearing up to make a point," Vanessa said, her eyes still meeting his, restrained, shrewd.

"Okay," he went on. "Say I were to drop dead, right here and now. Heart attack or something."

Vanessa's nose wrinkled a little as she frowned.

"I'd be dead... in this universe. Because a clot happened to get snagged in the exact blood vessel that it cut power to my heart and killed me. But think of this. In countless other universes, that blood clot had a fractionally different shape, or my blood vessel was a tiny bit wider, or... you get the point, right? There are a million worlds with a million living Darrolls, where I go on to be twenty or thirty or forty or older, get married, have kids. What does it matter? What does it matter that one Darroll Martock, in one dimension, has cashed in his chips? There's plenty more. An infinite number. What does one life matter, Vanessa? One life out of a million?"

Vanessa broke eye contact with him and looked into the middle distance, as though contemplating those million other universes.

"When you put it like that it sounds sobering," she said slowly. "As though everything and everyone is one grain of sand on a big old infinite beach."

He caught hold of her hand. "But we are, Vanessa. That's the thing. We're nothing. All of us are nothing, repeated and replicated, over and over again – "

He realised that he was babbling, and forced himself to fall silent.

She kept hold of his hand, using it to pull him up against her. Her other hand reached behind his head, and she kissed him, deeply and passionately, with her tongue sliding between his lips.

"You're not nothing to me, Darroll," she said when the kiss was finally over. "I love you because you're the only guy I know who thinks that way... who could think of thinking that way. You may be only one of a million Darrolls, and I may be only one of a million Vanessas, but you're the only one that this particular Vanessa has, and that's the way I like it. Oh, shit, I have to move it," she added in alarm as she caught sight of the time, "or my parents will ground me for a decade."

After she'd hurried away, Darroll sat on his bed, thinking about what it had been like when he was only one Darroll, before the accident and the swirls and Horsehead and everything. The difference was so enormous that it felt like a butterfly trying to recall what it was like to be a caterpillar; there were no terms of reference for him to work from, no words that he could find to even start describing it.

So he abandoned the attempt to find the words, and instead picked up the mutilated copy of Archie, turning over its pages. He looked at that comic book for a long time, staring at the headless figures of Archie and Betty and Reggie Mantle, thoughts winding through his head in intricate spirals.

42

Friday afternoon, he was cleaning out his locker. He could never understand how the hell his locker grew so full of garbage, candy wrappers and screwed-up bits of paper and shit. He sure didn't put them there. Perhaps Ed Crowe had a skeleton key and snuck around the lockers while nobody was looking, filling them full of crap. Or perhaps the school lockers were a dimensional gateway. That would have felt like a stupid idea, once upon a time, before Darroll became a trans-dimensional traveller himself.

He could just picture all the shit from other worlds, swept around the multiverse in a huge multi-dimensional sargasso like water round a plughole, to be spat out here and give Darroll the job of having to clean it out and throw it away every few weeks. And then it probably dropped through the bottom of the trashcan and back into the swirl of garbage again. Trash cannot be created or destroyed, he mused. It can only be moved around. He'd have to ask Horsehead that, next time he saw him.

Darroll's existentialism was interrupted by someone coming up behind him and touching him on the shoulder. Not a jab or a poke, just a slight touch to draw his attention. Of all people, it was Patsy Young.

"Hey, Darroll," she said. Darroll didn't think she'd ever used his first name before.

"At your service," he drawled, and she actually smiled.

"You're a funny bastard, did anyone ever tell you?"

"Frequently. I'm going to move to New York and do stand-up. I'm the next Bill Hicks."

"Look," Patsy said, "a few of us are getting together tonight. There will be beer. You wanna come? You can bring the goth goddess too."

"I guess Ed's gonna be there?"

"Course Ed's gonna be there. You'll be fine, though. This isn't some sting operation," Patsy said, which shook Darroll, because that was exactly what he had been wondering.

It was no particular secret, among teenagers at least, that Ed Crowe's drinking parties took place in one of the closed-down buildings in Muldoon. It was only a little way down the street from the doorway where he'd taken refuge, that time the swirls took him in the Oldsmobile.

That evening, he drove the Oldsmobile down there, parked in the lot by Celebration Burger and went inside to collect Vanessa. For someone who waxed self-righteous about how fast food was unhealthy for the mind and body, she sure put away plenty of hamburgers. Darroll didn't mind, though. So she was a hypocrite. So was everyone. So was he. He was about to go and drink beer he hated with a bunch of people he despised, just in order to cut and slash his way one more rung up the social ladder, and if that wasn't hypocrisy he didn't know what was.

Darroll and Vanessa left the Oldsmobile in Celebration Burger's lot and walked up Third Street to Crowe's speakeasy. He sidled around the building and thumped on the door in back, Vanessa at his shoulder. Ed Crowe opened it in person.

"Well hey," he said. "Captain Pencilneck and his best girl."

Darroll suppressed the immediate urge to simply jerk the door closed and shut Ed Crowe's face in it. "Ha de ha ha," he said, affecting to take the insult as a joke. "Patsy said this was the place?"

"Yeah, it's the place," Ed said, letting the door open further. Darroll stepped cautiously forward, into the lion's den.

The building had once been some kind of showroom. Now it was malodorous, creaky and probably unsafe. Candles cast a dim light over the back room to which Ed directed the newcomers. It reminded Darroll of the disused farmhouse where the Psychopath Club sometimes met.

The candlelight flickered over the faces of Patsy Young, Kirk Mondschein and Dig Doyle. Ed Crowe took his seat alongside Patsy on the mortal remains of a sofa, and gestured at a shapeless mass in one corner that proved, upon inspection, to be a bean-bag. Vanessa sat on it, which didn't leave much room for Darroll, but he leant partly on the bean-bag and partly on the wall, and managed to achieve stability.

It was pretty lame, all things considered. Darroll felt stupid for having envied Ed Crowe his social life. There were a couple of six-packs of beer in the middle of the room; Dig Doyle, they learned, had some means of stealing them from the gas station down by the interstate. Doyle kept giving Darroll and Vanessa sour looks, as if to say that he hadn't gone to the trouble of stealing them just to see them vanish down the throats of interlopers.

Ed Crowe and Patsy Young spent most of the time canoodling on the sofa, and since Doyle didn't appear inclined to be social, that left the conversational department in charge of Kirk Mondschein. Banal was not the word. Darroll took a beer, partly to be conformist and partly from actual curiosity, but it tasted like soapy water. He set it aside unobtrusively. Patsy, Ed and Dig all drank, and Patsy and Ed became more and more amorous. Vanessa drank, too, but rather than pawing at Darroll, she kept up her conversational end and observed. Darroll was so glad he was dating her rather than Patsy Young.

After a couple of hours, Ed made it clear that the party was at an end. Even Kirk Mondschein could figure that he wanted the rest of them to get lost so he could nail Patsy Young on the sofa. Adding the empty bottles to a pile of them in the other corner, Darroll and Vanessa got the hell out of there alongside Doyle and Mondschein. Doyle took straight off, leaving Mondschein grinning stupidly at them outside the back door. It was dark by now, but Darroll could see his face well enough to figure that he was imagining what Ed and Patsy were up to inside.

"That was fun, huh?" he said.

"Good times, Moonshine, good times," Vanessa said, with just enough sarcasm for Darroll to detect and for Mondschein to miss. A little thrill shot through Darroll. God, Vanessa was the best.

"You guys meet in there all the time?" Darroll asked casually.

"Yeah, s'right," Mondschein confirmed. "Good place to hide out. Nobody knows 'bout it." Wrong again, Moonshine, thought Darroll.

"Don't you go telling anybody, now," Mondschein warned, "or Ed'll be mad with ya. And when Ed gets mad, you sure know about it, yeah?"

"Secret's safe with us, right, Vanessa?" said Darroll. Plans and possibilities were beginning to coalesce in his head. They continued to do so as he walked back down to Celebration Burger, and as he drove first Vanessa, and then himself, home.

43

The swirls came twice more in the next few weeks, but both times, they found Darroll in school. Frustrating. When he dimension-hopped in school, he always seemed to arrive in a universe where he'd been killed in the accident, making him appear in class as a revenant ghost. The first few times, he'd had fun spooking people, advancing on them menacingly as though to take them away to the grave with him, intoning threats and prophecies in spectral tones.

But it grew old quickly. There were only so many ways he could wave his arms at people, only so many ways he could warn them that they'd soon be in their coffins like him. And they all responded the same way, almost every time. He was so sick of hearing Debbie Bloch shriek like a factory whistle. He had stored up a few home truths ready for Mr Tidmarsh, should he meet the principal on any of these excursions, but they always seemed to happen in class. His zingers remained undelivered.

But a few weeks down the line, the swirls finally came at home in the evening.

He'd been waiting for this. He'd planned ahead for it, planned very carefully.

He hopped out of his chair quickly and made a dive for his closet. That would give him some privacy for the shift. Also, there was a bag in the closet that he was going to need.

"I'll be right back out!" he promised Vanessa, who was lying on his bed with her sketchbook and the glue-stick and the dismembered comic books. She was drawing Moose Mason being shot at point-blank range by a machine gun, ludicrous numbers of bullets going in his body one side and out the other. Some of the bullets had smiley faces drawn on them.

She said something that he couldn't hear, partly because of the distraction of the swirls and partly because he was pulling the closet door closed behind him. The swirls were getting stronger. Where the hell was that bag? He only had seconds.

He found it and snatched it up, holding it tightly to his chest as he fell down to his knees and the swirls jerked him away on their wild ride.

The first thing he checked, when the swirls left him alone, was to note there was a thread of light under the closet door. By now he knew what that signified. The room beyond was occupied. And presumably it was occupied by himself.

He regained his feet, and took a couple of moments to compose himself and straighten his hair, smiling at the thought of sprucing himself up to meet his own double. Then, with a deep breath, he pushed the door open and stepped out.

From the look on his double's face, he wasn't used to having his own doppelganger suddenly step out of the closet.

"Hi, Darroll," said Darroll to Darroll Two.

Darroll Two, staring at Darroll, moved one hand to touch himself on the opposite arm.

"No need to pinch yourself," he went on. "You are not dreaming. Everything is gonna be just fine."

Darroll Two's arms dropped to his side, one of them still holding a comic book. Darroll tilted his head to look at it. "Spiderman? With great power comes great responsibility, right? Or at least that's what they want you to think."

Darroll Two finally found his voice. "What the hell is this? Are you me? From the future or something? Do you own a time machine?"

"Close but no cigar," Darroll told him. "You can't go forward or back in time. But you can go sideways. I need to ask you a question or two, Darroll, okay?"

That was rhetorical, really, but Darroll Two nodded slowly, suspicion replacing astonishment on his features.

"You got an Oldsmobile 88, right? Your father bought it you last birthday? Piece of shit present from a piece of shit parent?"

Darroll Two nodded again. "Yeah... yeah, it sucks, I guess."

"You had an accident in it, ever?"

Darroll Two shook his head this time. "Any dings in the paintwork were there already."

"Okay," said Darroll. "In that case the easiest thing to do is to show you this."

He reached up to his head and pushed the hair back from the little plate which covered the hole that the fence-post had punched in his skull. Darroll Two's eyes widened a little. "What the hell's that?"

"Long story short," Darroll said, "I put that car into a ditch and gave myself a hole in the head. Don't know how I didn't kill myself." He decided against telling Darroll Two about how many universes he'd seen where the accident had had exactly that result. "And somehow... what happened to me has jolted me loose in time. Every so often, I pull a stunt like this. I fall out of my own dimension, I turn up in another place where I don't belong, and I get to meet myself."

Darroll Two licked his lips, weighing the situation.

"I know how unlikely it seems," Darroll continued. "And I know what you're thinking, because I am you and you are me. Or at least, you are the me I would have been if I hadn't crashed my car. You be careful of ice in that thing," he added. "Fucking ice is everywhere in winter, here."

"Go on," said Darroll Two. He still looked thoroughly suspicious.

"So that's my story. I still don't know whether it's actually happening, or whether it's all just a delusion caused by my having a big ol' hole in my head. It'd be funny if it was all in my imagination, yeah? And you didn't really exist?"

"I do exist," Darroll Two objected.

"Yeah, but if I was imagining you, that's exactly what I'd imagine you saying. Anyhoo, another question for you," Darroll said. "What's your life like at school? Pretty shitty, I bet? Do you get grief from Ed Crowe, and those jerks who go round with him?"

He knew before his duplicate answered, from the look on his face, what the answer would be. This Darroll had just driven to school the day of the accident, hadn't swerved off the road, hadn't nearly killed himself, had had one more day the same as any other in the vast game of musical chairs that was high school. The game where you grabbed a chair and sat there, trying not to be seen, trying just to survive. No matter that the seat of the chair was covered with nails and tacks sticking into your ass, you kept sitting there because there were always fewer chairs than there were people trying to sit down. And every now and again someone came and took a chair away, but the music kept on playing. That was high school. High school in every dimension he'd seen.

"God, yes," said Darroll Two. "Ed Crowe is the biggest asshole in Straus High, and that is fucking saying something."

"Good, good," said Darroll. "Hold that thought. Do you hang out with Chuck Milne and people like that?"

"Sometimes."

"Okay then." Darroll fell silent a moment, planning what he had to do, and what he needed to tell his doppelganger to do. "In a few moments I'm gonna be leaving the house, and I don't expect you'll see me again."

"What? Why not?"

"Because I'll be going back where I came from. I'm afraid you can't come with me," Darroll apologised. "But with luck, once I'm back home, your life, your life here, will be a bit better, okay?" An afterthought hit him suddenly, and he added, "Speaking of which, did you realise Vanessa Murchison is sweet on you?"

"Fuck off," was Darroll Two's succinct reply to that. Darroll wondered whether he was right. Perhaps in this world Vanessa was uninterested in Darroll. Perhaps she wasn't such a fucking goth, even. Perhaps she was a cheerleader. Anything was possible.

So Darroll shrugged. "Just saying. That's not exactly important. But this is." He fixed his twin with a stern look. "Once I'm out of this house, get on the phone to Chuck Milne or Rowdy Serxner, and get together with them. Get them to come over here, ideally. Spend tonight hanging out with them. And with your mother too, if you can bear that. You have to believe me, Darroll. This is fucking crucial. I'm not here to get you into the shit, and if you want to avoid the shit, boy, do not be alone tonight. Under no circumstances must you be out of other people's sight tonight. Do you understand?"

"Why –"

"Never fucking mind why. You'll know why, tomorrow. You have to trust me on this. Swear to me you'll do it, Darroll."

"Okay, okay, jesus, I swear," said Darroll Two. "Does it matter what I do?"

"Nope. Read comics with them, watch television, hell, you can even play Dungeons and Dragons. Do Chuck and Rowdy always pester you to play that dumb game, like they do me? Okay, then." He did a quick mental check to ensure he'd forgotten nothing, while watching his duplicate closely to make sure his words had sunk home. They seemed to have.

"Gimme your hand, Darroll," he invited Darroll Two, and Darroll Two lifted the hand that wasn't holding Spiderman.

"Sorry I can't stay to get to know you better," he said, "but time is pressing." Funny how time can be infinite sideways and yet so short when measured going forward, he thought to himself as he shook hands, and then tucked the bag under his arm. "I'm out of here. You get on that phone."

The Oldsmobile was sitting outside the house, but he couldn't take it, of course. Instead he walked up the street and towards the centre of Muldoon, keeping his head down and his shoulders hunched, thinking. His plan was a little vague at this point, necessarily so, because he never knew what time of day he would be swirled away, or what day of the week.

He made his first point of call Celebration Burger. He walked past, glancing through the windows, looking for one particular person. But it was quiet inside, and none of the patrons were who he was looking for.

He continued around the block and made for the disused showroom, sneaking quietly round the back of the building. He put his ear to the door, and he hit the jackpot. They weren't even trying to keep quiet in there. Stupid bastards. Stupid, stupid bastards.

He retreated from the door and hunkered down behind a row of three big trash cans. It stank down there, and he wondered for a moment if there were rats. Town like Muldoon, probably only the rats were happy here.

He waited, and waited some more, fidgeting around and trying to avoid cramp. Christ, were they going to be in there all night?

Eventually the door opened, and he peeked carefully to see who was coming out. It was Digby Doyle, on his own. Darroll waited for him to turn around the building and head for the street, but instead, he turned the other way, towards Darroll and the trash cans. Darroll's heart thumped as Dig walked closer. This wasn't part of his plan. It could blow the whole thing wide open if Dig found him so soon.

Just as it seemed inevitable he'd be discovered crouching there, Dig came to a halt and turned to face the blank back wall of the building, then unzipped his fly. Relief flooded over Darroll, followed by the unpleasant realisation that his hiding place was downhill from where Dig was standing.

Doyle had apparently drunk a lot of beer, judging by how much urine came trickling down toward the trash cans. Darroll didn't dare move. The little stream of liquid passed within a few inches of his left foot and found a dirty, half-clogged little drain. It disappeared down that, to Darroll's considerable relief, and no doubt to Doyle's as well.

Finally Doyle farted, shook himself, and zipped his jeans back up. Then he turned away from Darroll. Was he going back inside? He finally headed back around to the street.

Darroll climbed back to his feet, glancing at his watch, and picked up the bag he'd brought with him. Was it safe to press ahead with the plan, if Ed's party was about to break up? Maybe it had already finished; maybe Dig was the last one out. He decided that if it went sour, he could always abort. There would be other times. Other chances.

He stepped inside the building.

His breathing was growing faster as adrenalin began to shoot around his blood vessels. He tried to summon up the memory of Tidmarsh, lying in his own blood on his own office floor, and the way it had made him feel. Somehow he couldn't do it. The only face that would come into focus on his mental screen was Louis Vickery, with that damn bow tie of his, telling him to go back home and put Muldoon on the map. Well, he was going to do that, right enough.

The dim light from inside and the sound of conversation told him that, as he hoped, there were people still in here. He followed both of those clues into the party room with the fragmentary furnishings, and there was Ed Crowe, one arm around Patsy Young, his hand practically on her boob. They were both laughing, and so was Kirk Mondschein. They stopped laughing when they saw Darroll appear in the doorway, the candles framing him in shadow.

"Martock?" Ed spat the word out, like an old time cowboy getting rid of a wad of slimy tobacco into a cuspidor.

"Little me," Darroll confirmed.

"What the fuck are you doing here?" Ed dropped Patsy, who lurched a little, and began to head for Darroll with an air that promised trouble when he came within reach. Darroll used the hand that wasn't holding his bag to raise one palm to Ed Crowe, like a traffic cop.

"Wait a moment, Crowe," he said, surprised at how confident he sounded. The Darroll he'd left behind in his bedroom earlier would never have sounded like that. Certainly he wouldn't have been capable of making Ed Crowe stop dead in his tracks. But Darroll himself knew how. Darroll had charisma.

And stop dead Ed Crowe did. "Yeah? What?"

"I need to talk," Darroll said. "To you guys. Mega important shit. I'm not even joking."

Ed grunted. "So talk. It'd better be good."

Darroll looked over at Kirk Mondschein, who was standing there uncertainly, looking uncertain whether he ought to be there or not. Darroll had to suppress a sudden surge of sympathy for Moonshine, the temptation to tell him to go take a hike. That wasn't the way a real psychopath would think. If Mondschein was going to hang around Ed Crowe, like a small, stupid satellite circling a large, stupid planet, then Mondschein would reap the consequences of living a satellite life.

So Darroll leant on the door frame casually. "Okay, here's the situation," he said, his eyes on Ed Crowe, not Kirk or Patsy. "You guys haven't exactly always gotten along with me and my friends. That pisses me off. See, Ed, I know you believe you have a reputation to keep up as the tough guy at Straus. I'm not out to challenge that. I'd be dumb to try. What I'm proposing is just that you go easy on me and my best buds, and if you want to use your muscle, well, it's not like there aren't other people you can use it on. And if you're wondering why you should listen to me rather than pounding me into gravel, here's why." He reached into the bag.

Ed Crowe looked at him, and the bag, suspiciously.

Darroll's hand came out of the bag holding a bottle. "I know you guys appreciate a little drinking party now and again," he said, trying to keep his grip on the bottle casual, and not let his fingers clutch it so hard his knuckles whitened. "Beer's okay, but did you guys ever sample bourbon?"

Patsy Young reacted first. "What the hell? Where did you get bourbon from?"

"Never you mind where I got it from," said Darroll, who had found the bottle, dusty and half full, in a box in the garage at home with some of his father's junk. "I figured you guys might be less inclined to beat up on me, if I shared it with you. A peace offering. Tell me I'm right, huh?" He tilted his head on one side jauntily and looked at Ed Crowe, from whose sails the wind was plainly departing.

Again it was Patsy who spoke. "I guess that's fair," she said.

Ed nodded. "Yeah, that's fair," he echoed. "Who'd you want us to leave alone?"

"Me, of course. Chuck Milne. Rowdy Serxner. And Joe Boardman."

"Joe Boardman?" Ed scowled. "You want me to keep my hands off that faggot?"

"I want you to keep your hands off all of those people," Darroll reiterated. He was uncomfortably aware that if he blew the negotiations here, Ed could lay him out flat, using only one hand, take the bourbon and kick his ass out the door. Of course, he had precautions against things going wrong, but he wanted the plan to work. For his own pride's sake, apart from anything else.

"Fine," Ed sighed, "you found my price, Martock. I'll lay off Boardman, long as he stays out of my way and doesn't flutter his fucking fairy eyelashes at me."

"He won't," Darroll said assuredly. "I guarantee that your personal space will remain free of Boardman's eyelashes. Now, shall we drink to this... non-aggression pact?"

Crowe smiled. "Yeah, let's see what kind of shit this brand is." He took the bottle from Darroll and looked at the label, though Darroll was sure Crowe didn't know one bourbon from another. Probably not from rye.

"Okay!" said Mondschein, pumping a fist in the air. "I dunno about you, Ed, but I like this stuff."

Ed sat down on the sofa, still holding the bottle, and Patsy joined him, leaving Darroll and Mondschein to find as much comfort as they could amid the old cushions and bean-bags scattered on the floor. "Pull up," Ed told them, "because I'm fucked if I'm getting up to pass this bottle round."

He uncorked it as Mondschein and Darroll dragged themselves closer to the sofa, Mondschein resting his back against the end of it.

"Whoo," Crowe said after he'd taken a slug. "That's got a kick to it. Try this, Patsy." He passed her the bottle by means of hooking a thumb into the top of her cleavage, and sliding it down between her breasts. Patsy yelped and hauled it back out. "Fuck off, Ed! That thing's cold."

Moonshine chortled dutifully as Patsy took her turn at the bottle.

"Is it meant to burn like that?" she asked.

"Sure it is," Ed said before Darroll could reassure her. "Forget beer, this is better."

Patsy shrugged and passed the bottle to Kirk. I see I'm still bottom of the totem pole far as these guys are concerned, Darroll thought. For now.

When the bottle finally came to Darroll, he tilted it to his lips, but didn't drink any. He kept an eye on the others as he did so, but none of them seemed to notice anything amiss, or to wonder why he was wearing gloves. It was dark in there; the candles didn't light the room worth a damn. And everyone wore gloves half the year in Muldoon, anyway, because otherwise your fingers would freeze off.

As the bottle travelled around, Patsy started telling a long and unfunny story. Some girl from Straus had had sex with her own cousin, or maybe she'd claimed she had in order to sound cool and then tried to take it back when everyone acted like it was gross. Cousins are totally incest, right? Darroll was too busy watching the level of the bourbon going down to catch the girl's name when Patsy first mentioned it, and then as the story continued, she didn't say it again. Toward the end of the story she started to get incoherent, and let her head fall onto Ed Crowe's shoulder. Ed himself wasn't in a much better state; Darroll could tell, because he didn't start pawing at Patsy when she began to snore.

Kirk annexed the bottle from Ed, without Ed objecting, and looked up over the arm of the sofa at them.

"Fuck, Martock," he slurred, "this stuff's powerful."

"Isn't it, though?" Darroll said. Ed's head was tilted back and his mouth had dropped open. Two down, one to go.

"Mah uncle had some bourbon one time," Kirk said. Darroll noticed that Kirk's accent was drifting further and further south the more he drank from the bottle. Darroll wondered whether he'd fall unconscious before his voice reached Texas. "It was mighty good but... but not like this." He thrust the bottle in Ed's direction. Ed remained oblivious, so Kirk swung his arm around to pass it to Darroll instead.

He didn't even bother with the charade of lifting it to his lips as he listened to Kirk burble aimlessly about his family and their drinking habits. He held onto the bottle for as short a time as he thought was safe, about a minute, then sent it back toward Kirk.

Drink it, damn you, he commanded Moonshine mentally. Drink it and pass out like the others. Jesus, how much can this guy take on board?

He'd bought it online, a chemical that was sold as alloy wheel cleaner, but which he had learned with fascination also served very well as a knock-out mixture. He had topped up the bourbon bottle with it, but he was starting to wonder whether he'd put enough of the chemical into the bottle. He'd read up on it as much as he could, on several different web pages, but he wasn't some kind of drug baron, measuring everything out in cold precise glass containers in a big laboratory.

It felt like forever, but it was only five minutes more before Kirk Mondschein stopped talking and started making grunting, rattling snores. Darroll watched him for a minute to make sure he was really out, and that the noise he was making didn't rouse Ed or Patsy.

"Ed?" he said, then repeated it, louder. No response.

Looked like he was good to go.

44

His first step was to pick up the bottle, go outside, and tip the remaining liquid down the drain to mix with Digby Doyle's piss. As the mixture of bourbon and cleaning chemical tricked away through the grate he squinted down, wondering where the drain led and whether there was any way of detecting the adulterated liquor. Too bad if there was. Even if they found it in the drain, what could they do? His double in this world hadn't ordered any wheel cleaner, hadn't made any tell-tale web searches. And he would be gone. They couldn't pin this on his double, and they couldn't catch him.

He dropped the bottle over the wall at the back of the lot behind the building, into the bushes beyond. So much for the bottle.

Back inside, Patsy Young, like Crowe and Mondschein, was still passed out. He bent over her and dragged her off the sofa. If she wakes up, he thought to himself, I have to decide whether to off her straight away, or try and tell her I was worried because she passed out and was trying to revive her.

But she didn't wake up.

He laid her on the bean-bag, face down.

He licked his lips with distaste, and then passed onto the next stage of his plan. This involved unfastening Patsy's jeans and hauling them down to her ankles, then doing the same with her panties. She had a big zit on her right butt cheek, which he had to resist the temptation to squeeze.

Somehow Darroll found it easier to arrange Kirk Mondschein in a similar way, bare-assed, pants round his knees, his body resting on Patsy's. Darroll snuck a quick look at Kirk's crotch out of curiosity, to see whether his pubes were as blond as the rest of his hair. They were.

He stood surveying his work for a moment, critically, trying to imagine it through the eye of a police officer. It looked convincing to him. On to the next movement of the symphony.

He took the last item but one out of the bag, the kitchen knife, a smile spreading over his face. No hesitation, now, and no doubt. Unhurriedly and carefully, he cut Patsy Young's throat, followed by Kirk Mondschein's. He tried not to get too much blood on him, but it was hard; the blood went everywhere. It was surprising just how much of it there was in what felt like no time. Could he smell it? Was the scent in his nostrils real, or imagination?

Okay. We're half way there. Now to finish the tableau. He imagined himself as Ed Crowe, coming into the hideaway only to find Kirk Mondschein nuts-deep in his girlfriend. Or about to be so, anyway, he corrected himself; he was pretty sure that the forensic evidence could prove that Kirk hadn't actually had his dick in her. But that didn't matter. Say Ed interrupted them before they actually got down to it.

Adjusting grip upon the knife, he began to stab savagely at the bodies of Kirk and Patsy Young. He found himself baring his teeth, realising he was veering towards the dangerous line that separated rational control from simple animal frenzy. He tried to calm himself, but blood was singing in his ears like choirs of angels. He was panting for breath by the time he judged that he'd done enough.

He had expected to be jerked back home by now, but there was no sign of the swirls returning. What if this was the one time they decided not to come for him? What if he was stuck here forever?

There was a lot of blood on him. Such a lot.

His sudden attack of nerves made the knife drop from his hand, and he had to stoop quickly and retrieve it, only narrowly avoiding kneeling in the blood next to it. That would have blown it, for sure.

Stepping all the more carefully, he turned his attention back to Ed Crowe, who was still sleeping like a baby on the sofa. A massively overgrown, ugly baby. He took Crowe's unprotesting hand and wrapped it round the knife, trying to make the nerveless fingers hold it in a realistic way. He knew that a smart cop might smell a rat if the fingerprints weren't just right on the handle. Next he dropped it on the sofa alongside him, still expecting every moment to find the swirls coming to take him away, ha-ha.

Still they didn't.

Why didn't they? A sudden thrill shot through him. Was Horsehead watching him, holding the swirls back? Or was this to be the one occasion where the swirls didn't come at all? Was he to be marooned here, in a universe with a nervous duplicate and with the blood of two murdered teenagers on his hands? That would put Muldoon on the map, all right.

He pushed the fears away from his mind, with such force that he let out a grunt of effort, and reached for the bag once more, to retrieve the final item from it. Even in this grisly room of death, he felt slightly nauseated as he fished out Ed Crowe's dirty jockstrap. Holding it carefully in his gloved hand, he rubbed the nasty thing down the crack of Kirk Mondschein's ass, then repeated the procedure with Patsy Young's intimate areas. That, he reckoned, should give the forensic scientists some food for thought. He noticed one of Ed's pubic hairs, carefully detached it from the jockstrap, and tucked it safely into Kirk's asscrack. He dabbed the jockstrap on the knife handle, too, and finally tossed it into a corner.

Still no swirls? Still no sweet chariot to carry him home?

Ed Crowe was snoring peacefully.

He left the candles there to burn themselves out. He didn't exactly care if the place burned down. All he cared about was getting out and getting home.

If the swirls wouldn't take him away, his own legs would have to.

He slid out of the back door, the bag under his arm. What the hell was he going to do? He couldn't let himself be seen. He was meant to be a mile away, at home with his mother, with other witnesses to prove a rock solid alibi. He wasn't meant to still be here, covered in blood and –

There was movement in the empty space behind the building. He thought his heart was going to stop.

"Hello, Darroll."

It was Horsehead. It was only Horsehead.

"What the fuck?" he snarled at him between his teeth. "You scared me to death."

"Better scared to death than stabbed, surely?" said Horsehead mildly.

"How... how did you know?"

Of course, Horsehead ignored the direct question. He stood there, staring down at Darroll, until Darroll cracked and broke eye contact.

"Listen," he said to Horsehead, "I have to get back home. Why aren't I back home?"

Horsehead shrugged. "I was curious. Your plan was intriguing. I wanted you to have chance to follow it through to its end."

"Yes, well," Darroll snapped, "it's all done and dusted, and I need to get the fuck out of here."

"I suppose you do," said Horsehead, still casual, still relaxed. For the amount of concern Horsehead showed for the murderer or for his victims, they might as well have been talking about the weather. Darroll wondered for a second what would happen if he turned back into the building, retrieved the knife, and shoved it right into Horsehead's fucking eye.

"Don't," said Horsehead, as though he'd read the thought. "It would not be pleasant for either of us. Just run along home."

As he spoke the word 'home', the familiar sensation finally, finally, began to well up inside Darroll. The fuzziness and the swirls swooped in towards him like an old friend greeting him, an old friend too long gone. He had never been so glad to abandon himself to their gentle care.

When he found himself back in his bedroom closet, he checked the time just in case, this once, he had returned to a moment other than the one he'd left. But as always, it was exactly the same time. As he looked at his watch, a cold hand grabbed his stomach and squeezed. He'd forgotten something, after all.

With all his careful planning, he'd forgotten something.

He'd forgotten that Vanessa was there in his bedroom when he'd departed from this universe. So of course she was still there when he came back, tired and dirty, stained with Patsy Young and Kirk Mondschein's blood.

He pushed the door open a tiny crack. There she was, still working on her sketchbook, her tongue poking a fraction out of the corner of her mouth with the intensity of her concentration.

If she looked up and saw him, it would spell disaster. She couldn't fail to see that Darroll had gone into the closet clean and neat, and come out dishevelled, bloodstained and exhausted.

Darroll's heart lurched for a second as she continued to sit there, her focus on her art. He couldn't hide inside the closet for any length of time. He had to come out, and one moment was as good as another.

So he went for it, striding around Vanessa with big, long steps. "Dusty in there," he drawled as casually as he could. "I need a shower."

"Mmhm," was all Vanessa said, still not looking up, as Darroll reached the door and passed through it. He jerked it closed behind him and leant on it for a moment, taking in vast, silent whoops of breath. Christ, that had been close. How the hell had he overlooked that Vanessa would be in his room when he returned?

He'd sneered at all those murderers he'd read of, who had given themselves away through obvious, careless oversights, and all the time he'd been no better himself. Only luck had saved him. Luck, and the fact that once Vanessa became absorbed in a drawing, it took a lot to distract her. What would he have done if Vanessa had seen him covered in blood? Would he have had to kill her as well? Right here in his own universe?

No. Nobody was dead, here; and nobody was going to be dead, Vanessa Murchison least of all. He could have killed almost anyone else without a qualm if he had to, but not her. Not Vanessa.

With no further delay, he headed for the shower. He tore off his clothes and stepped inside. For a second he ran it cold, thinking of Vanessa and the train. But then he turned it up nice and hot, clouds of steam obscuring the room as he watched the blood that had landed on him run away down the drain, first red, then faintly pink, and finally clear water.

He imagined Vanessa screaming at the sight of his blood-covered clothes, lying on the floor, and the cops being called, and the blood being identified as Patsy and Kirk's. What would the cops do when Patsy and Kirk were both found, hale and hearty and not covered in stab wounds? When no murder victims were to be found in this dimension's Muldoon at all? They'd be baffled, and have to release him.

But all the same, he wanted to avoid the bother it would cause.

When he finished in the shower, he looked in the mirror, wondering whether he'd see anything different. The mark of Cain on his face, perhaps, or a neon sign above his head saying KILLER. But everything was perfectly normal.

He kicked the bloodied clothes into a heap in the corner, put on a bathrobe and returned to his bedroom. Vanessa had finished her sketch of Moose Mason and affixed a comic-book head upon it with Darroll's glue stick.

"You were in there a long time," she remarked.

"I like to be clean," he said.

"Well, I gotta go," she said, sliding her sketchbook back into her bag. "See you tomorrow?"

Once she'd kissed him and departed, he towelled himself off and put on clean clothes. Then he shoved the bloodstained garments he'd been wearing into a grocery bag. He tucked that into a second grocery bag, and then into the bag he'd taken with him between worlds. He looked at the clock. It was past ten at night, now, but he didn't want to wait till morning. And he realised he wanted to be outside, free under the sky and stars, not shut up in his room.

He left the house via the garage, quietly. At least this time, he could use the automobile. He patted it. To think how he'd despised it when he first saw it. And it was thanks to this rusty old heap of Detroit iron that he had the power he possessed. The greatest power in the world, and not one single fucking shred of responsibility, so take that, Peter Parker.

He kept carefully to the speed limit as he drove into town. There were few other vehicles and no cops as he cruised into Muldoon and parked outside Celebration Burger.

Climbing out of the car, he left it unlocked. Everyone left their cars unlocked outside the burger joint. Nobody stole anything in Muldoon. It was a law-abiding city. All except for him. He looked across the street at the big mural he'd once defaced. It seemed years ago. The decorated wall sat there placidly. It showed no signs of vandalism, of course, because in this universe Darroll had never laid a hand upon the mural.

He leaned on the side of his car and stared at the mural for several minutes, lost in his own thoughts, until he realised a couple of people were approaching. God, it was Ed Crowe and Patsy Young. And they were drunk. Presumably on beer rather than bourbon, in this world, but drunk nonetheless.

For a few steps Ed and Patsy would walk together, then Ed would grab for her butt or her boob and she'd squeal, and run a few steps ahead, and Ed would chase her. Then they'd drop back to walking. And then the cycle would begin again. Everything ran in cycles, Darroll thought. You can break the cycle at one point or another, but it always goes back to how it was before. He could spend lifetime after lifetime revenging himself on Alvin Tidmarsh, or Ed Crowe, or the entire town of Muldoon and its murals, and still there would never be an end of it. There were a million million Ed Crowes and a million million Muldoons, stretching away into infinity in every direction.

Ed saw him across the street, and lurched over toward him.

"Yo, Darroll," he grinned. "I was just making out with Patsy. You been making out with Vanessa? What base does she let you get to, huh?"

Patsy came over in Ed's wake, and evidently heard at least some of that. "Lord's sakes, Ed, keep your mouth shut, will ya?" She looked at Darroll with a mix of annoyance and embarrassment, a look he'd seen many times before. Her expression was so mundane, so everyday. He could hardly believe that only an hour or two ago, he had killed this woman.

All of a sudden, he realised how tired he was. "Don't worry," he muttered to Patsy. Like it mattered whether he gossiped. Everyone in Straus High knew that Ed Crowe and Patsy Young were fucking like porn stars. "You gonna be alright to get home?"

Patsy nodded, and tugged at Ed. "Come on, champ," she said, "you'll have such a head in the morning."

Darroll watched them meander away. Having a hangover tomorrow was pretty damn mild for this world's Ed Crowe, he thought, compared to what was in store for his counterpart. As they dwindled out of sight, he opened his car door, took the bag out, and walked around the side of Celebration Burger, breathing through his mouth to avoid inhaling the stale, oily scent that surrounded the dumpster. With a quick movement, he lobbed the bag of bloody clothes into the refuse container and heard the dull sound of it landing amid the cardboard boxes and drums of vegetable oil.

Lord, he was exhausted.

Still, there appeared no reason now why he shouldn't go back home and get his head down, and so he did just that.

45

At first, when Darroll saw Alvin Tidmarsh or Patsy Young around Straus High, he had to remind himself that he really had killed them. They were not just so alive, but so unchanged. Patsy was still a bitch, and Tidmarsh was still a martinet.

But why would they be anything else than what they always had been? They didn't know that in another universe, their counterparts had come to a sudden violent end, or that he, mild-mannered Darroll Martock, the silent and unexpected avenger, had been behind their deaths.

It was so depressing. It made him feel as though the effort he'd put in carrying out his massacres had gone for nothing. Sure, there was a world where Straus High had a new principal, who had to be better than the old one because nobody could be as bad as Tidmarsh, but what good did that do Darroll himself, or his friends, in this world?

He had an uncomfortable suspicion that a real, true psychopath wouldn't confine his crimes to other universes. A proper psychopath wouldn't rely on having a reliable and unimpeachable means of escaping from justice. A proper psychopath would probably have made his presence known in this, his home dimension, and to hell with the risk of being caught.

But the thought made his toes curl.

At least he still had Vanessa, and the other club members. It was Vanessa's turn to address the next meeting, in fact. She'd discussed with Darroll who should be the subject of the speech, and between them they'd settled on a guy who progressed from being a pro-footballer, right here in the Midwest, to killing a bunch of women along a freeway in Oregon. "Everyone always figures that psychopaths look the part," Vanessa said, as they looked at a photograph of the killer. "Does that guy look like a killer to you?"

Actually, Darroll thought he did, but then again, he looked at a killer every day in the mirror. Though he was still afraid that he was no oil painting, he didn't think he looked like a killer himself. Perhaps all murderers thought that.

That Saturday, he arrived at the Boardman house quite early, and had to spend fifteen minutes talking to the Boardman family while he waited for the others to show up. They seemed to like him, for some reason. It didn't feel right that such normal people should get along with a guy like him. At least Julie Boardman had gotten the hint and stopped pressing iced tea upon him.

After a while, Rowdy and Beth showed up, and along with Joe they went down to their usual meeting place in the basement, to set the chairs in a circle. The gloom and clutter made Darroll think of the abandoned building in town, where he'd put an end to Patsy Young and Kirk Mondschein and framed up Ed Crowe for their murders. Over in the corner was the dusty lavatory where he'd first experienced the swirls. It hardly felt possible that it was less than a year ago.

Chuck Milne came clattering down the stairs with his usual shambling, roly-poly gait, and there was the usual chorus of greetings as he chose his usual chair. They all had usual chairs, nowadays. The Club was coming dangerously close to falling into a rut.

"Hey, Chuck," said Rowdy, "how do you make a unicorn cry?"

Chuck shrugged. "Is that a real question, or the first line of a joke?"

"It's a real question."

"It's a good one," Beth said, contemplatively. "If there's an answer I don't know it."

Darroll searched Rowdy's face for signs of jocularity. He found none. As always, Rowdy's face was as large, as plain and as devoid of feature as a field of grass, before the cows came to eat the grass and shit everywhere.

"Me neither," he said. Another question to ask Horsehead. Perhaps deliver it as a joke and see whether he had an answer.

"It's a spell component, in game," Rowdy explained. "Right, Chuck? It costs a buttload of gold, because unicorn tears are massively rare. So I was wondering whether you could farm them, like with cows, only instead of milking them, you make them cry and collect their tears. And then sell them to magicians."

Joe Boardman gave Rowdy a scornful look. "It's just a Dungeons and Dragons thing? Jesus, Serxner, you and Chuck ever gonna outgrow that?"

Chuck and Rowdy both began to protest at this slighting of their beloved hobby. Darroll mentally tuned it out. This wasn't what the Club was supposed to be about. He began to wonder how he could shake it up, whether it was necessary to kick it out of the comfort zone it was settling into.

Maybe he didn't even need the Club any more. He was doing pretty damn fine, now. He had Vanessa, and he had himself and his secret power, and he had self-confidence and charisma – the self-confidence and charisma he'd once thought so far beyond his reach that it was futile even to wish for them. Coach said he'd be trying him on the baseball team before summer. And then in a year there'd be college. Vanessa was going to study art. Perhaps he could wheedle his father into letting him apply to the same college, wherever it was. He'd have to ask Vanessa when she arrived.

Up above, there was some noise. Darroll glanced at his watch and found that Vanessa was half an hour late arriving. He started to rehearse a smartass remark to greet her with, to chide her for being so tardy.

But he didn't get to use it, because the noise above hadn't been Vanessa, after all. It had been two armed cops arriving to grab him, and handcuff him, and haul him away, while Joe and his parents and the rest of the Psychopath Club ran around in astonished confusion, and Rowdy tried to argue with the cops and was told to shut the fuck up, and Darroll kept yelling about his rights, and Chuck Milne got up in the face of one of the cops and told him that Darroll was his best buddy and he couldn't ever kill anybody anyhow, and the cop smacked Chuck in the face and told him that Darroll had murdered Vanessa Murchison right under her parents' noses, and even when Beth Vines tried to speak nobody shut up and let her be heard this time. And Darroll began to realise what must have happened, and that he was in the shit now. Deep, deep in the shit.

46

Darroll spent most of his time in the detention centre with his head down, his own thoughts keeping him company. He wondered periodically what the hell would happen when the swirls came next and he appeared in another world's jail cell, and what the hell the guards would do when they found him there, a detainee with no reason to be locked up. Would they keep him a prisoner while they tried to figure out who the hell he was and how he'd come to be locked up in a cell where he had no business being? Or would they just let him out and tell him to get lost?

If he did get out, would he be able to remain free? Depressingly, he suspected that he wouldn't. Within a few hours, or a couple of days at most, he'd do something or meet someone that caused sufficient change in that continuum. It would dislodge him, like a man spitting out an unexpected chicken bone in his dinner, and bang, there he would be, back in his own universe once more, and back in this cell.

He'd have to be some kind of hermit. Dig a hole in the back of beyond and live in it. Someplace that made even Muldoon look like the bright lights. What a prospect. No. What awaited him in the cell could be no worse than that.

Sometimes he thought about Vanessa. There were worlds, countless worlds, in which she was still alive and well, getting ready to go to art camp, looking forward to her destined career in graphic design. Some of those universes she'd drop out and find something else to do. Some of them she'd succeed. Some of them she'd probably make a big name of herself. It wasn't as though she didn't have the talent. Those drawings of hers, with Archie Comics heads pasted to them. So incongruous but so right. And that other one, the one tucked away in his bedside drawer at home, the one with her life-blood from the railroad accident spattered all over it. He wondered whether the cops had found that, and if they'd destroyed it trying to analyse it. That thought brought a hot flush over him, every time it came to him.

But most of those worlds with a living Vanessa also had a living Darroll, and the ones that didn't, had a dead Darroll. He couldn't hope for escape in that direction.

Other times, he thought about his other self. Because that was who had killed Vanessa. It couldn't be anyone else. Why? Why the fuck, Darroll? He wanted to meet his doppelganger, wanted to take him by the throat and shake him like a puppy with a chew toy, and then he wanted to kill him unhurriedly and painfully. But most of all he wanted to know why. Had the other Darroll been dumped by his version of Vanessa? Or did he come from a universe where Vanessa had never been Darroll's girlfriend? Had he asked her, and been turned down? Darroll dwelt on that thought, spending hours picking at it like a man with a dental abscess. Would he himself have been so devastated if Vanessa had refused his advances? Would he have been enough of a psychopath to seek her out in other universes for vengeance, as he himself had sought out Mr Tidmarsh and Ed Crowe and Patsy Young?

Perhaps the other Darroll was a complete, full-scale evil twin. Perhaps he was steadily working his way through everyone he knew, every time the swirls carried him to the shores of another sea, every time he found himself in a different universe with a get-out-of-jail-free card in his pocket. Perhaps the other Darroll had killed not only Vanessa, but all the others, ticking them off a list like groceries. Chuck and Beth and Joe and Rowdy, and his mother, and perhaps his father (that would have been fun). Dig Doyle. Kirk Mondschein. Rodney Liebscher and his brother, and Mr Spears and the other teachers at Straus High. Louis Vickery, strangled with his own bow tie. And Mr Vines, on display in his own funeral home, his own final client, like the barber in the old riddle about the town where the barber shaved everyone.

Darroll could pass hours at a time in such thoughts, and he did, because there was nothing else to do. His confinement irked him, of course, but he found it surprisingly easy to accept. Most of the time he was left alone, and if there was one thing he had learned to be good at in his life, it was enjoying his own company.

He was lying on his bed one day, eyes closed, when he sensed the presence of someone else in the cell. He had heard nothing, there had been no sound of the lock turning or the door moving; but he knew when he opened his eyes he would see somebody there. And that being so, he could take a good guess at who he would see.

So he didn't bother opening his eyes before speaking. "Hi, Horsehead."

"Good afternoon, Darroll," said the familiar velvet voice.

He did open his eyes now and saw Horsehead standing over him, looking down.

"Happy birthday."

It was his birthday, though he'd tried to forget it, and had three parts succeeded. Seventeen years old, woo-hoo.

"So what kept you?" said Darroll, sitting up on the bed. "And what the hell are you doing here now? Come to gloat? Come to claim my soul? You're a bit early for that. There's no death penalty in this state. It could be fifty years before you get to collect."

"Your soul, if it exists," Horsehead said, unmoved, "is not of interest to me."

"I wish I believed that," Darroll said, and there was an uneasy silence for a few moments before he shook his head, and rose to his feet. "You know what happened, don't you?" he said, stepping closer to Horsehead.

"I know."

"I didn't kill Vanessa. I loved her."

"I know that, too."

"But I did kill Mr Tidmarsh. And Patsy Young. So I guess what goes around comes around, huh? The scales of justice. They may bob around for a while, but in the end, they balance out, right?"

"Perhaps."

"What do you mean, perhaps?"

Horsehead sat down on the bed. It was the first time Darroll could remember where Horsehead had been looking up at him, rather than vice versa.

"If there's anything you can do about this whole situation,"

Darroll said, looking Horsehead right in the eye, "you'd better damn well do it in a hurry. You got me into this," he added with a surge of anger.

"I did not," Horsehead corrected him in a voice no louder than anything else he had said since appearing in the cell. "You had free will. Every Darroll Martock who finds himself slipstreaming between worlds has free will. You are fascinating to watch, Darroll, you and your doubles. You are like a bag full of marbles dropped on a hard floor. You all bounce away, in different directions. Some of you roll further than others. Some of them are lost to my sight, and I never find them again. Others are... picked up by other hands than mine, and they are lost to me too. But I have been watching as many of you as I can, because you fascinate me. Like that bag of marbles, you all look alike; the same size, the same shape, the same materials. But the streak of colour at the heart of each marble is different. No two are quite the same."

"Very poetic," Darroll drawled. "And as usual it still tells me nothing about who you are, or what you are, or what your powers are." He stepped up and pushed his face into Horsehead's. "Answer me one goddamn straight question, just one, just for one time in your life, whatever your fucking life is anyway. Can you get me out of this?"

"Yes."

He had expected Horsehead to dodge the question, or to answer it with a question of his own, like normal. He wasn't prepared for that positive monosyllable, and Darroll was at a loss for a continuation. It was Horsehead who broke the silence, this time.

"Yes," he repeated. "I can, if you want it enough."

"Want it?" Darroll gave a sharp, sardonic laugh. "Who wouldn't want to get out of this situation?"

"But why do you want it, Darroll?"

Darroll was about to give Horsehead a curt answer, but he paused.

"Christ... I don't know why, actually. I don't have anything to live for. My father doesn't give a damn for me, my mother... you know my mother and what she's like. And the one person who brought any light to my life, who gave it any meaning, has died. Twice."

"Everyone dies eventually," Horsehead pointed out gently. "You are dead yourself in more universes than you are alive."

"Well, thanks a bundle for that news."

"If I were to... extract you from this situation," Horsehead went on, "there would be a price to pay, and your life would change considerably."

Darroll nodded slowly, trying to read Horsehead's expression. Normally Horsehead's body language was close enough to human that he could read it. But this time? A poker face, a long brown poker face.

"Two questions," he said. "Would I have any freedom?"

"Yes. You would have freedom. What is the other question?"

"Would I see Vanessa Murchison again?"

"Most likely."

"That's good enough for me," Darroll said, without a moment's further thought. "I don't care what the price is. You say it's not about my soul, and I don't know if I believe that. But even if it is about my soul, you can take the fucking thing. If it comes down to a choice between Vanessa Murchison and my soul... I know which of the two has done me more good."

He'd just thought to himself that he couldn't read Horsehead's face, but he realised he was wrong when Horsehead smiled and the warmth of the smile lit the room up.

It lit him up too. The warmth, the glow, suffused him. It grew warmer, and more radiant, and brighter and brighter, until he had to close his eyes against it.

47

The mailboy was whistling softly to himself through the gap in his front teeth as he pushed open the door and entered Detectives Carpenter and Lynan's office. Lynan had been trying to identify the mailboy's tune for the eight months he'd been delivering the detectives' mail, and he'd not managed to figure it out, not even once. Lynan thought he was pretty well versed when it came to matters musical, so Lynan's conclusion was that the mailboy was a lousy whistler.

Without missing a note, the mailboy dropped a bundle of documents on the corner of Lynan's desk, and left the room. As usual, he ignored the black plastic in-tray, even though it had a big label on it saying IN. Lynan picked up the bundle and removed the rubber band. Then he opened his desk drawer and wrapped the band around the two inch thick ball of other bands that already inhabited the drawer. Lynan never threw an elastic band away. Lynan never threw anything away.

Carpenter used to plead with Lynan to write notes and memoes on fresh paper, of which they had reams and reams right there, not to mention boxes of the stuff by the photocopier down the hall. But Lynan always reused the reverse side of old documents. Carpenter was always coming in from a call and finding a note from Lynan on his desk, written on the back of a shopping list from 2001, or a mistyped arrest form from 1995. It drove Carpenter mad. When Lynan was out, and Carpenter took a message for him, Carpenter sent Lynan an email. Carpenter sometimes wondered if Lynan knew how to use email. Maybe Lynan's computer had millions of messages from Carpenter and the Chief and the other members of the force, going back all the way to when the department first got computers. Which was, let's see, maybe five years, and say two messages a day, three hundred and sixty five days a year, don't forget leap years, five times two times three hundred and –

"Mail for you," Lynan said, waving some at Carpenter. Carpenter stretched out across the cramped office and plucked his envelopes from Lynan's hand.

Lynan opened a large envelope. Its bright shade of sickly orange showed it to be an internal missive, rather than one that had arrived via the ordinary postal service.

"Oh, hey," he said, " this is the lab reports on the Martock case."

Carpenter, who had been about to open his first envelope, dropped it on his desk and paid instant attention to Lynan. "Yeah? What do they say?"

Lynan read through the document slowly enough to annoy Carpenter, who prided himself on speed-reading. You practically had to be a speed reader, the way the police department threw info at you in this day and age, and expected you to read and memorise every goddamn line.

Finally Lynan threw the papers down. "This makes no kind of fucking sense, Carp."

"How'd you mean?"

Lynan got up, pulled open a drawer, and grabbed a fat bundle of documents, spilling out of a manila file folder. He threw them onto his desk next to the forensic reports, and flipped several pages back and forth, comparing data. His hand went up to his head, and his hair grew more and more ruffled as he read. Finally he dropped back into his chair.

"This is how I mean," he said. "You just be the jury for a moment, here, and I'll be prosecutor."

"If you like."

"One-thirty or so Saturday afternoon. Martock arrives at the Murchison household, north end of Second in Muldoon. Sue Ellen Murchison lets him in. He's there to see the deceased, Vanessa Murchison, his girlfriend of several months. So notice," he said, looking up from the papers and fixing Carpenter eye to eye, "that straight away we have positive witness identification. Mrs Murchison had seen Martock dozens of times, and she's prepared to swear it was him. Also, Jeremiah Murchison, the father, didn't see Martock at the door, but heard him speak to his wife, and will testify that he recognised his voice."

"Looking good so far, then," Carpenter said.

"What's more," Lynan carried on, "Mrs Murchison says that Martock appeared out of breath. Quote, tense and worried, unquote. She actually asked if he was okay. He said yes, he just needed to see Vanessa. At this point, Vanessa Murchison shouted downstairs to ask if it was Martock at the door. Mrs Murchison returned to the lounge and Martock went upstairs to Vanessa's room."

"Mmhm?"

"Within five minutes, the Murchison parents were alerted by screams from upstairs. Mr Murchison ran up the stairs, and found his daughter in her bedroom, on the bed, bleeding profusely. He dialled 911 and attempted to administer first aid, but Vanessa Murchison was dead by the time an ambulance arrived. Call time, by the way, is logged at 1341 hours, and the ambulance was there at 1347."

"Where was Martock?" asked Carpenter, and Lynan smiled humourlessly.

"I'll come to that presently. Meantime... the local law arrived on the scene at, uh, 1356. Crime scene was secured and this office was brought in. Forensics did the usual sweep of the room, also of the late Vanessa Murchison's cadaver. The room was full of positive results from Martock. His spoor was all over, including his hair on the pillows of Vanessa's bed." He picked up the forensic report and once more flipped its pages. "Furthermore, Vanessa very helpfully fought back when she was attacked. Seems she was a feisty type, poor girl." He held up a photograph from the manila folder. "This was her, a few weeks before."

Carpenter took the photo and looked at it. "Fat girls often are," he remarked. "They get given a hard time for being overweight, and if it doesn't break them it toughens them up." He passed the photo, with Vanessa Murchison smiling the smile she would never smile again, back to Lynan.

"She scratched her attacker up good and hard," Lynan said, referring again to the forensic folder. "Under her fingernails, the lab found so much material they practically did a dance for joy. Skin, blood, even a beard hair. All positive DNA matches for Martock."

Carpenter was starting to look askance at Lynan. "So if there's all this evidence, what're you acting so unhappy about?"

"Following the arrest of Darroll Martock," Lynan went on, disregarding Carpenter's question and flicking through to another page in his paperwork, "we also tossed his room, forensically. DNA from Murchison was found in various places. In his walk-in closet, we found a Colt pistol, unlicensed, plus ammunition. Recently fired, the lab says. It had Martock's prints on it, and nobody else's. And furthermore," he said, looking Carpenter in the eye again, "there was an original drawing, heavily bloodstained, of a vampire and a young woman. Guess whose the blood was?"

"Vanessa Murchison's?"

"Give that cop a promotion. Yes, Vanessa Murchison's." He closed the folder in front of him and pushed it away to the back of his desk, as though its presence annoyed him. "So, Carp. You're the jury. Think Martock's guilty?"

Carpenter looked at Lynan with the air of a man suspecting a trick question. "Certainly looks that way, doesn't it? Juries these days believe DNA evidence. They've seen CSI on TV, half the time they think forensics are more important than all the other shit we have to wade through to get a case together."

"Okay," Lynan said. "Hold that thought, and I'm gonna put on the other hat. I now appear before you for the defense." He cleared his throat self-consciously. Carpenter raised an eyebrow, and waited.

"Martock was apprehended at 1422 the same afternoon, in the basement of a house belonging to the Boardman family, Joseph Boardman being a friend of Martock's and of Vanessa's also. When given his Miranda warning, Martock said…" Lynan pulled the document folder back to himself, and flipped pages. "… said, 'Oh shit, I'm in mega-trouble now, aren't I?' When asked if this was a confession, he said, 'I swear I didn't kill her. I know who did but you'll never believe me and I'm going to carry the can.' After which he shut his cakehole, and refused to comment further without a lawyer. Except for one more thing. Five minutes after his previous statement, he asked the arresting officer to give him a physical examination."

"A what?"

"A physical examination. He started to get undressed, right there and then."

Carpenter was frowning again. "Are you trying to tell me Martock's crazy? Is he gonna be too nuts to plead?"

"Not a bit of it," Lynan said. "That little weasel's as sane as you or I, and he's got cunning up the wazoo. He was absolutely insistent that the officer check him over physically for, quote, any sign of physical injury or harm. I spoke to the cop who was with him at the time. He figured Martock was worried we were gonna beat a confession out of him or something. He didn't see any harm in it, so he looked Martock over. It was his opinion that the prisoner was free from any physical injury or outward sign of harm."

"Hey, wait. Didn't forensics – "

"Yes, forensics did. So here's a nice contradiction to swallow. The dead girl clawed her attacker enough to make him bleed. To make his face bleed – remember that beard hair? And here's Darroll Martock, standing in front of a police officer in nothing but his tighty whities, and the police officer enters a statement that Martock has no physical injury to his face, or to any other part of his body."

Carpenter sat on the desk next to Lynan's and looked at his colleague. "That's kind of peculiar."

"It's more than peculiar, it's fucking unbelievable," growled Lynan. "And you know what bites me about it? It's as if Martock knew there was going to be DNA evidence against him, and wanted to be able to challenge it. How could he know there was DNA evidence if he hadn't left it there himself when he was knifing his girlfriend to death? And before you ask, he isn't a twin. He's an only child."

Carpenter had no answer to that, and Lynan continued.

"Now, you were asking where Martock was when Jerry Murchison ran upstairs and found his daughter dying. That, Carp, is a reasonable question, a question any jury would ask. And the answer is..." Lynan paused for effect, before slapping his open palm down on the desk. "The answer is, *we don't know*. He went up those stairs, but he didn't come back down them, or out of the door. The foot of the stairs in that house is visible from the chair where Mrs Murchison was sitting, and she saw nobody go downstairs or out the front door between Martock going up, and the time she heard her daughter start screaming."

"Windows?"

"The window in Vanessa's room was closed. I guess it's possible that Martock opened it, jumped out, landed on his feet and raced away from the scene. But the only fingerprints on the window latch were Vanessa's, and there were no forensic traces at all of anyone having been out the window or over the window ledge. And right under that second floor window is a flower bed. Beautiful soft soil, perfect for prints. No trace of any disturbance or anyone jumping into it."

Carpenter stood up from the desk and walked around Lynan. "Any other windows on the second floor he could have jumped from?"

"All dusted. No sign of egress from any of them. It's like the guy vanished into thin air. Oh, and just to add to the fun? He took the knife with him. No murder weapon was found in the room, or on Martock, or among his possessions, or anywhere since. Forensics know pretty much everything about the blade, its length and width and shape, hell, they almost know what factory made it. But we don't have the murder weapon, and that's always a tough one in a trial like this."

Lynan rose to his feet as well, and confronted Carpenter. He had to look up three inches; Carpenter was bigger and heavier than Lynan. "So that's the forensic evidence nicely knocked off-centre. Why don't we destroy the witness evidence too? Why, sure, let's do just that." He drew a deep breath. "At the same time that the Murchisons put Martock on their front doorstep asking to see Vanessa, we also have six witnesses who all say he was in the Boardman family basement, and had been there almost an hour. The Boardman parents and Joseph their son, plus three more friends of Martock."

"Jesus. You have to be kidding."

"I only wish, Carp, I only wish. The kids are all friends of Martock, so I suppose it's possible we could claim they were all clubbing together to protect their murderous little buddy out of fear or loyalty... but the parents too? I don't buy it, and a jury won't buy it."

Carpenter was looking blank by now. Lynan pressed on.

"And there's more." He flipped pages again. "Nobody I interviewed says anything that suggests Martock had any argument with Vanessa. In fact they all say they were regular little love-birds. She wasn't a virgin, but she wasn't pregnant, either. There was no known financial incentive for Martock to kill her."

"Murders still happen between couples," Carpenter interjected.

"Yeah, but I'd like some semblance of a motive we can wave around in court."

"Were they gang members?"

"Christ, Carp, have you ever been to Muldoon? Biggest gang you'll find there is the high school football team. Speaking of high schools," Lynan continued, "I interviewed Alvin Tidmarsh, Martock's school principal. When I mentioned Martock's name, he damn near spat in my eye. Said he was a rebellious, stubborn student who was unpopular with his peers, disruptive to the school's process and morale, and in his opinion..." He ran a finger down the page looking for a quote. "Ah. He said that if there was one kid at Straus High who was gonna come to a bad end, it was Darroll Martock. He gave Tidmarsh the creeps."

"You can't throw a teenager in the house because he gave his principal the creeps," Carpenter interjected. "Hell, I was a tearaway in school myself."

"Exactly. Martock's got no record, never been in trouble with the law before. Sure, we can get him for possessing the gun, but there's no evidence that he ever shot anyone with it. And while we're on the subject of the gun... you know I said it was a Colt pistol?"

"I heard you. What kind? Forty-five?"

"Ha, ha," said Lynan. "Forty-five be damned. This was a Colt forty-two."

"Colt forty-two? I never heard of those."

"No. Neither did I. Neither did the lab. And guess what? Neither have Colt. The lab actually rang Colt to ask, and they said Colt Manufacturing have never made a .42 calibre firearm."

"So it's some knock-off?"

"Maybe, though the lab said it looked good quality. You could take it for a forty-five easily. Identical design, a fraction smaller. Just one more weirdness about this whole freaky case. Not that it matters, I suppose, since Vanessa Murchison wasn't shot. We haven't been able to place Martock with any blade. Even his mom's kitchen knives are all present and correct." Lynan shook his head in frustration and confusion. "Oh, and here's one last thing. That pencil drawing of the vampire? With Vanessa Murchison's blood on it?"

"Yeah?"

"Two things. One: forensics say that the blood is Vanessa's, for sure. But they also say that the blood was at least two months old. The blood on that drawing could not have come from Vanessa Murchison on the day of her death."

"You're kidding me, Lynan."

"I wish. And secondly, the drawing in question? It was by Vanessa Murchison herself."

"Signed, huh?"

"No. But we have evidence from multiple sources that it was her work. Donna Pulleyn, who taught her art at Straus, says the style's unmistakeable. And furthermore a couple of those kids in the Boardman basement say the same, that it's clearly her work. Elizabeth Vines and... uh... Rowdy Serxner."

"Rowdy Serxner?"

"Yeah, that's his actual name. Christ alone knows what his parents were thinking. And no, there was no blood on the drawing when Vines and Serxner saw it. Now I suppose that if we wanted to pursue every obvious blind alley in this case," Lynan went on, "we could call in an expert witness on fine art. But you don't want to know how much their hourly rate is."

"Take ours, add a zero?"

"More than that, even. And at the end of the day, I don't see that it matters who drew it. We know Vanessa spilled blood on it, some time in the past, and whether she spilled ink on it too won't alter the case a damn either way. So there you have it. We have conclusive proof that Darroll Martock and nobody else murdered Vanessa Murchison, and we have equally conclusive proof that he couldn't have."

Lynan threw himself back into his chair and pushed the paperwork away from him once more. As he did so, the telephone rang on his desk. He reached for the receiver, and Carpenter reached for the documents.

"Detective Division, Lynan... Hi, Huxley... Yeah... Yeah, that would be me – What? Are you fucking kidding me?" Lynan snarled into the phone. Carpenter looked up from the folder he was flicking through, then back down at the documents.

"He can't! That's impossible! You fucking goons must've – " He fell silent for a few seconds, then spoke again, in a dangerous, low voice. "I am gonna be coming over to see you guys, and by Christ you had better have a fucking good explanation by the time I get there. Otherwise, I am personally gonna see to it that you get busted back down so far that you're cleaning the drunk tank shithouse for the rest of your lives. Yes... Yes, I will be seeing you, Huxley. And I may be the last thing you ever see, God help you." He slammed the phone back down and looked up to meet Carpenter's eyes and the unspoken question they contained.

"That was the detention centre," he said in slow and measured tones. "They were calling to say that Darroll Martock has escaped from their custody, having managed to get out of a locked cell without unlocking it, and without leaving any clue to his means of departure. I don't fucking believe this."

"Me neither," Carpenter echoed. "When's the last time they lost someone from there?"

"Like, never. And if they did, it was while the prisoner was in transit to court, or on exercise, or something. Not from a fucking locked cell!" He jumped to his feet and looked around. "Where's my jacket? I'm not going over there without a coat. It's way cold out there today. Same as always."

"Hold on a second." Carpenter folded open the document wallet. "You said there was a pencil drawing of a vampire and a woman?"

"Yeah. By Murchison."

"This one?" Carpenter extracted an item from among its fellows, a sheet of paper sealed in a transparent plastic forensic wrapper. Tags attached to it gave it a number, a date and an identity.

"I guess. Why?"

Carpenter turned the sheet of paper to face Lynan.

"Since when do vampires look like this? And that isn't a girl with him, either."

Lynan leaned closer to look at the drawing, his mouth dropping slightly open.

"But... This is insane." He took a quick look at the evidence tag. "That isn't the drawing from Martock's room. That's Martock himself, right there –"

Lynan's finger stabbed at the drawing.

Earlier that day, the likenesses of a vampire and a young woman had been sealed in the plastic evidence folder, like two flies in a block of amber. Now they were both gone, and two other figures had taken their place.

One was a young dark-haired man, whose thin face was split with a sardonic smile, as though he were looking up out of the paper and sneering at the viewer.

The second was taller than Darroll, his hands resting casually but protectively on his shoulders. He was neatly dressed in a shirt and tie. Where his head should have been, rising out of the collar of his shirt, there sprouted instead a horse's head.

It was turned slightly to one side so that one eye was invisible. The other eye, like Darroll's eyes, was looking straight out of the drawing, at the viewer.

The horse's eye held the answers to all of Lynan and Carpenter's questions, and to a million more besides.

But the horse's mouth was firmly, eternally closed.

ACKNOWLEDGEMENTS

A salute to those who not only had faith but kept the faith, including Russell Copeland, Stuart Dickson, Claire Brialey, Alice Dryden, Mike Rees, Emmy Gregory, Kitty Keighley, Michael Dobson, John D. Berry, and the members of InTheBar, Days Are For Writing and Greenwich Writers.